A View to Die For

Carolyn Maddux

Steamer Press

Steamer Press

First Steamer Press Edition October 2022

Copyright 2022 by Carolyn Maddux

All rights reserved.

Published in the United States by Steamer Press, San Diego.

Book design by Bojan Kratofil

Book Cover Art by Lauren Kent

Book Cover Design by Julia Kent

Steamer Press Trade Paperback

ISBN 978-1-7347719-2-3

eBook ISBN 978-1-7347719-3-0

Library of Congress No. applied for

www.SteamerPress.com

To the Readers:

Those of you familiar with Santa Catalina Island will realize that I have taken some liberties with the island's terrain, and no doubt with many other details. To those of you who find such liberties annoying, I would echo Samuel Johnson's response to James Boswell: "I wish you could have looked over my book before the printer, but it could not easily be. I suspect some mistakes; but as I deal, perhaps, more in notions than in facts, the matter is not great." As a former journalist, I'm not sure I agree with Johnson's conclusion; the matter is great, the devil is in the details, and I beg your forbearance.

All the characters in this book are completely and utterly fictional, with the exception of Dr. Robert Michael Pyle, who did visit Catalina in June, 2008, as part of his Butterfly Big Year as chronicled in *Mariposa Road,* and who kindly agreed to make a cameo appearance on the hillside above Avalon in this book.

Prologue

Friday, June 6, 2008

Two people stood on a peak high above a brilliant blue harbor on an island that could have been Mediterranean but wasn't.

A drowsy sun, making its leisurely descent into the Pacific Ocean, shone blandly across the western slopes of Santa Catalina Island. A light wind stirred the grass, still streaked with green after a late spring rain. Swallows chattered overhead. Smudges on the horizon to the east, across the water, marked the urban sprawl of California's Los Angeles County. The low-slung sun picked out vague golden shapes of the Port of Long Beach cranes and derricks.

"Look at that view!" Warner Kendall Hayden said. It sounded like a command as he gestured around him.

"It's lovely," the other said in a guarded voice. From where they stood, they looked across the seaward end of the town of Avalon. At the center pier, glass-bottomed boats and submarines awaited tourists for the evening cruises while yachts, each at its pristine white buoy, rode at anchor on the deep azure waters. Minute figures moved along the promenade above the waterfront. Above them, houses on the hillside appeared like stacked blocks. Zane Grey's pueblo-style home, long since reworked as a quiet hotel, sprawled among eucalyptus and junipers. Nearby, Chimes Tower looked like something from a Spanish mission. Below it, the last rays of sun made the red-tiled roof of Avalon's landmark casino glow like coals. Home to the legendary Avalon Ballroom, the Casino served this week as headquarters of the Avalon Plein-Air Festival.

"Lovely," Hayden echoed, "but going to get lovelier. Imagine you're sitting on a balcony, drinking in the view and a double martini." He raised an imaginary glass. Involuntarily, his companion stepped back from the rush of alcohol on his breath. Wavy-haired, well barbered, fit and stylish, Hayden wore a silk jacket and slacks in keeping with the place he described, not the tangle of toyon and lemonberry where he stood gesturing. "Imagine white stucco, wrought iron railings, fountains with Catalina tiles. Like Wrigley did it, with everything highest quality, but up to date. And beautiful, with bougainvillea, giant aloes, palms. Like the best of Avalon, but up here where you can see everything, all the way to Long Beach."

"I thought you could only build in Avalon. Would the Island Conservancy—"

"That's the beauty of it," Hayden interrupted, smiling. "You'd think it was in the Conservancy. Everybody here does. Guy I bought it from thought it was. But it's a sweet little exception." He chuckled. "He owned it for decades and didn't ever check it out, poor fool. Charles Willis. His grandfather was a friend of Wrigley's. He'd got hold of this piece of ground when Wrigley bought the rest, but he didn't get moving on it soon enough. The Great Depression hit." He shrugged. "Still, he got his development plans submitted to the county—and approved. Signed and sealed. And since it's still in the county, there's not much can stop me."

"But the county has its regulations, too."

Hayden's smile became a grin. Wolflike, thought his companion, who moved a few steps away. Hayden continued,

"Oh, yeah. L.A. County has its regulations. But this—it's grandfathered in. I've had my team of land-use attorneys go over it to make sure. They're the best, and they all said it's bulletproof.

"Bulletproof!" he repeated, shading his eyes as he looked to the west. "If Elbert Willis, Charlie's old granddad, had gone ahead with things, instead of trying to grow his capital with one more investment in '29, there'd be some fancy houses up here. Too bad he never finished his subdivision. But as long as I keep the land in one parcel, I can do multiple-occupancy." Hayden rubbed his hands together as he paced and talked.

"Old Charlie—he thought it was just useless land he could never do anything with. Now his grandpa—oh, Elbert had plans. A colony of elegant houses for the movie stars, ballplayers, high rollers. Great plans, but he lost the money he needed to build them. Died of the disappointment."

"Really?"

"Oh, yeah. Typical Depression story. Jumped out the window of his hotel room in San Francisco. And then he only got a couple of paragraphs in the *Examiner*. Everybody was doing it back then.

"Family thought the deed was like all his other paper: worthless stock. The daughter died and left her share to her brother, Charlie's dad." Hayden stooped down, picked at a grass seed that clung to his slacks, and brushed it off. "Charlie's old man died in Australia, or maybe it was New Zealand, I forget which. And so Charlie inherited it, back in the beginning of the '60s. The amazing thing is none of them let it go back to the county for taxes. They all just paid them year after year."

"I wonder why."

"Sentiment, maybe," Hayden shrugged. "Family tradition. Inertia. Who knows. Taxes weren't much, anyhow; somebody at the L.A. County treasurer's office listed it in conservancy status, along with the rest of the upland. But that's the joke; it's not in the Island Conservancy." He picked a stem of blue lupine absently and plucked away the individual pea-like blossoms as he talked. "I got to know old Charlie through a lawyer friend I swap favors with now and again. He owed me one, and said maybe I should check out this piece of property Charlie had. So we did some research, and it looked like a little gold mine.

"Old Charlie, he was hoping to buy his way into one of those assisted living places, and he was short by a good bit. He jumped at the price I offered him, told me he had to be honest and say he didn't think it would ever be usable, but I said I'd take a risk on it." He chuckled. "Said I could always donate it to the county and use it as a tax writeoff. Made him feel really good about it—a win-win thing. Sweet, huh?"

"And he had no idea it wasn't in the Conservancy?"

Hayden laughed. "Not a practical sort, our Charlie. He was an English teacher."

There was a short silence. "What, English teachers are impractical?"

"Idealists, most of them," Hayden said dismissively. "I dated one once. Save-the-whales sort of person. Head in the clouds. Sweet girl, pretty too." He smiled reminiscently. "But not practical. You have to be practical to get on in this world." His companion studied him for a moment, then turned away and appeared to survey the hilltop where they stood. There was a long silence. "So what is it you're planning up here? You said multiple occupancy. You mean condos, or a hotel?"

"Oh, yeah." Hayden grinned. "A luxury hotel. Big. Cantilevered out off the mountaintop in both directions. Avalon Bay below you this way, and Lover's Cove, and—come over here—Pebbly Beach in that direction. Just think about it. All by itself up top here — solitary splendor. Just like old Elbert planned: big stars, athletes, politicians, big-company CEOs. But just visiting, not living here. Luxury suites, fancy spa, masseuses. A big-name chef, gourmet food, and a totally killer view."

"But wouldn't you have a whole lot of opposition?"

Hayden shook his head. "People might whine about it now, the Conservancy folks will make a little fuss, but after a while they'll love the idea of all those people with big money coming in. They'll find out it's worth bending a few rules."

"Bending the rules? You'd do that?"

Hayden frowned. "You one of those whale-savers too?"

"No, I'm just—ah—surprised. That you could." There was a pause.

Hayden laughed again, a harsh sound the wind carried off quickly. "Oh, I've done my homework. I'm not worried about the planning commission or the council. Or the Conservancy. I know the pressure points." He gave the other a penetrating look. "And some people are beginning to find out what I know. They're lining up behind it, or will be when—" He stopped himself, switched gears, smiled again. "And there's that perfect deed: Bulletproof.

"So then," Hayden said, "the lawyers are going to be coming to me to try to cut a deal. Oh, I'll make a concession here and there, just to play the game." There was a warning note in his laugh. "But in the end, I'll have exactly what I want."

"Amazing," said the other. "A view like that in both directions. It's gorgeous from here. Can we go farther out? See more of Avalon?"

"Yeah. Sure we can. That's not much of a trail, but it's walkable if you're careful. You can see the whole bay. Yeah, it's an outlook to knock your socks off. But watch your step. You don't get vertigo, do you?"

"Not that I know of. But what about you?" Hayden still exuded an aura of martini. "Are you okay out here?"

"Oh, hell, yes. I'm fine." Hayden laughed. "A coupla doubles are nothing." Picking up his pace, he shouldered ahead. "And I know this piece of ground like the back of my hand. It's stable enough, but it drops way off. You wouldn't want to fall off the edge right here. It's a long way down."

"I suppose it is."

"And here we are," he crowed. "Look at that."

"Oh!" The curve of the bay, intersected by its docks, the tile-topped casino on its point and the dense little downtown, all appeared below them.

Warner Kendall Hayden moved to the edge, breathed an expansive sigh and gestured wider. "A view to die for, isn't it?"

Chapter 1

John Katsaros ended most of his evenings with a hike up into one of the hillsides where he could look out over the little city of Avalon. He loved the challenge of the steep streets as he strolled among the homes of his friends whose houses overlooked the town. He stood now, as the sun sank behind the western hillside and lights came on one by one, looking out over the curving harbor. With the onset of summer, it was filling with boats of all sizes; he noted a couple of big yachts that hadn't been there that morning. He gazed at Cabrillo Mole, the rock jetty that served as dock for the passenger boats from San Pedro, Long Beach and Dana Point, and thought about the sea bass he'd caught from the end of the mole the week before. Probably the end of good fishing there until fall, he thought, looking at the cloudless sky.

The last Express had pulled out from the mole as he closed the door on his little house on Descanso Avenue, made his way across the plaza to Metropole Avenue, and climbed the steps to Calle del Sol. Pausing to catch his breath before he took the Burma Trail that zigzagged up the hill to East Whittley, he'd watched late-flying hummingbirds still nectaring among the fragrant shrubs on the steep banks.

Making his way along the high west edge of the valley, John strolled past the home his friend Edgar Ruiz had recently completed. He smiled, thinking of how successfully Edgar had transformed the summer house that had belonged to his wife's parents, a typical mid-century multi-level cantilevered over the steep slope, into a model of efficiency with nearly invisible solar panels. No lights were on, but John was startled to hear the sound of weeping coming from a window at the back of the house. He scratched his head. Edgar and his wife, Alice Ann, were one of the most loving couples he knew, and over-the-moon happy to be expecting a baby. He shrugged. Perhaps Alice was watching something on television. After all, his beloved Celestina was doing that now, declining a walk in favor of—what was it on Friday nights? *Dancing with the Stars?*

He continued along, looping back to Whittley. He was just approaching Roger Cameron's house when he heard a door open and caught a glimpse of Roger, a biologist with the Island Conservancy, emerging. He prepared himself for the usual pleasantries but was surprised to see Roger duck into an alcove at the sound of his approaching footsteps. And then the man disappeared. He pondered that as he continued his walk. In a few minutes, he heard Roger's golf cart start up. Another mystery, John thought. It wasn't starting from the Camerons' driveway, but from a street corner above their home.

And now he was back at the bottom of the Burma Trail. He leaned against the wall at the upper end of Calle del Sol. Something was stirring in the quiet evening air, he thought, and despite the warmth of the evening, he shivered.

He was so lost in thought that he started when he heard his name called and saw his neighbor, Fred Paige, striding up the short end of Beacon Street toward him.

"Evening, Fred." John waved and half-turned away, but it became apparent that his neighbor was intent on joining him.

John wasn't looking for company, but he knew Fred Paige was lonely. Fred and his wife, Evelyn, had retired a year earlier to their island vacation house, but Evelyn had died in March.

"You walk up here every evening?" Fred asked.

"Most evenings. Tonight I walked up the Burma Trail to East Whittley." John indicated the narrow sidewalk that zigzagged up the hillside between homes and apartments that cantilevered out from the rocky slope. "Celestina's watching TV, but—well," John grinned, "I don't really like television. When it's not one of her program nights, Stina and I walk together, but not usually that far."

Fred mopped his brow with a rumpled handkerchief. "I'm out of shape. When Evvie was so sick, there wasn't much chance to get out."

John clapped his friend on the shoulder. The two stood for a moment, looking out over the harbor and the ocean beyond. "It's so peaceful when the last boat leaves," Fred observed. John's brow furrowed, but he nodded, and the two men descended the stairs, strolled east to Sumner Avenue, turned, and began to walk toward the harbor.

Behind them, from the fire station, a siren sounded. Doors opened and people stepped out onto their porches to peer up into the canyon. The siren stopped short.

"Practice?" Fred asked.

"Hope so," John said. A year earlier, in the spring of 2007, a huge wildfire in the chaparral had burned to the edge of Avalon, threatening the town and blackening the hills above it. A fire truck rolled by, no lights flashing. "Yep. Looks like everything's okay."

John was surprised to realize how his muscles had tightened at the sound of the siren, how easily his internal alarm sounded. He recalled helping his friend Andrea, a caterer, shuttle food to fire crews and volunteers and Marines who battled the blaze. He remembered the Express boats that ran through the night ferrying terrified residents evacuated from their homes to shelters in Long Beach, and the flames that turned the night sky orange as they snaked down the canyons toward the town. But he recalled the way everyone had pulled together. Was it the return of fire season that fueled his anxiety? He didn't think so.

Despite the terror, the fire had united everyone in a common effort. It didn't feel the same this spring. John shook his head as he thought about conversations half overheard during recent weeks in restaurants and shops, wondering and sometimes worried and angry talk. "Toyon Ridge." "That bigshot and his big resort." He thought about how those conversations would stop short any time men in business suits appeared.

"That bigshot from Colorado." John had met that developer, briefly, at a Rotary gathering. Hayden, his name was. Andrea had summed him up: "Too friendly, too well-groomed, too smooth. Much too smooth," she said with a shudder. He had mentioned meeting Hayden to Lexi, his granddaughter, only to see her smile disappear. She'd shuddered, too.

He remembered seeing normally friendly people casting uneasy looks at strangers in a town where strangers were the locals' bread and butter. This wasn't the easy Avalon he'd known all his life.

"Hullo! Lovely evening." Another voice retrieved him from his musings. He and Fred returned the greeting as a couple approached, a man carrying a pair of easels over one shoulder and two backpacks over the other, a woman carefully carrying two canvases.

"Painters? Isn't it late?" Fred asked as they continued on their way.

"Catching the evening light on the mole or the casino, probably. The Plein-Air Festival's starting, and there'll be painters everywhere for the next week," John said.

"Plein-Air?"

"Painting on the scene, outdoors. It's always been big here. There used to be a plein-air event every year. They'd end with an auction of the work the artists did here."

"Is that where you got that painting by your stairway? It looks like Stagecoach Road."

"It is. And no, we didn't get it at the festival, but the painter—Jill Reinhardt—lives here on the island. In fact, she's heading up the revival of the festival this year. Back when she was just getting established, she used to have a seconds show every fall. We got it there. To my mind, her seconds are better than a lot of what you see in the galleries now. I should have bought more when she was affordable."

Their companionable walk took them past a small craftsman bungalow Edgar Ruiz used as the office for his construction firm. It was growing dark now, but the "Open" sign still hung in Edgar's window. Edgar served on the city council, and was still finishing The Arroyo, a small development of eight eco-homes bermed into the hillside above town, homes with grass roofs and solar energy. Of course he would have to work late sometimes. But John thought again of the sound of weeping he had heard at the Ruiz home above them on the hillside.

The porchlight of the bungalow shone through a tangle of red and purple and coral bougainvillea that draped the porch rails. The vine vibrated as the door opened. Ruiz emerged, and reached back to turn the sign in the door's little window over to read "closed."

"*Buenas noches, amigo!*" John called out.

Ruiz jumped, and the face he turned to the two men was blank. But he mustered a smile. "Oh, *bueno*, Zorba! Good evening!"

"*Cómo estás*, Edgar? Do you know my neighbor, Fred Paige?" he asked. "Fred, Edgar Ruiz." The two men shook hands.

"I'm glad to meet you. You're on the council, aren't you?" Fred asked. "I'm just now getting a sense of how the city runs. I liked what you said in that forum last week, about being a sustainable community. We're so small out here, and with the council on board with that, and the Conservancy controlling development outside the city, we've got a good start."

Fred seemed unaware that the smile had left Edgar Ruiz's face. Lines John hadn't noticed before creased Edgar's forehead, tightened around the mouth in a face John had always thought of as a smooth oval. "Speaking of the Conservancy," Fred added, "what's all this we're hearing about some developer from Colorado building a big fancy resort on the bluff up above the Inn? The city and the Conservancy wouldn't approve that, would it?"

Edgar Ruiz shut his eyes for a moment, drawing a breath. When he spoke, it was with difficulty. "The problem," he said, "is that the land in question isn't in the Conservancy. It isn't in the city, either, although of course the county will ask our planning commission to weigh in on the environmental reviews. And we hope we will have some effect."

"I hope so too," Fred said. "People say it'll have a spa and a racquetball court and a rooftop swimming pool," he continued, oblivious to Ruiz's discomfort. "People say this Colorado guy's bringing in a gourmet chef. People say it'll make the Inn look like nothing at all, and put the place up the canyon out of business."

"People," John reminded him, "will say anything."

But Fred was warming to his subject. "Some people are saying that bringing in tourists with more money will be a good thing. And some are saying it'll ruin the island. Myself, I think you get big money in here, you get a lot of pressure to change the rules. Don't you think so?" he asked Ruiz.

"There's always a danger of that," Ruiz said carefully. "But we have to keep an open mind until we hear more from this Mr. Hayden."

"We're keeping you from your family. We'd better be going," John prompted. "Good night, Edgar." After another round of pleasantries and hand-shaking, he and Paige continued their walk toward home.

"A place like that would change the whole feel of the island, don't you think?" Fred persisted. John's thoughts were of the strained look on Edgar Ruiz's face, the stories that were circulating about the Mount Ada development, the polarizing of opinions around Avalon. Fred went on, "You get a bunch of high-rollers coming in to some big plushy resort and the next thing they'll want to buy houses here."

"There's an old Greek saying," John said finally. "God ascends stairs and descends stairs. The island's always changing."

"Not all change is good," Fred said. He tried to laugh at himself. "You know how it is with us newcomers. Last one in pull up the drawbridge! But the people that resort will bring here—" The pitch of his voice rose, and John could hear the fear in it. "They'll buy up anything that's for sale, buy it at any price. And that'll drive taxes up, and then people like us won't be able to afford to live here." He shook his head. "Somebody ought to shoot that Hayden."

John turned to face him, his intake of breath audible. "Just kidding, of course," Fred said.

"Of course." John clapped him on the shoulder. "But you are right, my friend. Not all change is good." John sighed, and then they walked in silence.

Chapter 2

The next block provided a diversion. "Just look at this, Fred." John paused at a storefront where a discreet hanging sign announced Photography by Yoshimoto. "My granddaughter Alexia's—Lexi's—studio." He beamed, his smile illuminated by the soft lighting in the window full of framed photographs. "The delight of our lives, to have Lexi living here on the island."

In one of the pictures, a bride and groom posed in front of the Casino. In another, bride and bridesmaids, cheek to cheek in a circle shot from above, formed a bouquet of faces in a close-up whose background was the Wrigley Botanical Garden. In a third, another wedding party stood in silhouette on a high ridge against the intense blue of a clear sky. To one side of the display hung a scenic shot of waves breaking against rocky island cliffs turned molten gold in dawn light. Opposite it hung a stunning portrait of island caterer Andrea Benet with a tray of exquisite fruit tarts.

"Beautiful work," Fred said. "That tray of desserts looks pretty good too."

"That's our friend Andrea." John smiled proudly. "She came to the island ten or twelve years ago and invested with a friend of hers who ran a little catering shop. After just a couple of months, the friend decamped and left Andrea high and dry with the business. And the bills. She barely knew anyone here, but she was a worker. She got the business going all on her own."

In fact, John and Celestina had taken to the tall, intense young woman and lent a hand and a bit of capital to help her salvage the faltering enterprise. "Oh, we introduced her to a couple good suppliers we knew, a cheese importer and a little network of family farms," John said. "Now she's the go-to caterer, and she has a beautiful gourmet shop, just moved to the front street. She's got the best location, right on Crescent where everybody's walking by. Does a nice latte in there too, if you ever get tired of the coffee at Chuck's." Andrea's catering company, Insula, had thrived, and her gourmet shop, La Cucina, drew well-heeled tourists to its imported pastas and cheeses, California organic olive oils and tapenades, and upscale corkscrews, whisks, zesters and other gadgets.

"Andrea's like family," John continued. "And four years ago, when our granddaughter moved out here, Andrea took Lexi under her wing. She introduced her to some other business owners who hired her to do publicity shots, and when Andrea got booked to cater weddings, she recommended Lexi for the wedding photography. So our little Lexi is doing very well."

"She's good," Fred said, nodding at the display. "You must be proud of her."

John nodded. "She finished school in Santa Barbara, then paid her own way to get her Master of Fine Arts at the Art Institute in Chicago. She'd like to do fine-art photography but weddings are building her reputation right now—and her bank account." He grinned.

"She grow up here on the island?"

"Nope. Her mom—our daughter Sofia—hated our trips out here when the kids were growing up. Our boys would head for the boat at the drop of a hat, but poor Sofie got seasick. And once we'd get here, she'd be miserable the whole time, dreading the trip back.

"But the funny thing," he mused, as much to himself as to his companion, "is that she loved the family business. She had to divide her summers between working in our markets on the mainland and coming to our place on the island, and she was mostly in the markets. And happy to be there. The boys hated the business. They hated hauling produce, they hated stocking shelves, they hated waiting on customers. Even as a youngster, Sofie hung out in the markets and couldn't wait to be old enough to work in them. By then we'd morphed into more specialty markets than grocery stores. She got her degree in business and has been with the chain ever since college. When we opened the first deli, it was Sofie that came up with the name Zorba's."

"Oh, my gosh. So that's why people call you Zorba. I thought it was just 'cause you were Greek."

"That, too."

"Oh, man, there's a lot of those places. I used to go to one in Lancaster. So that was yours! Great gyros, I remember. And what do you call that marinated lamb on skewers?"

"*Souvlakia.*"

"That. Yeah. Great stuff. No wonder all those meals you and Celestina brought over for Evvie and me were so good."

"Stina loves to cook," John said.

"I hope you know how much we appreciated that. We were still so new here when Evvie got sick, and you treated us as if we'd been neighbors for years."

"Neighbors are neighbors. We were just sorry we didn't have time to get to know Evvie better. She was a brave lady."

Fred nodded. They walked in companionable silence for a moment. Then he returned to the earlier subject. "So now your daughter runs the whole Zorba's chain?"

"Sofie and her husband. He's been the force that grew it, actually."

"How come there's not a Zorba's out here? Is there a rule against franchises?"

"Actually, Terry—my son-in-law—and I ran the numbers on one. Wouldn't fly. Not enough people year-round, too small a niche."

"Darn. Would have been nice."

"Yep. Greek delis run by a Nisei named Teruo Yoshimoto." John chuckled. "And Lexi's their daughter. Lucky they got to the point they could come to the island by helicopter, or we wouldn't have seen much of Sofie. Now Lexi, she loves the boats, loves the island, always has. It's wonderful to have her here."

They were just turning away from the window when a young man sauntered up. "Great photos, huh?" the slight, dark-haired youngster observed.

"Hello, Rhys. Just now getting off duty?" John greeted him.

"Yeah. Bunch of petty stuff, bunch of dumb reports to write." The slender young detective looked inquiringly at Fred. "I haven't met you," he said, extending his hand. "Rhys MacFarlane."

"Fred Paige. Glad to meet you, Mr. MacFarlane." They shook hands.

"Officer MacFarlane. Detective MacFarlane," John interposed.

"Just Rhys will do fine. Since you're a friend of Zorba's."

18

"So congratulations are in order," John said, clapping Rhys on the shoulder. "Rhys here," he added, turning to John, "just got his promotion to detective." And to Rhys, he said, "Fred's our neighbor. Moved here last fall."

"Well, if you've been here that long and I haven't met you, that's a good thing, I guess," Rhys said with a laugh that he choked off abruptly. "Oh, wait. Didn't I see an obituary? Your wife?" Fred nodded. "I'm so sorry," the officer added.

"Yes. Well." Fred looked awkward. "I haven't been out much. Until this last little while." He smiled. "I'll try to stay out of trouble."

"And I'll try to keep my foot out of my mouth, but I doubt I'll have much luck. It's nice to meet you, Fred. G'night, John." Followed by the sounds of their echoed "Good night," Detective MacFarlane ambled off down a side street.

"Nice youngster," John said to Fred. "Friend of Lexi's. Might be a little more than a friend, I'm thinking. Trouble with a half-Japanese granddaughter, you know? Inscrutable."

"Ah, kids these days. They don't commit themselves." They proceeded along, now and again meeting friends of John's who were introduced to Fred. "You know everyone," Fred commented.

"A place this small, it's family," John told him.

"You love it, don't you?"

"I do. It's usually so peaceful, so removed from everything. It doesn't feel that way now, though. And when something is worrying people, that worries me, too. Something, my friend, is not quite right."

"What do you mean?"

"People are worrying. Edgar is; I've never seen him tightened up like that. Our friend Andrea was, too, when I saw her this morning. There is something—a tension in the air. Don't you feel it?"

"Perhaps I'm too new here," Fred said. "But now that you mention it, Mr. Ruiz seemed pretty uptight, especially when I mentioned that Mount Ada project."

"Exactly." John put his hand on his friend's shoulder. "And perhaps I am an old man with too much time and too much imagination," he said. "Let's go home."

Their walk quickly brought them to the Katsaros house, a white-stuccoed two-story home. Like the other houses on Descanso Avenue, it had originally been one of the tourist cottages William Wrigley had built after he acquired the Catalina Island Company, and the island itself, in 1919. Like most of the others, it had been expanded, then rebuilt. John indicated a pair of chairs in the tiny side garden. "Want a sit and a cup of decaf?" he asked, knowing Fred dreaded going back to an empty house.

"Thanks."

When John emerged from the house with two steaming mugs of coffee, Fred was prowling the little patio illuminated by lanterns in the trellis overhead, looking at the tiles that bordered it. "These look like the real thing," he said.

"Oh, yeah. At one point my grandfather did some work for the tile factory that Wrigley had down on Pebbly Beach. He got seconds for next to nothing, still had a couple of boxes of them in the house when he died. I used some of those when I built the patio here."

"Wow," Fred said, looking up at the bougainvillea-covered trellis. "This is really beautiful."

"Thanks." John smiled. "I love bougainvillea. You know, I used to think it was native to California. But it's not. Explorers found it in Brazil and Peru. Now it's everywhere. About ten years back, Stina and I visited Zakynthos, the island where my grandfather had lived. We stayed at a little hotel on a hillside that was covered with it."

"Tell me about your grandfather."

Nothing could have pleased John more. "His name was Pero Katsaros. He came to California in 1899. There was a huge exodus from Eastern Europe at the turn of the century. At first he worked on a railroad crew. It was probably there that he met a couple of other young men from the Peloponnesus who introduced him to Catalina."

"Peloponnesus." Fred chewed on the word. "That's a part of Greece, right?"

"The southern peninsula of Greece," John explained. "And you know, when we got there we could see why he felt at home here. Los Angeles County is a lot like the mainland he had known growing up, those few times he went there. He grew up on an island off the coast, a small fishing village. It was a place that had gotten poorer and more isolated over the years. So he managed to get passage to America. And then war broke out in 1912, and he'd made just enough to get back home again."

"That was the war in the Balkans?"

"You know your history." John smiled. "It was the end of the Ottoman Empire. So many of the Greeks who came here went back there to fight. When Pero came back to California, he brought a wife, Iola, and a child."

"They had a baby? That was fast."

"No. Peter was four. Iola was a widow. Her husband was a friend of Pero's from the village where they were born. In fact, they fought together, and Pero was with him when he took a bullet and died. Promised him he'd take care of Iola and the boy." He put his coffee cup down. "Pero adopted her son. That was my Dad, Peter. He adored his new father; that part of things went well. But Iola wasn't impressed with the shack my *pappoús*—my grandfather—lived in. That fall, there was a bad fire, and his place burned up, along with about half of Avalon. She persuaded him to move to the mainland and even found herself a job in a laundry run by a Greek family. Pero drove truck for them that winter. But he couldn't settle into city life."

"They moved back here?"

John shook his head. "No. Iola wanted good schools for my dad, and she liked being in touch with other people from Greece. So she stayed in Long Beach, and my *pappoús* built another cabin here, and they lived apart for most of the year. My dad spent his summers on the island with him. She'd come too, for a while, but she was sick. She didn't tell anyone, not until she couldn't hide how she was coughing blood. Then they both—my dad and his father—blamed themselves for not staying with her."

"Oh." Fred's voice reflected his own sorrow. "But there's no telling, really, when it comes to blame, is there?"

"No, my friend. There is not."

22

Chapter 3

Saturday, June 7

Morning shadows and patches of bright sunlight played across the broad shoulders of Avalon Planning Commissioner Andrew Martin, who sat hunched at a glass table on his patio, head in his hands.

Before him was a letter on gray vellum stationery with a silver gilt letterhead: Hayden Development LLC. It had arrived three days earlier, and by now it might as well have been etched in his brain. Nevertheless he read, once more, the last two lines of a letter whose opening paragraphs described an upscale resort, lavish in its conception, on a promontory in what Andrew Martin had assumed was part of the Island Conservancy at the upper edge of Avalon.

By now you have probably heard of the plans for this property. That the land proposed for this project is not in the Conservancy may have come as something of a surprise to you, as it has to many.

And then that final, damning, damned paragraph, clearly no afterthought:

But you may also be surprised by the possibility that ICE could arrest any non-citizens in your employ whose documentation cannot be authenticated.

That was all. It was enough. Non-sequitur and not. A threat, not even veiled. He folded the letter and looked away. He didn't see how the sun dappled the deck of the elegant eco-home with shadows of eucalyptus boughs that danced in the light breeze, or gaze at the raked-gravel walkway between rows of aloes and deep-red euphorbias that led away from the deck and patio.

He saw the faces of his friends, his crew who tended the plants and worked on his landscaping projects: Armando. Juan. Santiago. Brothers. They had lived in Orange County for years, worked for his friend Jerry Bruce in Jerry's avocado orchard. When Jerry sold the orchard in 1999, and Andy bought a nursery on Catalina, the Lopez brothers were happy to hire on with him. They worked hard, had families, attended church, coached kids' soccer at school. They had Social Security numbers, absolutely clean records: not so much as a drunk-driving arrest among them. He didn't know whether they were legal or not. In 1999, nobody asked.

Of course, he supposed, he had known. What he didn't know was whether he had acted in time.

Had that bastard Hayden already contacted the feds?

Was everything he'd tried to do to prevent Hayden blowing the whistle a waste of effort? He could only hope he had been in time, but hope was such a frail thing.

In his mind, he saw gray concrete walls and tiny cells. He breathed their aura of despondency and hopelessness. ICE: the perfect acronym, he reflected: the new U.S. Immigration and Customs Enforcement, even more hopelessly bureaucratic than its predecessor agency, Immigration and Naturalization Service. He recalled visits with his parish priest to Mira Loma, the detention center in Lancaster, when members of the parish had been arrested: the despairing eyes, the endless questions about wives and children left without support, the hopelessness where there had been hope and determination, a modest living, even

24

the possibility of another amnesty and a way to become a new U.S. citizen.

"Andy?"

"Out here." Quickly, he shuffled a pile of papers, shoving the gray envelope into a manila folder marked "April minutes." Not that the letter with the Denver return address had anything to do with the minutes of the planning commission. Nothing and everything. The smell of coffee wafted onto the morning air through the sliding door. So did his wife's voice. "Shall I bring breakfast out?" Andy blotted his face quickly with a handkerchief, pressed fingertips to his temples, and shook his head to clear it. He took a deep breath.

"Sure, sweetheart."

Sarah Martin emerged from the kitchen, casual in jeans and a gauzy blouse, her long russet hair pulled into a knot at the back of her neck. She carried a tray with a carafe, a bowl of strawberries, and a plate of pecan-caramel rolls from Fibonacci, his favorite bakery. "You don't even have a coffee mug," she observed.

She gave Andy a long, appraising look. He could use a haircut. His dark hair was rumpled as if he'd been running his hands through it. His face looked bruised. She loved the broad planes of his cheekbones, the square of his high forehead. But there were shadows under the eyes, and a slackness along his jaw. Suddenly she could see him as he might look ten years from now. Twenty. She smiled at him.

"Not yet. I'll get one." Andy moved past her into the house. Sarah looked after him and sighed. She moved the stack of papers onto a chair, set out plates, and sipped from her own mug, Fiesta ware, tangerine. She gazed steadily at Andy as he returned from the kitchen with his coffee mug. He avoided her eyes.

Sarah put strawberries and a roll onto a plate and passed it to him. "Tough night?"

"Yeah."

"You were pretty late."

"Yeah."

"You look shot. Stressed."

"Yeah."

"Want to tell me about it?"

"Not much to tell you." Andy pulled the syrupy roll apart, dropped the pieces back to the plate, licked his fingers. "Had to meet with Roger, talk about an issue that's on the next agenda for the commission, and deal with some messy details." He shook his head again. "It's too complicated." He bit into a strawberry, nibbled the tip off, put the stem end back onto his plate.

"Complicated how? Is it that developer you've been worrying about?"

"Oh, hell. Yes, it's him. And now—he—" He stopped himself. "I really can't talk about it now, Sarah. Forgive me, darling. I've just got to think things through." Andy played with the half-eaten berry, picked it up, let it fall back onto the plate.

"He can't get his project past the planning commission," she said with certainty. "And certainly not past the city council."

"That's not the problem, Sarah! He—" Again, Andy stopped himself in mid-sentence. He stood. It seemed to Sarah that he shook himself mentally, pulling away from their talk, from her. "I've got to get over to the nursery. I need to meet with the planting crew first thing."

"You haven't eaten."

"I can't. No time. Sorry, darling."

Andy wiped his fingers on a flowered napkin, picked up a leather case, stuffed papers into it. He kissed the top of her head, grazed the sliding glass door with his shoulder and moved quickly through the kitchen. In a moment Sarah heard the door close. Heard the garage door whine itself open. Heard wheels crunch on gravel as Andy urged his electric cart up the drive and away.

Sarah picked up the abandoned breakfast and carried it to the kitchen. She tossed the picked-apart bun into the trash can and tipped the strawberries into her compost container before returning to the deck with her cooling coffee. She folded the blanket that lay tossed aside on the big lounge on the deck. He'd obviously awakened early. She'd heard him drive in sometime after midnight, heard the sigh of his sleep- apnea machine start up. She had meant to go in to him then, but decided not to; her sense of guilt was too great, her sense of loss even greater.

She had not slept, and heard him rise and prowl the deck at dawn. Sarah wondered where Andy had really been, wondered whom he had spent the long evening with, wondered what drove him, after such a late night, to rise so early.

She knew he hadn't been in the Conservancy office with Roger Cameron.

It was she who had spent the evening with Roger.

Chapter 4

The phone in his office in the Conservancy headquarters rang. Two rings, then silence. Roger Cameron lifted his head and glared at it. He hadn't expected to hear that signal again. It was over; they'd agreed on that. Parted as they began, as friends. About that part of last night, Roger felt good.

He wasn't sure how it had started, that thing with Sarah Martin. Some sort of insane magnetism. He loved his wife, had no intention of leaving her, couldn't bear the idea of how hurt she would be if she discovered his infidelity. He cringed as he thought how he had rationalized the affair: Margaret, who had for years responded to his every whim, seemed to have lost interest in him. She had seemed distant at times, lost in thought, bringing more work home. There were more and more nights when she said she was too tired for sex. But of course he loved her. And respected her. Everyone did.

He liked Andrew Martin, for Christ's sake; liked and respected him, too. He'd worked with Andy on every project the city and the Conservancy and the Island Company took on. He would never have set out to betray his Margaret, or Andy.

But somehow he and Sarah had taken to meeting, first just for walks, identifying some of the plants that grew only on Catalina, watching the hummingbirds, recording the emergence of the butterflies. He was flattered by her interest in the native plants and animals, and her admiration of his expertise as he pointed out the difference between species of grasses, the host plants for the indigenous butterflies. How often had he heard the trite phrase about one thing leading to another? That was about the size of it. One thing and another had led him and Sarah, three weeks earlier, to manage a guilty weekend in Monterey at a conference on ecotourism. They had booked separate rooms but hadn't planned on using one of them much. And when the one colleague of Roger's who'd planned to attend had come down with flu and cancelled, they had thought they wouldn't even worry, but they had worried all the same.

It was after that conference that they had come to their senses, realizing that what they had couldn't last, acknowledging the risks they took, but still reluctant to give up their stolen time together. Each tryst was one last time. Last night, walking the paths around the conservancy office, they had finally pledged to stop seeing each other.

He hadn't told her about the letter, and was relieved that she hadn't argued when he suggested they break off the affair now, once and for all. It had been his suggestion, hadn't it?

Better, he thought, to let her believe he felt the way she'd told him she did: in love or whatever it was, but still committed to their marriages. Thrilling at the prospect of being together whenever they could, but terrified at the prospect of discovery. Unwilling to face the thought of divorce, hurting her husband, his wife. And in the end, tired of the constant watchfulness, tired of the fear that someone would begin to talk.

Roger and Sarah had parted without even a last kiss, a kiss which might have erased their resolve. His resolve.

Of course, Roger admitted to himself, there was also fear: terror of the threat posed by Warner Kendall Hayden. Hayden, whose intrusive resort must be stopped at any cost, and who wanted Roger's support.

There were the letters.

Hayden's letters. Gray vellum, engraved, Hayden Development LLC letterhead. At first glance the first was an overview of a proposed resort above the Wrigley mansion, above the city limits, on the second summit of Mount Ada, overlooking the bay. He knew the site, and he'd heard about the project from a city planner and a couple of the county planning commission members. He didn't think it would make it through the planning process. Too big, too intrusive, out of scale for the island. Too likely to impact sensitive habitat.

His hackles had risen at the penultimate paragraph.

Hayden was going too far:

We will appreciate the support of the Conservancy as we go forward with this project, and perhaps we can continue in several cooperative ventures to bring additional tourism and revenue to the island: a new heliport, outback camping areas with cabins and spa facilities, four-wheel trails, adventure sites in the undeveloped interior, and more.

Support of the Conservancy. Why should he think he'd get their support? Presumptuous and portentous as that statement was, it was the conclusion of that letter that got Roger Cameron's attention, the conclusion that arrested his breathing, the conclusion that he had been rereading in his mind every waking moment since.

I would like to meet with you. I can show you photographs of the resort site and development plan, pictures of several of our finished projects, and perhaps most interesting to you, a photograph that a friend of mine took last month at the Casa del Mar in Monterey.

At their first meeting, Hayden had smoothly intimated that an extramarital affair was nothing out of the ordinary, but immediately moved to the assertion that he had been unable to bring his all-terrain vehicle to the island—silly regulation, that. He was sure, he'd said, that Roger would loan him one of the Conservancy's four-wheel-drive pickups. And Roger had loaned his pickup.

But of course it didn't stop there; Hayden had sent a second letter asking for a statement from Roger, representing the Conservancy, in support of his project.

Outright blackmail. Roger was dismayed at the intensity of his own rage. I will look forward to meeting you again soon, Hayden had written. Oh, yes. Wouldn't he just.

The telephone repeated: Two rings, silence, and then the usual progression of double rings. Roger glanced toward the conference room where visiting biologists were assembling the week's phenology report: Two observers from the Institute for Wildlife Study watching two eagles' nests on the west end were sure both chicks were thriving. A female Allen's hummingbird was making a nest in a young scrub oak near the parking lot, either an early start on a second brood or because her first brood had failed. Staff members counting butterflies had left word that the population of the endemic Avalon hairstreak butterfly looked strong in spite of habitat lost to last year's fire.

"Back in a minute," he mumbled in their general direction as he walked quickly out the back door and onto the trail that ran diagonally away from the building and parking area. He pulled his cell from his pocket and tapped a key. She answered instantly.

"Roger? I'm so glad you phoned back."

"Sarah. I'm surprised to hear from you."

"I know. I know, Rog." The words came in a rush. "I know we said we wouldn't, and I wouldn't have called, but I had to talk to you. Something's happening, Roger, something about

31

a development plan for property up beyond the Inn. It might be in the Conservancy, or maybe even in the city. Something's going on with it that's got Andy really upset."

Tell me about it, Roger thought grimly.

"And he's not telling me the truth about where he was last night. He said he was with you."

"I don't suppose you told him the truth about where you were last night either," Roger said reasonably.

"But—"

"It's good we made the decision we did last night," Roger added.

"To stop—What's that got to do with it?" Sarah sounded confused.

"Nothing. Nothing at all." Roger all but choked. "I hope," he added, then wished he hadn't said it.

"What do you mean?"

"Don't worry about it," he said weakly.

"Roger."

"Nothing, really."

"Rog, we have to talk." Sarah's voice became shrill.

"I know," he said. "But not right now."

Chapter 5

Andrea Benet paced around the polished floors of La Cucina. "I can't believe what I've done. Oh, damn," she mumbled, then stopped short. "I'm talking to myself. I never talk to myself!"

After lengthy negotiations with the Island Company, Andrea had recently relocated her boutique kitchen shop and deli to new quarters that also housed the office of her catering company, Insula, on the Avalon beachfront promenade. What should have been a time of profound satisfaction, however, was anything but satisfying.

As Andrea paced, her moving figure was reflected in one after another of the framed photos Lexi Yoshimoto had taken of buffet tables and specialty items, all favorite selections of Andrea's catering patrons. As if seen in a pier-glass, her reflection appeared to cross a steamy golden paella, then a tapas tray, a shrimp-and-kiwi salad with cilantro, a centerpiece made of skewers of fruit cut in flower shapes, an array of exquisite little tart shells filled with layered chocolate mousse and ganache. And then back again, over and over.

It should have been a source of pleasure for Andrea to see the colorful display of spatulas, stirrers and scrapers, whisks and zesters and frenchers and melon ballers she had assembled after they were delivered the previous morning. She didn't even look at it, nor at the row of vegetable-hued pastas like candy sticks in their tall jars, nor at the newly arranged ranks of tapenades and olives and capers her assistant, Francesca, had painstakingly reorganized according to size. Francesca loved order, dusted three times a day, cleaned display-case glass between customers. Ordinarily Andrea would have moved a jar out of line to encourage label-readers, or adjusted a utensil to a more pleasing illusion of casualness. Today she walked through the shop as if it belonged to someone else. Soon Francesca would arrive, and Andrea would be free to leave.

To deal with what she'd already done. To do what needed doing. Whatever that was.

"Stupid. Impulsive. Don't you ever think?" She realized to her chagrin that she was still berating herself out loud.

Five-ten, rail-thin with a striking mane of flax-blonde hair, Andrea paced, turned, and paced some more. Shadows darkened the half-moons beneath her ice-blue eyes. She had a headache. Normally a sound sleeper, she showed the effects of nights spent tossing, turning, and wishing she could rewrite her own history.

The moment handsome, self-assured Warner Hayden had first appeared on Catalina, Andrea had felt an unreasonable tightening inside. There was something about the man she found intimidating. Dangerous, but not the kind of danger she was all too often attracted to. His classic profile, his dark wavy hair graying perfectly at the temples, his impeccable tailoring, his air of complacent confidence, all worried her, even before he began revealing his plans. She had suddenly feared for the well-regulated life of the Island. She hadn't seen the personal threat then, but some instinct in her had recognized incipient trouble.

It must have been three months ago, she reflected, when Hayden first showed up at an Island Company reception for a retiring long-time board member, Carl Schilling. She had watched Hayden arrive with Schilling's sister on his arm. She watched him as he was introduced to Schilling, saw how he worked the crowd, moving from Schilling to his successor. Then members of the Conservancy board, the mayor, the Chamber of Commerce CEO. Hayden smiled, shook hands, proffered business cards, held eye contact. He laid a companionable hand on an arm, not too long, clasped an elbow, was glad to have met them, looked forward to seeing them again. And then he was beside her as she refilled a tapas tray. He sampled the squid in wine with fennel. "This is wonderful," he told her, taking her in with a bold sweeping glance, before turning to the next platter. "And what do you call this?"

"That's a Spanish tortilla," she told him. "Potatoes and eggs."

"Nothing like a Mexican tortilla," he observed. "Delicious. But not surprising. I understand you're the premier caterer on the island."

What was the answer to that one? She simply smiled and would have turned back to her work, but he'd forestalled her with that hand-on-the-arm gesture she had noticed.

"I'd like your card if you have one with you."

"I don't. I'm sorry." She did, but she wasn't going to let dishes get empty while she went to get one from her kit, and she didn't want his card, either. "We're called Insula. We're in the phone book."

"You're better at cooking than marketing yourself," he said casually. "But I have the impression you don't need to market yourself."

She had turned away, then, to collect empty plates that grazers had left on the end of the table, and hurried into the kitchen. When she returned with a refilled bowl of stuffed green olives, he was still there, looking at her, looking through her. She felt her face flushing. "I didn't get a chance to introduce myself. I'm Warner Hayden. I own property up above the Inn at Mount Ada. I have big plans for it." He smiled, making eye contact. "I'd like to include you in them. A high-class resort hotel needs a high-class food-service director. And don't tell me this is so sudden. I've done my research." Again, that smile.

"I'm a caterer, Mr. Hayden. And I'm sorry, I'm very busy."

"Perhaps we can discuss it at leisure over a drink when this little event winds down."

"I'm short-staffed tonight, and I'll be handling the cleanup." Immediately she regretted saying that; what if he offered to stay and help? But that wasn't Hayden's style.

"Another time then. I rarely take no for an answer, Ms. Benet."

As if that hadn't been bad enough, Andrea had found herself seated next to Warner Hayden at the annual Conservancy Ball. Andrea had hired two experienced teams, a prep crew and a quartet of excellent waiters, from the mainland to bolster her own crew catering the event, with its farm-to-table menu featuring fire-roasted vegetables, paellas cooked at the buffet table, and creme brulee, all in keeping with the Earth, Wind and Fire theme of the party. Francesca had volunteered to oversee the serving so that Andrea could accept the Conservancy's invitation to attend the ball as its guest.

"I'm so glad to have this chance to continue our conversation," Hayden had said after their host had done the unnecessary introductions. And, a captive audience, she'd had to listen while he outlined his plans for the hilltop site: the sixty luxurious rooms and thirty suites of varying size and opulence. The lap pool and the diving pool set among bowers of bougainvillea and grapevines. Spacious west-side balconies overlooking Avalon harbor and, on the east side of the building, balconies that overlooked Pebbly Beach.

"It's a waste," he said, "to have those industrial sites so close to that great beach: the power plant, the de-sal facility. Necessary, but hardly decorative. There are places where they could be nicely out of sight. I'm betting I can get the Island Company people lined up. By the time the resort's built, they'll be eating out of my hand. We can move the industry to where it won't be an eyesore. With my place as the new model, we can get some really upscale tourism going here."

Hayden mistook Andrea's raised eyebrows for interest. He continued, his voice rising above the big-band music and starting murmured conversations among other parties of revelers within earshot.

"The island's a natural for the pricey-adventure crowd. Helicopter them in, give them deluxe camping in yurts or those white canvas tents on decks with spas and masseuses and gourmet meals. Horseback trips with chuckwagons. Ziplines. Sailing trips with stays in Two Harbors. That'll do a lot more for the island than a bunch of scientists trying to root up broom and make the buffalos practice birth control. And bring in a lot more money than the day trippers who come over and buy a hamburger or a smoothie and a couple of postcards."

Then, as if she had been hanging on his every word, he smoothly excused himself. "I've got to go put big bids on some of the auction stuff. Jolly up the conservationists. Be back in a bit."

Andrea had watched as he made his rounds, exercising his smooth campaigner routine, but before he had returned to his place, she had fled the table.

She continued pacing her shop now, not noticing that it was several minutes past ten a.m., that weekend visitors were strolling in throngs along Crescent Avenue, and that she hadn't opened the doors. She felt as if she carried a weight on her shoulders. It was all happening, the unraveling she'd seen coming. Her own unraveling as well.

For four days, she'd been chewing on the letter Warner Hayden had sent. Opening it, she had assumed it was a form letter that went to all the members of the planning commission. He wrote of his plans for a hotel at the top of the bluff. While the Inn at Mount Ada was luxurious, his hotel and spa would be over-the-top opulent. But the letter continued. *I still hold out hopes that you will grace us with your culinary skills.* And it went on, from bad to worse.

I understand you are a candidate for the city council, so I am particularly interested in cultivating your support. And I suspect you will be particularly interested in supporting this project. It would be a shame if a bit of Oregon history should shadow the election process. Conservation is one thing; ecoterrorism another, don't you think?

Andrea knew the wording by heart. And it had made her angry, murderously angry. The smooth, smiling, elegant, slimy blackmailing bastard! She had never considered killing someone before. Oregon had been an accident. Reading the letter, Andrea had cringed, realizing the evil that she had sensed when she first met Warner Hayden had somehow become manifest: she knew now how it was that people could commit assault, even murder, deliberate, calculating murder. She, Andrea, the planning commission's negotiator and mediator, a dedicated pacifist: she could do that. Thinking about it made her hurt inside. Her cheeks flamed with it. Her heart raced with it. She paced and paced.

She had to stop thinking about it. She had to put it all away from her.

Like the spikes in the trees marked for cutting in that virgin forest in Oregon, like the headlines when the cutter had lost an eye when his chainsaw hit a spike and kicked back, like the arrest and its aftermath, like the somber meeting of Green Cell Number Three—her impulsive response to Warner Hayden's letter was something she simply must put behind her. She had to stow it away with those other memories in the bottom drawer of her mind, and forbid herself to go there.

She had to.

The sound of Francesca's key in the lock stopped Andrea's pacing and remembering. "Good morning! It's a beautiful day! And look what I've brought!" Francesca sang out, then stopped. "Andrea, what's wrong?"

"Nothing. Nothing. I've just been thinking about—about the Plein-Air breakfast and reception, wondering if we're really ready for them. Oh—Your displays are beautiful, Francesca. You're amazing. Can you manage here alone this morning? I've got something—something I have to take care of."

Without waiting for a response, Andrea bolted out the door.

Her assistant looked after her, worried.

"It's that damned developer," Francesca muttered, and turned on the "OPEN" sign.

Chapter 6

In his office in a two-story cottage a block inland from Andrea's new shop, Avalon City Councilman Edgar Ruiz also paced.

Edgar was up for re-election to the city council. A dwindling pile of yard signs lay on a table, green on cream, heavy recycled paper, not the plastic signs suddenly so ubiquitous across the country. Four years ago he had been amazed when he won, an upstart newcomer whose wife had inherited the family home on the island. As a builder who had worked his way up from roofing jobs in high school, he'd captured the islanders' respect and their imaginations with his environmental-design certification and his vision for development. Now he was challenged by a long-time islander who, his friends told Edgar, didn't have a ghost of a chance. He looked at the pile of signs without seeing them.

He thought back to his childhood, living simply but happily in Texas, then California, his parents hopeful, he and his little sisters doing well in school despite frequent moves. And then the long stretch after his father had been stopped for a defective taillight, could produce no driver's license because his wallet had been stolen from his worksite, and was deported to Mexico. Edgar, just starting high school, had worked afternoons and weekends and summers on a roofing crew to help his mother, a housekeeper at a nursing home. Somehow they'd managed to keep themselves and his two sisters fed and clothed.

During that time he'd been approached repeatedly by drug dealers who hoped Edgar would fall for easy cash and carry marijuana and heroin into the school. He'd resisted. In part, he remembered, his resolve had been bolstered when his English teacher had assigned the class a story by Washington Irving about a greedy New Englander who sold his soul to the devil in order to become wealthy. Ironic, he thought, that the story stuck with him. "And now Old Scratch has got me too," he mused out loud.

His reflections were interrupted. The bell on his door announced the arrival of two high-school girls, one blonde, one brunette, both wearing cropped tops and tight jeans with holes in the knees. "Hi, Mr. Ruiz," the brunette said. "We're part of the group that volunteered to work on your campaign. So we'd like to get a start on it and put up signs for you if you've got any left."

"Of course," he said automatically. "There they are. Here's a stapler; the stakes are in a bucket just outside the door. I think there are plenty. Oh!—And thank you," he remembered to add. He mustered a smile as the girls each took a dozen signs and trotted out the door, their flip-flops pattering on the tiles.

He looked after them, seeing in his mind's eye his beloved Alice Ann. Sweet Alice, whom he'd married when she wasn't much older than these girls. They had met in the community college where he was taking business classes and she was beginning coursework for a teaching certificate. She had taught kindergarten while he took classes on environmental planning and worked for a home-building contractor. She understood when he passed up better-paying jobs to take a position on with a green construction team, and cheered him on to get his own eco-building and design certification.

When Alice's grandparents died and left Alice their Santa Catalina home, the Ruizes moved to Avalon and Edgar realized he'd found the perfect place for his dream of building eco-homes. Bermed houses with solar panels, water-harvesting roofs, and drought-resistant landscaping had a market here, beautiful houses that people could live in with clear consciences about their impact on the earth, on this dry island's fragile ecosystem. And then the heart-breaker: he'd found it all but impossible to get conventional funding for the neighborhood of green homes he had envisioned for the hill above the golf course.

That was when, unwittingly, he'd made his pact with the devil. He sighed, looking at the letter that lay on his desk.

Edgar had all but given up on his dream of eco-homes on the island when a mortgage broker from San Diego, Aiden Rosen of Northside Mortgage, had phoned him out of the blue. A friend who owned property in Avalon, Rosen told Edgar, had heard about his project and thought it had merit. He was willing to invest in something with Ruiz's design principles secured by his LEED certification. The mysterious investor had charged Rosen's firm with underwriting the project on his behalf and offering a low interest rate because of its green plan. If Edgar would come in to his office, they could discuss the risks and the potential.

And so it was that The Arroyo, a community of eight green-built homes, became a reality. Edgar Ruiz, with his knowledge of environmentally-friendly building techniques and environmental issues, was not only accepted into the Avalon community but became a leader. Friends encouraged him to run for city council and he had run unopposed. He was delighted to share his training and his convictions with his public. And then, to fill his cup to overflowing, Alice Ann had announced that after ten years of diminishing hope, they were expecting a baby in the fall. Edgar Ruiz was a proud and contented man until the devil, Warner Hayden, arrived to claim his soul.

For several years, Ruiz had imagined meeting Rosen's mysterious property owner. He had envisioned someone from the field of science, possibly a college professor just about to retire, someone with a lot or possibly a parcel of land somewhere in the last unbuilt part of the town of Avalon who would show up in his office some day, telling him about his friendship with Aiden Rosen, and asking Edgar to build a new home on his property. One of Edgar's favorite daydreams was designing that home.

His benefactor, when he had appeared in Edgar's office several weeks earlier, was a landowner, to be sure. But he was no scientist, and he wasn't there to engage Edgar to build a green home, or anything else. Instead, Warner Kendall Hayden made it clear he was, in fact, the investor who had funded the loan Ruiz got for The Arroyo, and that the piece of property he owned was the promontory above the former Wrigley mansion. He smiled when Edgar expressed amazement. "You and just about everyone else on the island thought it was part of the Conservancy. Surprise," he said, unsmiling.

Ruiz had, of course, thanked him for backing the mortgage that enabled him to build The Arroyo. "Now the price of my vote of confidence in your project," Hayden said with a deprecatory shrug, "is simply your confidence in mine. Your vote, when my project comes up." He had described the over-the-top resort he proposed to build on that property.

No, he said, he didn't plan to offer Ruiz work on the resort project. "I don't want to compromise your integrity in any way," he had said, offering a grim smile. "Oh, I'd be happy to show you the plans, and the site, if you're interested. But they aren't as green as I'm sure you'd like. And it would be conflict of interest for you to be involved in the construction, of course.

"No, I would say your interest lies in the terms of your contract with Northside Mortgage," he added, and his smile as he turned to leave could have could have frozen the freesias blooming in the sun-drenched courtyard of Edgar's cottage office.

Sure enough, in the fine print of the contract between Edgar Ruiz, builder, and Northside Mortgage, was a brief clause providing that the second-party provider of the above-mentioned financing could, with six months' notice, raise the interest rate on the outstanding balance of the loan to the maximum allowed by law, a figure several percentage points above what Ruiz was paying. And although two of his buyers at The Arroyo had paid cash, Ruiz was carrying contracts on balances of varying sizes for the remaining six, and slightly over a million dollars remained outstanding to Northside. Not a huge burden at the present, but more than he could handle if the interest rate went up by more than three percent. Which it would, if he didn't cast his vote in favor of Hayden's project. Edgar resumed his prowling. He thought about what he'd found, exploring ways he might raise the extra interest on his payments. It could mean leaving the island, where his shy Alice Ann had bloomed among childhood friends, and where they had looked forward to raising the coming child. Alice Ann had fretted over the debt they were carrying while the homes he'd built were being paid off, her fears reawakened

44

with every dire prognostication about impending recession, every report that showed a slowing housing market. He couldn't bear thinking about her reaction to the huge increase in monthly payments he would have to make.

For a week, Ruiz had lain awake at night going over Hayden's plan in his mind. Huge, ostentatious, with the potential to put the Inn and several other smaller but elegant lodgings run by locals, islanders, friends, out of business. On the basis of construction and engineering alone it would require half a dozen variances from Avalon code. It represented everything he had worked against as a green builder: gross consumption, destruction of habitat, division in the Avalon community. He could only imagine the shock his fellow council members would register if he supported it, and his despair if he did so against the beliefs he valued most.

And what his fear had led to: that was something he couldn't bear to think about. He stopped pacing and sat resolutely at his drafting table. All he could do now was to step up the schedule on two new homes planned for the remaining property parcels at The Arroyo and hope for cash buyers. And, he thought miserably, hope against hope that his impulsive Friday-evening visit to Hayden's room at the Inn hadn't been witnessed.

Chapter 7

There's something about the light in Southern California that has long attracted artists. Add to that the romantic aspects of the South Channel Islands in their splendid isolation and Santa Catalina's colorful history, peopled as it has been with the Wrigley wealth, the stunning casino with its fabled ballroom, and the island's long association with movie stars, writers, artists and artisans. It's hardly surprising that Catalina has drawn plein-air painters through the years to work alone or to take part in festivals that culminated in wet-paint sales in the stunning Avalon Ballroom.

Maribeth Phillips, assistant director of the 2008 Plein-Air Festival, was anything but grateful for that long tradition as she sat at a computer in a borrowed office in the middle of Avalon on that Saturday morning. So much work, so many complications in the attempt to revive the traditional paint- in: she felt tension in every fiber of her body. On her screen was the list of Plein-Air Festival artists and the various hosts—hotels, bed-and-breakfast establishments and local artists and art-lovers who offered spare rooms—that provided housing for them. Beside her was a list of tasks at hand: Formatting the auction sheets as the painters titled and described their works-in-progress. Listing those they would finish in time for the Wet Paint Show that climaxed the week-long gathering of artists. Getting press releases to the mainland newspapers as well as the *Catalina Islander*. Meeting with the Chamber of Commerce to discuss the sale. And on and on.

A free-lance writer for travel magazines, Maribeth was used to deadlines, and the chaos of the plein-air event energized her. But there were, she conceded, moments when the artists were, well, wearing. She pulled her thoughts back to the updates on the artists' housing. Two French watercolorists had decamped from the Pueblo Hotel and moved into a bed-and-breakfast across town. They were paying their own way, to be sure, but there would be ruffled feathers to smooth if the revival of the festival was to continue into the future and its organizers were to expect the hoteliers to help sponsor future events.

Maribeth wrote a placatory note to the Pueblo people, and carefully made a copy which she added to her files.

Jill Reinhardt burst into the office, waving a handful of notes written on everything from paper napkins to the embossed stationery of one of the grand old hotels.

"Maribeth, have you talked to Andrea about the buffet? How in the world did we lumber ourselves with such a collection of difficulties?" the festival director asked rhetorically. "We've got two gluten-intolerants, two lactose intolerants, and a goddamned vegan. And now that blasted Viktor announces that he's allergic to everything in the nightshade family: tomatoes, tomatillos, eggplants, potatoes. Tomatoes and potatoes, for God's sake. Whatever happened to the kind of artists like Alfred Bierstadt, camping out and eating gathered greens and squirrels roasted on a stick over the campfire?" Jill stomped across the room, dropping her load of papers on a desk and running her hands through her close-cropped red hair.

"Bierstadt had a whole raft of people to carry his painter's umbrellas and his huge paintbox." Maribeth laughed. It occurred to Jill that her right-hand woman had a cackle that sounded just like Julia Child's. "He probably brought cooks to prepare his gathered greens and his roast ground-squirrel," Maribeth said, "and complained if it was burnt."

"Seriously, Maribeth. Can you possibly explain to me why I thought it was so brilliant to bring back the Plein-Air Festival? I have absolutely had it with my fellow artists. First Damien Seale's appendix bursts so he and Roberta cancel at the last minute, after all the work I did to get Novella Winter to take artists at Calendula House.

"Now we're two days into this thing and already Bianca and Viktor aren't speaking. Eve Jones is complaining that her hosts are distracting her from her work—she says they keep asking her to show little Maggie how to draw flowers and trees. And the folks at the Pueblo are miffed. Those French guys, whose names I can't keep straight, apparently expected to find Zane Grey at the Pueblo, if I understand them right, which I probably don't. One of them is ruffled about something, though, and they've moved out, and I've just spent half an hour convincing the Pueblo people we had nothing to do with the move, that we didn't know what it was about."

"I know," Maribeth said. "They've talked to me, too. I told them the same thing. Who can understand the French mind-set?"

"*Oui, en effet!*" Jill agreed. "And now," she moaned, "Carl Merriman's hounding me to set up an interview with Ellen Storey."

"Oh, great," Maribeth said. "Everybody knows she hates being interviewed."

48

"Right. Just as much as she hates being asked to paint to order."

"Where's she painting this morning? I should go out and warn her."

"I think she was planning to paint at that viewpoint she likes on the road to the airport, but she's not out today. She told Bianca she had a migraine. And I don't think she even knew yet that Carl's going to be stalking her."

Ellen Storey was the headliner for the revived festival. Jill and Maribeth were elated when she had agreed to come to Catalina. Ellen not only sold oil paintings for five figures but piloted her own plane, a snappy little Cessna Columbia. Even the Los Angeles papers had sent cameramen out on Wednesday to record the little buttercup-yellow plane's perfect touch-down on the tricky strip at Catalina's famed Airport in the Sky.

"It's good she came early, then," Maribeth commented. "Migraines can take a while to get over. She seemed kind of preoccupied yesterday. Maybe she felt it coming on. She was in great spirits when she got here."

"She's always kind of moody, though. Apparently has been ever since she lost her sister."

"A sister?" Maribeth turned from her computer. "I didn't know she had one."

"She doesn't, not any more."

"What happened?"

"I only know what I've read in the papers over the years, and a little bit from Andrea," Jill began.

"Andrea? She knows her?"

"I think they met in France, when Andrea was training in restaurants over there. Ellen's been here to paint before,

49

remember? And Andrea helped me persuade her to come for the festival."

"Oh. I'm sorry, I interrupted you. You were talking about Ellen's sister?"

"Her name was Elise, and she was apparently as brilliant at writing as Ellen is at painting. She got a PEN emerging writer award, she had stories in *Harper's* and the *New Yorker*, and she was teaching at one of the liberal arts colleges in New England. All this was in her early 20s, while Ellen was still in France. Then Elise had some kind of breakdown. Their parents had both died, so Ellen came home and took care of her."

"Home from France." Maribeth looked stricken. "That had to have been hard. But it was her sister; I can see how she had to."

"I suppose so," Jill said. "You'd know about that; you and your sisters are close. I envy that," Jill said. "Ellen kept painting, and got more and more recognition, but poor Elise couldn't write any more. She couldn't even teach. Ellen brought her out to Carmel about 20 years ago, thinking the change, the light and the sea, might help. For a while she seemed better, happier. And then she drowned. Nobody's ever said, but I suppose it was suicide."

"I wonder what happened to cause her breakdown."

"I don't know. I never heard Ellen talk about it. She sold the California house, and ever since, she's divided her time between France and New Mexico. She has a stone house in a little town on the Lot River in Quercy, and an apartment in Taos."

"And you said she's painted here on the island before?"

"Oh, yeah. One of her most famous pictures is the view from up above the Inn. The town and the bay in a light fog, very Impressionist, very beautiful. It's had a lot of attention."

"I think I saw it as an illustration in one of the plein-air books," Maribeth nodded.

"You know," Jill added, "she did that series of Woman in a White Dress pictures: wherever she painted, there was always a figure in a white dress somewhere. It got to be kind of a cult thing. But after her sister died, there weren't any more women in white. I thought maybe that would affect her prices, but she kept on selling really well. And the paintings she did here were marvelous, especially the one of the bay. She loved that view." Jill got up and stretched. "I'm guessing that's why she was willing to come be part of this festival; she's usually pretty much a loner. I think she was painting up there yesterday."

"Mmm. She said she got something started yesterday. I wonder why she didn't stay at the Inn if she's so fond of the view."

Jill shrugged. "She's got a waterfront view down at the Mariner. None of our other painters can afford the Inn, and maybe she didn't want to seem exclusive."

"We're lucky to have her, anyhow. And there should be some real competition for her work at the Wet Paint Show Sunday," Maribeth said. "Right. We've got to make sure everyone has a chance to bid on the pictures with no pre-sales. I've already fended off that Hayden person."

"Hayden? You mean the developer?"

"That's the one. He said he'll pay any price for a Story painting for his office. His office, for God's sake. Ellen told me he even asked her to paint a bigger version of that view from the bluff above the Inn. Came on to her at the cocktail bar the first night she was here. She was furious to find out that it was a developer who owns the property up there, and I think she was even more furious at his request."

"Really?"

"Well, yes. I mean—" she shook her head. "Asking Ellen Storey to paint a big version of something she's already done, so he can hang it in his office. How pretentious can some people get?"

"Maybe that's what she was being moody about."

"Could be. I'm just glad she wasn't staying at the Inn. She might have up and left the island." Jill perched on the edge of her desk, arched her back, and reached behind her to try to massage away some of the tension from her lower back.

"For somebody who seems so smooth, he seems to have rubbed a lot of people the wrong way," Maribeth observed. "You practically snarled when you said 'that Hayden person.' But he's certainly good-looking." She looked wistful. "I'm not sure I could have turned him down."

Jill laughed. "I don't think he's much used to being turned down."

Chapter 8

Jill and Maribeth continued their review of Plein-Air Festival woes. "Mr. DiMercurio can't drive tomorrow after all," Maribeth said, looking at her transportation schedule. "Can we get Lucy to fill in?" Various islanders, eager to feel a part of the arts community, had signed up to provide transport to artists who wanted to paint in places they couldn't walk to from downtown Avalon.

"Depends on who wants to go where. She's got a cart, but not a car." Jill ran her hands through her hair.

"Bummer. The French guys want to go to Two Harbors, and the guy from Georgia wants to go to the airport. Do we have any other volunteers on our list with cars and interior permits?"

"There's Andrea," Jill said slowly, "but I think she's going over town this afternoon. Said she was going to help her mom get ready for her move to one of those retirement communities. Maybe we can get them on one of the Island Company buses. Who else needs transport?"

Maribeth looked at her notes. "Eve wants to paint in the botanical garden, I think."

"We can loan her a cart for that. I think everybody else will be working in town or on the beach. Viktor might want to go down to Pebbly Beach, but he'll probably want to walk."

"Say, what's going on between him and Bianca?"

"Are they actually rowing, or is Viktor just sulking?" Jill asked, bending forward in a series of stretches.

"Sulking, I guess. He is, but that's putting it mildly," Maribeth said. "Sulking noticeably. She's ignoring him, he's looking daggers. And Thursday evening, she was having an ever-so-cozy drink with Warner Hayden in the lounge at the Inn. Maybe she was just trying to get to Viktor. Although," she added thoughtfully, "it looked to me like she was really warming up to Mr. Hayden. Practically purring. Well, who wouldn't?"

"Quite a few I could name," Jill said.

"Maybe she's going to paint a picture for him." Maribeth shuffled the papers in her file and shoved it into her desk.

"Oh, great. That's all we need." Jill went from rubbing her lower back to rubbing the back of her neck.

"Plein-Air: The Soap Opera." Maribeth rose from her computer. "Let me." She moved behind Jill and massaged her neck and shoulders. "Sheesh. Your muscles are so tight it's a wonder they don't snap. Lean into me." She kneaded in silence for a moment. "It's funny, isn't it? Bianca and Viktor were such a pair of lovebirds when they were at the last Plein-Air. In fact, they met here, didn't they? Remember how they went off together arm in arm, and told us all they were going to buy a van and drive across Canada together?"

"Ye-es. Well, that was years ago." Both fell silent as Maribeth focused her attention on Jill's neck and shoulder muscles.

"Better?"

"Yes. Much better. Thanks." Jill slid off the desk and went to stand at the window, and Maribeth returned to the computer.

"Viktor's been with Bianca every time she's come back to paint here, though, hasn't he?" Maribeth asked.

"Right, but we haven't had to assume responsibility for them. I think they're one of those couples that simply thrives on the old cycle: fight, kiss, make up." Jill clasped her hands and looked pensive. "It can't be easy for them, actually. Bianca's kind of skyrocketing; there's no denying that she's a personality, even if it's a difficult one. And her work has had a lot of attention from the critics. She's been hung in some pretty major galleries, while Viktor—well, his stuff hasn't. Not recently. The critics hate his new seascapes. He'd like to think he's the next Guy Rose, and his technique is great, but his colors—agh! It's not going to happen with all those grays and browns he's been putting in his cliffs. And his sands. And his waves."

Maribeth shrugged. "Viktor Sentik's Brown Period." She paused. "They're still a couple, though. After all, we contacted them at the same address, and they arrived together, and they're sharing a suite. But you're right; I don't suppose Viktor appreciated the fact that Carl featured Ellen and Bianca in the *Islander* story on the festival. Ignored Viktor altogether, and compared Bianca to Frida Kahlo."

Jill snorted. "Everybody compares Bianca to Frida Kahlo. I'm not sure why. Her work's more like Emily Carr's than Frida's. And did you ever see her paint a portrait of herself?"

"But she does look a little like Kahlo. Those dark eyes and straight-across eyebrows. If she braided her hair, she'd be a ringer."

"She would. And it's beginning to look like Viktor and Bianca are having a Diego Rivera-Frida Kahlo relationship. Maybe that's the point. Messy, those people." Her hands returned to the back of her neck, then she ran her fingers through her hair. "It's not going to make Viktor's work any brighter if his sweetie goes all soppy over that smarmy Hayden."

"I still want to know what you have against Mr. Hayden," Maribeth complained. "You really can't blame him for wanting an Ellen Storey oil painting. And look. He's rich, he's successful, he's handsome. Seems to me he has a lot going for him. And that big resort like he's got planned—gosh, it sounds just amazing. Spas and big suites. That would bring some money to the island. Some nice rich customers for our artists."

Jill turned from the window and stretched again. "You mean you think we're going to let ourselves in for more seasons of this?" She turned and smiled at her assistant. "Maybe you're right, Maribeth. But we don't need him getting our artists upset. The man just gets my back up. There's something about him—he—oh, I don't know." She shrugged, reached over, and shut her computer off.

"Come on," she said to Maribeth. "Let's go tell Andrea about all our allergy people and see what she can do to accommodate them. She headed for the door. "Maybe we'll get lucky and she'll have some new appetizers she needs taste-tested."

"You go," Maribeth said. "I've got to get these auction programs started. If Andrea's got something wonderful to sample, you can bring me a taste."

Chapter 9

Fred Paige, with time on his hands, had become a regular at Chuck's. The intentionally scruffy coffee shop near the pier where the locals hung out was, in fact, named Fisherman Joe's. The locals, however, had been calling it Chuck's as long as John could remember. And no matter who owned the shop or who poured out the thick black brew, the regulars called him Chuck.

John Katsaros sat over a cooling mug of oily black coffee. Fred installed himself on the stool next to him. Over the till, next to the fly-spotted NO TALKING POLITICS sign, hung a photograph of John's grandfather sitting on a rock where the landmark Casino would be built in 1929. Fred pointed to it and said to John, "Chuck here tells me that guy in the photo's your granddad that you were telling me about."

"Yep." John stirred his coffee thoughtfully. "He was a fisherman, you said?"

"Fisherman and handyman," John answered. "Not long after he came to California, he came out here with a couple of friends. Adrastos and Stefon," he said reminiscently, rolling the words on his tongue, tasting their familar foreignness. "Stefon had a fishing boat, and after a while, my grandfather bought it so Stefon could go back to Greece with a dowry for his sister. It gave him an excuse to come out and live here. He had a little fishing shack up on the hill. It was the back end of town back then."

"Guess it must have seemed a little like home," Fred observed, holding out his cup for a refill and settling in for some conversation.

"Yeh. That was when the Island Company was just forming, before Wrigley. The Banning brothers owned it then, and they were making Avalon into a place for tourists. Granddad helped the Bannings build their Greek amphitheater, and he took tourists fishing. That was before the Balkan Wars started."

"When he married your grandmother," Fred recalled.

John watched the current Chuck, whose name was actually Allen, industriously wiping the counter with a bar towel. "How about another fill-up?" He held his mug out, nodded at Allen, blew across the top of the brimming cup, and thought about the grandmother he'd never known, wondering what it had been like for her, raising her son almost alone in a strange country.

"The boy must have been pretty young when she died," Fred prompted, fishing for more of John's story.

"He was. Just fifteen. He—Peter—my dad—stayed on the island with his father then. He would probably have lived for years like my *pappoús* did, bachelors fishing, diving, hunting goats and working for whoever was developing the island. But one day, when Pero's friend Adrastos came out to visit, he brought his daughter." John smiled. "And that changed everything."

"Yeah?"

John smiled. "He fell for Alia, and I guess she felt the same way; they were married a year later."

"And they lived on the island?"

"No," John said. "When my dad said he wanted to marry Alia, my *pappoús* told him, 'Don't end up like me, alone. You live where your wife wants to live.'

"By the time they got married," John continued, "she was already working in her father's grocery store. Adrastos had started importing foods he loved from home: Kalamata olives, cured meats, Feta and Mizithra cheeses. His wife, Phoebe, made Greek breads. It was a good business. My dad worked for him for a while in Palos Verdes. Then my mom persuaded her father to set my dad up with another store. They bought a little grocery in Long Beach, and that's where my sister, Elena, and I were born."

"So you grew up in Long Beach?"

"Yep. And then when Mom's parents retired and went back to Greece, Mom and Dad took their first store on too. Of course we came out to the island whenever we could. I loved visiting *Pappoús* Pero out here, and so did Elena. And by golly, he left us kids his house, the one he built after the fire. He'd built onto it. Elena and I and our families would both come out on holidays. Our parents, too, whenever they could leave the store, or stores. When Elena moved to Colorado with her husband, Stina and I bought their half of the house."

"You were in the grocery business all along?"

"Uh-huh." John nodded. "More specialty markets than groceries by then. We'd added one in L.A. and one in Gardena. That's how it all started. The next step was the first deli. The first Zorba's."

"Makes me hungry just thinking about it." Fred laughed, but John heard the wistfulness in his voice.

"Come over and have dinner with us tonight. Stina makes wonderful egg-lemon soup she serves with swordfish. *Parasoupa avoglemono.* We get swordfish fresh off the boat down here at the dock."

"Sounds great."

"Bring your appetite." John stood up, realizing Celestina would be home soon from her morning's work folding bulletins at church. Unlike Pero, who didn't bother with church, Peter had gone to church with his mother and had raised his own children in the Orthodox Church. John and Stina, far enough removed from Greek tradition, had settled comfortably in at the Roman Catholic Church of St. Catherine of Alexandria when they moved to the island.

He headed for home, but hadn't gone far when Andrea hailed him. "Zorba! I've been looking for you! Do you have a minute?" One look at her anxious face made him aware it might be more than a minute she wanted.

Chapter 10

They sat companionably on Adirondack chairs on John's front porch. "I'm in a mess," Andrea confessed. "You know about the plans for a big hotel up above the Inn?"

"I've heard some," John conceded. "And you've met Mr. Hayden?"

"I've met him. Briefly." His tone conveyed all that needed to be conveyed; Andrea was reassured that their opinions were the same.

"John, he—he threatened me. It was blackmail, more or less. And I—well, I didn't handle it right."

She had intended to tell him everything, but she realized she couldn't. There were some things a friend shouldn't be burdened with knowing, and at the back of her mind, she realized she couldn't risk the possibility, even if it was slight, that she would strain their friendship too far if she told him what she'd done. John waited for her to continue, sitting totally still, his hands relaxed in his lap. The silence grew longer than she could stand. She backtracked.

"Do you believe in evil, John?"

"I wish I didn't, but yes, I do. Why do you ask?"

"The moment I saw Warner Kendall Hayden, before I knew anything about that travesty of a resort he's been planning to build on the promontory, I knew something evil was going to happen. Was happening," she corrected herself.

John nodded. "And where there is one evil, often others follow."

She looked at him, but he didn't elaborate. "I don't know how he found out," she said, looking away, "but he knew things about me that no one on the island knows. Well, you know some of it, John. When I was at Reed, I got involved with a pretty radical group. We protested some logging in the Coast Range."

"Yes."

"And we did more than that. We vandalized a couple of bulldozers, and we put spikes in some gorgeous old-growth trees that were marked for cutting."

"I knew you went to jail as a protest against the clearcuts."

"It wasn't just a protest, John. We were arrested for assault. One of the loggers," she said, choking on tears, "was—injured. Badly. His chainsaw hit a spike and bounced back. It cut him in the face. He lost the sight in one eye." She stopped and blew her nose. "We were so stupid."

John said nothing, just reached over and took Andrea's hand.

"We weren't jailed just for trespassing and protesting. When we were identified in court, the prosecutor said he intended to charge us with felony assault."

"And did he?"

"No. He probably should have. But some of our parents got together and hired an attorney who told the judge the timber company knew those trees had been spiked and didn't tell their crews. They sent them in to cut knowing they were in danger. So the judge ordered us released pending charges. And then there was a big community groundswell of support for us, and nothing was ever filed." She smiled wryly, wiping her eyes. "The county prosecutor was up for re-election.

"But our cell—our group—dissolved, and the same parents who hired the lawyer set up a fund for the logger who was injured. I guess we all did some growing up."

"I guess you did."

"And now it's come back to haunt me. Hayden's been using it to put pressure on me."

"To support his project?"

"Yes. And to work for him."

"Work for him?"

"Be director of food service in his horrible resort. I can't imagine anything worse."

"And he's threatened you with exposure?"

"Yes."

"Andrea, that's extortion. You should tell the police. If you have to, tell the community the whole story. Beat him to the punch, as they say. I don't think it would be that big a shock to people here."

"You think that?" She thought for a long time. "I suppose you're right."

"Then do it."

"It's too late for that. I've done something else stupid—" She paled. "I can't talk about it. I'm sorry." She rose as if to bolt away, but stopped herself and turned back. "I'll think about it on the boat, John. I've got to go over town. Mom needs some help with some things and I have to see the Island Company people first thing Monday morning about a couple of issues." She bent over and kissed John on the cheek. "Thank you. Thank you for always being here for me. I hope you know how much I have always appreciated you." She hugged him. And then she did bolt.

John watched her stride off. He sighed and went indoors, where Celestina was chopping vegetables for a lunchtime salad. "Our friend Andrea is disturbed," he said. "I'm afraid she has done something she wishes she had not done."

"Our friend Andrea," Stina echoed him, "is very smart, but—." She paused. "But I think she cares about this island too much for her own good," she concluded, kissing John on the forehead. She knew it annoyed him that she was taller than he, and she thought a little irritation might divert him from worrying.

"It is not possible to care too much about this island," he told her firmly. But he returned her kiss.

Then he remembered his invitation to Fred and kissed her again.

"I almost forgot," he said. "I invited Fred to dinner tonight. Could you be persuaded to make *parasoupa avoglemono*?"

Chapter 11

While Andrea had been searching for John, and then finding him, Jill had been searching for Andrea. Now she returned to her office, where Maribeth was already back at the computer, finishing the design for a new set of posters advertising Sunday's Wet Paint Show. "Can't find her anywhere. She's not in the store and not in the catering office. Francesca says she took off like a scalded cat. This seems to be one of those days."

"You need to paint. There's nothing going on here that I can't take care of," Maribeth said. "Go on. Get your chair and your paintbox and your easel and get the heck out of here so I can get these posters done and printed. And up."

"I promised update notices to the *Times* and the *Press-Telegram*."

"Done. You've been gone for a while."

"Well, Francesca was letting off a little bit of steam, so I had to hear her out. She was railing about your beautiful friend, Mr. Hayden. He seems to have Andrea worked into some sort of lather, and if Andrea's upset, Francesca gets all mother-hennish. I hope Mr. Hayden stays out of her way for a bit." She picked up a paper from the desk. "Anyhow, thanks. You're amazing. I wasn't looking forward to writing press releases."

"Go paint," Maribeth said.

Jill loaded up her gear. Once out the door, she stopped, mentally reviewing where the invited painters were most likely to be. And least likely. She stopped at Fibonacci, bought a ciabatta sandwich and a bottle of water, and headed for Descanso Beach.

There, to her surprise, she found Eve Jones hard at work. She had been there for some time, Jill guessed, once she'd seen the extent to which Eve had progressed on a view of the Casino. It dominated the canvas, with a brilliant teal harbor and palms morphing into the green of the hillside. Eve was doing a masterful job with the shadows below the elaborate balconies, but she smiled up at Jill and invited her to set up her easel beside her.

"Not the casino for me this morning," Jill said. "I'll join you but I'll face the other way: I'm in the mood for water and rocks, I think."

They painted side by side for a while, both absorbed enough to keep conversation at a minimum. Jill offered Eve half her sandwich, an offer gratefully accepted. Once they had eaten, they tossed the remnants to a watchful gull and resumed painting.

Their concentration was broken by a shriek from a nearby bench. "SHIT!"

They looked over at a young woman, clearly a tourist, in a too-tight turquoise top and shorts. She saw their wide eyes and explained, "Goddamned seagull. Bulls-eye on my ice cream cone." The girl skittered away to toss the dripping, desecrated dessert into a beachside garbage receptacle.

"Shit, indeed," Eve mouthed. Jill repressed a chortle. "I wonder if that was our seagull."

"If it was, then she got a bit of our lunch."

A moment later a shadow fell across Jill's canvas. The young woman, bereft of her waffle cone and ice cream, was looking for diversion.

"What a chicken-shit place this is. Five bucks for a goddamned ice-cream and then the damned bird craps all over it. The place is one big rip-off."

She took their silence as assent and approached. "What're you doing?" she asked.

"Painting."

"Like pictures?"

"Mmm hmm," Jill answered absently.

"Wow," the young woman said. "You're artists." She looked at Eve's work. "Oh! That's the Casino! Hey, do you know what time it opens?"

"I think the museum on the other side of the building is open now," Jill said. "The main part is only open for public events."

"Well what kind of casino is that?" the young woman asked, tossing her long, bleach-streaked ringlets. "You mean even the slots aren't open now?"

"Oh—ah, no. It's not that kind of a casino. It's an events center. Conservancy Ball, weddings, the Plein-Air Festival art sale next weekend, that kind of thing. There are movies in the theatre downstairs every night, and once a year there's a silent-film festival with the Page organ."

The girl stared at them, open-mouthed. "No gambling?" she asked finally.

"No."

"What a chicken-shit place this is," the girl exclaimed and teetered off on wedge-heeled sandals.

"Great vocabulary," Jill murmured.

"She could at least make it seagull-shit," Eve said. "I suppose we ought to feel a little bit guilty about that."

"Not a bit of it," Jill said. Once again, they turned to their work.

A middle-aged blonde woman wandered up and looked over Eve's shoulder, then moved behind Jill and watched as she wielded her palette knife to contour the rocks. The painters braced themselves for more inanity.

"Are these for sale?"

"Not yet. They will be next Sunday if they turn out all right."

"Why Sunday?"

"That's the Wet Paint Sale for the Plein-Air artists. You'll find us all over the island this coming week."

"Oh, really. That's interesting. I've never watched someone paint before." Jill hoped the woman would tire of watching soon; conversation didn't help her work. A younger woman approached, unseen. She slipped an arm around the other woman. "Emilie!" the older woman shrieked. "I didn't expect you so soon! I'd have been at the dock."

"I'm not early, Mother. I think time got away from you. Did you have your meeting with Lexi?"

"Oh, God, yes. Her work's beautiful, of course, but I found her just a bit, well, temperamental. She's certainly got her rules."

"Mum, let's let these ladies get on with their painting. You can tell me all about it on the way to the hotel. Where are we staying? I'll have to get hold of Lexi and set up a time to get together."

"Oh, darling, I've got a salon appointment for this afternoon."

"That's all right. You get beautiful, and I'll go talk to Lexi."

"But darling…" The two moved down the beach toward town, the mother's querulous voice audible from time to time for moments afterward.

"Another island wedding in the works," Jill murmured.

"At least she didn't ask me to show her how to paint," Eve said.

Jill rubbed her temples and ordered herself to relax.

"It's interesting, being here with so many other painters." Eve had changed the subject, and Jill breathed a sigh of relief, but judged her relief premature when Eve went on, disingenuous. "It's a real honor, getting to rub shoulders with painters like Ellen Storey and Bianca Alvorado and Viktor Sentik. I think Viktor's work is amazing, beautiful. I just wish Bianca wouldn't give him such a hard time. I mean she kind of rubs her successes in, any chance she gets. It must be hard for them to work with all that conflict going on. How do you choose who's invited, anyway?"

"For the earlier festivals, we just contacted painters we knew, but now we work through PAPA," Jill said, referring to the recently organized Plein-Air Painters of America organization.

"How about René and that other Frenchman, the one with the double-barreled name?"

"Jean-Marc? They're people Ellen met painting at Limoux last year. They've had work in one of the galleries where she shows her work in Taos. She recommended them, and they've been nice to work with." Jill didn't mention their decamping from the Pueblo, fearing that Eve might decide to follow suit and leave her housing. She could feel tension beginning to tighten the muscles in her neck again.

But Eve didn't continue her queries. Instead, she returned to laying titanium white against the dark diagonals of the casino shadows. Jill relaxed into her painting, and the two artists continued to work in a companionable silence until the light changed and it was time to go to dinner.

Chapter 12

The breeze was cool against her face as Alexia Yoshimoto jogged along the service road, yellowed grass giving way to bare ground underfoot. She'd hit a level spot after covering steeper ground on the paved road. She had turned off behind the Mount Ada Inn and was running along the hillside above the east end of town. It was a route she chose when she needed to get away from her worries and concentrate only on the road ahead of her. Right now, Lexi appreciated the cool breaths of air that met her at the inner turns where the arroyos were deepest.

Lexi needed cooling off.

Her shining, bobbed black hair bounced with each step. Her skin flushed with exertion. She mopped at her face with a bandana, then tucked it back under the belt of her running shorts.

Since early afternoon, the diminutive young photographer had considered committing a murder, a horrid, gruesome, bloody one. Her potential victim was a mother of a bride. Lexi's wedding photography garnered her awards and satisfaction, but she hadn't chosen an easy line of work.

Brides-to-be were typically indecisive, Lexi had come to realize. Jittery, prone to roller-coasters of emotion, and often impractical, they were still, at the root of things, happy. They were in love, and Lexi could excuse their dithering and their mood swings. Parents of the wedding couple were another matter. She'd encountered moms who were exacting, irrational, inflexible, often cheap, often whiny, and always demanding, either trying to relive their own weddings or improve upon them. And fathers of the bride—sometimes they were even worse. Reluctant to give up the daughters they still saw as little girls, they'd been passed over by their daughters in favor of the successful rival, the hapless groom. And afflicted with a rising tide of debt, wedding-dads frequently covered their panic with anger and bluster. She wondered if she was really prepared to stay with photography if her livelihood had to depend on weddings.

When she had set up her studio two years earlier, Lexi had aimed for a career in quality portraiture and landscape work. Friends advised her that the money was in advertising photography, but fashion didn't interest Lexi and she certainly wasn't about to spend her life focusing her Canon EOS 5D Mark II on furniture or handmade glassware or even high-end real estate. The other option was weddings, and on Catalina, there were always plenty of those.

Having settled for that, at least for the time being, Lexi set about becoming the best wedding photographer in the region. Her edgy compositions and careful workmanship were propelling her to the upper registers. She could always turn down a job, and sometimes she did, but when she agreed to work with a couple, the couple's parents usually came along with the job. She wasn't at the level yet where she could set her own terms. When she reached that point, maybe these meetings with mothers-of-the-bride-to-be would become a thing of the past. Lexi worked at unclenching her jaw as she ran through the familiar landscape: sun and shadow, blue and sage-green, greasewood and laurel and prickly-pear cactus.

Lexi liked to meet with her clients over lunch, to get a feel for their taste, the way they interacted. On this particular day, she had planned to meet with the mother-daughter duo of Emilie and Vivian Oleson at Swordfish before moving on to her studio to show them the video displays she prepared at the beginning of each job. Lexi always insisted on paying her own way at these planning luncheons. She knew this one would be troublesome when she arrived to find the mother of the bride already at the table, alone with a half-finished glass of white wine in front of her and a fretful set of lines between her brows. Vivian had greeted Lexi with the news that her daughter wouldn't be arriving on the island until later in the afternoon.

Actually, Lexi knew that part of the change in plans. She and Emilie Oleson had been friends, though not close ones, in college before Lexi took off for Chicago, and had crossed paths in the company of mutual friends since Lexi returned to California. They'd talked on the phone at mid-morning after Emilie had overslept and realized she'd have to catch a later boat to the island. Lexi knew it would be just Emilie's mom, but hadn't realized Vivian Oleson would have begun on the wine.

"I'd like to make a couple of things totally clear before you meet with Emilie," Vivian told Lexi, draining her glass. "First off, the family pictures before the ceremony. Our family situation is a bit—awkward. Claude—my second husband—adopted Emilie, and she'd always regarded him as her father, even after he and I divorced. So he's in, and I suppose that can't be helped. I gather you know Emilie. She's a darling, but she's so—naive, I suppose. She insisted on having Claude escort her down the aisle. Wedding traditions, father-of-the-bride, all that sweetness-and-light stuff," she added mordantly, signaling to the waiter to refill her wine glass. "No getting around that. But I expect you to make sure that his—that his current wife is not in the photos of Emilie and her family. Poor Emilie will feel she can't say no if the little broad crowds in. I've made it clear what I expect, but if it's left up to Emilie, she'll fluff it, and her pictures will be spoiled."

"Will that spoil them for Emilie? Are you sure about what Emilie wants?" Lexi had the impression that Emilie and her stepmother, Dottie, were on friendly terms.

"I know what I want, and I'm footing the photography bill," Vivian Oleson had snapped, gulping her wine. "I'm paying you enough. You can certainly do that much. I don't want that woman in any of the pictures." Great. She'd lost most of her afternoon, what with setting up a meeting with Emilie at short notice, and now she'd have to come up with options to work around the Oleson woman's ultimatum. The last thing a bride needed was that sort of an issue an hour before the wedding.

Vivian Oleson's second pronouncement was even more annoying: She wanted to be present for the entire wedding-morning photo shoot as the bride dressed. Lexi's brides usually preferred to have only the maid of honor in on the actual dressing, with the mother, in her own finery, brought in for a mother-daughter portrait and an informal, putting on jewelry or a veil, at the last moment.

Lexi knew the size of the dressing room in the Wrigley house, now the Inn, where the wedding was to be held. Two women plus Lexi and her photography equipment would just be workable. Four would be almost impossibly awkward, and Vivian Oleson didn't strike Lexi as someone who would be easy to maneuver around. Damn mothers of the bride anyway. No doubt they'd had to cope with their own mothers, so couldn't they remember that and back off a bit? She supposed not. But she'd been firm about the dressing-room photos. Vivian had received her ultimatum with an ill-tempered grimace.

And then she'd delivered the her closing salvo.

"I've said our family is complicated. I just heard from Emilie's actual father," she said. "He wants to come to the wedding, too. And I will not have that bastard there. While I was pregnant with Emilie, he had a girlfriend on the side. I found out when my check for nursery things bounced; he'd paid for his slut's abortion. He made no effort to see Emilie when she was a tiny little girl. He sent child-support payments, I'll grant you that, though his heavy-duty lawyer made sure they weren't what they might have been, considering his income. Can you think of any reason he should be at her wedding?"

"Not really," Lexi had responded, uncomfortable with the overload of information.

"I think he wants to buy his way into Emilie's life. Can you you recommend a guard service I can hire to keep him away?" That, Lexi had said, was outside her area of expertise. Later, at a meeting over iced tea in her studio with Emilie, Lexi didn't find things any easier. The poor girl was quaking with misery. Obviously, her mother had declared her intentions to Emilie, too.

"I actually think my mother's enjoying all this drama," the bride-to-be had confessed. "Actually, I don't want to see my birth father there, either. I mean, what an awkward time to be introduced. I've never known him aside from what my mother said, and none of that was good, but then it wouldn't be, would it? But hired guards? Really?

"All I want is a nice, pleasant wedding," she murmured. "I'm much more worried about the situation with Daddy and

Dottie; I don't want them hurt. And Mother will try her best to see that that happens." She had begun to cry then.

Now, as she tried to exercise away her irritation, Lexi recalled her efforts to calm Emilie. She wouldn't let Vivian call all the shots, she had assured the girl. Emilie obviously wanted her father and stepmother to feel included in her big day. Lexi had laid out a sort of plan to include Claude Oleson's wife of five years in a few shots Vivian wasn't buying. She offered Emilie a rock-bottom price for the extra photos.

But it still wouldn't be easy. She envisioned explaining to an elaborately coiffed and gowned Vivian that no, these photographs would not appear on her bill.

As for the extra father, surely he wouldn't try to be part of the photography scene. Oh, she hoped not. Maybe she should research a good guard service. She lengthened her stride. Enough, she told herself. Don't think. Just breathe. Just run. They'll sort it out. It's not your worry.

Lexi pounded along the road. This leg of the path was rough, and she couldn't afford a sprain or a sprawl with a full shooting schedule, half a dozen June brides with weddings large and small, ahead. A buzzing noise caught her attention. A cloud of flies swirled among the shrubbery just above the trail. She slowed to a walk. Breathed in an odor, sweetish, foul. Runners know the odor of roadkill. Something was dead. Fox? Deer? What would account for a dead animal here? She set off again, then returned, curious in spite of the smell. She parted the branches of ceanothis that screened whatever it was from the trail.

She saw the shoe first. A dress shoe. Black wingtip, slender, leather-soled, elegant. She drew a deep breath, pushed aside the shrubbery, and forced herself to look. A man sprawled there, fetched up against the thick greasewood bush. If the shrub hadn't stopped him, he'd have been right in the middle of the track, she thought irrelevantly, and I'd have tripped over him.

He might have been sleeping but for the awkward angles of his limbs and the fact that people in silk suits didn't sleep rough. His face was turned away, the head arced back. Lexi swallowed down a wave of nausea. She felt sure she knew who she was looking at, knew that dark wavy hair, that sleekly fitting gray silk suit. Now she saw that where the hair grew streaked with white at the temple, it was darkened with blood that coagulated on the ear and made a black track across the bit of visible cheek. The flies moved across it. The impeccable suit was rucked and stained, dusted with dirt and bits of twigs. But Lexi felt certain the dead man — and surely he was dead? — was Warner Hayden, the land developer who'd been on the island off and on over recent weeks, the real estate magician with the luxury resort dream, the smart businessman who'd pressured her to work on publicity for his resort. A resort, she knew, he'd planned to build on the promontory above where she stood. Above where he lay.

Crumpled, bloodstained, and dead.

Chapter 13

Lexi wrested her flip-phone from her pocket. One bar. She dialed 911, hoping the signal would be strong enough.

A familiar voice answered. "Nine-one-one. What is your emergency?" Relief flooded through her, gratitude that she had an answer, and that it was someone she knew: Rhys MacFarlane, the Los Angeles Sheriff's Office's youngest detective. Apparently the dispatcher was already off duty. Like Lexi, Rhys was a fervent incomer who had made the island his home as well as his workplace.

"Rhys! It's Lexi. I'm on the trail back of Mount Ada. Rhys, there's a b-body here. Just off the road. It l-looks like he fell down the cliff." As she stuttered out her message, the horror returned, and the revulsion.

"Are you okay?" Rhys asked.

"Yes. Well, no, not really." She struggled to continue. "Rhys, it's a man in a suit. I think it might be that developer who wants to build a resort up on top here. Hayden. He's bloody. There are flies. His head—" She stopped. She couldn't stop her voice from rising to shrillness, and she didn't want Detective Rhys MacFarlane to think she was an hysterical female.

"Never mind. You don't have to tell me. I was just filling in at the desk for a minute; I'll leave right now, as soon as I get a patrol deputy and paramedics alerted. I'll be there as soon as I can."

"Paramedics? Rhys, he really looks dead."

"Standard procedure."

"Do I have to stay here?"

"I think so. I'm sorry. Please stay, but not too close. Find a place to sit down. I have to call over town and mobilize the troops. Lexi? You doing okay?"

"Uh—yeah." Her voice shook.

"Breathe deep," Rhys said. "Hang in there. I'll be up just as soon as I can."

She heard a click. And there she was, alone in the chapparal with a man who, alive, had filled her with discomfort, even fear.

Dead was worse.

Lexi had first seen Warner Kendall Hayden at an Island Company reception, where she noticed him talking to her friend Andrea Benet. He was strikingly handsome, but Andrea wasn't responding to him like a woman attracted. Later, he'd been talking with Roger Cameron, the lead biologist with the Conservancy, and a couple of city commissioners. She'd wondered briefly who he was. When she mentioned him to Andrea, Andrea had shuddered.

"Too groomed, too smooth, too sleek," Andrea had said. "Like a snake. I think he's trouble."

A week later, the man was back on the island for several days, staying at the Inn. He'd spotted Lexi there with clients, had smoothly inserted himself into their group, introduced himself, and asked her to come have a drink with him to talk about a job he had in mind. He'd made it clear he knew more about her than what was on her website, and that made her uneasy. She could see him now, smiling, telling her about his plans for "the luxury resort of your dreams." Her dreams? Hardly.

He intended to build his luxury resort at the top of Mount Ada, a peak she particularly loved for its outlook, a wonderful place for portrait photography when her subjects were fit enough to hike the firebreak up to the top. She told him so. He'd mistaken her fervor for enthusiasm, and described how his first project would be a new road to the top. He wanted her to photograph his mockups, he'd said. "I know you've got just the right eye to superimpose them on photographs of the site." She had explained that she wasn't interested in advertising work, but he cut her off. "You're a businesswoman," he'd said. "You can't turn down lucrative work." His "you can't" had nettled her, and she had shaken her head as he, ignoring her response, added, "Especially a job which might well lead to a series of larger projects," as if that was the last word on the subject.

He went on to tell her he was aware that she had deep roots on the island, and then changed the subject to Avalon's beauty and the movie stars and magnates who had been part of its development. He'd been easy, charming, friendly. Magnetic, she thought, and she'd been half-flattered, half revolted. More than half revolted, though she couldn't say exactly why. Perhaps it was that smooth self-assurance.

She'd been disgusted with herself for not giving him an immediate, emphatic, this-is-final "no," but she had planned to. Soon. She did not want to work for him. Would not work for him. If this body was who she thought it was, she wouldn't have to explain that.

It was curious, she thought, that she could be thinking this way in the presence of something as grotesque, as horrible, as out of place on her beautiful, well-ordered island as a dead body.

"Oh, Rhys, hurry," Lexi murmured as she began to pace on the trail.

Her heart was hammering. She could hear it, pounding, thudding. She heard her breathing become harsh and heavy. And then she realized it wasn't her own breathing she heard. There were crashing sounds in the brush, and the sound of rocks rolling down the nearby fire trail, as if the steep ground was uprooting itself and getting ready to cover the horror that lay at her feet. The moving hillside became a person, a man, half running, half sliding down the slope. She gaped as he pulled up short. His reddened face looked dark against unruly white hair and beard. Sweat patched his shirt. He carried a butterfly net, and wore a backpack and a camera slung across his chest and belly. "I'm sorry; I didn't mean to startle you. I'm trying to get to the ferry on time, and I got lost up there," he said and started to edge past her, then stopped. He followed her gaze downward. "Oh my God. What's this? You—"

He caught her as her knees buckled.

Chapter 14

Lexi came to quickly enough to help the bearded stranger move her into a sitting position on a stone covered with a straggling growth of rock phlox. She felt sick. His grasp was comforting, although she realized he too was shaking.

"Thank you," she managed.

"Of course. I don't suppose you have a phone?"

"Somewhere here," she said. "I've already called the police. Rhys—a deputy's on his way. It may take a while for him to get up here. Can you—"

"Oh, lord. I was running for the ferry. I need to be in Santa Barbara tonight. There's a conference in the morning." He looked at her pale face and slumped. "I'll stay with you until the police get here. Assuming you want me to."

"Please."

Please, please, Lexi thought, don't let him be a murderer.

"Unless that's an obvious heart attack back there, I suppose I'll have to stick around for a bit anyway. It wouldn't do to go running off. I'm Bob Pyle, by the way. I'm a lepidopterist."

Seeing the color begin to return to Lexi's cheeks, and realizing it was helping to give her something to think about besides that lifeless form in the brush, he continued. "I live in Washington— the state, that is—but I'm going all over the country, covering as much ground as I can to look for butterflies. I'm calling it my Butterfly Big Year, recording as many species as I can in twelve months. I was up on the top of the island looking for the Avalon Hairstreak. Found several, in fact. But one of your nice rangers sent me on a short-cut back to Avalon and I think I lost my way. Seems like I've been heading for the boat for a couple of hours."

"Thank you for turning up here," Lexi said, extending her hand. The butterfly collector reached out his own and shook hers gently. She tried to smile. "I'm Lexi Yoshimoto. I was just running along this path—and it will get you to the Express if you head back the way I was coming and then run down the paved road. But I appreciate you staying. I've never—" She couldn't summon the words.

"I haven't either. The scientist in me wants to go investigate, but I can't make myself go back there."

"Rhys won't want us back there messing up the scene anyway," she said quickly. "In case it's—in case there's foul play involved somehow. Well, any unattended death, I guess. They'll have to have someone from the coroner's office or something. Probably even before they can move him." She wondered as she said it if that were true, and if so, where she had come by the information.

"Do you have any idea who it is?"

"I think so. I think it's a man called Warner Hayden. He's been on the island a lot over the last month or more. He owns property up top, and he's been planning to develop it, to put in a luxury resort with a spa and heaven knows what all. It's going to be something really deluxe, to hear him tell it. Was going to be, I guess."

"But he wouldn't have been able to build something like that, really, would he? With the island in conservancy status?"

"I think I heard that his property was outside the Conservancy boundary. Everybody had always thought it was part of the Island Conservancy, but I guess it was some kind of exception. It would still have to go through a lot of planning approvals, though, with the county and the city planning commission and probably the city council."

"Anything up there would foul up butterfly habitat. Among other things."

"I suppose so."

"Two species here on the island aren't found anywhere else: the endemic Hairstreak and the Catalina Orange-tip. You probably know all that," he added apologetically. "It would be a terrible thing to destroy any of their habitat. If their host plants are destroyed in even a relatively small area, it could threaten their survival. I don't know where his property is, but he could have been setting out to destroy enough habitat to wipe out a species."

Lexi looked at him intently. "You aren't one of those eco-extremists, are you? Stop at nothing to stop him if he was threatening butterfly habitat?" She smiled to let him know she was kidding. Probably.

Pyle laughed. "I'm a pretty peace-loving guy. I came back today—I was here late last month, but all I found were painted ladies and swallowtails—to try to find the avalona and the orange-tip. This is the only place they live. I found avalona up there on West Mountain—lots of them this time. You don't have an orange-tip anywhere about you, do you?"

When Lexi didn't answer, he returned to her question. "No, I'm not an eco-terrorist. If I went around knocking off everybody who destroyed sensitive habitat, I'd have been in the slammer long before this."

She smiled, then, and loosed a nervous laugh of relief.

They were deep in a discussion of clearcutting on Western Washington hillsides, Orange County orchards torn up to make room for subdivisions, and the impact of farm insecticides and genetic modification on migratory Monarch butterflies when Rhys MacFarlane, red-faced and sweating, came sprinting up the trail. Lexi jumped up and took a few steps to meet him.

"I'm glad I found you!" he panted, encircling her in a bear hug. "Are you okay?"

She nodded.

"You're pale. You should be sitting down. I tried to phone to let you know I was on the way, and to make sure where you were. But your phone said it was out of service. You must be in a dead zone.

"Oh!" He had noticed the bearded stranger still sitting on his rock beside the trail, butterfly net at his side. "Is this— And you thought—"

"No, Rhys. This isn't the body in the brush. This is Bob Pyle. He just got here. He's a—"

"Oh, my gosh! Dr. Robert Michael Pyle? No wonder you look familiar. The Audubon butterfly guides. And *The Thunder Tree*? Gosh! Wow. I'm glad to meet you!"

"Rhys." Lexi put out a hand to get his attention. "There really is a body."

"Oh. Oh yeah." His already flushed face reddened still more. "Of course. I'm sorry you had to—You two stay here, if you don't mind, and I'll just go check the—"

"Rhys, Bob has to catch the Express in an hour if he's going to get off the island tonight."

"It won't take long," Rhys said. "Can you—"

"Of course," the butterfly hunter said quickly.

"Thanks. Just keep an eye on her, will you? This has to be pretty awful for you, Lexi." With a quick smile for the two of them, the deputy loped off.

"If you miss the Express, I'm sure you could stay with my friend Andrea," Lexi said. "I live in the upstairs part of her house. It used to be my grandparents' place."

"Did you grow up here?"

"No, I grew up in San Diego. But my *pappoús*, my grandpa, grew up on Catalina and it was his parents' place. He kept it, and he and my *yiayia*—my grandma—retired back here. He started the Zorba's delis." She spoke with fondness and pride, and the color began to return to her cheeks. "The whole family comes out in the summers, and I always wanted to live here year-round."

Bob Pyle sought to keep her talking. "Have you been working here long?"

Lexi nodded. "Almost three years."

"And it's good with all your family around?"

"Oh, only my grandparents are here. My parents moved to Hawaii while I was still in college. When I wanted to set up my business here—I'm a photographer—my *pappoús* and *yiayia* made their top floor an apartment with a separate entrance for me. It's on the hill on the west side of town. Now they've got a smaller place down nearer the beach, in the flats. Easier to walk to everything. My friend Andrea bought their original house, and I kept my apartment—that is, I rent from her. Andrea's got a spare room, though, and I'm sure you could stay," Lexi said. "She's a caterer, and she has a really classy little kitchen shop called Cucina."

"A chain of delis, a caterer and a kitchen shop. Your people sound like a good crowd to hang with."

Lexi laughed, then cut herself off, shamefaced. "Yeah. Thank you. It's nice to talk about something besides—" she nodded in the direction of what lay up the trail— "him."

"It is. And I appreciate the offer of housing. I'm still hoping I can catch that boat, though. I really need to drive to Santa Barbara tonight. I'm supposed to be staying with the woman who's helping to underwrite this butterfly odyssey. And tomorrow morning there'll be leps from all over the country meeting up there. They're expecting a review of what I've found in the first four months."

"It's still quite a way down to town."

Rhys returned. "Looks like he fell," he said. "I'd guess it was an accident, considering that slope, but it's too early to tell for sure." he added. "A couple of quick questions for you, Dr. Pyle. Were you staying on the island?"

"No. I came over on the first boat this morning."

"And you're here for—?"

Dr. Pyle quickly outlined his Butterfly Big Year project.

"Did you know anything about this man's development plans?"

"No. Lexi here told me a little, but that's all I know."

Rhys nodded. "I don't think I have any reason to insist that you stay. I'll call my sergeant to get his approval, though, so I'll need to ask you to stop at the sheriff's station on your way to the boat to confirm that. We'll need you to give the watch deputy a phone number where we can reach you tomorrow if we have questions for you, and then we'll let you be on your way. Lexi can show you the quickest route down," he said, nodding to her.

"And if you miss the boat to San Pedro," Rhys added, "there'll be one to Long Beach in just a little while. You can take a taxi to the San Pedro terminal."

Pyle smiled wryly. "There goes the budget. Looks like it'll be back to eating peanuts and sleeping in the car. But thanks, Officer MacFarlane."

"Rhys, please. And hey, it was really great to meet you."

He watched wistfully as Lexi and the lepidopterist moved quickly down the trail toward Avalon, fingered a message into his Blackberry, then turned back toward the dusty corpse in the brush.

Chapter 15

Dusk was settling over the island as Rhys MacFarlane began what would be a long night. After talking on his phone with the watch commander, who had just got off the afternoon boat in Long Beach, the young detective had his marching orders. He'd phoned the sheriff's station and asked that his fellow detective, Ted Price, be dispatched to the scene. He'd found it simple to confirm, if unofficially, the identity of the dead man. The contents of a slim wallet and a silver card case in the inside pockets of his suit both indicated that the deceased was Warner Kendall Hayden, 55, of Denver, Colorado. Once he had some assistance, he could set about securing the area. Not long after Lexi and Robert Pyle left, Rhys was relieved to see one of the island paramedics, Seth Forman, come jogging along the track. Forman murmured over the contusions and bruises visible on the dead man's head and torso.

"Do you have to cut away his clothes?" Rhys asked.

"If we were treating him, we would. In this case we'll hold off until we get him to the morgue," Forman said. "I can see enough to say he sustained most of these injuries as he came down from up there." He glanced up at the steep escarpment. "He chose the steepest slope around here to fall down—or get pushed off of."

"Pushed—What makes you say that?"

"The big drop—that part of the bluff that's actually a cliff— is on the property that Hayden owned. He knew the property, was perfectly well aware of where it dropped off. He was going to develop it into some high-class resort. Okay, he might have gotten careless. Or he might have gotten into some kind of an altercation with someone up there. He wasn't keeping his plans a secret. A lot of people were beginning to hear about them. And a lot of those people weren't happy."

"Really." Rhys was a young officer, but he'd learned that you could find out more from letting people talk than by asking questions.

"Oh, yeah. It wasn't just the project. Francesca says she's never seen so many people so uptight about a guy. I've met him. Just. I'm not exactly in the mover-and-shaker league, so he didn't give me much more than the time of day. Evening, actually: it was at that farewell reception for Carl. Making over Carl's sister Cora like anything, and it looked like he was making some kind of play for Andrea Benet, too. He was pleasant enough, in a silvery-tongued high-roller sort of way, but hell, the Island's got lots of those, resident and nonresident. Francesca said Andrea was upset the next morning, though. Don't know what that was all about, but Francesca thinks there's something really—I don't know—off about him. Was off about him. I guess there can't be much wrong about a corpse except he's dead."

"So we might not have an accidental death here."

"It'll be interesting to know what the med examiner's going to find. Have you talked to Homicide yet?"

"Still waiting. So Mr. Hayden, here—could he have had a heart attack and fallen?"

"Maybe. I couldn't say that, either, until after the M.E.'s seen him. But he hasn't puked all over himself and I don't see any other signs that suggest a cardiac."

"Any idea about when he died?"

"Rigor's gone off; it would, in this heat. Can't really tell how long, but I'd guess maybe 24 hours. Maybe less."

MacFarlane felt a sinking sensation. "Could it have been this morning?"

"Possibly, but I doubt it. That'd be a stretch."

Still, MacFarlane was concerned. A second call to his commander yielded no results. Out of range, the display on his phone said. He hoped he wasn't going to catch it for letting Dr. Robert Pyle leave the island. He looked around, disgusted. "I don't suppose you carry tape with you. I'm not going to have enough—we'll have to secure the trail, both sides. And we ought to tape all the way to the top, too. By the time we get up there, there won't be enough light to see anything that could help us."

Forman nodded. Then he straightened and stretched. "Well, we can't remove him until investigators have had at the area, and I expect they'll want to look around here and up top before I get the all-clear. Probably won't happen until morning. Oh well. That's the nice thing about dead bodies: there's no hurry." He nodded toward the still, crumpled figure. "He's not going anywhere. Guess that's all we can do at the moment."

"We're stuck here, then," Rhys said. "We'd better not tromp around here any more, but we can't just go leaving him."

"Not if you want to keep your job," Forman said with a grin. "Your first go-round with one of these?"

"Yeah," Rhys said, feeling foolish.

"Your timing stinks," were the first words Rhys heard from homicide chief Red Garrick. The relief he'd felt when his cell phone vibrated didn't take long to dissipate. He suspected he could have heard Garrick's howls all the way from Monterey Park without the phone. "Geez. As if you didn't know we've got a serial killer over here, ranging all over the whole damned county. A hiker in Ritter Ranch Park Wednesday, woman, stabbed and raped. A biologist in Antelope Valley Thursday, bludgeoned. Yesterday, a couple of senior citizens in their travel trailer at Castaic Lake, one stabbed, the other stabbed and beaten. Or beaten and stabbed. Another one this morning, just outside Acton. A birdwatcher or something. Just for variety, this one's shot. Then raped.

"All hell's broken loose in L.A. County," he continued. "And all our teams were already assigned to other shit. We've called Bill Stanley in from vacation. Yesler's in Norway, for God's sake, and Tebo is still in the hospital. And now you, MacFuckingFarlane, you have to get into the act with another body."

"Yes, sir," said MacFarlane. "I'm sorry."

"Not half as sorry as I am. Who's seen him? Forman, I suppose? He there?"

"Yes, sir."

"Put him on, will you?"

Gratefully, MacFarlane passed the phone to the paramedic and listened to the exchange as Forman provided what details he could. He handed the cell back to Rhys with a wry grin.

"Sounds like one of your hoity visitors got a snootful and fell off a cliff," the chief snorted. "But until we confirm, Detective MacFarlane, you treat it as a crime scene."

"At least it doesn't look like this is one of your serials," MacFarlane said hopefully.

"You an expert in homicides now, Detective?"

"No, sir. But the evidence…"

Garrick ignored him. "Well, only D.I. we can send you is Jimmy Canham. We can spare Detective Inspector Canham.

Only it better be an accident, because even an ass like Canham is needed over here with what we've got going."

That sounded ominous. "Thank you, sir," Rhys said. There was a silence. Rhys waited. "One more thing," Garrick said. "We sure as hell can't get anybody out there till tomorrow, so you better secure the scene damn well. Make sure nobody comes in and steals your precious evidence. Or your precious corpse." The line went dead.

Rhys, with Seth's help, had used up all his crime-scene tape by the time Detective Ted Price came puffing up the trail. He needs more exercise, Rhys thought. Well, he'll get it now. Price was only ten years older than his fellow detective, but with his big ex-footballer frame and an incipient potbelly, he made the slender, blue-eyed MacFarlane, with his shock of curly black hair, look like a schoolboy.

"Hey, man, thanks for coming up."

"Oh, any time. Sheesh," Price grumbled. "Linda'd just brought me a chocolate brownie sundae. I left her eating it. At least I got to finish my burger." He pulled four rolls of yellow crime-scene tape out of his knapsack.

MacFarlane and Forman briefed Price as to what they'd learned thus far. "The guy ended up here. It'll be pretty easy to see the path his body took coming down."

Forman agreed to stay near the body while they secured the chute down which Hayden had slid and rolled before coming to rest above the trail.

"We'll tape about twenty or twenty-five feet away from the path each side, and broaden it out up top," Rhys said. "Then one of us is going to have to spend the night up there where he fell from—or got pushed from—to make sure nobody comes messing with the scene. And one of us gets to come back down and spend the night with Seth and our corpse." Price groaned. "Yeah, well, at least you've had dinner," Rhys muttered, winding the gaudy tape around the boughs of greasewood, Toyon and lemonade berry as he worked his way up the steep hillside, paralleling the route of Hayden's descent. The two officers worked in silence for a time.

"Hey, Rhys." MacFarlane was two-thirds of the way up the slope, Price a bit below on the other side. "Somebody else came down here. There's a diagonal cutting along here toward where Hayden slid down. Lots of places where ground gave way. Looks fresh."

"Oh, yeah. There was a butterfly hunter trying to take a short-cut to the mole. Famous lepidopterist, in fact."

"Yeah? Think he murdered our man?"

"No."

"Don't be too sure. Some of these insect people are pretty extreme, eco-terrorists with bug nets. Threaten a butterfly or a newt or an old-growth tree and they go ballistic."

"Whoa, Price, don't get ahead of yourself. We don't know anybody killed him. This is just precautionary. Probably the M.E. will find out he died of a heart attack or was stoned and fell off the bluff."

"You better hope so. If it's murder, Garrick's going to be gunning for you." Price snickered.

"Yeah? Sounded like he was happy to send us D.I. Canham."

"Canham? He still with the force? Shit!"

"Something to look forward to," Rhys muttered. "We better hope this was an accident."

"Cheer up," Price said. "From what I hear, our Warner Hayden was asking to be killed."

Chapter 16

Sunday, June 8

By early morning, fog had risen from the ocean to enfold Santa Catalina. At their posts on the trail under the bluff, where the body lay quietly enough, Deputy Coroner Seth Forman and Sheriff's Detective Ted Price flung off blankets, got up and walked stiffly up and down the trail as they had done from time to time through the night. Nothing more than a flighty deer had stirred on their watch. In unison, they checked the vacuum flasks that lay beside their folding chairs. Empty, both of them.

"Now that we can see if anyone's coming along, one of us could go get some coffee," Forman suggested. "Flip you for it: heads I go, tails you stay." When Price protested, he laughed. "Just checking to see if you're awake." He looked at his watch. "Never mind. Day shift's due in half an hour. Want me to phone and ask them to bring up coffee?"

"Nah. I think I want a warm shower and a long nap more'n I want more coffee," Price mumbled. Shaking out the blanket, he rewrapped himself and began to walk mechanically up and down the section of trail between the barrier cones they had put in place the previous evening.

Forman, bundling himself in his own blanket, subsided into his folding canvas chair, wincing as he tried to find a comfortable position. "I'm getting too old for this kind of thing," he muttered. The only answer was the croaking call of ravens.

On the bluff overlooking the Avalon harbor, Detective Rhys MacFarlane was pacing too, hands in his pockets, shivering in the fog which thickened and seemed to muffle the chatter of swallows somewhere overhead. His cell phone vibrated. Price, disgusted, was on the other end, reporting that Homicide had phoned. Despite the identification found on the body, the detectives would need to find someone closer to Hayden than his island contacts and the ID in his jacket to confirm his identity. "There have been identity thefts, they tell me," Price said, his annoyance audible.

"So one of us'll have to search Hayden's room. We'll need to come up with a next of kin or a long-time acquaintance. I'll go, if you like. It's almost light enough that Seth can see if anybody approaches down here. Give it a little longer and I'll go on over to the Inn and make sure nobody goes into that room.

"Seth says he can stay here till four," Price added.

Rhys heard another voice protesting in the background, but couldn't hear what Seth said. "Why four?" he asked.

"That's when he goes on duty," Price laughed.

"Oh. Right." Rhys realized cold and lack of sleep were taking their toll on his brain. "Sorry I missed that one." He resumed his pacing.

Manzanita and ceanothus bushes emerged from the fog as Rhys neared them; he found that they kept taking on the aspect of crouching figures ready to leap into his path or sidle away down the murky slope.

And then one of them did move; he was sure of it. The shape took on human form as it moved toward him.

"Sheriff's Department," he shouted. "Hold it right there. Don't move until I tell you." He tensed as he approached the now-immobile figure. Involuntarily, his hand moved toward his holster.

"Rhys! It's me—Lexi!"

"Lexi!" Relief coursed through him, but he checked the impulse to run to her. "You shouldn't be here." His voice was stern. "It isn't even six yet. And this is a crime scene."

"I know. Well, actually, it's after six. The coffee bar's open. And you've been up here all night. I've brought you a latte and a muffin from Buckwheat." She approached and he could smell the coffee.

"Mmm. I'd hug you for that, but my jacket's soaking from the fog. And you really shouldn't be here, Lexi."

"I know," she said miserably. He moved closer and saw that her eyes were shadowed, as if she hadn't slept any more than he had on his long night's watch. "I had to come ask you something. Something about"—she swallowed—"about what happened here."

"Lexi, until we re sure this was an accident, I can't answer questions about it. Not even questions from you."

"But Rhys, he's dead, and it might be my fault."

"What do you mean? Wait—don't answer me yet." But he couldn't let Lexi think he suspected her of doing anything criminal. Not Lexi. He couldn't suspect her of being anything but what she was: her beautiful, perfect self. Never mind procedure. She was looking at him intently, her expression confused, her eyes wide. He felt the world slide out of focus and back in again.

"Okay, tell me about it," he said. "But could you let me have that latte?"

It was already only lukewarm, but he drank it gratefully as she began to speak with uncharacteristic difficulty.

"Rhys, when I looked into the brush and saw him—Mr. Hayden—I didn't really know he was dead. I mean I thought he was, he looked—but I—I didn't do anything to make certain. I didn't even think about it. I didn't feel for a pulse. I didn't try to find out if he was breathing." She covered her face with her hands. "I don't think I could have made myself touch him." She looked up at him then. "But—oh, Rhys! What if he was still alive, and I didn't do anything to help? What if he could hear me, but couldn't speak?"

"Oh, Lexi! Look—I'm sorry if I didn't make it clear yesterday. Your instinct was right, of course. He was dead; there was nothing you could have done except suffer more horrors. I should have told you—he'd been dead for quite a while. Seth confirmed that." He suspected that shock had affected her thinking.

When she still looked doubtful, he reminded her, "You recognized that smell, remember? And I'd guess he never gained consciousness after he fell. And anyway, you know we couldn't have got here any faster than we did even if he had been alive." He took her hands in his. They were ice cold. "Would it help to talk to Seth? I can have him call you when he's relieved here."

"Oh, no, Rhys. I don't need to bother Seth. It's bad enough that I bothered you."

"Bother me? You could never bother me." He realized he was blushing. "And you brought me coffee."

"That was really an excuse. I simply had to find out…" her voice trailed off.

"Uh, Lexi?"

"Yes?" She looked up at him with that direct gaze that took his breath away, but not so completely that he lost his voice.

"Didn't you say you brought a muffin too?"

"Oh, yeah! Yes, I did. It's pecan bran. I hope I didn't squash it." She extricated it from a capacious pocket in her jacket. Still warm in its double napkin, it smelled of honey and cinnamon. "Here."

"You're an angel. But I'm going to have to send you away now, before my relief shows up. This still could be a crime scene. You don't need to tell anybody you came up here," he added sheepishly. "I'd never hear the last of it, taking a breakfast delivery at the scene of an investigation."

Chapter 17

Once again Rhys MacFarlane watched Lexi's slender figure retreat into the distance. The fog soon swallowed her up. He shivered, and as if shaken into life, his cell phone vibrated. "MacFarlane? Detective Inspector Jim Canham here. Homicide. Understand you got a guy that rolled down a hill on you." He chuckled. "Doesn't sound to me like you got anything worth investigating out there, but hell, a nice boat trip and a day on Catalina, with comp time 'cause it's a weekend? Sounds okay to me."

Someone must have approached, because Canham's voice suddenly became more official. "I'll be getting on the morning boat with a photographer. If the situation warrants, we'll call out the rest of the team, but I doubt we'll need to do that. You still out there with the body?"

"Yes, sir. Well, others are with the body; I'm making sure nobody comes into the area he fell from."

"Well, somebody will have to stick around till we arrive. Don't let that body of yours get up and wander off. What do you know about him?"

"His name was—is—Warner Kendall Hayden, sir. From what I hear, he was a real estate developer who had a parcel of land up above the upper edge of Avalon. It's property everyone around here seems to have assumed was in the Conservancy, but turns out it's not."

"Never mind all that stuff. This Mr. Hayden. Developer. What about him."

Rhys took a deep breath. "I've heard he was bringing a lot of pressure on the county, and local planners and council members, to approve his project—some kind of an ultra-posh resort."

"So... a resort. On a destination island. Doesn't sound like much of an issue."

"On Catalina, it's a big issue. He'd have to get through a long process. People thought that land was Conservancy, and they still think of it that way."

"Hmph. So he'd been around for—for how long, MacFarlane?"

"A few weeks. Actually, two or three months, off and on. Mostly on, the last couple of weeks."

"That's a pretty wide window. You met him?"

"We don't exactly move in the same circles, sir."

"No, I wouldn't think so." Canham chuckled unpleasantly. "Was he living over there?"

"On the island? I don't think so. Price called a friend who waits tables at the Inn and she said he'd been staying there, but she'd been away for a month so she didn't know for how long."

"So you don't know how long he's been on the island." Canham left a long pause, a condemning silence. "But you think—what? Somebody maybe wanted that land for something else? Or something against him? Maybe he was the kind of person who got people's backs up?"

"What little I've heard indicated he was very smooth and charming, sir. Maybe too much so."

"So somebody wasn't charmed?"

"I'm not sure, sir. General impression is he was a—" Rhys stopped and searched for the right words. "A pretty high-pressure kind of guy."

"Aren't they all?"

Rhys thought of Edgar Ruiz. "Not on Catalina. I mean—"

"Oh, God. No, not in the perfect little island world. Okay, assuming he wasn't all sweetness and light, what makes you think he didn't just fall off the ledge or cliff or whatever it was?"

"Well, sir, well, people like that make enemies sometimes. And Seth—the responding paramedic, I mean—said the physical evidence was inconclusive. He said it didn't look like heart attack or stroke. He thought we should investigate further."

"Oh, he did."

"He—"

"I assume," Canham cut in, "that you secured the room where this guy was staying?"

"I've been up here at the scene all night, sir, but we had one of the night shift guys tape the door."

"Well, I'm glad to hear you knew enough to do that." Canham's voice dripped sarcasm. "And who's relieving you at the site?"

"Two fire department volunteers. Commander didn't want to pull the day patrol off duty on a Sunday in tourist season."

Rhys could almost see the sneer as Canham spoke again. "God. Only on an island. And what are you doing next, Detective MacFarlane?" It sounded like a test question.

"Sir, your department instructed us to go to his room—Hayden's room—and look for information that will lead us to his next of kin or someone to confirm identification. I was going to meet Detective Price there."

"Shit. Well, do what you have to for that, but God help you if you rubes mess up evidence before my photographer and I get there. We'll be out on the ten o'clock boat."

"Sir, we…" Rhys realized the call had ended. He pocketed the phone and began walking again.

Half an hour later, the two wide-awake volunteers eagerly in place and the Chimes Tower bells sounding eight o'clock, Rhys met Seth at the Inn. The assistant manager, his crooked tie a sign of hasty dressing, regarded Rhys with raised eyebrows and ushered him through a door beside the reception desk and into a parlor to join Seth. A mirror over a miniature fireplace formed a portrait frame for the two: wan, hollow-eyed and unshaven.

"Can I offer you coffee, gentlemen?" the manager asked. They thanked him, and explained their need for a key to Warner Hayden's room. He disappeared briefly, and reappeared with two mugs of coffee and a key with a leather fob.

"Thank you. And for the coffee. We'd appreciate it," MacFarlane said, "if you wouldn't mention anything about Mr. Hayden's death until Detective Inspector Canham arrives. We are assuming, of course, that it's accidental, but we need to be certain of that, and if there should have to be an investigation…" He didn't finish the sentence, partly because of caution, partly because of exhaustion.

"Of course." Their host handed over the key. "Room 5," he said. "To your left. One of your people came in last night and taped the door. You'll find the room hasn't been slept in; the maid reported that yesterday morning, and I told her to leave things as they were. It's not unusual, when a guest is here for an extended period of time, for him—or her—" he added with a tilt of the head, "to be away for a night or two. A trip over town, a visit to a friend." He shrugged and shared a knowing smile. "We wouldn't have thought there was anything out of the ordinary."

"No one else has asked after Mr. Hayden?" Rhys thought to ask before they moved back into the hallway. "Called him, maybe? Or left messages?"

"Not that I know of."

"Or asked for a key to the room?"

"I'll ask the staff."

It wasn't until they'd moved quietly down the hall and entered Hayden's room that MacFarlane realized the answer he'd received to his last question wasn't exactly an answer.

Room 5 was immaculate, the bed neatly made up with the coverlet turned back. It clearly hadn't been slept in.

A search of drawers in the desk turned up a stack of files, which Rhys would have loved to search through, but there was no time now, and there was no need to look beyond the leather-bound calendar, gilt edged, which lay atop the stack. He riffled through it, and saw that it appeared to have nothing but cryptic notations on the date pages. Those could wait. He turned back to the first page, which he saw was custom-printed with the owner's name, business address, and contact information. Under the notation "In event of emergency please notify" was the name Harold Keith and three telephone numbers. The first number was the same number as that listed for Hayden Development, LLC.

The "Next of Kin" line was empty.

Chapter 18

Taking the leather-bound calendar from the desk in Hayden's room, MacFarlane and Forman resealed the room with "No Entry" tape and headed for the sheriff's station downtown. Seth Forman made the call to the first number. Rhys, realizing the boat bearing Canham and his photographer would be coming in shortly, retired to the restroom to wash his face and straighten his uniform.

"No answer at number one," Forman told him as he returned to the office. "We could hardly expect him to be at work on a Sunday. I'm guessing the second was his home, but we get no answer there, either. Not even a message. Looks like there are folks too high-class for voicemail. So—I'm assuming the one with the C is a cell phone. Should've called that one first, I guess." He dialed and, getting an answer, nodded.

Rhys heard the deputy coroner introduce himself, confirm that he was speaking with Harold Keith, and explain, "I'm very sorry to bother you, but there has been an accident, and we need to know if Mr. Warner Hayden has next of kin we can reach."

There was an audible response from the telephone, and Forman said, "Yes, it's very serious. He was found dead yesterday afternoon. Apparently he had fallen from a cliff." He took his notebook from his pocket, then turned to Rhys and gestured for a pen. "Single. No children?" There was a lengthy response. "Okay. Any siblings you know of?" Rhys handed

Forman his pen and Forman wrote busily. "Okay. In that case, is there any chance, Mr. Keith, that as his business partner you would be able to come out and identify him?" Rhys could hear a rise in the vocal timbre at the other end of the line. "Yes?" The gabble became less audible. "Yes, an ex-wife would qualify as next of kin. Yes, I do. Go ahead. San Diego. Vivian Oleson, O-L-E-S-O-N, 619–" he wrote busily. "Thank—" The voice was continuing. "Oh. Not at home? You–Do you have a cell number for her? No? Do you have any idea where she is? Oh!" He put down the pen and turned toward Rhys as the voice on the phone continued a rapid buzz. His face was taut with excitement.

"No, sir, I think we can take it from here. Thank you very much, Mr. Keith."

His eyes were wide as he hung up the phone and stood. "The ex-wife. He says she's gone to meet her daughter to plan a wedding—here."

"Here?"

"Hayden's ex-wife is here, Rhys. On Catalina."

Rhys sat down. Hard. "You've got to be kidding."

"Nope. Heard it with my own ears."

"I don't get it. How does he know that?"

"Keith? She'd phoned him. Apparently her daughter is Hayden's, from a very short marriage. Ms. Oleson called the firm to try to find out if Hayden would be on the island when she was here. Keith said she explained that she was checking because she was hoping to avoid seeing him."

"I'll call the Express. Find out when she sailed. I'll bet she wasn't trying to avoid him at all. A wedding? I don't think so. That's a funeral she's planning, Forman! Bet we've got it, just like that. Woah," he crowed. "I can't wait to see Canham's face when he steps off the boat and we've got it sewed up." Rhys MacFarlane was almost dancing as he picked up the telephone and dialed.

Forman headed for the restroom.

When he returned, Rhys was still on the phone, but he had subsided into a chair, a punctured balloon. "Thank you," he said expressionlessly, hanging up.

He looked up at Seth. "Morning boat from Long Beach. Yesterday. I just verified it. And if I weren't so sleepy, I'd have picked up on the name when you spelled it out. Mrs. Oleson. It really is a wedding. Her daughter Emilie is someone Lexi knew in college. She—she was meeting with Lexi about the wedding photography yesterday." He looked even more deflated.

"Hey, sorry, buddy. If there's no celebrating to be done, I think I'll pass on attending Canham's arrival. I'm going to go home and clean up. Maybe catch a nap. Call me if you need anything more."

The two left the station, Seth heading home, Rhys dragging his feet toward the dock.

Chapter 19

When Rhys met the Express, it was clear that his concerns were well-founded. Detective Inspector James Canham didn't walk, he swaggered. He didn't speak, he shouted. Flushed and bulgy-eyed, he bellowed at Rhys MacFarlane before he'd finished descending the gangplank. "You MacFarlane?" he demanded.

"Yes, sir."

"Rice, is it?"

"It's pronounced Reese, sir."

"Oh. What kind of name is that?"

"It's Welsh, sir."

Canham was in his face now. Rhys took a step backward. "Well, don't back your way off the pier," Canham laughed. "Right now, you and Gospel here are all I've got to work with. And to look at you, there's not much I'm going to get out of you." He turned away, leaving MacFarlane painfully aware of his bleary eyes, unshaven face and rumpled uniform. He probably smelled, too.

A tall man carrying a tripod and case stepped around Canham's bulky frame and extended a hand. "I am Officer Gospel Oni. Photo guy. From Nigeria, if you are wondering about the name and the accent. Our schoolmasters were from England."

"Rhys MacFarlane."

"Sheriff's detective?"

"Oh, right. Sorry. I'm not clicking on all four."

"I shouldn't think so. I am not up to much and I got four hours of sleep before this gentleman called me out. And you have been working for how long now? Thirty hours?"

"Close to it." MacFarlane smiled wearily.

"You two done with your pity party yet?" D.I. Canham barked another loud laugh. "We've got work to do. Where you keeping this body of evidence, MacFarlane?"

"We didn't move it, sir," Rhys said, gesturing toward the slope that rose steeply above them. "I've got a car waiting at the station. Let's go." He led the way, hoping their procession didn't attract too much attention. Fortunately, crowds of tourists intent on finding restrooms, coffee shops or their hotels seemed to take police presence in their stride.

An hour later, Canham's face was even redder. The body's inconsiderate roll to a landing place inaccessible by vehicle angered him. The stench and the buzzing rise of several hundred flies when MacFarlane and the reserve officer lifted the blanket angered him. The battered condition of the body angered him. "You idiots, this is all bruises and contusions, exactly what you'd expect when a person has a significant fall." He shaded his eyes and looked upwards. "How far did he come?"

"About three hundred feet, more or less. There's a steep drop from the top of forty feet or so, then a kind of a sloping ledge, then a sort of chute where there must have been a little landslide, probably after a fire. If he'd come down onto the ledge a few feet either direction, he'd likely have gotten caught on the brush well above here and maybe nobody would've ever found him."

"Guess you lucked out. Or maybe not." Canham took off his jacket and stood back, watching Oni haul his tripod around to shoot the body from each angle.

A fire department volunteer was on hand with a stretcher and body bag, ready to help his fellow reserve officer remove Warner Kendall Hayden from the hillside when Oni was finished. "Called the hospital," he told MacFarlane. "They've got the morgue room cooling. And we've got people on tap to move the body to Pebbly Beach for the copter this afternoon."

It occurred to Rhys that Hayden had planned to memorialize himself with his huge, high-end resort. The hillside had become another sort of memorial. He turned to Canham. "After they take the body away, I suppose you want to have a look around up top, sir?"

"No, I do not want to have a look around up top. I think this whole frigging thing is a waste of time. But I suppose I'd better do it, just to make sure your corpse here didn't leave a suicide note, or that a murderous eco-nut isn't up there bragging and begging to be arrested." Rhys gave a sort of gasp and raised his hand involuntarily in a classroom gesture.

"What." Canham glared at him.

"I should have told you before, sir. Someone else came down the hill just after the body was found. Will you need to talk to him?"

"Oh, really. Good of you to remember. Did he have a smoking gun?"

"No, he had a butterfly net. Named Marsha." Behind Canham, under the bush where he'd folded himself and his camera for a closeup, Oni made a choking sound, suppressing a laugh. Rhys realized he sounded ridiculous, and shook his head, trying to clear the fog. "Sorry. It's in my report, sir."

"Yes, well. I only had time to skim it during the crossing."

"He was sick," said Oni, flashing a grin over his shoulder.

He hunched himself back into the brush for a close-up Rhys didn't want to see.

"Helluva tide-rip out there this morning, swells from the west and wind from the east," Canham said, his exophthalmic glare as accusing as if it were Rhys who'd ordered the weather.

"Hung over," Oni mouthed behind Canham's back.

"So who was this Marsha person hanging around up here? A local?"

"No sir. I'm sorry to be confusing. The person was a lepidopterist."

"Say that in English."

"A scientist who studies butterflies," Rhys responded blandly.

Canham's brow darkened. "So you've got this butterfly freak named Marsha flitting around out here."

"Uh, no, sir. The lepidopterist—the person studying butterflies—is Dr. Robert Michael Pyle. He's written a lot of books about butterflies, sir. That's how I knew his butterfly net is named Marsha." Canham's expression told him his explanations were not making things better.

"God deliver us from idiots," he thundered. Then he paused and appeared to be thinking. "Hmph. Some of those eco-freaks don't care about people, only lizards and birdies and little fishies. And trees. Do you know how long he'd been hanging around on the island?"

"Just yesterday, sir. He said he came on the first morning boat. He—"

"So he says," Canham interrupted. "According to paramedic friend, your Mr. Hayden's been dead since the night before. You better hope it wasn't murder, though, and I am going to call and request an autopsy. You've let a pretty important witness go off to who-knows-where. On his word," he snorted. "For which you have no corroboration. You don't know when he came to the island, do you?"

"Not at this time, sir," Rhys said, shamefaced. "We have contact information where we can reach him today if we need it, sir."

"And then there's the person who found him," Canham said, ignoring him. "Always suspicious, finding a body. Especially one that was off in the bushes. How did they know where to look? What do we know about that person, Rice?"

MacFarlane took a deep breath. "A local photographer, Lexi Yoshimoto."

"Know anything more about her?"

Young, beautiful, too fine and lovely to be mixed up with a stinking corpse, Rhys thought. "She's lived on the island for several years," he said. "Great photographer, does a lot of weddings."

"What was she doing out here?"

"Running. This trail is one the locals use a lot."

"She have anything to do with Hayden here?"

"I'm not aware that she did," MacFarlane said. "I'm sure she knew who he was. Most people did."

"So yeah. Let's get ourselves up to where you think he fell from. I trust there's a road up there if this guy was going to develop the property?"

"There's a firebreak. We can get in there with the four-wheel rig," Rhys assured him. "Unless you want to go up the way I went last night. It's shorter." He gestured at the steep, rubbly slope. Canham looked hopeful for a moment, then showed it was possible to get even more red-faced than he already was.

Oni guffawed.

Score, Rhys thought. But I'll pay for it.

He smiled at Canham. "It's not so hard if you grab onto the brush and pull yourself up. Just don't grab for the cactus."

"No thanks," Canham said coldly. "Come on. Let's move out. Once we're back to the truck I'll phone the coroner's office."

"Yes, sir," said MacFarlane and Oni in unison.

Once on the ridge, Canham prowled restlessly along the track while MacFarlane showed Oni a patch of roughened grass he'd noticed the previous evening. Oni dutifully photographed it.

"I'd like to look at the ledge below this area again," MacFarlane said to Canham. "The light was failing by the time I'd worked my way up here yesterday."

Before the D.I. was able to answer, Rhys's phone buzzed. It was Price. "I'm up at the golf course. I did a little asking around at the Inn, and a couple of people saw Hayden Friday evening. He had cocktails served with a lady friend up there. Don't know who she was. He told the waiter he'd be having dinner at the golf course. Staff there confirmed. Said he had a couple of martinis. At least. He wasn't with anyone when he left about eight o'clock."

"Okay. See what else you can pick up, especially about who he was with. And thanks." He pocketed the phone.

"Well?" Canham was in his face again, looking expectant.

Rhys relayed what Price had told him.

"There. See? He got a little looped, came up to gloat, and fell over the edge. It'd be damned easy to do."

"With respect, sir, it'd be easy to shove someone off here, too," MacFarlane said, wishing he had the nerve to demonstrate. "So. If we move along here about 50 yards, the ledge slants up and it's an easy scramble down to reach it, and we could—"

"Look," Canham broke in. "We haven't come across a damned thing that indicates this was any more than an accident. A stupid accident, but that's it. Not," he added jubilantly, "unless the medical examiner finds something more than those bruises and contusions. And I don't think we missed a gunshot wound. So no, MacFarlane. We are not going to go messing about on ledges, and then maybe down a little farther in case there's a cigarette butt or maybe a little curare dart.

"No, my guess is alcohol and maybe a little something else. High roller stuff. But you, young Rice MacFarlane. Since you're so all-fired eager to process a murder here, you are going to accompany Mr. Hayden to Boyle Heights."

"Sir?"

"I'm sending you along to the morgue with the body. The post-mortem is scheduled for five-thirty this afternoon. Give or take a few hours." For the first time, Rhys saw him smile. "If you're really lucky, the M.E. will find a slab for you to sleep on."

Chapter 20

Most of the plein-air artists gathered late Sunday afternoon in the Santa Catalina Hotel near the harbor in Avalon. It was early for dinner, but at 4 p.m. the fog had rolled back in, sending those painters who were still at work hurrying to their hotel rooms or hosts' spare rooms to stow their paints and paintings. Now they occupied three tables in one corner of the hotel's main dining room. The maitre d' steered other early diners to the far side of the room, for already the noise level among the painters' group made him cringe.

Maribeth Phillips sat at a table with Viktor Sentik and Eve Jones. A fourth place at the table remained vacant. Eve alternated between trying to draw Viktor out of his gloomy preoccupation with the empty chair and assuming a brittle vivacity as she chatted with Maribeth. Ordinarily maintaining an outdated boho-chic look with torn leggings under oversized sweaters or enormous poet shirts, Eve had actually taken the time to put on makeup and a dress. Her eyes, shadowed with turquoise behind her wide-framed glasses, darted from time to time toward the doorway. Maribeth considered the import of these efforts and wasn't happy with her conclusion.

"It's been the most beautiful day," Eve babbled artlessly. "We were out on—what's it called—Descanso Beach? That means rest, doesn't it?" Maribeth nodded. Viktor didn't answer. Eve stared at him for a moment, fiddling with the pale shoulder-length curls she usually kept tamed in a tight ponytail. Then she turned to Maribeth. "But we weren't resting. Jill was painting there too for a while, and we were working quite hard, really. It was so lovely, beautiful light, really wonderful for painting, and I'm almost done with that canvas now. Just a few finishing touches to the Casino building.

"It's such a lovely building. This morning it looked almost bluish. Maybe that was the light playing off the water. That ocean is such a brilliant blue-green color; I'm sure people who see my picture will think it never could have looked like that." She turned back to Viktor. "I've seen pictures and heard so much about the Casino, but I was surprised to discover that it's not a casino at all. Just like that poor girl whose ice cream got seagull-bombed, I thought there would be roulette wheels and card tables." She gave a self-deprecating laugh. She turned to Viktor and described the scene with the girl and the gull. He drained his glass of wine and looked moodily toward the door of the dining room.

"So what happened there? At the casino?" she asked Maribeth. "Did the city make a rule against gambling?"

Maribeth smiled at her. "It never was a casino in that sense," she explained. "It was built to house a ballroom, a movie theatre, and exhibition space."

"But why call it a casino?" She turned to Viktor. "Doesn't that seem a little misleading?"

Viktor raised his thick, well-arched eyebrows and glanced at her, then away. "It's an Italian word," he said. "It simply means a public gathering place."

"Oh!" Eve said. "I didn't know that. I do love learning new things." She beamed a smile at Viktor, who sighed and returned his gaze to the empty chair. Then at his empty wine glass.

116

Maribeth suppressed a snort. She didn't know Eve well enough to know whether she was witnessing simplicity or an ingenue act, but she was pretty sure it wasn't impressing Victor Sentik. To fill the awkward silence, Maribeth asked Eve, "Did you know it's the second casino built on that space?"

"No. Really?"

"There used to be a rounded rock there; it was called Sugar Loaf Point. You've probably seen pictures of it. Actually, it shows up in several of the early plein-air paintings. There's one by Granville Redmond painted at the turn of the century—the old century—in a gallery in Carmel. And quite a lot of others, painted it—Ernest Narjot, and George Henry Clements."

"I'm such a neophyte. I don't know any of those names," Eve murmured. "Oh, Redmond, yes. But that was a long time ago."

"Well, yes. All of the paintings that show Sugar Loaf Rock were done a long time ago," Maribeth told her. "One of the early developers had part of it blasted away to build a hotel, but then the hotel, the St. Catherine, was built in the canyon above Descanso Beach instead. When Wrigley bought most of the island, he built the Sugarloaf Casino with a ballroom and classrooms for a high school."

"A ballroom and high-school classrooms!" Eve giggled. "What an odd combination!"

"I guess so. But it wasn't big enough." Maribeth, sensing desperation in Viktor's contemplation of his empty glass, signaled a hovering waiter for another bottle of Cabernet. "It was octagonal, but only a story and a half tall, and the town was growing. So a few years later he built another, the current one—with a movie theatre, one of the first theatres designed for the talking films that were just coming out."

117

"Wow. Seems sort of wasteful to have a whole new building," Eve said, glancing at Viktor. He didn't respond.

"Well, Wrigley had the old one moved and used it in his bird park. Now," Maribeth added, "it's been recycled again: the frame is a play area for a preschool."

Eve cocked her head. "So when was the current casino built? I forgot the first films were silent."

"They finished it in May of 1929, the spring before the Great Depression began."

"Oh, the Depression," Eve said. "That must have been an awful time."

Pouring red wine, Maribeth nodded, wishing Viktor would drag himself out of his own Great Depression and give her a hand with the conversation.

Mercifully, the maitre d' arrived with an hors d'oeuvre tray.

At the next table, conversation was more general. Ellen Storey, apparently recovered from her migraine, sat with three of the younger painters who had discovered that among them, they almost represented the four corners of the country: Washington State, New Hampshire, and Georgia, in addition to Ellen's New Mexico. "And of course here we are in Southern California, surely the farthest corner of all," said the New Englander. She had hung her signature Panama hat on the back of her chair, and a cropped cut emphasized her elegant head. Her black skin showed blue highlights in the low glow of the restaurant's illumination.

"Three coastal painters and you," drawled the lanky, gel-spiked Georgian, smiling at Ellen. He didn't notice that she flinched slightly. He had just joined the faculty at the

Savannah College of Art and Design and wore a maroon fleece vest with the SCAD emblem. Earlier, he had been resplendent in a purple T-shirt bearing the same name. Now he turned to the short, owlish painter from the Evergreen State. "What I can't figure out," he drawled, "is how you can be a plein-air painter in Washin'ton when it rains all the time."

"Watercolor," smiled the Washingtonian. He had ordered two bottles of a good Pinot Noir. He grinned at Ellen and refilled her glass.

Ellen smiled back and relaxed in her chair. Fine-boned, gray-eyed, she wore a blue linen tunic that contrasted with the long, dark hair she bundled into a loose knot at the nape of her neck. A salt-and-pepper streak ran from the hairline above her right eye over the top of her head. A tiny asymmetrical heart charm sparkled from a silver chain bracelet as she raised her glass.

"Is it really very rainy where you live?"

"Actually, yes. About 75 inches a year. My home looks out over Willapa Bay."

"Willapa!" exclaimed the New Englander. "I just read the loveliest book about the Willapa Hills."

"*Wintergreen*?"

"That's it!" She was delighted. "Do you know the author?"

"Bob Pyle? Yes, I do. He's quite a public figure up our way."

"Dr. Pyle?" The man from Savannah came to attention. "I ran into him yesterday, up on the top of the island. He was looking for some local butterfly, he said. Hairnet or bluestreak or something." He laughed at his own wit.

"Oh, my gosh. This must have been a stop on his Butterfly Big Year." Willapa nodded at Savannah. "He's doing a butterfly version of the Birding Big Year. I didn't realize he'd be here when we were. I'm sorry I missed seeing him."

"What's this Big Year thing?" New Hampshire leaned forward.

"He's spending the whole year going all over the country looking for as many of the different butterflies as he can find."

"I wonder how many species there are in the country."

"About eight hundred, I think." Ellen said. "Don't ask me why I think that. The older you get, the more unrelated facts you discover you've picked up along the way."

"Eight hundred different butterflies. Fifty states. Wow."

"Wouldn't it be fun to do that with painting?"

"Oh, yeah! Drive all over the country, stop and paint wherever you can, see how many canvases you can cover?"

"In all fifty states. California and the Gulf Coast in winter, Alaska and Maine in the summer."

"And when would you do Washington? When does it stop raining?"

"End of July."

"For two days?"

"Three, sometimes. If we're lucky."

"I wonder who we could get to finance it." Laughing, they began to toss out the possibilities: National Endowment, Pew Center, Warhol Foundation.

"We can hire a grant writer."

"With what?"

Ellen sat back, watching the three of them, smiling at their interaction.

At a third table, the two young Frenchmen, René and Jean-Marc, looked up from an enjoyable argument about which shade of blue was best for painting the Catalina sky to see Jill Reinhardt arrive at their table. "A good day painting, gentlemen?" she inquired.

"*Mais oui,*" responded the dark-browed René.

"Indeed yes," said the cadaverous, blond Jean-Marc. "Today it is a very good day."

"I understand," Jill began, "that you have made a change in your accommodation. Was there a problem where you were, at the Pueblo?"

"A mere misunderstanding." Jean-Marc looked uncomfortable. "And then we received such a very kind offer."

"About this misunderstanding," Jill said, refusing to be diverted.

René, however, burst into a noisy laugh.

"Jean-Marc, he does not know the literature so well as he thinks he does. He sees this Pueblo on the list and he reads somewhere that it is associated with the very famous author Zane Grey, so he chooses that place in order to acquire an autograph for his *petit amie*—his girlfriend?—Simone. Simone studies English literature at *l' Ecole Normale Supériure*, you see. But poor Jean-Marc, he does not do his homework. So he is here wanting the autograph of a man many decades dead, and he is laughed at. By a desk clerk!" He loosed his raucous laugh again. Jean-Marc's face blotched most unbecomingly.

"*Taisez-vous!*" he muttered. Turning to Jill, he tried to smile. "A woman who was at the opening reception tells us that she has the rooms for rent, that two artists who were to be there did not come, and that she will make us la *petite- déjeuner* each morning! And so we move to Mrs. Winter's house." His smile faded as he saw Jill's expression.

"*Alors!* Have we made *un faux pas?*"

"Well, you see, the festival arranges lodging and most of the places have made special prices for us. We like to keep them happy, and the people at the hotel weren't happy yesterday." That was an understatement, Jill reflected. "But then no one should have been rude to you. So don't worry about it. What's done is done. And the good thing is that you're making up for the Seales, the couple who had to cancel, at Calendula House. I'm sure Mrs. Winter is delighted, and you're fortunate. She's a wonderful host."

Meanwhile, René had begun a bantering exchange with Isaiah and Ariel, two middle-aged painters from San Francisco and Oakland who had taken their places at the table, all talking about the afternoon's quality of light which the Californians said was unique to their coast and René said was identical to that of the Cote d'Azur. "Here is the shoreline looking *exactement* as our Cap Ferrat," he asserted grandly.

"Except for all the houses and cars and crowds," Isaiah said.

Whatever René's retort might have been, it was lost. Every head was turned to the door. Bianca Alvorado stood there, backlit by the hallway chandeliers, racked with sobs.

122

Chapter 21

As the diners watched, Bianca drew a lacy handkerchief from her shoulder bag, wiped her eyes, drew a series of deep shuddering breaths, and tucked the handkerchief back into her bag. She squared her shoulders and looked around the room, commanding everyone's attention, painters and tourists alike.

"I am late," Bianca announced to the group at large.

She wore an emerald-green sundress with a wide flaring skirt and had wound her braided black hair into a crown, Kahlo-style. "But in our hotel, I have heard such terrible news just now. Terrible."

Viktor pulled out the chair next to him and half-rose, expecting Bianca to come and sit down. But she swept past him to Jill's table. "I am simply desolate," she said, looking around the room. "I can hardly believe it. My friend that I meet just days ago, when we arrive, Warner Hayden—I am sure some of you know him, this beautiful man, he has fall—fell—off a cliff. He was up where he was going to build his beautiful big resort, and he fell, and he—he is dead." She uttered the last phrase on a choked sob. But she didn't dissolve into tears again.

"I am sorry," she added, looking around with a pitiful effort at a smile. "It is just so dreadful. It has knock me right over."

Viktor came to stand with her, solicitous, holding her elbow. She leaned into his shoulder.

"Where did you hear this?" someone asked.

"In the hotel. I am just leaving my room when the woman at the end of the hall opens her door and is looking up and down the hallway. She ask me if I have seen her daughter—I think she tells me the girl is call Amy or Emily. She—the daughter—has gone off to try to get for her mother some tranquilizers. She looks just so dreadful." By now Bianca had the attention of the entire group. Viktor returned to his seat as she continued her narrative.

"So I tell her I think I have something in my room, and I take her there, and I give her a Valium, and some water. She is shaking, poor thing, so I ask her if she wants to tell me about it. 'My husband—my former husband—is dead,' she says. And can you believe it? She is the former wife of Warner Hayden. Her name is Vivian Oleson."

Bianca's voice rose as she continued her narrative. "She comes here to this island to help her daughter plan a wedding, and then the police, they come to her and say she must identify this man she has not seen for many years. She must go with the police and look at him, dead. What a thing!"

Viktor had begun to relax in his chair. He smiled a little knowing smile as Bianca continued, speaking as she walked between the tables to the one where he sat.

"I am so upset as well, hearing this news, but of course I try not to let her know that. She says they are divorced long ago, and since then she has remarried, and now she is divorced again. And this daughter of hers who is grown, she is his daughter."

There were furrowed brows and murmurs as her listeners tried to sort out Bianca's pronouns. Someone asked, "So if she hasn't seen him for so long, why is Mrs. Oleson so upset?"

"Oh," said Bianca grandly, "if you have love a person deeply, that love remains a part of your *psique*—your psyche."

"Or not," René said in an aside to Isaiah. "Maybe she pushed him."

Isaiah grinned. "Hell hath no fury, right?"

"Oh, God, Bianca's doing her Frida thing again," Eve muttered to Maribeth, glaring, but Maribeth continued to watch Bianca and didn't answer. Somewhere in the room, someone dropped a fork or a spoon. Bianca didn't turn to look. "And so she has to go, poor woman, to the hospital, to their very cold morgue room, and identify the body. It is most horrible for her," Bianca continued, ignoring the mumbling. "She say he is all dirt and dust and bruises and blood. They don't even clean him up and make him look nice. It is very hard for her. She say she can see bits of blood on his face still, and there has been blood coming out his ear. And his clothes, his beautiful suit all ruined. Eugh!" she gave a little gasp of disgust.

The company of artists had gone quiet, except for the occasional clink as someone refilled a wineglass. Several of the diners unconsciously pushed their plates away as Bianca continued her recitation. "Rocks and dust do a terrible thing to a silk suit. And to the handsome face." She wiped her eyes. "Imagine you have been marry to this man and you see him all dead like that."

"Imagine you have been married to this man and divorced from this man and maybe you aren't sad at all," the painter from New Hampshire whispered to the one from Willapa Bay.

"And then the daughter comes back, and she too begins to weep, and Warner is not even ever in her life," Bianca continued. "And here is one more horrible thing." She gestured with an outstretched hand, like a Flamenco dancer. Viktor stood as she moved again toward the place next to him at the table. "The person who finds him, finds his body out on the hillside, is the photographer who was going to make the daughter's wedding pictures. The mother has just meet with this photographer person yesterday."

Bianca picked up Viktor's wineglass and drank deeply. "Oh, that wedding will bring back such awful memories now! But maybe they will get a different photographer. I would." She shuddered and Viktor put his arm around her. "It is just too terrible, too sad. Such a waste. Such a beautiful man. And all those wonderful plans for that lovely place, that palace he was going to build." Her voice began to rise and tremble.

Maribeth and Jill, facing one another across their respective tables, exchanged glances. Jill was relieved to see that while Maribeth looked somber, she was composed. She hoped Maribeth had only been impressed with the man, not smitten. Jill turned toward Ellen, who had turned back to her plate and was buttering a roll. Ellen looked somber, too, but Jill thought she sensed relief in her demeanor and posture. Now, she thought, Ellen would no longer have to cope with Hayden's importunate angling for the painting he wanted.

A babble of conversation rose then, but Bianca's voice still sounded above the others.

"Such a lovely man," Bianca lamented, rubbing her shoulders cozily against Viktor's. "So charming, so handsome, and so much money."

Chapter 22

Detective Rhys MacFarlane never approached the Los Angeles County Department of Coroner on Mission Road without thinking what an odd name it had—what became of the missing "the," he wondered—and how unfit the building seemed for its function. Built as a general hospital in 1910, it was an extravaganza of red brick and pale marble, Romanesque scrolls and curliques. Its striped facade, he thought, might have been more appropriate to a vast amusement arcade than to a hospital, or now, to the offices pertinent to a morgue.

But then, MacFarlane reflected, it housed not only the coroner's offices but a gift shop called Skeletons in the Closet that sold everything from toe tags and tee-shirts to blankets marked L.A. County Medical Examiner. He wondered if people didn't find it offensive in an environment where most visitors were coping with shock and loss.

Each year, the coroner's office dealt with some 20,000 sudden, unusual or violent deaths. Warner Hayden's death, Rhys thought, might well have fit all three categories. But of course Hayden's body wasn't being dealt with in the jolly red-brick part of the building. Autopsies were conducted in one of the suitably gray and forbidding wings . Modern and capacious when they were added, they felt to Rhys as ancient as the main building, but gloomier. In the lobby of the first annex, he waited for the medical examiner. He shivered in a chill that stank of formaldehyde and other, less sterile, substances.

"You don't look much better than some of these folks I've been cutting up," a voice said. One of the medical examiners, Dr. Amy Porcuincula, approached, smiling up at him with friendly dark eyes. "I gather you've had a couple of long days."

"And a longer night in between," said Rhys, relieved to be dealing with a pleasant M.E. He'd met several during training sessions, including some he was happy not to have working on his case.

"There's a cot in one of the old examining rooms. You can catch a few hours sleep; I've got two in cold storage waiting for me before I get to your man. Second door down that hallway." She gestured with a gloved hand. Then, noticing Rhys's involuntary shudder, she added, "It hasn't had any corpses in it lately. It's set up for the medic on night duty, but we're working day and night to keep the stiffs from stacking up in the hallways. Nobody gets to sleep anywhere any more. You look dead on your feet. Have you eaten?"

"I had a sandwich on the boat coming over."

"Good. I'm glad you're not starving, but even if you were, I wouldn't recommend the sandwiches in our vending machine. I swear the vendor people rely on the formaldehyde in here to keep them from rotting. Coffee? Decaf?"

"The cot, I think. Before I fall on my face."

"Good man." She saluted and turned back to the autopsy room, a maze of stainless-steel tables and cabinetry, where several of her cohort bent over bodies in various stages of procedures: evisceration, storage of organs, brain examination. There was a low murmur of voices as examiners dictated their findings into recorders. Rhys averted his gaze to Dr. Porcuincula. She was a little less slender than Lexi, but had the same dark hair and petite charm. He wondered what had sent her into forensic

128

pathology; a morgue had none of the hopeful aspects of medicine that pediatrics, family practice, even oncology offered. As if sensing his gaze, she turned toward him at the door. "Would you like to be in on the examination, Detective MacFarlane? Or shall I bring you in when I've made my findings?"

Rhys hesitated only a moment. "Afterward, I think. I don't mind—"

"I understand. It's a lot of standing around with not much happening, but all of it revolting." She smiled broadly. "I'll wake you when I have some results to show you."

Detective Inspector Canham waved an anatomy book and raged while deputies MacFarlane and Pierce struggled to extricate ancient body parts from a greasewood thicket under the bovine gaze of a row of Catalina Island's buffalos. The buffalos stood around in a semicircle, their breath steaming in the cold air that bore an unpleasantly medicinal smell. One of them nibbled at his shoulder. Rhys, clutching the L.A. County Medical Examiner blanket closer, drifted toward consciousness. The troubled dream dissolved as someone shook him gently.

"I hate to wake you, Detective," Dr. Porcuincula said. "But I've finished with your Mr. Hayden." Rhys swung his legs over the edge of the cot and sat up, alternately rubbing his eyes and attempting to smooth his hair.

"It's okay," he said. "Thanks."

"I think you'll find my results interesting," the medical examiner told him. "I have the report on my computer. Come with me."

He followed, watching her rather than noting the bodies on shelves alongside the hallway, appreciating the feminine sway of her shapely hips and wondering once again how she had come to choose such a line of work. Back in the autopsy room, she was all professional as she turned to him at the examining table where a pale-green sheet covered the earthly remains of Warner Kendall Hayden. A laptop computer stood open on a small wheeled cart adjacent to the table.

"Here we are," she said, turning the laptop so that he could see the screen. "Blood alcohol level, .002. It would have been far higher at the time of death; most of it has metabolized, but for there to be even this much, it's pretty clear the gentleman had had several drinks before he met his demise."

Rhys swallowed. "An accident, then?"

"Bear with me," Dr. Porcuincula responded crisply. "Alcohol is just one factor here. I've sent out samples to toxicology, testing for cocaine and a few other things, and I'm guessing we'll find that our friend had a little of this or that in his system. Even at this remove, there's some inflammation of the nasal surfaces that suggests he used the odd hit of recreational cocaine."

"Okay," Rhys said. "And?"

She smiled. "And get to the good part? Are you ready for a look?"

Rhys took a breath, shifted his feet, and nodded.

The M.E. pulled back the sheet. "The neck is broken, and it would appear that that is consistent with a fall. No evidence of choking. See here?" She eased the head back on its neckrest and pointed with her probe at the junction of jawline and throat. "The hyoid is intact. Up to this point, what with the evidence of alcohol consumption and a possibility of cocaine, we would most likely say Mr. Hayden was the victim of an accidental fall.

130

"But here," she said. "Here's our little deal-breaker." She pointed to a bruise on Hayden's right temple. It looked like all the other bruises to Rhys: yellowing a bit at the edges, mottled, raw in places. "Look at the difference," she said. "Where these have small areas of deep haemotoma," she indicated bruises on the forehead and jaw before moving her gloved hand back to the bruise on the temple, "this one has more abraded surface and deeper discoloration. And beneath that, the skull is crushed.

"This injury," she said, looking up at Rhys, the smile gone now, "is the result of a directed impact with an irregular object, most likely a rock. Someone knew where to hit your victim. And it's quite possible, given the broken neck," she added, "that this gentleman was already dead when that someone smashed him in the head."

She re-covered the corpse. Rhys rubbed his chin. "After he was dead." He shook his head, hoping for some kind of clarity to emerge.

"That's right. The *coup de grace*." Dr. Porcuincula smiled wryly. "It's actually not that uncommon for a killer to want to be certain."

Chapter 23

Bianca Alvorado, despite her outpouring of grief, had been consuming rather a lot of wine at dinner. She had pushed the food around on her plate, but declared that she was far too upset to eat. Eventually, she had risen and rushed from the room. Glowering more darkly than ever, Viktor Sentik hauled himself slowly to his feet and followed her.

Bianca made her way unsteadily from the seafront hotel toward the smaller hotel where she and Viktor were staying. With no audience but Viktor, Bianca ceased her lamentations over the demise of Warner Kendall Hayden, but she sniffed loudly from time to time.

Viktor's natural taciturnity, or perhaps it was a cultivated trait to underscore his artistic bearing, did not lend itself to making comforting conversation with Bianca. She clung to his arm but still managed to stumble. "Ow! My ankle!"

There was no response.

"Viktor. Walk more slow. I have injure my ankle."

"Serves you right."

"Does WHAT?"

"Never mind. We're almost at the hotel now. Just take it easy." It was the most he had said all evening.

"'Take it easy,' he says. To me, who might have broken my ankle—ow!—because he was walking so quickly." Her voice rose. "And he says it serves me right." She groped for a handkerchief in Viktor's pocket and wiped at her eyes.

They were entering the lobby of The Bell, a small family hotel built in the 1940s. Viktor looked around. No one was in the bar, although laughter filtered in from the little central courtyard. Polite, well-behaved couples were enjoying the evening. He felt just a twinge of envy of these ordinary people, whose ordinary lives he generally scorned.

Bianca dropped his arm and hobbled with exaggerated difficulty toward the staircase. Grabbing the banister, she pulled herself laboriously from stair to stair, moaning softly, then limped to their room. Viktor, who had given up assisting her, moved ahead and deftly unlocked the door for her. Forgetting her limp, she sailed past him, then whirled to face him.

"So what is it you accuse me of?"

"Accuse you? Nothing."

"Nothing? I do not think so. You say it serves me right. For what? Tell me!"

"What do you think I'm accusing you of? Don't be silly."

"Silly? Hah! You are jealous."

"Jealous of what?"

"Of me. Of my enjoying the company, the courtship perhaps, of a gallant man. A handsome man. A cultivated man of business, who makes a good conversation, not sitting around looking gloomy."

"Cultivated? Gallant? Courtship? Hah! An opportunist shyster."

"What is this word shyster?"

"A crook, like as not."

"You speak ill of the dead." She sniffed and reached for a tissue.

"Don't go shedding fake tears."

She flared. "Fake? Why you think that they are fake?" She wiped at her eyes. "This was a man I was—was beginning to care about a good deal."

"This was a man you had known for two days. If you cared about anything it was his money."

"And that was another thing. Yes, he has—he had money, and he was not afraid to spend it. And now he is dead. And you, Viktor. You were jealous. You know you were."

"And if I was?"

"Then perhaps you push the man off the cliff to get rid of him. Did you, Viktor?" She rushed at him and clutched the front of his shirt in both hands. "Did you?"

He detached her hands, held them briefly in his own, and dropped them. "Bianca, dear, you are not worth killing for."

She grabbed the nearest movable object, an alarm clock, and flung it at his head. He ducked. The alarm clock shattered against the door. Viktor burst into harsh laughter.

Bianca stood for a moment, then joined in. They clung to one another, laughing uproariously, until the very ordinary people next door pounded on the wall. Then they went off, arm in arm, to the little bar downstairs. Bianca did not limp at all.

Chapter 24

Monday, June 9

Palm trees cast long shadows westward as the six o'clock Express chugged away from the Long Beach dock. Brown pelicans basked on pilings in the morning sun or coasted in kite-string procession over the rippling blue water as the boat passed seawalls and jetties on its way to the open ocean. Refreshed by a good, albeit short, night's sleep at his grandfather's place in Seal Beach, Rhys began to make notes.

D.I. Canham had phoned him after receiving word that the medical examiner was calling Hayden's death murder. He'd ordered Rhys to collect Hayden's appointment book, which was already in evidence, and to collect anything else of interest from the dead man's room at the Inn. "Go through the appointment book first. Follow up on anything that might give us a clue to who he saw the night he died."

"Yes, sir," Rhys had said. That seemed to him the obvious first step. "The appointment book's mostly in initials, so that won't be easy. We've already asked for records of any phone calls to or from his room. Unfortunately, the hotel doesn't have a switchboard any more, so we're dealing with the phone company. That'll take time."

Canham didn't seem to be listening. "I'll be over on the ten o'clock boat. I've arranged for a suite in the Islander for an operations center. I want you there when I arrive."

Oh, damn, Rhys thought. "Yes, sir."

"Oh, and I've got someone checking on that butterfly guy of yours. My source says he's quite the environmentalist. You'd better hope he's not taking the Monkey Wrench Gang thing a step farther. I'll see you in the op center at eleven. You and Price both."

"Yes, sir."

The deputy dutifully phoned the island office and passed the order along to Price. "Looks like it's you and me doing Canham's bidding," his fellow detective retorted.

"Right." Rhys ended the call and returned to his note-making, tapping into his Blackberry:

Scene: security? comb for anything? Fall path. Vehicle tracks?

H's clothes: all pockets.

Talk to wife. Locate daughter.

Comb hotel room.

Rhys sighed, stretched, got a coffee at the bar on the boat and returned to his seat.

Twenty minutes later, with a long to-do list for the day ahead, he was staring at his Blackberry when it vibrated. He looked at the message, then phoned. "What's up?"

"I bagged up the contents of Hayden's desk," Price told him. "Put them in evidence with what you already got. Calendar's pretty cryptic, all speedwriting and mostly just initials, no names, but there are some suggestive bits. Appears he met with Councilman Ruiz a couple of times in the past month. Also looks like he met with the city council and the planning committee, or at least went to their meetings. I guess we'll have to check the minutes to see if there's anything for us there."

"Ugh. But yeah. Can one of the reserves do that?"

"If Garrick hasn't got them all working on the mainland."

"Yeah. Wish the calendar were more help. We should probably check with his partner and see if he can tell us anything about their game plan, but when I talked to him at first, I had the impression he didn't know much about what Hayden was doing out here."

"Looks like the guy played it pretty close to his vest."

"I'm more worried about the scene," Rhys said. "I don't know what Canham's going to have us do, but I want to get back up to the top of the ridge before anything that might be there gets tromped on or blown away."

"I'll go now," Price said. "At least, I will as soon as I get everything from his desk here entered into evidence and make sure the room's still off limits. We'll have to go over it inch by inch. Meet you up there?"

"Fine. I just wish there were a couple more of us," Rhys grumbled. "Oh, well. Canham'll be here on the next boat."

"Yeah. Well," Price said, and what he didn't say spoke volumes. "See you."

The sun shone brilliantly on the green-going-gold landscape high above the Avalon harbor. The two deputies, gloved, had combed the area, stepping carefully and inspecting the ground beneath them for any signs of combat, of a fallen body, of anything out of place or indicative of human presence.

"Man, it looks like everybody on the island's been up here," Price complained. "Indents everywhere, but nothing you could really call a footprint." They paced in silence.

The only thing that caught their eyes as they probed the rim of the bluff was a small piece of crumpled green paper, inconspicuous in a clump of grass. It appeared to be a torn portion of a larger piece of notepaper. Wet with dew, it bore traces of ink but no message the deputies could discern.

"Interesting." Price carefully put the paper into a plastic bag. After no other evidence presented itself at the rim of the bluff, they slid, checking themselves by holding onto manzanita bushes, down to the grassy shelf that interrupted the long steep descent to the trail far below. Once there, they proceeded on hands and knees. A close inspection revealed areas of compressed grass.

"Wish we had that photographer back," Price said.

"Yeah. Blackberry photos are lousy."

"Better than nothing, I suppose."

"Couldn't prove it by me. Take notes, will you?"

Price typed into his Blackberry as MacFarlane measured and described the scuffs and areas of pressed-down vegetation. Once they'd identified the top of the chute down which Hayden's body had fallen and rolled, it became clear that he'd been dragged to the edge of the ledge. Suddenly, MacFarlane stopped his dictation in midsentence. "Oh."

"What?"

"Blood. I'm sure of it."

"Spatter?"

"Smear. Look here." MacFarlane pointed. Price looked. "Oh, yeah. And that's not all. Look over there."

"Oh, God. That's it." MacFarlane leaped to his feet.

"Well, that's where it was, anyhow." Price aimed his mobile's camera eye at the the place where grass had grown out from under a stone, making a pale star pattern in the turf.

"So now where's the blasted rock?"

"Someplace down there." Price waved an expansive hand. "Jeez. Couldn't our perp have just left it there?"

"With his name on it?"

"Uncooperative lot, perps."

Rhys looked over the bluff, then at his watch. "Not much time. The boat's probably almost halfway over."

"And we haven't checked for any castable vehicle tracks, either."

"Will you do that? I'll go on down and see if I can find that rock."

"It's a needle in a haystack."

"We could get a dog up here, maybe, but let me look first." Rhys checked his pockets, made sure he had gloves. "Meet you at the rig in half an hour."

Twenty-five minutes later, Price returned to the vehicle warm and frustrated, having found no identifiable tracks. There were some that were probably old tracks of rangers' rigs, and a more recent set that crossed and recrossed them, but nothing he could cast in the bone-dry earth. And there was no sign of MacFarlane. He phoned dispatch. "Anybody around who can go over to the Islander and help set up an op center?"

"Your D.I. Canham already called. Sounded pissed that you weren't here. Couple of the fire guys are over there putting in a file cabinet and an extra phone and computer desk."

"Thanks." He looked up. MacFarlane, flushed and dusty, blood seeping from a gash across his cheekbone, approached, grinning and holding up a plastic bag. "Got it!"

"How the heck?"

"Well, once I got down there I realized there was an awful lot of slope with an awful lot of rocks, so I didn't think there was going to be any joy just looking. And besides, we still might need to go over the area Hayden went sliding down. So I went back up to the bench with one of the rocks I'd looked at, and threw it, and then I went down to where it landed."

"And you found it there?"

"Nope. And I realized my throw might not be our murderer's throw at all. I was just starting to zigzag back up. I tripped on a rock, looked down and saw a fly walking across it. It's the right size, and there are traces of what I'm sure is blood. Just sheer dumb luck."

"Nice wound you got while you were at it."

"Huh?"

"You're bleeding, man. You must have gone straight through a couple of those manzanita bushes."

MacFarlane put a hand to his cheek and looked disbelievingly at the blood on his fingers.

"Just don't muck up the evidence with that," Price laughed. "Good going, Rhys!"

"And now, off to face the Canham."

The two officers got into their rig and headed off downhill.

Chapter 25

A frowning D.I. Canham greeted MacFarlane and Price in the sheriff's station. "We can go over to the Op Center," he said. "It's set up now, no thanks to you two."

"But sir," Price protested. "MacFarlane has the weapon. He found it."

"Weapon?"

"The rock."

"The. Rock. You just climbed up, or climbed down, and picked up the one rock out of a hundred thousand rocks on the damned hillside, and that's it."

"Well, yes, sir. More or less, sir. I—"

"You amaze me," Canham cut in. "You're supposed to be setting up an operations center, and dealing with Hayden's room, and you just go wandering out and—and what makes you think one rock out of a hundred thousand rocks on that damned hillside is the murder weapon?"

"Not exactly the murder weapon, if he was already dead, sir," MacFarlane put in. "More like the—"

"It seems to me," Canham thundered, "that if you fall off a cliff around here," he gestured at the surrounding hills, half of them barren in the wake of the fire, "you are going to fall on a rock."

"But the medical examiner—"

"Yes, yes, I know," Canham said. A look at his purpling face warned both deputies that Rhys's mild argument had only made things worse. "And," Canham added, "now that we have to assume we've got a murder on our hands, we're back to you, McFarlane, letting our prime suspect sail away to God knows where. Brilliant work, Deputy. Now we've got to go to hell and gone to get hold of the creep."

MacFarlane could feel the flush rising in his face. "Sir?"

"Your goddamned twit with the butterfly net."

"He really isn't a suspect, sir," MacFarlane said.

"Don't you tell me who is and who isn't a suspect," Canham roared. "Now listen. I see by your pitiful excuse for a report that this Pyle person told you he was only on the island for the day on Saturday."

"Yes, sir. We discussed it yesterday, sir. He came over on the morning boat."

"He told you he came on the morning boat. Did you bother to check that out?"

"No, sir. You gave us your opinion that we were looking at an accident, and so we didn't follow anything at that time. We're short-handed, sir, as you know."

Canham's visage went from red to purple. Jaw jutting, eyes bulging, he moved in on MacFarlane. His chest about an inch from MacFarlane's, he stared furiously down at the deputy. "You, MacFarlane, will not be shifting the blame on me for the negligence that passes for law enforcement on your little tourist-trap island. For your information," he continued triumphantly, "All I had to do was check the airlines—starting with A for Alaska. Bingo. Robert Pyle flew in to San Diego. Checked rental cars at the airport: Bingo. Now I had the license plate number. Called an associate in the San Pedro P.D., and there just happens to be a camera in the San Pedro parking lot of the Island Express."

He showed MacFarlane a photo. The deputy's stomach clenched. A typical surveillance-camera picture, it was grainy and dim, focused on a dark Hyundai Elantra. The time stamp said 2:11 a.m. Rhys could almost read the license number. "Wonder what happened to Powdermilk," he said aloud, then swallowed. He remembered that car, with its *Prairie Home Companion* name, from reading *Chasing Monarchs*. Clearly, such details were beyond Canham.

"What happened to WHAT?"

"Powdermilk. That's the name of Dr. Pyle's own car. A little Honda with about a million miles —"

"His car. He names his car. The nutcase even names his butterfly net." Once again, Canham was turning the shade of purple that Rhys and Price were learning boded no good. Muttering darkly, Canham snatched the photo out of Rhys's hand and handed it to Price.

"I am assuming," he said, "that at least you aren't too dazzled by the famous doctor of butterflies and his named car and his named butterfly net to follow up on this. I'll grant that one of you at least had the sense to have the guy leave a contact number at the station. Too damn bad he doesn't carry a cell phone, but that's your problem. I want you to find him, wherever he is now, and get him in here for questioning."

"Bring him in?"

"Get hold of him. I don't care how. Start with that woman in Santa Barbara. Find out where he was going from there. Get him back here, or send him to one of our officers over on the mainland, and preferably not on the taypayers' dime. In case I did not get through to you yesterday," he continued, lowering his voice to a spittly hiss, "there are plenty of eco-terrorists who put trees, and fish, and bugs, and butterflies, ahead of people. They will stop at nothing. So I want a police officer to talk to him wherever he is by now, and God help him if he doesn't show up. I want to know why this guy told us he was only on the island on Saturday."

"Yes, sir," Price said.

"And you." Canham aimed his glare at MacFarlane again. "I want you over in Hayden's room. I want a list of every damn thing in that room. I want to know what's there, and what's missing. I want you to check his calls. While you're doing that, I'm going to get the word out that we need to talk to anyone who saw Mr. Hayden Friday afternoon or evening." Canham turned to leave.

"Sir," MacFarlane said, "May I enter this into evidence before I go up to the Inn?" He held up the plastic bag containing the blood-marked rock.

"I'll do it," Canham snarled, and grabbed it.

Behind his back, Price was grinning from ear to ear.

Laboring though his list-making, Rhys was coming to realize that some people travel with more clothing than other people—people like sheriff's deputies, even detectives—might own in a dozen years.

He had gone through the pockets of three silk suits, one a pale blue-gray, one a silvery shade somewhere between light gray and tan, and one navy blue; four pairs of lightweight wool slacks; three sport coats and a couple of safari-type jackets, one poplin, one canvas; and four pairs of twill slacks. He'd checked out drawers filled with silk underwear, pristine cotton handkerchiefs, innumerable pairs of socks, at least a dozen shirts, a cashmere pullover, several name-brand polo shirts, and six pairs of shoes. He wrote in his notes that two pairs of twill slacks and one pair of sport shoes were dusty with an orange-tan dust like that of the hillside down which their owner's body had slid and rolled.

In a case stacked with Hayden's luggage, Rhys had also found a leather folder full of receipts, including numerous bar tabs and restaurant receipts and one receipt for barging "one all-terrain vehicle" from Long Beach to Pebbly Beach and back to the mainland. The files he'd noted all pertained to parcels of real estate, and he didn't see anything of particular interest. All the while, the certainty that something important was missing nagged at Rhys.

He went out to the parking lot at the Inn and found, to his surprise, a pickup with the Conservancy logo on the side, pale with the same dust as he'd found on the shoes and slacks.

"Oh, yes," said a groundsman who wandered up. "He rode the service roads and fire trails sometimes. He was going to bring his ATV out, but of course he couldn't. I heard he tried but the crew at the landing sent it back. I don't know how the hell he got hold of a Conservancy rig. You'd think they'd have come after it, hey?"

"Do you know where he went with it?" Rhys asked.

"Went up the fire trail that takes off just up the road. Went up above the cell tower up there, I think. Several times. Manager," the groundsman added, "wasn't happy."

It occurred to Rhys that if Hayden had been making it clear he planned to build a hotel on the hill above the Wrigley mansion-turned-Inn, the manager most certainly would not be happy. Rhys returned to the room and checked the drawers in the nightstands at each side of the king-sized bed. He found a desk calendar and a hotel notepad, and wondered why they hadn't been on the desk. He tore off the top pages of each to send off to the labs, where experts would check the paper for the imprints of notes or messages Hayden might have written. Something, anything, even the imprint of a phone number to give an idea of someone he might have met, someone who might have been with him on the peak, someone who might have shoved him off and then climbed down to the ledge to make sure he was dead before tumbling him through the chapparal.

And that's when it hit him.

A cell phone. Of course Hayden would have had a cell phone.

He phoned the operations center. No, all that was in evidence in the case so far were the appointment book already retrieved from Hayden's room, the bagged files and other contents of the desk drawers, his luggage, and the clothing, wallet and credit card case removed from his body at the morgue. McFarlane asked that someone contact the major phone carriers and, once they'd located Hayden's carrier, get a list of calls.

"They're not cooperative. And they're slow. But okay, we're on it."

Putting his phone down, Rhys drew a deep breath. He'd have to talk to Canham.

"MacFarlane?" The D.I.'s voice was harsh.

"Sir, it appears Mr. Hayden's cell phone wasn't on his body when he was found. And it isn't here in the room."

"And you only now thought of the phone, Deputy?"

"Yes, sir." Deputy. Not Detective, Deputy. McFarlane gritted his teeth.

"So where should you go looking for it, Deputy?"

"On the slope he went down, I'm thinking. Up on Mount Ada."

"You're the bloodhound, Rice."

"It's pronounced Reese, sir," Rhys said. "It's Welsh."

"Whatever. You seem to like rootling around up there. I'll need you till Price is free. He's putting the word out that we want to see anyone who saw or talked Hayden on Friday, try to find out when was the last time he was seen, what he might have been doing or planning on doing that evening. Then you go on up and see if it isn't maybe lying right next to where you found that rock."

"Yes, sir," MacFarlane said.

Chapter 26

The news of Warner Kendall Hayden's death moved across the island. Roger Cameron heard about it at an impromptu meeting called by the mayor. He arrived to find several members of his committee on road and trail development, members of the Avalon city council and the county planning commission. One of the city planning staff announced Hayden's demise with barely concealed jubilation. "Found dead near the bottom of the cliff below his own property. He'd apparently fallen and broken his neck."

Roger overheard a member of the conservancy board whisper "Deliverance!" to Avalon Councilman Edgar Ruiz as a buzz of excited comments and speculation arose.

Voices rose. Inevitably, there was speculation. Roger heard the words "steep" and "drunk" and "accident."

"Do you suppose," one of the councilmen asked seriously, "that someone pushed him?"

"I can think of a lot of people who'd have liked to," said another.

"Of course it's a terrible tragedy," the planner said, assuming a somber demeanor and looking around the table. "But from a planning point of view, it's, well, at least a reprieve."

There was a crescendo of agreement. Someone applauded, but stopped clapping when no one else joined in.

Into a brief silence, the mayor's voice rose definitively. "Unless the man has heirs who push the project, this will save the city a bundle in legal fees. And believe me, we weren't going to let that resort of his take shape without one hell of a fight."

"The first thing we should do," observed a member of the planning commission, "is get our attorney to see about closing that dratted loophole Hayden was so smug about. Get that property into conservancy status STAT."

"That's why I've called you to meet," the mayor agreed. "It's ridiculous that a development approval issued almost a hundred years ago and never acted upon until now should have any standing. There's got to be something that can be done about that. Are we in agreement that we ask the attorneys for the city and the Conservancy to work on that?"

Again, voices rose in agreement. The discussion continued, but it was a blur to Roger Cameron.

His first reaction had been panic. The picture! Why hadn't he managed to procure it? He'd thought there would be more time to effect that—he hadn't known how, but surely he should have managed something.

His second reaction was nearly as chilling. Hayden had pressured him into loaning him his Conservancy-owned four-wheel rig. What would the police make of that? And how would he get it back?

And then his two worries blended. What if someone other than Hayden and whoever took the photo or photos Hayden had written about had seen them? What if the police found out about the threats Hayden had made? Would that link him to the death? Of course it would.

That meant he must speak to Sarah. A week ago, the thought would have filled him with a heady surge of anticipation. Now he dreaded it. He recalled the shrill sound of her voice when she'd phoned him Saturday. He hoped she wasn't going to have second thoughts, become clingy and melodramatic. True, there hadn't been any drama when he had suggested they stop seeing one another—it had been he who suggested it, hadn't it? Strange that he couldn't recall the scene. Evidence, he told himself, that he had put the whole aberration from his orderly life behind him.

Even before Hayden's letter had appeared, Roger had reassessed the cost of the affair with Sarah. Once they had agreed to end it, Roger had made it a point to value, consciously, what he had risked losing: Margaret, her quiet support, her competent management of their home. The foundation for his life. He reminded himself with a scientist's rationality that he could expend his energy on causes the Conservancy stood for only because Margaret was there to see that all the rest of their family life was taken care of.

Sarah's ripe sexuality had energized him at a point when years and familiarity and, he had to admit, Margaret's increasing indifference to sex had dulled that aspect of his marriage. Sarah's growing interest in the natural world of the island and her admiration of his work on its behalf were flattering and bolstered his confidence at work. But none of that was worth sacrificing the orderly life of his science, his family, his associations, his place in the community.

It was unfortunate that he needed to talk to Sarah. He hadn't meant to tell her of Hayden's threat, but now it loomed darker, more onerous, because there was no way of knowing what Hayden had done with his information. He had to warn Sarah to be careful, that their guilty secret was not entirely secret. And he had to be sure she would never speak of it. Anywhere.

And another thought: what if Hayden had threatened Sarah too?

Against his will, he considered the possibility that she had received a letter like his. Was that why she'd agreed so readily that they should part? And had she—no, surely not. The backdrop to his thoughts, the blur of voices, rose again. He struggled to capture the thread of the conversation before people realized he had been miles away from the committee's conversation.

"I'm assuming, then, that we're agreed on that course." The mayor was speaking again. There was a murmur of assent.

"Councilman Ruiz?" The mayor's voice sounded an inquiring note. Roger looked across the polished table at Ruiz and was bemused to see that the councilman appeared to be as absent from the discussion as he had been just moments before. Ruiz's face, with its flaring mahogany cheekbones like an Aztec warrior's, was ashen, his expression blank. "Are you all right?" the mayor asked.

Roger watched a mirror of his own coming-to as Ruiz refocused. "Yes. Well, no. I'm sorry. A sinus headache, that's all. Yes, I'm entirely in agreement," the councilman said. "But I'm sorry. With this headache, I'm afraid I'm not much good to you all today. Please excuse me." Edgar Ruiz got up and stumbled from the room.

"Mr. Cameron? Do you agree?"

"Yes. Of course." Roger wondered what he'd agreed to, and forced himself to concentrate on each speaker as the session continued. The moment the meeting broke up, he too excused himself, declining his colleagues' suggestions of lunch or coffee, and fled.

Chapter 27

The conservancy headquarters was empty. His co-worker who had been at the committee meeting had gone out with the city's public-works crew to look at two trailheads due for regrading, and the rest of the staff was working on a post-burn assessment on the slope above and below the stagecoach road, so Roger asked Sarah to meet him in his office. She had sounded distressed when he telephoned. There were dark circles under her eyes when she walked through the door.

"Thank you for phoning," she said rather formally. "I've been hoping we could talk."

"Yes. Well." Roger found himself at a loss for words, but Sarah had an abundance of them, and they tumbled out in a rush.

"Roger, something's terribly wrong. That developer: he's got Andy all tied in knots. I don't know what it's about, but I've never seen Andy so upset. At first I thought it had something to do with us—my guilty conscience, I guess—but now I think he's afraid of something, desperately afraid."

She took a deep breath to continue, but Roger interrupted her.

"Sarah, listen. If you mean Warner Hayden, he's dead. He can't worry any of us any more."

Sarah looked at him blankly. Her expression reminded him of the shuttered countenance Ruiz had presented at the committee meeting.

"He was found near a trail—a road—down below his building site. No one's quite sure whether he fell or was pushed."

"Dead. Oh, God. Oh, it's worse than I thought." She sat down and put her hands over her face. He stood and looked at her. He realized she was wearing her hair loose. It didn't become her, he thought. It made her look older, unkempt, unlike Margaret with her elegant grooming and her sleek pale blonde bob. Suddenly, Sarah looked up at him.

"Any of us. You said he can't worry any of us. What did you mean?"

"Look, Sarah. I wasn't going to tell you about this. I didn't want to upset you. But Hayden, or rather one of his acquaintances, saw us in Monterey. It might have been a private eye; I don't know. But Hayden wrote to me and said he has a picture."

"Of us?"

"Yes. He threatened to make it public if I didn't support his big resort project. You asked me last week why I loaned him my pickup. That's why. He—did you get any kind of threat like that?"

"No," she said slowly. "No, I didn't. Did you see this picture he has?"

"No. I didn't see it, and now, of course, it could be anywhere."

Sarah thought for a moment. "Surely it can't be too damaging. So we were there. Can't we just say that we ran into each other and went out for a drink or whatever?"

"I can't imagine that Margaret would see it that way, or my staff." Beads of sweat stood out on Roger's tanned forehead.

Sara stared at him, trim crewcut and buttoned-down collar, and wondered what the attraction had been. He reminded her, she decided, of a mediocre actor portraying a Nazi officer as World War II rolled toward its conclusion in a B-grade film. "Maybe I can go break into his room before his next of kin come to claim his things," she said absently.

"Sarah, don't make light of this."

"I'm not."

"Nobody must ever hear of our, ah, indiscretion. There's so much at stake. The Conservancy. My family—uh—our families."

"Yes. I wondered if you remembered that I have a husband too."

"Well, of course. And you were talking about Andy being upset. You don't think he—he suspects—" He broke off, sounding strangled.

"No. I wondered at first, but I don't think so. He's been acting kind of frantic, worried, ever since the middle of last week. He said it had something to do with the nursery when I pushed him to explain, but he wouldn't say what. And Roger, he didn't get home until one o'clock Friday—no, Saturday morning. When he said he couldn't face his breakfast—that's so not like Andy!—I asked him what was going on, where he'd been so late. He said he'd been in a meeting—with you."

Seeing that Roger was fumbling for his phone, she realized he was about to check his calendar. "Roger. Please," she said coldly. "You were with me Friday evening. We were ending an affair, you might recall. So he wasn't with you. Unless you had a meeting with Andy after eleven p.m."

"No, no. Of course not. That's ridiculous. I—I wonder —"

"Wonder what?"

"Do you think Andy might have followed us?"

"No," Sarah said quickly. "I realized that when I first wondered if he—He trusts me completely. That's what makes what we did so shameful. A trust like that is a terrible thing to betray. And that's why I decided we had to end our—what did you call it—our indiscretion." It had been her idea to end it, hadn't it?

One thing was certain in Sarah's mind; she was going to get to the bottom of what was worrying her beloved Andy. She glared at Roger. "Besides, I love and trust him. So you didn't see him that night, and you don't have any idea what this might be about?"

"No," said Roger maliciously, "unless Hayden has a photo of him, too." Then, fearing he had gone too far, he backpedaled. "Sarah, this letter. This picture. You realize we both have a motive for murdering Hayden. It's important to be very careful, not to say anything to anyone about the photo. About us."

Sarah stalked to the door. She turned. "You can rely on me to be careful, Roger. I won't be speaking of the relationship we had to anyone. Except a priest." Seeing him blanch, she relented. "And you don't have to worry about that, either. I'm going over town tomorrow and I'll find a church I've never been to for making my confession."

Chapter 28

John Katsaros walked home from Charlie's, pacing slowly in the early afternoon sun. The sky was clear but it seemed to John that a pall had settled over the island like a blanket of cold fog. He shivered in spite of the heat. His friend Fred had met him as he left the coffee shop and asked, "Hey, Zorba, did you hear about that developer?"

"What about him?" John already knew about Hayden, and he was miserable. Rhys MacFarlane had phoned late Saturday afternoon to say Lexi had found Hayden's body, and was shaken: would he and Stina find her and make her stay the night with them? John had gone to Lexi's place and brought her home, knowing Andrea was away. Lexi had picked at her dinner, declined talking about her ordeal, and agreed meekly to spend the night. But at 6:30 Sunday morning, he and Stina had found her room empty. A note left on the table beside the hastily made bed said, "I'm off, but I'm fine. Don't worry."

So of course they worried. Lexi had returned an hour later, gone off to her studio for a couple of hours, and returned. She was uncharacteristically quiet, though in Andrea's absence she had agreed to spend the night with them again. She had left the house that morning for her studio, saying only that she had photos to sort and that she was going to offer to return Vivian Oleson's deposit, assuming that Emilie would not want to continue with plans for a wedding on the island. "My first cancellation," she said with a bitter smile as she left.

And his friend Andrea: he'd been surprised when she'd clammed up on him and bolted. That trip over town struck him as an escape, as a story hastily contrived. What was his dear friend Andrea hiding from him? It began to feel as though there were secrets behind every door. He only half-listened as Fred Paige described, in the lurid detail available only to those who had good imaginations and no facts at hand, how high-living Warner Kendall Hayden had tumbled from his own property, dead drunk, and been found dead by a jogger. Drunk, but maybe somebody had pushed him. Since he was going to build a bigger, better resort up there on that cliff, probably a lot of people would have liked to see it stopped.

"Motives all over the place," Fred said gleefully. "Even me."

John couldn't help but agree. He was glad to be able to turn away and go indoors.

The afternoon Express pulled in to the dock, churning the water around Cabrillo Mole into a pale aqua foam. Andrea disembarked trailing her overnight bag and carrying a briefcase. Any trip "over town"—the term Catalina Islanders use for visiting the mainland—made her grateful that she had settled in on the picturesque, craggy island with its dense little harbor city. Rounding the point into the boat-studded waters of Avalon, which might have been any Mediterranean resort town, always drew exclamations of delight from Island Express passengers. Andrea was always grateful that when she arrived she was home, but she enjoyed seeing the place anew through visitors' eyes each time she walked off the dock in the midst of a group of tourists.

The trip to town had come up suddenly, and was a welcome distraction. The final phase of the move to her new shop had involved renegotiation of a memorandum of understanding regarding utilities. There had been some lively discussion when she spoke with the Island Company's attorney by phone, and she had decided to deal with the MOU in person. And it was satisfying to help her mother discard extra belongings and prepare for the move to the pleasant senior-living complex she had found for what she insisted on calling her declining years.

Returning, Andrea felt that she had done well. Crossing over to the mainland on Saturday, she had feared that her preoccupation with Hayden—his importuning, his threats, her fears—might interfere with this final session with her new landlords. But as the two humps of the island mountains had receded beyond the wake of the Express, Andrea had come to a surprising conclusion: John was right. No one would be surprised if she went public with her college-days activism, her ill-advised spiking of trees, her jail time. She found herself feeling light, unencumbered with the worries and regrets that had plagued her. Hayden couldn't coerce her with a threat of exposure. A second forum was scheduled in the coming week, and she made some notes for a speech that would alienate a few supporters, she knew, but would clear the air once and for all. "Just look forward." How often had her beloved John Katsaros advised that? "You cannot set your foot twice in the same stream, so just look forward," he would tell her.

The first time he used the old Greek saying he was so fond of, she hadn't understood him. Hadn't she waded the same stream each time she walked the trail to Ben Weston Beach? She recalled the conversation when she'd countered his advice with that question. He had given her that level look she'd seen frequently since. "Andrea, Andrea. Just think about it." They had been sitting on a bench near the green pleasure pier. "Come out here," he had said, leading her wordlessly to the end of the pier. "The current comes past here. Look down now." She looked and saw the flashing sides of a school of fish as they turned in unison, catching the sunlight. "Jump in here now and you'd be swimming with those jack mackerel," he said, smiling. "Yesterday it was jellyfish. Tomorrow? We don't know what the current will bring us. The stream, whether it's a little creek or a river or an ocean current or the trickle out of my garden faucet, keeps moving onward. That's how life is, Andrea. Go forward with it."

She was going forward. As for the other worry, she would deal with it when the opportunity arose.

So she was smiling broadly as she walked along Crescent Avenue—she still thought of it as Front Street—toward La Cocina. When she caught sight of Francesca coming toward her, she grinned and hoisted her briefcase. "Signed, sealed, delivered," she shouted, quickening her pace.

She fell into step with Francesca. "They dropped that ridiculous provision about water rates. We got everything we wanted, and three years. Better than I'd hoped. I missed the noon boat, but it was worth it. And I used the time to go to Zorba's and check out that new line of cheeses Lexi was telling us about. I think we might want to switch wholesalers. I tasted a Graviera that's absolutely perfect, and a Myzithra that's ten times better than the one we're getting now." She didn't appear to notice that Francesca didn't respond with her usual enthusiasm. "Are we closed? Let's go down to the bar and celebrate."

"I have something to tell you first," Francesca said. She hesitated, then added quietly, "You'll probably still want to celebrate, but we shouldn't broadcast the reason. And actually part of it's rather awful."

"How mysterious." Andrea was still smiling as they entered the shop. Everything gleamed. "Was it a quiet day? Looks like you've polished everything twice. Those display cases look great."

"Actually we were pretty busy, but it all came in clumps, like it always does." Francesca shrugged. "Sit down."

"I'm sitting." Andrea climbed aboard one of the stools at the counter where customers waited for special orders, and drummed her fingers on the gleaming counter. Francesca tried hard not to look at the smudges her boss was making.

"It looks like you may not have to worry about that resort of Mr. Hayden's," Francesca began. Andrea's drumming fingers grew quiet. She stared at Francesca. "He's dead," Francesca said. "Of course everyone's speculating like mad, but for the moment the usual line is that he'd probably had too much to drink, went up to gloat over his view, and missed his step. Seth said he came down that one part of the slope that's pretty much a cliff."

"Seth was there?"

"He had to respond to the scene, so yeah. But you know how he is. Until the M.E. determines the cause of death, it's like living with a clam. And even now that there's an investigation going on, he's not saying much, but he did say the M.E. found evidence that somebody had finished him off, made sure he was dead."

"Did he say when—when it happened?" Andrea had gone pale. She was gripping the counter.

"Probably sometime Friday evening. By Saturday afternoon, when Lexi found him, rigor was just beginning to go off. Seth had to—"

Andrea interrupted. "Lexi? Lexi found him?"

"Yes, poor girl. Fainted into the arms of a stray butterfly hunter, she told us. We thought she needed company so she spent the night with John and Stina. She's—"

Francesca stopped her narrative abruptly. Andrea had jumped off the stool, pushed past her, and rushed into the lavatory. She had closed the door, but Francesca recognized the sounds. Andrea, who could weather the roughest winter crossings without so much as a touch of *mal de mer*, was being violently sick.

They evidently would do no celebrating at the cocktail bar this evening.

Chapter 29

Ted Price was still at the sheriff's station cataloguing evidence when the first person responded to the word that the sheriff's office wanted to hear from people who had seen Hayden on Friday. So it was Rhys MacFarlane who ushered Ellen Storey into the suite the team had requisitioned as a base of operations. "Ms. Storey is here, Inspector Canham," he said. Ellen stood in the doorway looking at Canham, who was seated at a two-drawer maple writing desk. It seemed far too small and delicate for him. She smiled ever so slightly, but said nothing. A moment passed before Canham stood, awkwardly, as if unaccustomed to the courtesy.

"You can sit down," he said, indicating the wing chair opposite his. He opened a folder as if to check on a file. "Ellen Storey. The painter."

"One of many this week," she said. He looked confused. "The Plein-Air Festival." He nodded. "You were asking who had seen Mr. Hayden on Friday."

"We're trying to track the movements of the deceased that day, yes."

"I saw him on Mount Ada, up beyond the Inn, half an hour or so before sunset," Ellen said briskly. "It might have been a little later. And I've only recently come to realize that the viewpoint I'd been painting from was probably on Mr. Hayden's property."

Canham looked at MacFarlane, who was seated, ready to take notes. Rhys nodded and wrote.

"You'd been painting out there for how long?"

"Since early afternoon, two or two-thirty. There's a certain light once the sun's in the west. I've painted in that place before, Inspector Canham."

"You mean during this—ah, this festival?"

"No, on earlier visits. This is the third—no, fourth time I've come to the island to paint."

"You were here at the earlier Plein-Air Festivals?"

"No. Just here painting on my own from time to time. It's been a popular place for painters for a century and more," she said.

"I see." There was a small silence. Ellen looked at him inquiringly, fingering the little heart charm she wore. Rhys wondered if Canham made her nervous.

"And was Mr. Hayden there while you were painting?"

"I don't think so." She furrowed her brow. "I get pretty engrossed when I'm painting, but I didn't see him until I had packed up my things—my easel and my big paintbox and the remnants of my lunch. Supper." She shrugged. "I brought a sandwich because I wanted to finish the piece in case the weather changed."

"Yes. And then?"

"I was just starting along the track—it's not much more than a game trail that intersects with the fire break above the Inn—when I saw him coming up the trail."

"Did you speak?"

"Yes. Just the usual pleasantries, and then he asked if I'd like him to help me carry my things back to the Inn, where I'd parked the golf cart I was using. I did not."

163

"You sound emphatic about that."

She smiled apologetically. "Yes, I'm afraid I was. He smelled of alcohol, Inspector. And, well, Mr. Hayden had approached me earlier about a matter I didn't care to discuss with him, and I didn't want a repetition of that conversation." Canham smiled gently but firmly. His smile broadened in the brief silence. Then, "I'm afraid I must ask you about that conversation," he said.

She dropped her gaze and leaned into the back of her chair, as if to create an inch or two more distance between herself and her interviewer, and fiddled with her bracelet as she spoke. "He wanted a painting for his office. There was a piece I'd already done. It's an expanse of harbor from almost the same place I was painting Friday. Until this trip, I'd always thought it was in the Conservancy."

"And that's where you were?"

"Yes. I had wanted to paint from that viewpoint just once more, and I was eager to finish it."

"Back to this painting he wanted. He wanted to buy one you'd painted already? I should think that would seem like a good thing."

Ellen pulled a white handkerchief from her jacket pocket, looked at it, fiddled with it for a second. Then she looked at Canham. She shrugged. "It already has an owner. Mr. Hayden wanted me to paint it again, but bigger, much bigger—paint it to size for a wall in his office." The last word came out with just the slightest suggestion of a hiss. "It sounds innocuous, out in the air, in words. It probably was. But I found his request offensive. As if I were—a decorator, not a painter."

"Not an artist." Canham watched for a reaction. She dropped her eyes but didn't answer. "And how long ago was this request?"

"Wednesday evening. I'd just arrived. I'd stopped downtown to say hello to Jill Reinhardt, who organized the festival. I'm sorry, you know who does what here." She paused.

"Actually, don't assume I know anything. Jill Reinhardt's a local?"

"A local artist. She was involved in the earlier festivals, and she's chairing this revival."

Canham nodded at MacFarlane. "Note that." The detective wrote busily. "Go on," Canham said to Ellen.

"Anyway, he saw us and insisted on buying us a drink."

"And made this offer that offended you."

"I'm sorry," she said again. "It's just a personal thing. Early in my career, Inspector, I did my share of commissioned paintings, subject and size to order. When my paintings began to sell—to sell well, I mean—I was relieved that I wouldn't have to do that again. That's all there is to it, really. Not enough to get all ruffled about. I was being silly, I expect."

"Back to Friday. Did he bring up the painting he wanted?"

"He said, 'I won't repeat my offer, but it still stands.' "

"And you refused him again?"

"I simply said 'Thank you. So does my answer.' I found his presence—ah— uncomfortable enough that I preferred to avoid a prolonged conversation. Especially since he'd been—"

"Drinking?"

She nodded.

"You could smell it, even outdoors?"

"Perhaps because we were outdoors. And he came—well, quite close enough, Inspector." She smiled at him.

165

"So you were going down the track—is it a track?"

"A rough trail. There's a fire lane that's shorter, but it's steeper."

"You were going down while he was coming up?"

"Yes."

"And did you see any kind of a vehicle?"

"No. I noticed there wasn't one. I heard that he sometimes came up in a four-wheel rig—loathesome things—and it's been chewing up the firebreak. I assume he had left it at the Inn, because I would have heard it if he'd used it."

"And you say he was coming along the trail, not the firebreak."

"Yes. The firebreak goes up the side of the mountain, but the trail intersects it. It connects with the service road that goes to those tower things—a cell tower, I think, and something else up higher. I'm assuming he came up the same path from the Inn that I was using."

"I see."

She sat composedly in the silence.

He leaned forward then, and looked at her for a moment before speaking. "We have to consider the possibility that he was intending to meet someone up there. Did he appear to be waiting for—or maybe looking for—someone?"

There was a pause. Ellen looked briefly at her hands before returning Canham's gaze. "No," she said. "I didn't have that impression." He let the silence lie between them. Then he nodded in MacFarlane's direction, but kept his eyes on Ellen.

"Did you think he might have been coming to look for you?"

"No, Inspector. It didn't occur to me."

"Even though he wanted one of your paintings."

"I think he was well aware of what my answer would be." Canham was silent again. Ellen waited.

"Is there anything else you'd like to tell me that might bear on this case, Ms. Storey?"

Her eyebrows rose slightly. "No, Inspector. I don't think so."

"Thank you for coming in. If anything occurs to you, anything at all, please come and tell us."

"I will, Inspector." She unfolded herself from the chair and left.

"What do you think, Rice?"

"Rhys, sir. About what, sir?"

"Did you notice the cool and collected Ms. Storey hesitated when I asked if she thought he might be waiting to meet someone there?"

"I–I suppose she did, a bit."

"I think she's protecting someone, Rice. We need to find out who that is. She may live in France and New Mexico, but she admitted she's been here before. It shouldn't be hard to figure out who she knows. Price is back, so now you get on up there and look for that cell phone."

Chapter 30

By the time Canham had finished interviewing Ellen Storey, the word had spread that he was looking for people who had seen Hayden on Friday. A small queue of eager witnesses sat on chairs in the hallway outside the room he was using.

Detective Price had spent a feverish hour on the station phone. He'd reached Dr. Robert Pyle's host in Santa Barbara only to learn that his quarry had flown to Seattle, driven home to Gray's River, and almost immediately left for Fairbanks, Alaska. Price had managed, through the airline, to be in touch with the rental-car agency Pyle had used and the Alaska State Troopers were alerted to the license numbers for the Ford Focus he'd rented. Now Price returned to the operations center, resignedly set to take notes.

First called from among the would-be witnesses fidgeting in their chairs was a waiter from the hotel. He had attended Hayden at breakfast. "So when he had finished," he told Canham, "I said, 'See you at lunch.' And he said, 'Probably not.'"

Price made careful notes.

"Did he indicate anything about what he was planning to do?" Canham asked.

"Not to me, sir."

Price stopped writing.

A small woman who cleaned rooms at the Inn reported that she had come to Hayden's room about 10, the time she usually cleaned. She had knocked, received no answer, and entered the room to discover Hayden there, on the telephone. "He was very rude," she said. "He told me to get out."

Price placed an asterisk beside that statement and wondered exactly what had made Hayden so irritated: interruption or the possibility that something might have been overheard? He hoped Rhys would get some response to his request for information about Hayden's incoming and outgoing phone calls. It began to look like that might be the only useful thing they'd get.

Then a volunteer from the Conservancy office added an observation that sounded more hopeful. Hayden, he said, had spent the early afternoon Friday in the conservancy's Nature Center at Avalon Canyon. "He had a kind of a grayish notebook and was writing a lot," he told Canham.

Price underlined "notebook" in his notes.

"Did anyone there talk to him?" Canham wanted to know.

"I think one of our botanists may have met with him. I know at one point I heard her door close and after a while he came back out to the main display room. But she's away now. She's at a conference in Phoenix this week."

Canham swallowed an expletive with difficulty and asked the volunteer to phone with any information the Conservancy might have to help them contact the botanist.

A young woman who worked as a ticket agent for submarine tours was next. She fingered the six earrings in one ear as she told Canham she had seen Hayden getting off the morning Express—she thought it might have been the boat from Dana Point. Or maybe it was Long Beach. She could never remember which boat came in first. She wasn't sure whether he had luggage with him. She wasn't sure whether he had a briefcase with him, either. And no, she didn't really know what Warner Hayden looked like, but she'd seen someone in a nice suit. She remembered the suit: pale linen, like in the movies. Canham dismissed her curtly.

"What do people think we're doing here, running a goddamned sideshow?" he spluttered.

Price went to the door and found an impatient Bianca Alvorado waiting her turn. She flounced into the interview room and he motioned her to a chair facing Canham, introducing the detective inspector to her. "Ms. Alvorado is another of the painters here for the Plein-Air Festival," he told Canham.

"I understand you've said you can help us discover where Mr. Hayden was just before his death Friday evening," Canham said.

"Oh, what tragedy!" Bianca fumbled in her bag for a handkerchief, a beautifully embroidered linen one with cutwork edges. She used it to good effect, wiping carefully at her eyes and fluttering her lashes at Canham over the edges of the kerchief. Price looked at her. The word "vamping" came to mind.

"I have much sorrow," Bianca intoned.

"When did you see Mr. Hayden last?" Canham asked, impatient.

"Last? Just before dinner. On that terrible Friday."

"And where was that?"

"In the Inn. The lovely hotel up on the hill. A far better place than where we poor artists are staying." Bianca tossed her head. "Drinks there are very expensive."

"You were having drinks there?"

"But yes! That is what I come to tell you. I have drinks— something called White Lady—there with poor Mr. Hayden."

"Was he drinking 'white ladies' too?"

"No, martinis."

"How many?"

"Only two. But—" She stopped.

"But they were doubles?"

She shifted uncomfortably. "Yes. But he is not drunk."

"Did you meet him there?"

"Oh, no. He is such a gentleman—he bring me there from where I stay, at The Bell. In the elegant golf car that the Inn has. I have been painting, rocks and sea, down at the Cove of Lovers. And that is where he finds me. He tells me he has been looking for me all day. We meet," she added archly, "and had drinks the night before too. So he comes to look for me. And I am at the perfect place, he says."

Bianca was warming to her theme. "He tells me I am a wonderful painter, and he will bid on everything I paint when he comes for the festival next Sunday. And now," she said plaintively, "he never lives to buy my pictures." She wiped at her eyes.

"So he met you at the beach where you were painting. And then?" Canham urged her on.

"I finish my picture—well, almost finish. He help me pack my paints, and then he drives me to The Bell in the beautiful golf car that looks like an old Triumph, not one of those nasty little ones they make us use. I change for dinner and then we go for drinks at his hotel."

"Do you know what time it was when he came to where you were painting?"

"No. I paint very intense. I only notice him after he has been there for a time. I do not know how long but he says he has been watching me paint."

"Do you know what time you left the beach?"

171

"No, but it is I think 5:30 when we leave my room at The Bell. I am glad it is still early because—never mind." Canham sat. Bianca remained silent and rolled her large eyes. It was cat and mouse. Price wondered who was playing whom. But Bianca caved. "My friend that I came with, Viktor, I was hoping he would not come to the room."

"And why was that?"

Bianca rolled her eyes. "Men. They are so—possessing. I do not want there to be a scene."

But if there had been, she'd have reveled in it, Price would bet.

"So then you went straight to the Inn at Mount Ivy?"

"Mount Ada."

"And did you go to Mr. Hayden's room?"

"Of course not. I—" Bianca stopped herself. "No. I did not go with him."

"Mr. Hayden went to his room?"

"For only a moment. He say something about dropping something off in his room. I did not see he have anything to drop off, so I think it might be a polite way of saying he needed to—to attend the restroom." Price had the impression that she was improvising. She was doing it well. He underlined "something to drop off."

"Were you going to have dinner with him?"

At this, Bianca's volubility failed. "I'm sorry; I do not understand."

"Were you planning to have dinner together?"

"Ah. No. He—I—no."

Canham wasn't content with that. He probed. "Did you think he was going to ask you to dinner?"

172

"He is—was—a lovely and generous gentleman. He says he wishes our evening could continue. I think—" Bianca seemed to cast about for the right words. "I think he have something else he have to do that night. A business appointing, perhaps."

"An appointment?"

"Appointment. Excuse me. Yes."

"Did he say what it was?"

"No."

"So you left?"

"Yes. He take me—took me—in his beautiful cart. Back to the Bell."

"So the last you saw him was at The Bell, not at the Inn."

"Yes. But he does not stay there, only drops me off."

"And that was it?"

Bianca's eyes widened. Her nostrils flared. "No, that was not 'it.' It is only a beginning. He say he wanted to be with me later. He say—oh, such lovely things he say to me. And then I wait, but he does not come. I do not hear anything. And then, the next night, I find out he is killed." She burst into howls, mopping at messy tears with her crumpled handkerchief.

Canham backed his chair away, stood, and looked baffled. Price got up too, grabbed a box of tissues and handed it to Canham. Canham handed it to Bianca, who continued to cry and mop at her eyes, darkening the tissues with drowned mascara. Then she leapt to her feet and grabbed Canham by the lapels.

"You police, you must find who did this."

Canham took her hands from his jacket and held them away from himself, almost as if they were about to dance some Victorian galop, Price thought.

"Do you have any idea who we ought to be looking for?"

It was an unorthodox question for this point in the interview, but it produced a startling result. Price quickly grabbed his notebook again.

"Yes! Yes, I do. I think you must look at Viktor! So jealous he is, and when a beautiful man like Mr. Hayden, who is handsome and wealthy, is interested in me, he is jealous. Oh, yes, he is jealous! Ask anyone! I think Viktor kills him for the love of me."

Canham folded his arms. He nodded at Price. "You take her back to her hotel, and put Mr. Sentik on our list. It looks like we'll have to talk to him."

"And then I shall lose him too!" Bianca wailed as Price took her gently by the arm and escorted her out the door. "It is too much!" She grabbed her handkerchief and applied it to her eyes again. "Oh, it is too much!"

Price agreed.

Chapter 31

The sun-drenched beach between the mole and the pier was crowded with people. Moms in swimsuits lay prone, tanning, while their children dug in the sand and whined for something more entertaining to do. Boyfriends and girlfriends on beach towels came as close to coupling as they dared. Middle-aged people who'd outgrown their middle-sized bathing suits bulged in beach chairs. Sunburned young men in baggy shorts lobbed volleyballs over the heads of the sun-bathers.

In the midst of it all, Viktor Sentik stood at his easel, painting a line of boats that bobbed at anchor. Next to him, seated in a folding chair beneath an artist's umbrella, Eve Jones captured the brash bluish green of the pier buildings and their reflection in the waves.

Hand in hand, a boy in a black tank top and shorts and a girl in a black mesh top and black miniskirt sidled up. They stood just behind Viktor and watched as he wielded his palette knife, putting highlights on waves.

"Boats," the girl said knowingly.

"Good call," the boy said sarcastically, and she hit at him half-heartedly. They looked soft, pale and out of joint, as though they spent their days in darkened rooms lit only by computers.

"Hey," her companion said to Viktor. "How come your water looks kind of tan when it's really blue? It looks prettier the way it really is."

Viktor glared and did not answer. He added a blob of dark green to the paint on his palette.

The couple sidled away to hover over Eve's painting. "Gee," the young man said. "That kind of looks like the wharf right over there. Water looks almost real." The girl hung on his arm and giggled. He addressed Eve. "That's pretty good. Hey, is there water all the way around this island?"

"All the way around? Yes," Eve said, straight-faced. "That's what makes it an island."

"Wow. So you have to take the boat if you want to go anywhere?" The young man picked at a stud in his lip.

Eve nodded. "Pretty much," she said. "There are some roads."

"Well if it's an island, where would they go?"

"To the airport," Viktor said. "Middle Ranch, Two Harbors, other beaches."

"Yeah? You get there on those little golf carts?"

"By bus, usually."

"Oh, wow. Thrills." The youth sneered.

The girl giggled and hung even more heavily on his arm. "Come on, Den. I want to ride the submarine." And off they went.

Viktor continued painting. Eve wiped her hands on a paint rag, picked up her purse and trotted off to one of the seafront shops. She pondered the chalkboard menu, then ordered a mango-peach smoothie. On an impulse, she told the youngster at the till, "Make that two, please." She returned to the beach and Viktor. "I didn't bring a lunch. Did you?"

"Nope."

"Here."

"Mmh. Thanks." He went on painting, but he stopped from time to time to consume the treat. He made no further comment.

Another hour passed, Eve content with Viktor's silent company, each intent on the work in progress. Eve had only a few more strokes to add to the edges of her canvas when Bianca planted herself between them.

"'Ello, Eve," she said. "Oh, very pretty.

"And Viktor, my love. I come to apologize. Oh, my poor Viktor, I have made things look bad for you. Oh, very bad. I am so sorry. It is that detective, the big one with the buggy-out eyes. He asks so many questions, and I tell him, I tell him Mr. Hayden make a little love to me and talk of buying my pictures, and then I—I tell him you are jealous."

"What?"

"You know this is true. But I am sorry I tell him, Viktor. Truly I am. You must forgive me, Viktor."

"Like hell." His voice was unemphatic, almost uninterested.

Eve listened, amazed.

"I know you would kill for me, dear Viktor, but I know you did not do this thing. And even if you did kill that beautiful man, I love you, I know you do it for the love of me. So you — Viktor, you must forgive me."

Eve took a deep breath. "Excuse me. I know it's none of my business, but that man Hayden, he was also putting the moves on the pretty little photographer. I saw them on Thursday. He was kind of imploring her."

"Oh, fooh! She was nothing to him," Bianca said grandly. "He had only eyes for me. And you are right. It is none of your business. This is between us, between me and Viktor. So kiss me, Viktor," she said, taking his wrists in her hands, sidestepping to avoid the sticky palette knife.

"Go away."

"You do not tell me to go away," Bianca blazed out, dropping his wrists, hands on hips.

"Oh, but I do." His voice rose. "Look here, Bianca, I am painting. I want to finish this picture."

And Bianca went.

Eve watched Viktor covertly. He was painting faster. He made longer strokes as he limned in more waves, darker, greener waves. She thought she saw a sort of fury in the way he attacked the canvas with his paint-laden knife, topping the waves with white foam. From a peaceful, even drab scene— Eve had to admit it had looked drab—it had deepened, hinted at impending storm, gathered life and intensity.

He is so intense, so sensitive, and that woman hurts him at every turn, she thought, and she packed away her paints with care. She rose, said goodbye to Viktor, and carried her finished canvas to the festival office. Then she combed her hair and set out for the sheriff's station.

Directed to the nearby operations center in The Islander, Eve joined the little queue of folks who had seen, or thought they had seen, Warner Kendall Hayden on the final day of his life. When she was admitted to Canham's presence, she nearly fled. But she took a deep breath, and the words fairly tumbled from her mouth of their own accord.

"Bianca Alvorado all but told us she accused Viktor Sentik of killing Mr. Hayden," she began, surprising herself. She hadn't meant to get into that part. "I didn't see Mr. Hayden on Friday, actually, Inspector, but I did see him on Thursday night," she continued hastily. "It was after dinner, over in the hotel where they have the meals for the festival painters.

"Some of us went into the lounge afterward, and he was there. Somebody pointed him out and said he was the developer who was going to build a big resort here. He was talking to that photographer, her name's Lexi something, she has the little studio on the street over there." She made a gesture in a generally westerly direction. "It was very clear he was making a pass at her," she told Canham. Well, it had kind of looked that way, hadn't it?

"Tell me exactly what you saw," the inspector suggested. What had she seen exactly? Eve wasn't altogether sure, and she hesitated. She almost said as much, but Canham rose and stood over her.

"He was kind of looming over her," she said, and realized that she had spoken without thinking. She looked off and up as if to bring the scene into better focus. "He had his hand on her—her shoulder, but it looked as if he was going to—well, I'm not sure. But she kept kind of edging away from him. And I could certainly see that she was angry," Eve told Inspector Canham. "Very angry."

Chapter 32

The little church looked almost deserted. The houses in the largely residential neighborhood were small and old but well tended. Jacaranda and bottle-brush trees lined the streets, casting long, cool shadows. Their castoff flowers had mostly been swept up. It seemed to Sarah Martin as if this might be a safe place. Still, she sat for a long time in the car, the engine idling, as she fought the impulse to flee, simply to drive away.

Finally, she got out of the car and made her way toward the church. She opened the heavy plank door and went in. Dust motes sparkled in the narrowing shaft of sunlight that the door allowed into the shadowy entry, the beam picking out a vertical row of posters on the mostly shadowed bulletin board. A bingo schedule, a poster with its asymmetrical heart symbol advertising a Right to Life demonstration, and another for a concert by a visiting Nigerian children's choir. It could have been any parish anywhere, she thought. She walked hesitantly into the cool vestibule and found what she was looking for.

She shivered as the door to the confessional clicked shut behind her. Immediately it seemed insufferably stuffy, improbably warm. Sarah lowered herself onto the cushioned kneeler, checked to be sure she had a handkerchief in her pocket, and positioned her clasped hands on the shelf.

Presently she heard the door behind the screen of dusty speaker-cloth slide open. She took a deep breath.

"Bless me, Father, for I have sinned."

She could see the shadowy image of the priest making the sign of the cross before her. What little light there was came from behind him; his face was invisible. She hoped hers was, too. She sank down a bit, resting on the backs of her calves. She closed her eyes, felt dizzy, and opened them again. The priest remained silent.

"Since my last confession, Father, I have missed Sunday Mass twice. I have let my mind wander, and I have been remiss in my duties to my family." Unexpectedly, the tears welled up and she choked on the last words.

The priest was silent as she wiped her eyes and blew her nose.

"Father—" Again, she choked into silence.

"Yes, my child. I think you have something much more important to tell me, perhaps something more difficult."

"Yes, I do, Father."

"Begin when you are ready." His voice sounded old, like brittle paper, but it was a kind voice.

The tears came again. She fumbled in her bag, found a packet of tissues, blew her nose again, and dabbed at her eyes. The tears kept coming but she spoke through them. "I have committed the sin of adultery, Father. I have let another man come into my life, and I—I am not worthy of the good man I married."

"Do you love him?"

"My husband? Yes. Yes, I do."

"And the other man? Do you love him also?"

"I don't think so, Father. No. I think it was—oh, I don't know. It sounds so adolescent to say I was infatuated. Temporary insanity, maybe." As soon as the words were out, they sounded impossibly stupid.

"It is easy for us to excuse our sins in such a way, my child. How long have you been committing this sin?"

"Two months. Not often." Silence. "Father," she continued desperately, "I sinned against God and against my husband, and I am truly, truly sorry."

"Before you can receive absolution, you must break off the adulterous relationship completely."

"I have done that, Father."

"Does he know? Your husband?"

"No, Father. I have told myself that I must confess to him, but I haven't, not yet."

"Good."

"Good?"

"My child, you are bearing a heavy burden. You called your husband a good man, so I assume he is blameless in this—in your adultery."

"Yes. Yes, he is."

"Can you think of a reason he must share this burden and this pain?"

She was silent for a moment. "No, Father."

"This, then, is your penance: You must not lay this burden on the shoulders of your husband. You must carry it yourself. First, go into the church and say the sorrowful mysteries of the Rosary."

"Is that all?"

"All? It will not be easy, my child."

"No, Father." It wouldn't, Sarah realized as she began the familiar words of the Act of Contrition. Her voice faltered when she came to the words "You, whom I should love above all things," but she regained control and continued, "I firmly intend, with your help, to do penance, to sin no more, and to avoid whatever leads me to sin."

She really did feel lighter, she decided, when she had heard the priest's gentle prayer of absolution. "Through the ministry of the Church," he intoned, "may God grant you pardon and peace." And he absolved her, telling her to go in peace.

As Sarah left the confessional, rosary in hand, the priest sighed. They never came, he reflected, until it was over. Were they repentant, or just regretful? Did they want absolution, or did they just want to talk about it to someone, even a priest?

But then, he reminded himself, listening was doing God's work.

As Sarah, relieved and burdened in equal parts, was parking her car in the Long Beach garage stall she and Andy rented near the Express dock, Roger Cameron was parking his golf cart in the driveway of the Cameron family's island home.

Roger's nerves were taut. First yesterday's news that Hayden was dead—surely Sarah couldn't have had anything to do with that, could she? She hadn't had a letter like he had. Had she? Or Andrew?—She had babbled something about Andrew and a letter. What might Andrew have done if he'd had a letter from Hayden about—about him and Sarah?

As if that weren't enough to worry about, there had been Margaret's cryptic call this afternoon.

"What time are you coming home today?" she had asked him. That was so unlike Margaret, always so self-reliant. She was accustomed to his demanding schedule, one that took him off to remote parts of the interior some days to monitor projects or populations. She never complained about his long hours, not even when they were longer than usual when he and Sarah—but that was over. He wouldn't think about that.

She had sounded anxious. Margaret, who was usually so calm and contained. As it happened, he told her, he would be able to leave work a little early. He'd be bringing some reports home to review before a habitat committee meeting tomorrow, but he didn't mention those. He should have finished them this morning, but he'd been too preoccupied to give them his full attention.

"Good," she had said. "We need to talk."

Roger disliked those words, and it seemed that he was always hearing them. Signaling trouble. What was it now? Had Margaret found out about Sarah? He should have told her before. He should have brought home flowers. He should have…. He should have resisted the affair with Sarah altogether. He knew that now. It was shoddy, stupid, sneaking around. He'd been flattered, diverted, that was all. If Margaret had found out, would she believe him when he told her it was over?

"We have to talk." Of course she must have found out about it. But it was over. Please let her believe that.

He squared his shoulders and went indoors.

He found Margaret in the kitchen, putting the finishing touches to what looked like chicken Caesar salads. She came toward him, her outfit unwrinkled at the end of the day, her silver-blond hair gleaming. She wore the pale coral-pink shell and pale gray slacks she had chosen when they vacationed in San Francisco last year. He remembered her pleasure when he'd suggested she shop for something as a souvenir of the holiday, and how beautifully they had fit her slender, curving body. They hung less snugly now, as if they had become a size too large. But Margaret was still more beautiful, Roger thought, than any woman he had ever known, fragile, lovely porcelain.

And like porcelain, he saw, her face was closed, expressionless.

184

She knew. He felt his insides clench. An impulse took hold of him. Not ordinarily demonstrative, Roger gave a sudden gulp and, taking Margaret's two hands in his, fell to his knees at her feet. "I'm so sorry, my dear, so terribly, terribly sorry," he sobbed, kissing her hands.

Margaret's eyes widened and she managed to gasp, "How did you know?—Did the doctor—?"

But Roger rushed on, unheeding. "I don't deserve you. I can't think what made me betray you, but it's over, I swear it's over. Margaret, my love, I never really loved anyone but you. Sarah was just a—a kind of madness. A kind of crazy impulse thing, that really didn't mean anything at all. That trip to Monterey—that was the only time.

"Oh, please, Margaret dear, forgive me. You—you and Lizzie and Eric—are my life. You've always made our home a haven. You've been my anchor. I can't believe that I nearly threw it away, but I'll never, never look at another woman again."

Only then could he turn his imploring face to hers. He saw that her face, pale as it usually was, had lost every bit of color. She turned away.

With her back to him, she said, "You've made what I was going to tell you much easier, Roger. Doctor Ziegler got my test results back this morning. I saw him at noon. It's cancer, all right, and it's spread to my spine and my liver. He says it's inoperable. I turned in my resignation at school this afternoon.

"I have perhaps six months left, maybe less. Now let's have dinner."

Chapter 33

Hot, dusty, and with no success in his search for a cell phone, Detective Rhys MacFarlane descended the slope from Mount Ada and walked down Wrigley Road. When he got into town, heading for the sheriff's station, he suddenly veered off and headed down Descanso. He'd stop and talk to his friend John, he thought, and with luck he'd find out how Lexi was doing. Besides, John had his finger on the town pulse better than anyone he knew.

Moments later, he was sitting on the quiet back deck with John and Stina, sipping lemonade and listening to the whistle of a departing Express.

"Nice, isn't it," John observed. Summer afternoons during the week, islanders can hear the tempo getting slower and the quiet growing with each boat that departs for the mainland.

The comfortable thing about John and Stina, Rhys thought, was that they understood he was on a case and didn't ask questions he shouldn't answer.

"It seems to me," Rhys said, "that hardly anyone wanted to see that resort built. There were a lot of people who didn't like Hayden. We've got way too many people with motives for this murder." And then he sat back to see what light John might cast on the case.

"You're kind of stuck, aren't you?" It was Stina who asked. He nodded. And waited. She did not volunteer anything more, but sat back, her mouth a taut line across her tanned face.

There was a silence. Rhys still waited.

"When Warner Hayden came to the island," John said finally, "it seems to me a kind of atmosphere came along with him. Do you believe in evil, Rhys? I don't know if Mr. Hayden was an evil man, but I think something dangerous came to Avalon when he came here. Or maybe it was here and he woke it up." He shrugged. "I see people—normally happy people—go tense when the talk turns to that resort. Conversations stop when certain people, people involved with the Conservancy or the city council, come by. People I've known for years are suddenly strung tight as bowstrings."

John put his lemonade glass aside and stood up, facing toward the water. "Now Hayden is dead, and maybe his project is dead too, but there is fear here, Rhys. Much too close. Our Lexi's afraid. Andrea's afraid. I saw Edgar Ruiz the other night, and I think he is afraid too. And Sarah and Andrew Martin. And there are others. I do not know if they are afraid for themselves, or whether they fear for others, but people are watching one another, looking over their shoulders. This is how evil works, I think."

He was quiet for a bit. Stina did not contradict him, as she often did, but sat watching him anxiously. "We must find who killed Hayden," John said at last.

"Will you help?" Rhys asked. "Will you tell me anything you notice?"

And then Stina spoke. "Things I notice," she said, "make me afraid." She rose abruptly, picked up empty lemonade glasses, and disappeared into her kitchen.

Rhys recognized an invitation to leave when he saw one. He got up, said his goodbyes, and made his way to the sheriff's station.

The parade of interviews was ending as Rhys arrived at the op center. "No joy with that one," Price said as a hotel clerk from The Bell left. "Corroborated the Alvorado woman's story about coming back at 5 with Hayden and leaving again, and said Sentik came in at six, left for dinner at seven. Nothing for us there.

"But I've got a few things of interest. Canham's taking the San Pedro boat over town. Linda's got a class tonight but she left dinner in the refrigerator. Let's go compare notes over a beer and whatever it is she cooked."

"You don't want me eating your dinner," Rhys protested, but it was only a *pro forma* protest. He knew Linda always cooked as if for an army, and Price, for heaven's sake, didn't need to eat all of it.

The rest of what Price had just said registered with him then. "Canham's taking the boat? You mean he's not staying over?"

"Nope. He's gonna be a commuter. Says his girlfriend's nervous with this serial killer loose." Price snickered.

"Price has a girlfriend?"

"So he says. Wonder what she's like, eh?"

Over two bottles of IPA, a plate of cold roast chicken and a pasta-and-veggie salad, deputies MacFarlane and Price compared notes. "So your luck on the slope ran out," Price said. "No phone, huh?"

"It could be anywhere up there," Rhys said, grimacing. He had a couple of new scratches on his face and a nasty gash in his forearm. "I clambered in and out of more tangles of half-dead scrub than I can believe. I went the whole way down the chute where he fell. *Nada.*"

188

"Weird. You can find a rock with a tiny bit of dried blood on it and you can't find a phone. Doesn't that make you wonder if there never was a phone up there?"

"Or if someone found it and took it."

"You mean someone might have got to the body before Lexi?"

"Could have, I suppose. But no, what I mean is someone who did the guy in. Who maybe had reason to take the phone." Rhys drained his beer. "Who'd maybe had conversations with him they didn't want known. Or who had called and lured him up there."

"Like an ex-wife. Damn. Too bad the Oleson woman didn't work out. That would all have fit so nicely."

"Water under the bridge." Rhys shrugged. "What we've got might fit someone else. Maybe we'll get some something helpful from the crime lab on that piece of a note that was up there. Let's look at your notes. I think we've got a pretty wide field of suspects."

"Too wide." Price got up, rinsed his plate, stacked the two of them in the sink and then pulled his notebook from his pocket. "Well," he said, "about every second so-called witness we had in there was some kind of kook. Including a couple of the Plein-Air artists. First we had the Mexican woman, the flamboyant one, ranting on about how her boyfriend probably killed Hayden because he was jealous of Hayden's interest in her. And then—this is weird—another one of them came in. Woman named Eve Jones. Wanted to tell us how she'd seen Hayden putting the moves on Lexi, and how angry that seemed to make Lexi." He eyed MacFarlane.

Rhys was sitting very still.

"Hey, I didn't mean it was weird that Hayden should make a play for Lexi. Anybody would. I would if I weren't a happily married man. But it looked to me like this Eve person was trying to protect the Mexican woman's boyfriend, Viktor something-or-other."

Rhys tried to make light of it. "Ah, those artists," he said. But inwardly he seethed at the idea of Hayden—the jerk was old, for God's sake—putting his paws on Lexi. Good thing the guy was dead.

"Really, there were only two things that kind of grabbed my attention," Price continued. "The first was a maid at the Inn. She said Hayden seemed really upset when she opened the door and he was on the phone. Made me wonder if he was afraid she'd overheard something. Do we have anything going on the phone calls?"

"The hotel's system is one of those phone-company things. Too bad switchboards are a thing of the past. That would make it so easy. But we should have something back from the phone people tomorrow."

"Good. Then—and I think this might really be a breakthrough—a volunteer from the Conservancy center came in. Don't know how he heard about us but he said Hayden was in the center for quite a while Friday afternoon. He was taking notes of some sort in a notebook, grayish, not very thick, and the volunteer thinks he may have been talking with one of the lead biologists. Only problem is she's left town."

"The volunteer?"

"No, the volunteer was a guy," Price said. "Old retired guy, used to teach high-school science, I think. No, the biologist. She's at a conference in Phoenix."

"Can we call her?"

"Canham asked the guy to phone in if he could get hold of contact information for this woman. I don't think he called in, though. We can go up to the center tomorrow and follow up if we don't hear." Price yawned. "So—when you went through the stuff in Hayden's room, or up there on the slope, did you find any kind of a notebook?"

"Nothing aside from that calendar we got when we first went into the room. That was kind of light-colored leather, wasn't it? Doesn't seem like something somebody would describe as 'grayish.' And it was a full eight by ten or more. Nothing in there except for times and initials anyway," Rhys said. "We'll have to follow those up, of course, but it doesn't seem like that calendar would have been what your volunteer saw."

"So it's hurry up and wait."

"Yeah."

Price yawned again. "That's probably good. We both need a good night's sleep."

Once again, Rhys recognized the signal. Asking Price to thank his wife for the dinner, he left. He'd intended to go home and get some sleep. Walking home, however, Rhys kept thinking about the mysterious notebook. He knew he'd gone through Hayden's room thoroughly. If only he had more of a description. It occurred to him that Lexi did volunteer photo work with the Conservancy and spent a good deal of time in the center. She might well know the names of the volunteers. If he could get in touch with the man, and if the guy was observant enough, he might be able to tell them more about the notebook, or at least eliminate Hayden's calendar. Or he might come up with a way to reach the absent biologist. He realized it was an excuse, but it was as good as any. He climbed a side street to the house Andrea and Lexi shared, took the path that zigzagged up the hillside, and knocked on the door of the upper floor.

Lexi opened the door and smiled when she saw who it was. "Hello, Rhys. Come on in."

Rhys stepped over the threshold and saw that Andrea was there as well. "We're having a nightcap. Chai. Do you want a cup?" Lexi asked.

"Mm. Sounds good."

Andrea rose and greeted Rhys warmly enough, but there was a wary look in her eyes and she put her mug down on the coffee table. "No second cup for me, Lexi. I've got some bills I need to go over. Days in the shop are never long enough." She quickly slipped down the stairs. Rhys heard the lock on the door click as she closed it.

"Did I scare her off?"

Lexi winced. "What do you mean?"

"She seemed like she didn't want to see me."

"Oh. I think she was ready to go," Lexi said quickly, but she didn't sound convincing. Rhys was tempted to ask what was up. but he resisted, remembering that listening was more rewarding than asking questions, and recalling too that it wasn't really that long since Lexi had had the miserable experience of finding Hayden's body. He wasn't going to push her for information.

Turning the conversation away from Andrea, he asked Lexi about the people who worked as volunteers at the Conservancy center. She seemed to relax at that. Two of them, she said, were retired men; and yes, she knew their names. The one who had taught science was called Schoenberg.

Could he borrow her phone? His mobile was all but out of power. He could, and did, and hit it lucky on the first call. The notebook, Mr. Schoenberg recalled, was a small one, he thought about five by eight, and very slim. Probably a Moleskine, he said, and dark gray. Hayden was wearing a bush-style jacket, and he slipped the notebook into his pocket when he left the building, Schoenberg added. Rhys thanked him and put the phone on the counter Lexi had taken it from.

"Was that a help?" Lexi asked, handing him a mug that steamed and gave off a fragrance of cinnamon, ginger, clove, and cardamom.

"Oh, yes. It was. So's this. Thanks, Lexi."

She sat down, then. After a moment, she asked, "How's your case going?"

"Frustrating."

"Ah."

"I'd love to tell you all about it, but—"

"You can't. I know. I heard today that I'm a suspect."

"You know I don't suspect you."

"That detective inspector—he does. Me, and Andrea, and Edgar. And others, too, maybe even that gloomy-looking painter."

Rhys shook his head. "And Bob Pyle the butterfly guy. He really seems to have it in for him. And half a dozen other people. I even heard him wondering about the director of the Conservancy."

"Well, we know he wasn't around on the weekend, at least."

"We do?"

"Rhys, he's on his honeymoon."

"Of course. You took the wedding pictures, what, a week ago?" She nodded.

"So where did they go?" he asked.

"To Florence and Madrid. And now I expect you'll go check that out," she said with sudden bitterness, getting up and looking out the window over the town whose lights glimmered in the darkness.

"Lexi." His voice was pleading.

"I'm sorry, Rhys. You're such a good friend. I'm just out of sorts." She turned and gave him a quick hug. "We're all on edge. We're all watching each other. Anytime anyone makes a comment about the—the murder, we chew on it to see if it means something else. It's awful. We've just got to find who did it."

Rhys knew morning would come far too soon. He suppressed a yawn that had nothing to do with present company and took Lexi's hand. "I've got to go. Tomorrow's another day, and you're right. We've got to solve this. I'm glad you said 'we.' Don't do anything silly, but if you hear anything that might help, tell me. Okay?"

"Of course okay." She kissed him on the cheek.

He staggered out into the warm night, dizzy with fatigue and the feel of Lexi's warm lips on his cheek.

Then he thought about her words. "You're such a good friend." Damn.

Chapter 34

Tuesday, June 10

Thin skeins of fog lay across the harbor, and the last of the higher fog layer was breaking into drifting clouds that grew smaller as Viktor Sentik watched them. He had wakened early and taken a cup of coffee down to the beach, then walked to the end of the pier. Who, he wondered, had decided on that violent blueish-green color? After strolling the seafront, he had returned to the hotel where the plein-air painters gathered, and stood now at the edge of the broad patio where the early risers were gathered at breakfast, watching the mingling and listening to the babble of voices.

The week of painting was well under way, and the group was happily recounting accomplishments. The two Frenchmen had gone to two Two Harbors, where Jean-Marc had painted a view of the isthmus and René had created a landscape featuring Banning House and prickly-pear cactus. Jean-Marc, if he couldn't meet the writer of Wild West stories, had at least seen bison and reported happily that he'd sketched, for his girlfriend, the buffaloes whose ancestors were brought to the island to feature in a film of one of Zane Grey's stories.

Maribeth and Jill exchanged amused glances. Another misapprehension, but they needn't disabuse him of what little he could salvage of his longed-for Zane Grey connection.

Ellen ambled in, talking with the man from Southwest Washington. "How're you doing? Are you getting used to dust and heat instead of rain?"

"Makes it easy to dry a canvas. What's hard is getting any work done with all the spectators."

"Where were you painting?"

"In the canyon up from the boatyard."

"The one with the Quonset huts?"

"Yeah. I love the colors in that little neighborhood. But the kids came and watched first, and then pretty soon everybody kind of came in procession, one by one, and they wanted to comment, and make suggestions. You know the kind of thing: 'How come you left out that tree?' or 'Why don't you paint that garden? It's prettier than the huts.' I like the place, even the rusty junk."

Ellen smiled. "You do it well. You're brave to do neighborhoods. I thought I was away from it all when I went up to the lookout on the stagecoach road. It's a great view, lovely eucalyptus trees, but all day people would drive up and pile out. I cringed every time one of the buses came along. I thought I was in a Tom Robbins novel."

Her companion was quiet for a moment. Then the penny dropped, and he laughed. "*Another Roadside Attraction.*"

"Oh, right," laughed the woman from New England, joining them. "And the questions. 'How do you know what colors to put in your picture?' 'How long did it take you to paint that?' 'Is it hard, being an artist?'"

"What do you say to that one?"

"I said, 'Oh, absolutely!' and then, of course, there's the inevitable. 'Do you make a lot of money being an artist?'" There was a burst of laughter.

Viktor scanned the group. There was no sign of Bianca. She often slept late, skipping breakfast. It wasn't good for her to do that, but he couldn't convince her that coffee alone wasn't a suitable start for the day. He joined the queue at the buffet table.

"How's it going?" Viktor wasn't sure whether the speaker was Jean-Marc or René. He hadn't bothered to distinguish any difference between the two French painters.

"Well, the painting aspect of things is okay."

"And?" Jean-Marc/René asked with polite interest as he loaded his plate with eggs and sausages.

"Agh. My lovely roommate has chosen to accuse me of murdering that accursed high-roller developer. Just because she had a crush on him."

"I am so sorry." Jean-Marc/René added two apricot-filled Danish and several chunks of fresh pineapple to his plate. "That is terrible."

"That," said Viktor, "is life with Bianca."

He finished filling his plate and retired to a small table at the far end of the patio, where he presented a portrait of gloom while, in fact, he enjoyed the lavish spread the islanders offered to fortify the painters against a long day of work. He considered his options for the day's painting: fishermen on Cabrillo Mole, the view from the Chimes Tower, kayaks at Descanso Beach, or some of the working areas on Pebbly Beach.

"Viktor." Eve, wearing a paint-daubed gauze shirt and jeans with ventilated knees, appeared at his elbow. Her hair was down and she'd actually put on a bit of lipstick. "May I join you for a moment?"

"Uh—yes, I suppose so."

She hesitated. After yesterday, she'd hoped for a little more enthusiasm.

"Victor, I heard Bianca accusing you yesterday of murdering that developer, that man who was going to build a resort up above the Inn. She—that's so unfair. I know you didn't do it." She sat down opposite him.

"Do you?" Viktor knitted his brows, then looked past Eve so fixedly that she glanced over her shoulder. "And what makes you think that?"

"Because you're a good person. And because—well, I've been hearing things. Around. There were a lot of people who didn't like that man. And I saw why. I saw him putting the moves on that photographer, the Eurasian girl who's got that studio over on Sumner. And I saw the way she looked at him."

"And why are you telling me this?"

"Because that's someone who had a motive to murder him. To shove him off the cliff. After all, in murder mysteries, it's often the person who reports finding the body who did it. How else would she know where to find him on that hillside?"

"Are you playing detective now, Eve?"

"No, I'm just—what do they call it? Assisting the police?"

"What do you mean?"

"I mean, Viktor, that I talked to the detective inspector." She shuddered a little. "Not a very nice person, I don't think. But I wanted to give him someone to think about besides you."

She looked pleased with herself, and expectant. She looked into Viktor's face.

"That was a silly thing to do."

"Silly? To make an effort to clear your name?" She extended her hands toward him, but when he did not respond she folded them before her on the table.

Viktor shook his head and sighed. Eve glared. "Viktor, you can't go on letting Bianca try to ruin your life. She's making you terribly unhappy. And now accusing you: that's just inexcusable. You shouldn't stand for it."

"Eve," Viktor said, reaching out at last and putting one of his long, paint-stained hands over hers. "Eve, I think you are making a mistake, a mistake about Bianca and me. She isn't trying to get me into trouble. She's just letting off steam."

"You're defending her when she does something like that?"

"Not defending, just understanding."

"Well she doesn't deserve you," Eve burst out.

"I think," Viktor said, "that you should stop before you say anything more. You don't understand how things are with Bianca and me. We give each other a lot of—latitude, I guess you'd say. And yes, we get mad, but it's part of how we are. Eve, I love Bianca, and I know that she loves me. It may be a setup that's strange to you: I think you are a girl who'd like someone who sends you flowers and is constant and faithful and adoring.

"Bianca and I would be bored to death in a relationship like that."

Seeing that tears were welling up in Eve's eyes, Viktor added, "And I think you should notice that one of those Frenchmen has been looking at you longingly for days, and you haven't even noticed him. Now let's forget that we even had this conversation, shall we?"

Eve rose, whirled around and ran.

Viktor looked regretfully at the last sausage on his plate, gone cold while he'd been extricating himself from Eve's adoration. He picked up his plate and cup and ambled off in search of Bianca.

Chapter 35

Maribeth had watched as Eve slipped away from the larger group and joined Viktor. She had seen the way Eve leaned in toward him, how she had spoken to him, and the way she had recoiled at whatever his rejoinder was.

She wondered, as Eve bolted away and ran up the street, whether she should go after her. She decided not. What, after all, could she say?

Eve, she observed, was heading toward her hosts' home. For Eve's sake, Maribeth hoped the Robesons were all out for the day. She checked with the hotel's food service to make sure box lunches were available and then she returned to the office the Conservancy had loaned to Jill and her for the duration of the Plein Air Festival. She rearranged the transportation schedule.

Ten minutes later, as she had begun work on the wet-paint auction list, the phone rang. It was Eve, and she sounded remarkably cheerful.

"What can I do for you, Eve?"

"I know I didn't sign on for transport today, but do you have someone who could give me a ride up to Three Palms?"

"If you don't mind riding along when Jenny takes Isaiah and Ariel down to Pebbly Beach, you're on," Maribeth said. "She can drive you up Wrigley Road on her way back. She has the big cart, so there'll be plenty of room for you and your gear."

"Perfect," said Eve. "Oh," she added. "I should check. Is anyone else painting up there today?"

"No."

"Good. Thanks. I'd like a little time by myself."

"Did you order a lunch?"

"No, but Lucille's packing me what she calls a snack. Fruit salad and a ham croissant."

"Be sure and take plenty of water."

Relief again. Disaster averted, for the time being at least. Eve was, she decided, pathetically naive, but an excellent painter. And Three Palms, a pull-out on Wrigley Road virtually next door to the Inn at Mount Ada, sat on a promontory that offered a bit more view of the town. Eve, Maribeth thought, would find it served her well. It was a favorite spot among painters, and a pleasant place to paint if you didn't mind the occasional cart rocketing around the sharp curve in the road.

Eve would recover. Maribeth turned to other tasks.

While Eve settled herself to paint, Detective Inspector Canham explained to the two local detectives just exactly why lepidopterist Robert Michael Pyle was the obvious candidate for murderer. "I've been checking him out," he told MacFarlane and Price. "He's got roots in Colorado. That's where Hayden's headquarters are located. No doubt he's had someone checking into this resort plan. Might even have some history with Hayden and his projects. He made no bones about the fact that he came to the island looking for some rare butterfly that's only found here."

"But sir, he's—"

Canham silenced Rhys with a warning palm-out gesture. "I know. You're a fan. Get over it. This Pyle—he's worked with enough eco-groups that he knows damn well just writing letters and testifying before commissions isn't going to stop a big project that will benefit everybody. I wouldn't put it past him to find a convenient way to short-circuit the whole thing." He smacked a fist into his palm. "Isn't it just too much of a coincidence that he got here when Hayden was here?"

"But sir, this wasn't his first time on—" MacFarlane began.

"My point exactly," Canham said. "He's been here before."

"But I talked to—" Rhys blurted, but the phone rang.

Canham grabbed it.

"It's who? Oh, God. Not again. Give me just a minute, then put her on." He set the phone down, swiveled in his chair, and looked at MacFarlane and Price. "It's that Jones woman. She was in yesterday and gave us a big story about Hayden putting the moves on that cute little photographer. The one that found the body. Of course, one does wonder why she was where she was when she was, as if she wanted it found.

"We'll have to look into that. See what was going on with her and Hayden," Canham ordered. "Still, my money's on the butterfly guy."

The phone made an impatient noise and Canham's voice changed. "D.I. Canham here. Is that you, Miss Jones?"

The telephone made more noises.

"Did you pick it up? Good. Leave it right where it is." There was another brief exchange and then Canham hung up.

"Okay, MacFarlane. Got a little errand for you. The Jones woman says she found a cell phone just off the road up near the Inn. Let's hope it's Hayden's. Off you go."

Eve Jones waved as MacFarlane drove up. "It's over here. I was just setting up my easel, and the sun reflected off it, or I probably wouldn't have noticed it. I didn't pick it up, in case it's evidence or something. But I don't suppose it has anything to do with your case," she added.

"Good thinking." Rhys smiled at her. He marked the place where the phone lay, then picked it up carefully in a gloved hand. It was covered with fine dust. He figured there was no chance of lifting prints. He slipped it into a plastic bag.

"We've been looking for Mr. Hayden's phone," he told Eve. She looked delighted. "Thank you so much. This could be really important."

"Oh, good."

"He was staying at the Inn," Rhys mused, eyeing the marked spot where the top-of-the-line Blackberry had lain. "And when he was around town, he was driving one of their carts. It looks to me like if somebody came around the curve fast enough, and it was on his lap or in a loose pocket, centrifugal force could have sent it flying right about there. Great job, Miss Jones."

"Is it really his?"

"We won't know until we take it in. Doesn't look to me like it's in working order, but it might just have run down. These phones with all the bells and whistles seem to run out of power at the drop of a hat."

Eve nodded agreement. "Mine's always out of battery. Or out of range."

"Well," Rhys said, "I won't keep you from your painting any longer. Thanks again."

He headed back down the hill, feeling optimistic for the first time since he'd taken Lexi's panicked call from the hillside.

Lexi. Why in the world would that pleasant young woman have tried to implicate Lexi in this murder?

Chapter 36

The power cords for the Blackberries the Los Angeles County deputies used weren't compatible with the very new, very sleek—and very damaged—model everyone hoped was Warner Hayden's, but the desk clerk at the Islander produced one from a drawerful of cords he kept for guests who'd forgotten theirs at home.

Once in the sheriff's station, MacFarlane and Price tested the phone for prints while Canham paced. They'd been hopeful, but they couldn't come up with a single print, not Hayden's, if it was his, much less the prints of anyone else who might have handled the phone.

"Damn dust," Canham said. "Well, what are you waiting for? Plug the blasted thing in."

They plugged in the phone. Nothing happened.

"Shit. You get what looks like the big break and it's nothing. Not so much as a single effing print to show us who had it. Or," Canham snapped his fingers. "Or your little blonde painter lady took it when she bumped him off. Think she was crafty enough to wipe it clean and then jostle it around to make it look like it was there all along? She's been trying to get involved with this thing for the last couple of days, hanging around, coming up with theories. That's a hallmark of murderers, wanting to get in on the investigation to revel in the confusion they've caused. What do you think?" he asked hopefully. No one answered.

"I think he's desperate for a lead," Price muttered.

"Could be nobody else was involved with that phone," MacFarlane pointed out. "Hayden used a Conservancy pickup in the hills, borrowed it from Roger Cameron. Surprising he could wangle that," he added thoughtfully. He picked up the phone in its bag. "But when he was around town, he was driving the Inn's classy cart, the one that looks like a classic sportscar. If he took that turn fast in the cart, and he didn't have it in a secure pocket, or if he'd been using it and it was lying loose on the dash or the floor, centrifugal force would have landed it just about where Eve Jones found it."

"You hope," Canham said. "Still, we'd better check her Friday-evening whereabouts."

"So what do we do now?" Price asked.

"I guess we'll have to wait till tonight. I can take it in to the tech at the main office," Canham said, disgusted. "Just put it in evidence."

Rhys did so, bagging and numbering it. But as he was entering it into the evidence log, one of the foot-patrol officers spoke up.

"Hey, MacFarlane," he said. "There's a guy named Thad Powell—I think he's over on Metropole—who does computer repair. I'm not sure it's an official business, but people go to him when they lose their files. He's really good. He rescued my hard drive when we got a virus that wiped everything out, and I'm pretty sure I heard someone say he'd managed to retrieve some contacts out of a squashed cell phone." He looked at Rhys. Rhys looked at Canham.

Reluctantly, Canham nodded. "Can't hurt. Try him."

The young patrolman grinned, wrote his name in the evidence book, grabbed the phone in its bag, and loped off.

Canham, MacFarlane and Price returned to the operations center, where Price mounted a photo of the phone on the wall map. "Wonder when Alaska's finest are going to find your wandering bug doctor," Canham said.

"Sir, I phoned Roger Cameron last night to confirm that it was a Conservancy truck Hayden was using," MacFarlane said.

"You're quick to change the subject," Canham growled. "Well, go on."

"Cameron admitted it was the one he uses, seemed uncomfortable about it. We need to look into that—it seems pretty irregular. Then I asked him about butterfly habitat along the crest of Mount Ada. He says there's not a lot of silver-leaf lotus or even St. Catherine's lace up on that peak. He says you'll find the occasional hairstreak up there but it's not prime avalona habitat."

"So you're still working to disprove my theory," Canham grumbled. "Okay, so maybe it's not the butterfly. Maybe it's just a general thing. These goddamned environmentalists—"

Once again, the phone rang and cut off the conversation. Rhys answered, but the call was for Price. He listened to Price's side of the conversation, trying to keep from smiling as the gist of it became evident.

"You found him? At Bonanza Creek? Oh, good."

Canham stirred, muttering.

"Slept in the car? Got there at—you said 1:30? That's a.m.?" Price was scribbling furiously.

"Oh, really. San Pedro police? At four? Oh, great. That'll help a lot. Thank you, Sergeant. We've put you to a lot of trouble, but you've told us what we need to know. Thanks very much."

"Sergeant Preston of the Yukon, I presume?" Canham had obviously worked out the answer in advance, too. His voice was harsh, his expression sour.

"Yes, sir. I mean no, sir. Sergeant Metz of the Alaska State Troopers. They got the alert to the parks in the area, and the license showed up on a campsite registration so a trooper was able to talk to Dr. Pyle. He told the trooper, ah," Price checked his notes, "that he'd missed the early ferry—his word—the first time he came over to Avalon, and it cut his time pretty short. Said the signage to the boat terminal was lousy. So this time he drove through to get to the dock the night before, and slept in the car in the parking lot. He told the trooper a San Pedro police officer woke him up at about four a.m. so I suppose we can get confirmation of his story."

"I don't think we need to," MacFarlane said. "I was trying to tell you when the call came in about the phone. I called the Express office early this morning. I should have done that earlier and it would have saved Alaska the trouble. The Express confirmed what Dr. Pyle said in the first place, sir. He was on the seven-o'clock boat from San Pedro, sir."

"Well, I'm glad you've got so much initiative, Rise-and-Shine MacFarlane," Canham said bitterly. "Okay, okay. So we scratch our best chance for an early solve. I hope you're happy. And since you've got so much energy, you can go back up and find out where the Jones woman says she was Friday night, and then check it out.

"Price, you find out where the street-beat guys took that phone, and go see if that computer geek's been able to get any information off Hayden's phone. If it is Hayden's phone. If he could even find out that much.

"I need coffee," Canham added. "God, this morning started early." He shouldered his way out. Price and MacFarlane looked at each other. The hotel's coffee shop was at one end of the building, the lounge in the other. Canham had lumbered off toward the lounge, not the coffee shop.

"Is the sun over the yardarm already?" Rhys looked at his watch.

Price guffawed.

"See you back here."

Price and MacFarlane, each with a take-out coffee in hand, returned to the op center simultaneously. The room was empty. Before they had a chance to confer, however, Canham returned. "Well?" He looked from one to the other.

"I think we can rule out Eve Jones," Rhys said. "She arrived on Thursday, and she did, apparently, see Hayden a couple of times, once Thursday before dinner and again when she was having coffee Friday. But she had dinner with her host family Friday evening, and spent the evening talking about art with the family. They have a daughter who's pretty much over the moon at having 'a real painter' staying with them. I phoned to confirm that she was there and unless she sneaked out and climbed up on that hill in the pitch dark after ten o'clock, Eve Jones is in the clear."

"Eh." Canham appeared preoccupied. "Over to you, Price. Uh, any joy with the phone?"

"As a matter of fact, yes. Some," Price said. "This tech—Mr. Powell—was amazing. He got the number of the phone and even a few of the calls. He was able to confirm that it's Hayden's. He said some of the circuits were damaged so most of the storage is gone, but he did retrieve outgoing calls for

208

two days, Tuesday and Wednesday of last week. I've written them down."

Price handed over the list of phone numbers Thad Powell had retrieved from Hayden's phone. "Too bad he could only get the numbers from two days, and not the last two days at that," Canham grumbled.

"And he couldn't get any indication of whether the calls were answered. But I was able to go online and ID the numbers. Take a look."

Wordlessly, Price moved the paper with the phone numbers and identifying names over to Rhys.

Hayden's office in Denver, a total of four times.

A private investigator in Denver, once.

A P.I. in Los Angeles, twice.

Roger Cameron, Conservancy biologist, twice. Edgar Ruiz, city council member, twice.

Andrew Martin, member of the planning commission, once.

Andrea Benet, caterer, twice.

Lexi Yoshimoto, photographer, three times. Rhys felt his stomach contract as if he'd been slugged.

Canham took the piece of paper and waved it under Rhys's nose. He leered. "Know anybody on this list?"

Chapter 37

Detective Inspector Canham smiled nastily. "I've got another errand for the EverReady Bunny here. MacFarlane, your M.E. friend with the Filipino name called while you were out. She says preliminary blood test results indicate an 'as yet undetermined'—I hate the way those medics won't commit themselves—'amount of cocaine.'"

"Really," Rhys said. "Do you think—"

Canham interrupted. "I want you to go back to Hayden's room and check all the drawers and even the carpets for traces. Damn, we need that phone information for contacts." He rubbed his temples and took a couple of deep breaths. "Price, I want you to bring in that pickup Hayden was using and check it from stem to stern. Then I want you to follow up with Roger Cameron. MacFarlane, when you get back from the Inn, you follow up with those calls to Colorado and L.A."

"Yes, sir." Rhys left.

Canham ruffled through a file folder and a stack of notes. "Oh, great," he grumbled. "Now you tell me Sentik's a dead end, in spite of all the blither that señorita of his gave us."

"Oh, right," Price agreed. "The bouncer at the bar here—he's engaged to one of the Plein Air organizers, so he knew he'd better lend a hand—said he virtually carried Viktor back to The Bell that night and tucked him in."

"Says here Hayden's got an ex-wife somewhere." Canham looked up from turning over notes and straightened his slouch. He was perspiring.

"Here on the island until yesterday afternoon," MacFarlane said.

"You knew about her? You let another likely suspect get away?" Canham half-rose from his seat, his face purpling.

"She didn't get here until Saturday," Price said quickly. "We thought the same thing when we found out there was an ex, and especially when we found out she was here. Thought maybe we'd have it in the bag before your boat got in. Pretty disappointing to discover she didn't come over until Saturday morning."

"Is that in your report?" Canham slumped back into his chair.

"It is, sir. Let me show you."

"Never mind," Canham snapped. "Well, looks like we'd better take a look at that photographer girl, the one the painter woman's trying to finger for this." He shuffled papers again. "I don't think she's given us anything to go on; I think she's just trying to take the heat off Sentik. Too bad he's a no-show." Canham spread the papers out on the table. "But in my long experience, it's not a bad idea to take a good long look at the person who finds the body. Get the Yoshimoto girl in here, will you, Price?"

"Surely you don't think she was involved."

Canham gave him a long look. "Don't be too sure," he said. "You wouldn't be the first cop to have the wool pulled over his eyes by a sweet little girl. She's got MacFarlane by the short hairs, whether he knows it or not, poor little sap. The only thing we've got going for us at this point is the list of people whose numbers Hayden phoned during two days last week. We need to know how each one of them is associated with him.

"So," Canham continued, "First the little photographer, I think. Then we'll need to get to Andrew Martin—he's on the planning commission, right? And Cameron; he's with the Conservancy. And there's that business with the truck; seems pretty irregular. Could be something there. And Ruiz. Edgar Ruiz. He works for the city?"

"He's on the city council."

"Right. Oh, yeah, then there's the Benet woman. Wonder what that's about? Maybe she's his supplier. There's got to be something in those phone calls that will take us forward in this case. I'm damned sick and tired of treading water here."

"Yes, sir." Price headed for Lexi Yoshimoto's studio.

The carpets in Hayden's room appeared pristine. So did the bathroom surfaces. Rhys wondered whether housekeeping had ignored the order to leave the room untouched. Finally, an upper drawer in one of the nightstands yielded a minute quantity of what Rhys supposed would be called an "unidentified white powdery substance." Wielding a brush to coax traces of it into a plastic envelope, Rhys looked at the Winsor and Newton label on the handle and realized his evidence kit was equipped with a fine-grade artist's brush. He laughed out loud as he thought of the dozens of Winsor and Newtons the plein air artists like Eve Jones and Bianca and Viktor were using here and there around the island while he used his for such a pedestrian project.

He assumed, though Canham hadn't explained, that the in-room evidence could be construed to indicate Hayden himself initiated the use of cocaine, probably used it routinely, rather than having been given it by someone as part of a plot to kill him. But still, Rhys reasoned, the cocaine, in addition to the alcohol, would have made him more confident, more careless, more susceptible to being shoved off his own precipice.

What was it that that phrase reminded him of?

"Hoist with his own petard," he answered himself. What was that from? *MacBeth? Hamlet?* He tried to recall the discussion from Humanities 101. Something about being caught in one's own snare. Was Hayden involved in some sort of plan that backfired? And was Roger Cameron involved? If not, why did Hayden have Cameron's rig?

He shook his head. The situation seemed more and more like a bad dream, and seeing Lexi's name on a list of Hayden's phone calls intensified the nightmarish aspect of it all. What he wouldn't give for a nice assignment involving the theft of a couple of Bougainvilleas. On his way back to the operations center, Rhys was rounding a corner when he caught sight of Lexi and Andrea walking quickly in the direction of the Katsaros home.

He could use a dose of Zorba's wisdom, he decided. And so he followed.

Celestina answered his knock. "You, too?" she queried.

Rhys fumbled in his brain for an explanation for his visit, but Stina made that unnecessary, simply enveloping him in a welcoming hug. Lexi and Andrea both turned startled faces toward him as she ushered him into the living room.

"Another young friend, John," she announced. "Now we have all three, and I think we all share the same worries. Sit down. I'm making coffee. I made *galaktoboureko* this morning. First time in months. Now I know why. Sit. No talking until I get back."

She dodged into the kitchen, returning quickly with a tray laden with mugs of coffee and plates with squares of creamy custard baked between layers of phyllo. The scent of orange and lemon made Rhys's mouth water, and he remembered he'd only had granola for breakfast. Before he could address the delicate pastry, however, he realized that Lexi's face was tear-streaked. "What's wrong?" he asked.

"What's wrong?" she wailed. "I've just been grilled by your horrible detective inspector, that's what's wrong. Rhys, it was awful." Stina handed her a box of tissues.

"I suppose I should say his bark is worse than his bite, or something," Rhys began, feeling lame. "Lexi, I'm sorry. He enjoys being intimidating."

"I shouldn't be such a wuss," she said, wiping her eyes and blowing her nose.

"The whole situation is awful," he said. "I have to say I'm discouraged. We keep running into dead ends with this thing. What am I missing here?"

"You'll find it," John assured him. He turned to Lexi, who was still sniffling. "Do you want to talk about it?"

"It's not enough to discover a disgusting dead body. Now it seems I'm a murder suspect. And what makes it so awful," she said tearfully, "is that I am glad he's dead. Hayden. He kept pestering me about doing photography for him. I told him no but he just kept at me."

"He was a horrible person," Andrea said, putting an arm around Lexi. "I think he deserved what he got. He made you feel like you'd already agreed to work for him even though it was the last thing in the world you'd want to do."

She looked at Rhys. "I suppose I'm next on the suspect list? Hayden wanted me to go to work for him as director of food service and catering for his wretched resort. And he—"

Lexi was still sobbing. "I feel so guilty. And then that man asked me for my alibi for Friday night. Alibi!"

"But you had one, didn't you?" Andrea said. Lexi sobbed all the harder.

"Yes. But Inspector Canham made it pretty clear that he was still suspicious."

"Oh, no," Rhys said. "Lexi, it's just routine. It's just because your phone number was on Hayden's phone when we finally found it. They're interviewing everybody whose number's on the phone. You and Edgar Ruiz and Andrew Martin and Roger Cameron and even Andrea."

Now two stricken faces were turned to his. Rhys swallowed. "I shouldn't have said that. What was I thinking?"

"You never heard it," Stina pronounced, looking at each of the younger women with a stern glare.

But their dismay had nothing to do with his breach of professionalism. What he saw on their two faces, he realized, was fear.

Back at the operations center after a stop at the sheriff's station where he entered the envelope with the bits of cocaine into evidence and filled out a crime lab routing slip, Rhys paused at the door to be sure another interview wasn't going on. Hearing nothing, he entered quietly. He looked with loathing at Canham, who was poring over a topographic map of Mount Ada. The detective inspector looked up.

"Well?"

"White powder in a drawer in the nightstand. Just traces."

"Enough."

"Sir, I—" Rhys paused. How did you approach your superior about an inappropriate interview?

Canham broke into Rhys's pause. "I talked to our little local photographer. She says she didn't answer the calls from Hayden. That's what she says. Admits he was putting the moves on her and that she didn't want to work for him. About Friday, she says she was having a long dinner with an old classmate. But hey, I'm thinking it'd be dirt easy for a little dish like that to persuade some old boyfriend to lie for her. She knows the terrain up there, too," he said, tapping the topo. Rhys noticed his pallor again. "I think it's conceivable that she could have found a way to lure Hayden up to the site, maybe with a little line or two of cocaine before they went up there to check out the photo ops." He laughed nastily.

"I can tell you this much," Rhys said. "I know she was having dinner with a girl she knew in college that night. And I sure as heck know she wouldn't—couldn't have killed anyone, even an old creep like Hayden. Inspector Canham, sir, you can't go treating her like a suspect. That's just not right!"

Canham took a step toward Rhys, then another, until they were face-to-face. He looked down at the young deputy.

"And what makes you think I am 'treating her like a suspect?' Hmm?"

"Sir, she said—"

"Were you in contact with this young woman? When you were supposed to be following up on telephone calls to Colorado and Los Angeles?"

"I ran into her when I—when I was on the way here," Rhys stammered.

"You ran into her. And you had this conversation on the street?"

"Actually, it was in a friend's home."

"Now look, Deputy Rice MacFarlane. I don't know how the hell you passed your detective test, but in my book, you just flunked out. Los Angeles County is not paying you to socialize on county time. And I am not putting up with you working at cross-purposes with an active investigation. If you intend to stay on this case, you will work in concert with the team, and under my direction, and that is that."

"Yes, sir," said MacFarlane as Canham swore and walked quickly from the room. He heard the restroom door bang.

Price showed up just as Canham returned to his desk. The inspector's face was gray and he was sweating as he listened to Price. "Nothing to report on the pickup, sir. Just dust, all matching the yellow soil up there. Nothing in or underneath it. Guys are checking it now for prints." Canham didn't answer. "You okay, sir?" Price asked, suddenly noticing that Canham wasn't reacting with his usual profane bluster.

"Yeah. No. Hell. You two carry on, follow up on those phone calls. I'm feeling rotten, and I'm going to try to catch the afternoon boat off of this damned island. You get onto those phone calls," he ordered vaguely. Price and MacFarlane looked after him as he walked out of the office.

Half an hour later, there was a call from the acting Commander. "I think you two are on your own for a while," he said. "Your D.I.'s up at the hospital, in the E.R. He came by to see if somebody could drive him to the boat but he collapsed here at the station. Good thing he didn't make it to the Express, actually. It wasn't pretty. Keep going on anything you've already got scheduled, and bring your reports up to date. I'll be back to you in a while when we know what's going on with him."

Chapter 38

Detective Ted Price sat at Canham's desk, paging through the inspector's files. "He hasn't got much in the way of notes here," Price said. "Any ideas beyond what we've been working on?"

"Nope. Except—"

"Except what?"

"After I deal with the calls on my list, do you mind if I go back to the hotel? I think we need to talk to every employee. There aren't that many, and I'd like to try establish a timetable. Find out who he hung out with, who he had coffee with, anything. Not just the day before he died, but all the time he was here. And I want to try one more look through the room to see if I can find—" He paused, at a loss.

"Find what?"

Rhys was saved from having to corral his thoughts by another call from the Commander. Price put the phone on speaker mode. "They've admitted Canham to the hospital. It's food poisoning. Probably salmonella."

"But they admitted him? Must be bad," Price said.

"They've got him on an IV hydration drip and they're going to keep him to monitor an irregular heartbeat. Probably just the result of the stress. His temp was almost a hundred and four."

"Wow."

"D. I. Canham was convinced it was poisoning. Thought he was the serial killer's latest victim." The Commander's voice held barely suppressed laughter, but he caught himself.

"Salmonella can be pretty rough on the system, so he could hardly be expected to think straight. His girlfriend's sick, too. They called to see what he'd eaten. Seems she'd bought a seafood salad at a deli for dinner, but left it on the counter. He was late getting home and that was just long enough for it to turn."

"Eww." Price rolled his eyes at MacFarlane as their supervisor continued.

"She only had a little of it, so she's just uncomfortable. Canham, apparently, had eaten the lion's share. So what have you two got going?"

"We're following up on the phone calls Mr. Powell was able to identify on Hayden's phone. I'm trying to see if we can pick up any leads from the people involved with Hayden's project. MacFarlane's going back to the Inn to make sure we have statements from everyone." When he and the Commander had finished their conversation, Price turned to MacFarlane. "I didn't mention your search for the unknown Something. What do you have in mind?"

"I don't know. It just seems to me that there's got to be something more. Something to explain why everybody tenses up at the mention of his name. And there are those cryptic initials in Hayden's calendar."

"Then let's just get on with those phone calls."

Calling the first number, Rhys spoke with a remarkably reticent associate of Hayden's who identified herself as Sylvia Woods. Yes, Hayden was in the habit of phoning in regularly to keep his firm updated on his whereabouts. No, she didn't think there were any troubling issues involved in those conversations. "It was all very much routine," she said primly.

On a whim, Rhys asked another question. "Will the project continue, now that he—that he is deceased?"

He had expected a glib "of course" or a brusque brush-off. But the voice at the other end of the line faltered. "I really can't say," Ms. Woods answered, and she sounded as if she resented having to say that. "You see, the Catalina project involved land Mr. Hayden had acquired on his own, rather than in the firm's name. I expect it will depend upon whoever inherits."

MacFarlane knew better than to ask a business associate who Hayden's heirs were. But it did suggest a line of inquiry. "Can you tell me who Mr. Hayden's attorney is?" he asked.

"Our firm is represented by Connelly, Farquhar and Dunham here in Denver," she said. Her voice was firm now. "As to Mr. Hayden's personal attorney, I'm afraid I cannot say."

Or won't, MacFarlane thought. He thanked her and ended the call.

He stared out the window, made some notes, and dialed again. The phone at the Denver private investigator's office informed him that the owner of that number was away from the office. He left a message. He fared better with the L.A. private eye, whose name, he was intrigued to discover, was Ella Ketchem. After Rhys identified himself, Ketchem was forthcoming. She'd been employed twice earlier in the spring by Hayden, she said, once to research Andrea Benet, and once to shadow Roger Cameron. She'd had little trouble determining that Andrea, while at college in Portland, had been part of a cell of eco-terrorists who called themselves the Green Chain. Their chief focus had been a former forest preserve that had been purchased by a timber company after the organization that had held it in conservancy status had gone bankrupt. They'd chained themselves to trees, put water in the gas tanks of bulldozers and spiked old-growth Douglas firs, she told MacFarlane.

"A logger was badly injured when his chainsaw hit a spike," the P.I. continued. "Andrea and four other members of the cell were initially charged with first-degree assault. Mr. Hayden was happy to have that information. After it came out that management of the timber company knew trees had been spiked but hired gyppo loggers to cut them anyway, the prosecution lowered the charges to reckless endangerment," she added. "He wasn't quite so happy to hear that. But there was some jail time and community service involved, and that seemed to be what he was looking for."

And Cameron?

"Mr. Hayden had me shadow him for three weeks. He was spending quite a bit of time with a woman who volunteered part-time at the Conservancy's center in Avalon," she said. "Then when I reported to Mr. Hayden that Mr. Cameron had registered for a conference in Monterey, he actually paid me to stay in the hotel where the conference was and to shadow him. The woman was with him, and as Mr. Hayden had requested, I took a photo of them. He paid a bonus for that."

"Do you know the name of the woman?"

"Sarah Martin. She registered at the hotel as Sara Mason. No h on the Sara."

Rhys glanced at his phone list again, but no number showed up for Sarah Martin. Still, the list Thad Powell had retrieved only represented two days in the cell-phone history of Warner Kendall Hayden. And Sarah Martin's husband's name was on the list.

"Did he seem to know what he was looking for when he hired you to shadow these people?" Rhys wondered aloud.

"I don't think so. In our line of work," she added drily, "if you shadow someone for long enough, you'll usually find something they don't want shared with the world. Mr. Hayden explained that he was considering hiring these people, but he wanted to be sure there would be no conflicts of interest. He seemed to have—" she paused, "high standards and deep pockets."

And the phone calls made to the aptly named Ms. Ketchem on Thursday and Friday?

"Mr. Hayden phoned me on Thursday, but I was in court all day. This phone—you've reached my cell number, of course—was switched over so he would only have had the out-of-office message from my answering service," she said. "I remember that he didn't leave a message, but just phoned again the next day."

"And the purpose of that call?"

"He said he wanted to engage me on another job. He made an appointment to see me this week—yesterday morning, in fact."

"Did he say anything about what he wanted you to do?"

"No, he was always rather secretive, only spoke of his assignments in person," she said, and he thought she sounded genuinely regretful. "But I gathered from yesterday's newspaper," she told Rhys, "that I could cancel that appointment."

By the time he'd written reports on his talks with Hayden's staffer and Ketchem, there was a call from the evidence department. The powder he'd found had field-tested positive for cocaine.

"No surprise, huh," Price commented. "While you were busy writing, I got in touch with the county planning department to find out just where this resort project is in terms of time—how soon it was likely to be approved or not approved. I went over and picked up a load of copies of documents. I'll check with the city and the Conservancy, too, while you're at the hotel. We need to get a handle on just exactly what this guy had going on, who he had on his side and who wanted to stop him."

"We need to look at Roger Cameron," Rhys told him. "That detective in L.A. had some interesting things to say. She provided him with a photo of Cameron and Sarah Martin in Monterey. They apparently were having an affair. And she'd ferreted out information on Andrea, too, for him. Some ecoterrorist activity when she was in college. I'm getting the impression that our lovely victim was pressuring people with the results of all this research. One thing you can't call him is a cheapskate."

"Jeez, no, I guess not. A rat, though."

"The P.I. said he explained that he had very high standards for prospective employees. I wonder who she thought she was kidding. Or maybe he had her snowed. Anyhow, now we have more motives."

"Little motives everywhere," Price agreed. "What we need is some hard evidence. Well, let's get cracking."

MacFarlane started with the manager of the Inn, making notes of employee schedules and contact information, and talking to those who were at work. None of them had anything new to tell him, but he gleaned bits of information in spite of that.

The maid who'd interrupted Hayden's phone call told MacFarlane that Hayden was habitually rude to the Mexican and Guatemalan employees. "My brother, he takes coffee in to

Mr. Hayden every morning, but if he sees him on the street, he don't even say hello."

MacFarlane inferred that it was Hayden doing the snubbing, but he asked, "Mr. Hayden, you mean? Acted like he didn't know your brother?"

"Yes. It's like he don't know who he is. You know, all us little brown people look alike." She shrugged philosophically.

The manager confirmed the earlier impression that Hayden, while he was staying for an extended period, was nevertheless away for a night or two at least once a week. No, he hadn't left any information about where he was when he was away, or any contact numbers; the hotel had his cell phone number, however. "I don't think we've had call to use it. Now, will that be all?" he added hopefully.

MacFarlane disappointed him, explaining that he would have to return to talk to the evening shift of employees. He mollified the manager by asking if late afternoon, when the shift first arrived, would be less disruptive.

"The porters will be busy, but it will be all right for front desk. I can stay to cover," the young man said, noting that two of the employees who had worked Friday evening had left the island to attend a wedding. He checked the work roster and said they'd both be back at work that evening. He sighed.

"You've been very discreet, but the word's out, of course, and it's a bit upsetting for everyone, guests especially."

He looked relieved when MacFarlane left the desk and began interviewing employees. A waiter who was a friend of Lexi's said—very apologetically—that he'd seen Hayden in conversation with Miss Yoshimoto downtown and that he seemed to be trying to convince her of something. She was shaking her head and Hayden was looking amused, like he

224

didn't believe her, the waiter added, eyeing MacFarlane carefully. Rhys, who was still discovering the strength of his feelings for Lexi, was surprised; was it that obvious to others? Or was there some other reason for the young man's apparent embarrassment?

The groundskeeper reiterated his assertion that the presence of the four-wheel pickup Hayden used was frowned on by the Inn's owners, observing that the manager had been told never to allow a vehicle like that on the premises again. "If he weren't setting out to be a competitor to us," the attendant added, "I think they'd have made him remove it. But they didn't want to look—ah—petty, I guess."

Once he'd interviewed everyone and attempted phoning those who were off duty and not likely to be asleep, Rhys searched Hayden's room again. He wasn't sure why. He felt certain there was a file, a notebook, something, that would provide more of a clue to Hayden's interaction with the people on his list. He was forming a picture of the developer that explained the island people's reaction to Hayden and his death. It might have been the project, but given Ms. Ketchem's revelations, he suspected other reasons.

Of course there might have been notes on Hayden's phone; some people seemed to use their cell phones for calendars and alarm clocks and notepads all in one. Too bad that Thad Powell hadn't been able to retrieve all the contents of that expensive Blackberry.

By the time he'd discovered exactly nothing in his search, MacFarlane realized that the Inn's evening crew was coming on duty. Again, he came up with little that was new until he spoke with a young woman who, he gathered, did general duties and assisted at the desk. She was busy with a newly arrived guest and he tried to make himself as inconspicuous as possible until a bellman scooped up the guest's bags and they disappeared down the hall. She rewarded his wait with information he wasn't sure he wanted.

"Yes," she said. "Friday evening there was a fair amount of coming and going. And I remember seeing Mr. Ruiz on Friday evening. I thought he might be joining someone in the lounge, but he didn't go there. A few minutes later one of our guests phoned and asked for an extra pillow, and when I went upstairs to the linen room, I saw him in the hall outside Mr. Hayden's room. And then he left."

"Not with Hayden?"

"No."

"Did you see Mr. Hayden leave earlier in the evening with anyone?"

"No. Someone mentioned seeing one of the artists in the cart he was driving sometime before dinner Friday—the pretty dark one that the newspaper wrote up a couple of weeks before the festival started—but I didn't see her in here. It was a busy evening; some new guests came in rather late, and there was a lot going on, one way and another."

"So what time was it when you saw Mr. Ruiz?"

"It was about eight o'clock, I think," she said. "I'm sorry I can't be more accurate than that."

"And he didn't go into Hayden's room."

"No."

"And did you see anyone else?"

"No," she said, but she said it in a drawn-out way that made it clear she wasn't sure.

"Anything at all?"

"Well," she said, "I can't be certain, but I thought I saw someone outside the entry, someone who didn't come in."

"Can you describe that person?"

"No. No, I couldn't see clearly, and I just caught a glimpse of… a woman, I think, but tall. I had an impression of someone tall and blonde."

Rhys thanked her, with the usual admonitions to be in touch if she thought of anything else at all, even if she couldn't see how it would be useful.

Once he had talked to everyone he could reach, Rhys returned to the operations center. Price was finishing work on a timeline for Hayden's proposed resort. A flow chart titled "Toyon Ridge Resort" outlined a series of steps; the project seemed to be about halfway through the stages of the application process.

Reviews were begun, and the applicant's Environmental Impact Study had been submitted to the county. However, Price had determined that some local entities had yet to comment on the EIS and two groups had already requested additional review time. One of those groups, not surprisingly, was the Island Conservancy. The request was signed by Roger Cameron.

Price had also come up with the names of Hayden's venture partners and a list of other participants in the project: architects, engineers, and attorneys specializing in land use. "No joy there," Price said, dejected. "I've talked to people in Colorado. They've checked out anyone in his partnership and anyone involved with any of his other projects who would benefit from his death. *Nada.* Actually, it could put a couple of investors in a financial bind, because there are bound to be some delays while his estate's settled. No motive there, I'm afraid.

"Even so," Price continued, "it's beginning to look like a possibility that—that the key to this whole thing is that project of his, one way or another. The people he upset, and the people who didn't want to see him pull it off. One of those people has to be the one we're looking for. We just need some solid leads."

Without Inspector Canham around to deflect him and with Price hard at work on the Toyon Ridge flow chart, MacFarlane ambled over to the evidence room to take another look at Hayden's belongings.

Pockets, he thought, recalling the Conservancy volunteer's observation. But there were no secret pockets in any of Hayden's clothing. An appointment book with only dates and initials. A dead Blackberry with almost no retrievable information. Files that appeared complex enough to contain a wealth of financial finagling but nothing that seemed relevant to their possessor's death. Empty luggage. So much luggage, MacFarlane thought again.

He was stacking the elegant suitcases when a thought occurred to him. He opened each case, flipped the tops back, unzipped each compartment, felt around the linings and along the joins of tops, bottoms, and sides. One case was two-layered, an overnight bag made to accommodate a laptop, and he paid especial attention to the bottom of the top half. Sure enough, feeling across it with both hands, he detected an unevenness in the thickness of the bottom. He took out his Swiss army knife and pried tentatively at the join between the lining and the back of the case. The lined bottom of the upper section came loose, and there, against the stiff plastic of the lower layer, lay exactly what the volunteer had described: a charcoal-gray Moleskine notebook.

Rhys unloosed a jubilant "aha!" and reconstructed the suitcase.

He opened the notebook. Out fell a manila envelope; inside that was a photograph of Roger Cameron and Sarah Martin, with the Casa del Mar identifiable in the background. He slid it back into the envelope. His jubilation dissolved as he began to read the contents of Warner Kendall Hayden's notebook.

Chapter 39

Back in the operations center, MacFarlane added his notes to the information gathered thus far. Price zeroed in first on the presence of Councilman Ruiz outside Hayden's hotel room Friday evening.

"Wonder what he was up to," he muttered. "Somehow I don't see him hobnobbing with Hayden. Any connection between him and this woman who says Hayden was down on Hispanics?"

"Not that I know of," Rhys said.

"We'll have to check it out. And find out if we can where he was on the rest of Friday evening. Then there's that sighting: a tall blonde. That could be Andrea. And you just found out what her connection with Hayden is."

"Mm hmm." Rhys nodded, but didn't add what he was thinking: that Andrea had complained that Hayden was pressuring her, too, to work for him.

Price looked at the clock. It was 4:30. "I suppose," he said, "that we ought to go up to the hospital and see how Canham's doing."

"And see what ridiculous orders he has for us?"

"Yep." MacFarlane grinned.

"Which doesn't mean we'll follow them, right?"

"Right."

The inspector was propped up against a bank of pillows, still pale, and nested in what looked like a cat's cradle of plastic tubes. If the two detectives thought their inspector would be mollified by Price's work on Hayden's business connections and the status of his proposed project, they were mistaken. "I don't remember asking you to do that," he grumbled. "Did you get those interviews done?"

"Yes, sir," they said in unison. They reported what Hayden's private investigator had revealed.

"So he was putting the thumbscrews on Cameron and that Benet woman," Canham said, shifting his shoulders in a massive shrug that threatened to unhook one of the IVs that dangled from a stand at the head of his hospital bed. "Sounds like it was his way of getting what he wanted. Damn that thing," he added, glaring at the IV stand. "Has to follow me around even when I take a leak. Blasted uncomfortable." He extended his arms, each with its tube taped into place. "Talk about imprisonment."

"Well, at least they let you get up to use the bathroom," Price said quickly, before any more details were forthcoming.

"Any leads on how Hayden was using this information he got?" Canham asked.

Now was the time to speak up, Rhys told himself. But the Moleskine remained in his pocket.

"Now look, MacFarlane," Canham said. "You can make amends for that breach of protocol this morning with the little photographer girl. You're in her confidence. I want you to find out from her anything more you can about this Andrea Benet. They share a house, right?"

"That's right. There's an upstairs apartment, and Lexi rents that." Rhys wondered where Canham got his information; he hadn't seemed to know or care anything about the island people, but perhaps he knew more than he was letting on. That was unsettling. "We should get going and let you get some rest, sir," he said, edging toward the door.

Canham ignored him. "And then there's Hayden's will to think about. Who benefits? That's always the first thing to think about. I had a guy watching for someone to file probate in Denver," Canham said smugly. "I was going to tell you about that earlier. He called this morning with the attorney's name. You get a call in to him. What do you know about the family situation now?"

"The ex-wife's gone back to San Diego but the daughter's still staying with friends here. The Slaughters," Price said. "Nice people."

"Nice people. Hmph. There are a lot of nice people on this damned island," Canham added darkly, "who know a lot more about this whole thing than they're letting on. And you two—you know these people. I want you to ferret it out of them."

"We'll put it on our to-do list," Price said. "We'll be going over this evening to talk to Roger Cameron."

"Yeah, right. Sorry to leave you on your own like this," Canham muttered. "They're going to keep me overnight." A nurse pattered in and glared at the uniformed officers.

"That's enough," she said crisply. "Our patient needs his rest."

MacFarlane and Price beat a hasty retreat.

While the two deputies were getting their marching orders from Detective Inspector Canham, Lexi was seeking counsel from her grandparents. John had phoned her with the news that Celestina was making moussaka for supper. Lexi had no late-afternoon appointments. She had brought a colander full of lettuce, spinach and baby kale leaves from the garden she and Andrea had made on terraces behind their house, and a paper bag containing their first tomatoes of the season.

Now, over plates of salad dressed with lemon and olive oil and the fragrant mixture of herbed ground lamb, eggplant and béchamel sauce, they discussed their worries.

"I haven't heard anything more from that horrible inspector," Lexi reported.

"He can't seriously suspect you," Celestina assured her.

"But Yiayia, I do have a motive. Mr. Hayden really was putting pressure on me to do photography for him, and I really, really didn't want to. And he acted as if I should be grateful. Like I should—find him attractive." She shuddered. "I found him—well, I couldn't stand being around him. He was so smug, and so sure of himself."

"Not at all like some men we might name," Celestina teased. Lexi flushed.

"Your nice young policeman doesn't think you're a suspect," Stina observed.

"But what if I can't convince the inspector? It puts Rhys in an awful position. I wish we could help him figure out who did it," Lexi said softly. "Pappoús, you know everything about everyone."

"But I do not know who did this," John said, "and it troubles me."

"Must you know everything all the time?" Stina was only half-joking. John held her gaze for a moment, then sighed.

"What troubles me," he said, "is that so long as we don't know who killed Mr. Hayden, we wonder. We wonder about each other. And we think about the bad things we know about the people here, instead of the good things. This is how evil spreads, with fear and mistrust. My *pappoús* used to say 'Who mistrusts most must be trusted least.' And so the good works and the trust that bind us as a community begin to erode away.

"If this murder is not solved," John added, wiping the last of the meat sauce from his plate with a crust of Stina's tangy bread, "suspicion will grow and grow, taking the place of the trust that has always bloomed here among us as neighbors. Like the broom on the hillsides, it will crowd out the good, the spirit of helpfulness, the sense of working toward what's best for the whole community." He began thoughtfully to chew the bread and pushed his plate away.

"And so we must do whatever we can to help your friend Rhys," Stina said.

"Okay," Lexi said. "Thank you." She looked happier than she had in days. Stina got up and began clearing away the empty plates. Lexi stood up to help her, but Stina waved her back to her chair.

"My place is the kitchen," she said. "I feel happy there. I'll bring coffee out in a while. You two stay here and solve the mystery."

Chapter 40

Once Stina had left the room, John turned a serious face to his granddaughter. "Lexi, I am very worried about our Andrea. Something is eating away at her. Not the business in Oregon, of that I am sure. But whatever it is, it is weighing on her too much."

He raised his eyebrows when Lexi nodded. "I am, too, Pappoús. She's so tense. She's like a spring set so tight it's going to break."

"Think about it, Lexi. When did this start?"

Lexi thought. Her grandfather saw her fingers moving. "A week and a half ago, I think?"

"So it didn't start when Mr. Hayden showed up."

"Not like this. Oh, she was upset, angry that he was pushing her to go to work for him, just like he was pushing me. In fact I think he wanted her more than he wanted me. At least I think he made more of a nuisance of himself, pushed a little harder. Well, face it." She shrugged and smiled. "There are lots of good photographers, but nobody cooks like Andrea. My *yiayia* excepted," she added quickly.

"I wonder what happened to move her from being annoyed to being so worried, so fearful?" John mused.

Lexi swallowed. Her grandfather waited.

She put her hands to her head, then looked at him, frowning as she concentrated. "There was a letter," she said, "and it made her mad, but I don't think it was that."

"A letter?"

"We'd both come home a little early and we were having tea on her deck," Lexi said. "She'd brought her bag from the shop out with her to show me a new catalog, and a couple of pieces of her other mail had slipped into the middle of it. One of them was a letter with the name of his company on it, and she kind of shrugged and said something like oh, no, now he's starting a letter campaign and laughed because his insisting she should be his chef was getting to be almost ludicrous. She said she'd read it later."

"And it was after that she began to be so upset?"

Lexi shook her head. "She was angry, then. But it was—she was worse when she got back from being over town and found out that he'd died. When she found out I'd found Mr. Hayden."

Lexi shuddered. John stood, took her hand, and said, "Come on. Let's go sit on the patio."

They moved outdoors. The wind had dropped, the floating clouds had thinned, and the evening was comfortably warm.

Lexi put her chin in her hands and thought hard. "She was better when she was angry, though. It was after he died that she stopped talking to me about him and started acting so—so worried. And I think she was avoiding people, too."

"Avoiding people?"

"Francesca said she kept leaving the shop. And once I even saw her cross the street to avoid Ellen, that artist friend of hers. It's like she's a hermit crab, crawling into her shell. Pappoús," Lexi said, "Should I try to find that letter?"

"No," John said. "I don't think so. That's an invasion we aren't ready for. At least not yet. Besides, I think I know what that's about, and there has to be something else."

"Oh," Lexi said. "Okay. Well, Rhys has just got to solve this murder. And if I can, I'll help him. Only I do hope," she said, turning an anxious face to her grandfather, "that it isn't—" She stopped. "I don't want it to be anyone we know."

Stina came around the corner of the house then. "Come indoors," she urged. "Coffee and dessert are ready, and—" She smiled at Lexi. "And there's a very nice police officer who has come to see you."

"So how is your investigation going? I don't suppose there's anything you're allowed to tell us," John said once they were seated around the table. In the center sat a plate of baklava swimming in its pool of cinnamon-and-lemon-scented honey. "I can say that we're following a couple of leads," Rhys said, "but to be honest, we're kind of floundering."

"I'm thinking you have a commanding officer who's not giving you much help."

"And I can't answer that one, either," said Rhys. "He's—"

"Oh, I know. And you don't need to." The two men shared a comradely, if wry, grin.

"Anyhow, he got food poisoning. He's spending the night in the hospital," Rhys said. "So he won't be intimidating you for a while," he said, smiling at Lexi. "Serves him right," he added.

"I'm going to leave you to it," Stina said. "I have a pasta project going on in the kitchen, and I don't want it to dry out."

"And I'm leaving, too," Lexi said, standing. "I've got wedding people coming in tomorrow afternoon and I need to sort about 600 photos before they arrive. Thank you for dinner, Yiayia," she called into the kitchen. "It was wonderful."

The men remained quiet until they heard the door close behind her.

"Is she—"

"Not a suspect," Rhys said. "I'm not sure Canham's altogether convinced, but it's not Lexi I'm worried about at this point."

John didn't respond but remained gazing at him. Rhys recognized the technique, and he'd done enough interviews to be wary of the instinct to fill a silence. Then he laughed at himself, for he'd sought out his trusted friend to do some unburdening. He thought about how best to begin and decided total honesty was all. He know what he told John wouldn't go beyond the walls of his dining room.

"Look, Zorba, I've got a problem. It's right here in this notebook." He told John how he'd felt certain something was missing from Warner Hayden's room, and how he'd searched and finally found the unobtrusive Moleskine journal.

"He had something on a number of people who had some kind of influence, and he kept track of each one: noted down the letters he'd sent, what kind of response he had, and whether and when they capitulated," Rhys said. "It's disgusting. He must have spent months, maybe years, tracking down these people's history, spying on them, fishing for things to hold over their heads, and then threatening them to get them to support his project. It was extortion. Blackmail." He stood up and paced as he continued.

"It gives us half a dozen people with a strong motive to do away with him. And none of them is someone I'd want to see accused. Especially Andrea. Add this to information we already have and it makes her look really bad. And Lexi—it's going to hit her hard if Andrea's under suspicion." Rhys shook his head.

"Zorba, I can't hurt Lexi." He sat down, facing John. "She's in no danger of being considered a suspect. She was with friends the night Hayden was murdered. And I cannot imagine that Andrea would do such a thing. But I have this notebook, and matching it up with initials in Hayden's calendar, we're finding out just how he operated. And we just keep adding to the list of people who had a motive to kill him. And Andrea's—well, the most likely if you look at what we've learned."

"So this is good and bad news? And what you're worrying about is Lexi?"

"Yes," said Rhys miserably. "She'd hate me if I had to produce evidence that convicted Andrea. I—I think I'm in love with your granddaughter. But it's no good, I suppose."

"You must let the lady speak for herself on that matter, my friend." John smiled.

Rhys took a deep breath. "But not now. Not with all this going on. And I can't see that she'll want anything to do with me if it turns out we have to—to—I mean we have to treat any suspect the same as any other. What an awful word. Suspect. I wish I'd never found that list," he said vehemently. "And worst of all, I can't see D. I. Canham handling the information with any kind of delicacy. He doesn't like Catalina and he doesn't like us. He'll take real pleasure in broadcasting what's in here. And yet I can't just sit on evidence. Zorba, what do I do?"

John gave him a long look and a gentle smile.

"You know what you have to do, my friend. You do not need me to tell you."

"I know."

And he left the Karatsos house with a feeling of dread.

Roger Cameron greeted Price and MacFarlane affably at the Conservancy headquarters, but ushered them quickly into his office, closing the door behind them. He pulled out two upholstered chairs before seating himself at his desk.

"Thank you for seeing us this evening," MacFarlane began. "We just need to clarify a few things involving people Warner

Hayden saw or talked to in the days before his death. Mostly it's just a rule-out thing," he added, when he saw Cameron swallow hard. "When did you last see Mr. Hayden, or talk with him?"

"Let me check," Cameron said, reaching for his desk calendar. "That would have been a council meeting, I suppose, about a week—ten days ago."

"Did you speak on the phone after that?"

"I don't think so." Cameron met MacFarlane's eyes. "No."

"The thing is," Price put in, "that your number showed up in Hayden's phone as one he called during the last two days of his life."

Cameron drew a deep breath. "He was very—ah—anxious to get support from those of us in the environmental community for—for his resort project."

"Anxious enough," MacFarlane asked, "to put pressure on some of you?"

"What do you mean?" Cameron had been leafing through the calendar without looking at it, but he put it down and pushed himself away from the desk, increasing the distance between himself and his questioners.

Price gave MacFarlane a quick look, the slightest shake of the head, and MacFarlane caught it. "He has been described as a very determined individual," he temporized. "Had he called often? Come by your field office, perhaps?"

"I think one of the assistants mentioned he'd been in the center on Canyon Road. I wasn't there at the time."

"And he was using your four-wheel vehicle, is that right?"

"Yes." Cameron drew breath. "I know that seems strange, but you see he wasn't able to bring his ATV over. We—I—his project was one the Conservancy didn't favor, but we—I— thought if we were—ah—hospitable, we might be able to work out some compromises that would benefit the island as a

240

whole. And he was only using it on the road and his own property. Which is not, as I'm sure you know by now, in the Conservancy."

"Of course," Price said encouragingly. Cameron looked relieved.

"Do you have any idea who might have felt so strongly about his project that they'd kill to stop him?" MacFarlane asked.

"No. None at all. I mean there are a number of us who would have taken any legal means we could to stop him. But not murder. No."

"Are you aware of any personal reasons anyone might have had for wanting him dead?" MacFarlane kept his tone neutral.

"No, no. I didn't really know him at all, so I couldn't say," Cameron said. A sheen on his forehead reflected the ceiling lights.

"And of course," MacFarlane said blandly, "we'll need to know where you were on Friday night between about eight p.m. and midnight."

"Home," Cameron said quickly. "My wife hasn't been very well. We spent a quiet evening at home."

"We'll leave it at that for now," Price said. "A notebook of Hayden's has turned up. It appears he was putting a rather unorthodox kind of pressure on a few people. So we may be back to you with a few more questions later."

A stunned Roger Cameron was left looking after them with horror.

"Nice redirection," Price told MacFarlane with a grin. "You didn't miss a beat. I'm betting that sometime tomorrow Mr. Cameron will come to us spilling the whole story of Hayden's blackmail. What I'm wondering is why he lied to us?"

"Maybe Hayden's call really didn't get through. He seems to spend a lot of time overseeing fieldwork."

"Maybe."

"So why did you warn me off questioning him about the photo and then mention the notebook?"

"Just upping the pressure. Mr. Cameron is not being straight with us, and I wonder if he's hiding more than the little romance on the side."

Roger Cameron sat staring at nothing for several minutes. Then he roused himself. "Damn," he said. "Why did I—" He picked up the telephone and dialed.

"Margaret, dear," he said. "I've just finished copying tomorrow morning's agenda and then I'll be on my way home. I hope you're feeling better."

When he spoke again, it was in a tired, almost tremulous voice. "Margaret, I need a tremendous favor from you. Sheriff's officers were here, and they asked about last Friday. I'd forgotten that I was working in the field Friday evening and I said I was home. It'd be awkward if I had to change my story now, I mean it would look unprofessional, so would you mind—if they come asking, which of course they're most unlikely to do—but if they should, would you just tell them we were at home, together? It'll make things so much simpler, darling. Thank you."

He hung up quickly, so quickly that he didn't hear Margaret's toneless response. "Oh, Roger, Roger. What have you done?"

He rubbed his temples, and left the office.

Chapter 41

Wednesday, June 11

Four scientists fidgeted impatiently in their chairs around a table in the Conservancy field office at 8:15 a.m. "Where's Cameron? He's always on time," one of them complained.

"He's getting flaky. He was always so responsible."

"Yeah. There was that loan of his pickup."

"The Conservancy's pickup, you mean."

"What on earth was that about?"

"I don't know, but now that Hayden's dead, and the police are involved, we probably won't see our rig for months."

"I always said it was a mistake to assign those rigs anyway. Back when we had a pool, he could never have done that."

"Yeah, we heard you. It's his responsibility to see we get it back, or get another."

"But where is he? He should have called if he was going to be this late."'

"He'll probably be here soon."

But Roger Cameron didn't appear. No one answered when an assistant phoned his home.

Half an hour later, two members of his staff drove to his house. No one answered when they knocked and called out, but when one of them turned the doorknob, the door opened. They looked at one another.

"Should we?"

"Why not?"

They went in, cautiously, calling, "Roger! Margaret! Anybody here?" All was silent. There was no answer from the man who lay face up on the floor in the white-carpeted living room, his white shirt stained the rusty color of dried blood, a look of mild astonishment on his wide-eyed face.

MacFarlane and Price waited unhappily for the arrival of Canham's homicide team from the mainland. MacFarlane spoke with Canham on the phone. "Yes, sir. Mrs. Cameron is missing. The cart Cameron drove is here in the driveway, but the family had a sedan, and it's missing too."

"Call the sheriff's station and have people start looking for it."

"We've done that, sir," MacFarlane said. "We've also looked and found no purse with cards or keys, and there's no overnight bag in the luggage set in the master closet. We assume she's left."

"You can't rule out kidnapping."

MacFarlane made no comment, but continued, "We've also got calls in to the Express and the heliport, and we've got Bay Watch making sure no boats leave the harbor. They've requested a copter to check the other moorages."

He had just hung up the phone after assuring Canham his investigative crew would report in to him at the hospital when his cell phone vibrated. He answered, listened, and pocketed the cell. "The Cameron car is down on Descanso," he told Price. "I'll follow up at the Express office. If she was on one of the boats I'll head out on the next one. Be in touch." He waved his cell phone and was gone.

L.A. County's teams were still stretched thin and working the still-unsolved serial spree. A jogger found strangled on a popular running route near a grade school in Quartz Hill had been added to the toll. Once the team arrived and went to work, Price went by to update Canham, still tethered to the IV stand in his hospital room. Canham's first response was to suggest that Roger Cameron could have been the serial killer's sixth victim.

"We don't think so, sir. It was a straightforward gunshot to the chest. And he was indoors."

"Well, then it's probably connected to Hayden's death. Where was Cameron Friday night?"

"Home, he said," MacFarlane answered. "We would have checked with Mrs. Cameron today."

"Cameron was one of the people whose number Hayden called, wasn't he?" Canham sounded as if the question had just occurred to him.

"Yes, sir. That's why we spoke with him last night."

"What if he'd figured out who killed Hayden, or saw something, and the killer realized it?"

"He didn't say anything when we talked to him that would suggest anything like that, sir," Price said.

"And he was in that notebook you were talking about, too," Canham said.

"Yes, sir."

"And what was the connection there?"

"It appeared that Hayden had an incriminating photo and was using it as leverage to get Cameron to support his project," Price said.

"And what did he say about that when you interviewed him?" Canham wanted to know.

"We, ah, didn't bring that up," Price said. "He seemed to be hedging, and we thought we'd let him sweat a little, see what a few hours of worrying about what we knew would bring out."

"Oh, you did, did you?" Canham's pale face was returning to its usual flushed condition. "Well, now we've got a second murder on our hands. That's what a few hours of worrying brought out. It's quite possible that his wife left and he shot himself rather than face..." Canham stopped, seemingly gathering his thoughts.

"Yes?"

"What if he killed Hayden to save his precious Conservancy-strangled island from this development?" Canham demanded. "What if your letting him sweat cost us a solution?"

"Where's the weapon?" Price asked reasonably.

Canham shrugged. "His wife heard the shot, didn't want him disgraced, and got rid of the gun?" His shoulders sagged. It wasn't hanging together. "We'll have to wait for the Medical Examiner," he said.

Price's phone rang. Canham listened. "You did? Good. Okay." He pocketed the phone. "MacFarlane's on the boat to Long Beach," he said. "They found the car downtown, just a few blocks from the dock, and Rhys checked the Express as soon as we knew. Margaret Cameron sailed on the eight o'clock boat. So MacFarlane went down, and—" The detective noticed that Canham had closed his eyes. He looked gray. "Are you okay, sir?"

"No, dammit," Canham snarled. "I'm not. I feel like hell. Salmonella can be fatal, you know. But we've got to hit this one running. Price, I want you to question all of Cameron's associates and see what you can find out."

Madly texting to the Conservancy office, the sheriff's station, and finally to Roger Cameron's assistant once he had boarded the midmorning boat, Rhys managed to ascertain that both the Camerons' children, a daughter and a son, attended the University of California Santa Barbara. The son, a freshman, lived in San Miguel Hall on campus, and the daughter, a junior, shared a house with three other girls just off campus. By the time the boat docked in Long Beach, Rhys had an address for Elizabeth Cameron and the license number of the black Kia her mother had rented at the Enterprise kiosk at the Long Beach landing.

He also had a car and driver. A rookie deputy named LaMont Trask and his aging patrol car were waiting for Rhys as he left the Express terminal. "I'll drive you, Detective MacFarlane," the youngster told him, obviously thrilled. "I'm assigned as your backup." He grinned, even white teeth gleaming in his dark face.

For the first time in days, Rhys MacFarlane didn't feel like the new kid on the block.

"Your—uh—Inspector Canham told us there's a suspect, sir," Trask said. "He said she's probably armed."

"He did, huh?" MacFarlane slid into the passenger seat.

"Armed and dangerous," Trask said. "Here we go."

Chapter 42

During the first part of the trip north, Deputy LaMont Trask stayed focused on the road, navigating the turns and exits to cross Ocean Boulevard, navigate Highway 710 and merge onto Highway 405. After the freeway crossed into the valley he turned his attention to his passenger.

"So do you like being a detective, sir?"

That one stumped Rhys for a moment. Certainly he'd been aiming toward the detective squad ever since community college, and being able to remain on the Catalina force after qualifying as a detective had been satisfying. His first case, a stolen luxury golf cart, had been almost too easy to solve, and he'd untangled the mysterious disappearance of nearly a hundred expensive shrubs whose trail led him to a little old lady who uprooted plants and took them home whenever she thought they were inappropriate to the place where they'd been planted. There wasn't a lot to challenge a detective on Santa Catalina most of the time; mostly things weren't much different from his deputy duties.

But now that one death, one murder, was stalled and had resulted in another, now that he was on the trail of a woman who may have killed her husband in cold blood, now that people he knew were potential suspects, Rhys wasn't quite so sure. "It's an adrenaline rush followed by hours and hours and hours of boring slogging down dead ends," he told the young deputy, realizing what a lame cliché he'd just uttered.

"Take today," he said. "We don't know what we're heading into. We don't know yet who murdered Roger Cameron. It could have been a domestic; we might find the killer when we get to her daughter's house. Or it could have been someone else, perhaps someone connected to our first murder, and Mrs. Cameron may simply have fled the horror of it. Our inspector is convinced that Mr. Cameron knew who murdered Warner Hayden, and the murderer has figured that out and bumped him off."

"What's your theory, sir?"

Being called "sir" made Rhys MacFarlane feel slightly silly, and he nearly looked over his shoulder to see who Trask was talking to. "Knowing what we know about Mr. Cameron, that he'd had an affair that someone knew about, at least Warner Hayden did, makes me think his wife did it."

"Isn't that usually the way of it, sir?"

"Yeah."

"That's pretty sad."

"Yes, it is, Trask."

"Are you married, sir?"

"Nope. Are you?"

"Engaged. My high-school sweetheart. Her name's Amara."

"Good for you." Rhys was envious.

"Soon as I get promoted, we'll be married. Ammy's a teacher. Kindergarten. She's amazing with kids."

The young deputy broke off his litany of praise of his beloved to maneuver the turns onto I-405. That accomplished, he asked Rhys, "So what do you think we'll find in Santa Barbara?"

"Could be just a bereaved wife in shock," Rhys said, thinking of the possibilities. "Didn't look like a suicide, and we didn't find a note, although that doesn't always signify. Could be our D.I. is right and Cameron was murdered because he knew something about the case we've been working on all week."

"Yeah, I heard you had a suspicious out there. But apparently not part of the series up in the mountains, huh?"

"Right. Ours is a high-flyer real estate developer named Hayden who wound up dead at the bottom of a cliff below his property. We're trying to figure out what's the connection. Mr. Cameron worked for the conservancy and for some reason had let Hayden use the Conservancy's four-wheel rig. They might have had some kind of agreement that went wrong. Or it might have been nothing like that, and it could very well be that we're on the path of a killer. We know from evidence in this other case that Mr. Cameron was cheating on her."

"You think she's dangerous, sir?"

"It's hard to say. She hardly seems like the type. But then, you never know what goes on in people's minds, do you? If she killed her husband, and it looks like that could be the case, then she could be. Or her kids could be so protective they won't let us see her. Then we'd have to back up and get a warrant. It's anybody's guess. We'll have to assume that she's got a gun, or they do—that we're walking into a powder keg. But something tells me that won't be the case. I can't tell you why."

"It's a small island over there. Sounds like you know her?"

"I can't say I really know her, but I've met her," Rhys said. "She's always seemed very calm and self-possessed. She's a high-school counselor, I think. She invited me to talk about a detective's job at a career assembly last winter. I knew her husband, too. It's hard to get your mind around something like this involving people you know."

"Any leads on this other murder you're investigating?"

Rhys welcomed the digression, but it reminded him that investigating the death of Warner Kendall Hayden involved people he knew, too, people in his everyday orbit, people he knew well, people he called his friends, and one person in particular with whom he wanted to be much more than friends.

He told Trask about how Lexi had found Hayden's body, and how it had begun to seem that there were perhaps a dozen people with a motive to kill Hayden.

"You ever see *Murder on the Orient Express*?" Trask asked.

"Is that the one about the guy who's killed on the train, and it turns out everybody was in on it?"

"Yeah."

"I read the book. Geez. I hope this doesn't turn out to be one of those." Rhys leaned back and rubbed at his forehead. "I'd have to testify against a whole lot of friends."

Chapter 43

By the time Trask had to turn all his attention to maneuvering the streets of Santa Barbara, MacFarlane had had the opportunity to talk through his list of potential suspects in the earlier murder. He found it had clarified his thinking. But now it was time to hone in on the homicide at hand.

"Pull over for a moment," he said as Trask approached the address they had for Elizabeth Cameron. "Let's figure out how we tackle this. We'll have to assume your armed-and-dangerous scenario, even if it makes us look pretty foolish."

They planned their approach, then slowly drove the final block to Elizabeth Cameron's home. The house, a modest rambler in white stucco with a tile roof and details that were intended to be mission-style, had a carport. In the driveway behind it sat a black Kia. Trask pulled in at an angle behind it, blocking any exit. The two officers got out of the car, hands at their holsters, and approached the house.

They rang the doorbell and immediately heard footsteps approaching. Margaret Cameron opened the door to them. There were shadows beneath her lustreless eyes, and hollows beneath her cheekbones. He realized her lithe slenderness had changed to painful thinness.

"You didn't take long," she said by way of greeting. "Your timing was good. Eric just arrived. I can explain things to all of you at once. You won't need those," she added, glancing at the hands they still held at hip level. "I threw the gun overboard on the trip across. I'm assuming you'll take me in, and once I've talked to the kids, I'm ready."

She led them through the house to a shaded patio where two blond young people sat toying with iced tea and staring at them apprehensively. Tears tracked down the cheeks of the girl, whose white-blonde hair was like her mother's but longer. "They know Roger is dead," Margaret said to the officers. "Now," she added, looking at her son and daughter, "comes the hard part."

"Before you begin," MacFarlane broke in, "I have to warn you…"

"That anything I say may be used in evidence? I'm aware of that, Detective MacFarlane."

"I have to say it anyway," he said, and did.

"Now may I begin?"

"Of course." He already had his notebook in hand.

Margaret Cameron pulled a chair out to face her children and sat. "I told you your father was dead," she said quietly. "What I really hate to tell you is that I shot him. I can't even begin to explain it."

"Mom, no!" Eric looked even more stricken than he had earlier.

"Because he was having an affair?" Elizabeth blurted.

"You knew about that, Lizzie? I didn't, until he told me night before last," Margaret said.

"I wasn't sure," the girl said, "but last time I was home—oh, never mind."

"Whatever happened, whatever's going to happen, we'll go through it with you, Mom." Eric went to stand behind his mother's chair, hands on her shoulders.

Elizabeth looked at him, appeared about to speak again, but put her hands over her mouth.

"There's more," Margaret said. "I was going to come up this weekend to tell you but then this—well, this kind of pushed things ahead. The thing is, Lizzie, Eric, I have cancer."

"Oh, no! Mom!"

"You'll get through this, Mom." Eric rubbed her shoulders.

"No, actually, I won't. I talked with the doctor day before yesterday. The cancer's far more advanced than we thought, and it's fast-growing. Surgery's not an option. Chemo will only prolong things, and I don't want that."

"But Mom—" Eric objected.

"Wait a minute," Elizabeth interrupted. "You got this news from the doctor day before yesterday, and then Dad told you he'd been having an affair?"

"Oh, my God," Eric said. "Mom—"

"Who—" Elizabeth began at the same time. Margaret cut them off brusquely.

"That doesn't matter. It's—I'm sorry. It's going to be terribly hard on you, losing both of us, and there will be publicity. I'm sorrier about that than anything. But your Aunt Mary is close by, you know, and I've spoken with her. She wants you for holidays and breaks and I've arranged with our attorney to have everything in trust for you. You'll have a tough time, but you'll get through it. Just keep your minds on your studies, and that'll help. I'm glad you're here and not in Long Beach; you can ignore the newspapers and you won't have to listen to the gossip."

Margaret turned to the officers again. "I know I can't ask you to leave us alone, but can you turn your heads while I say goodbye to my children? Then we'll be on our way."

254

Rhys gave Trask a significant look. Each of them stepped away to opposite ends of the patio. They heard quiet murmurs, then Elizabeth's sobs. Margaret Cameron approached and touched Rhys on the shoulder. "Let's go."

The officers escorted her to the patrol car and helped her into the back seat.

"I have a pillow and a blanket in the trunk," Trask said. "Let me get them for you. It's a long ride back."

"Thank you."

"Do you mind if I ask you a few more questions?" Rhys said as Trask pulled away from the house.

"Not at all."

"Did you know Warner Hayden?"

"The developer? I'd met him, yes." She sounded unsurprised.

"Did you know he'd been blackmailing your husband?"

"No, but I'm not surprised. That explains it, I suppose."

"Explains what?"

"His death. Hayden's. And the way Roger had been acting. Thank you for not bringing this up in front of the children. At least we can spare them that for now. I would never have thought that he could—" She stopped. Before Rhys could probe for the conclusion to the sentence, his cell phone vibrated.

"MacFarlane."

"Can you talk?" The voice on the phone was Price's.

"Yeah. Some. What's up?"

"She confess?"

"Yeah."

"Well, Roger Cameron is out as a suspect in Hayden's death, anyhow. Sarah Martin came in and told me she was

255

with Roger Friday evening," Price continued. "Said they were breaking it off."

"Sheesh. Does—" he stopped himself, not wanting Margaret to hear.

"Does her husband know? She says not. Well, anyhow, you've got Cameron's murderer; motive, confession, seems sewed up pretty tight. Bullet's consistent with the gun that was registered to Roger. Doesn't look like Margaret Cameron is covering for anybody."

"That's a relief." Rhys sighed. He turned to Margaret, who had closed her eyes. He opened his mouth to tell her her late husband was not Hayden's killer, but looked at her pale, ravaged face and said nothing. A few minutes later, he looked back at her again. She was sound asleep.

The ride south was a long and quiet one. Cushioned by the pillow and blanket Trask provided for her, Margaret Cameron continued to slumber. Unsure whether or how deeply she was sleeping, the two officers were mostly silent, speaking in quiet voices about inconsequential things: how dry the hillsides looked for this time of year, the prospects of anyone beating Brazil in the upcoming Confederations Cup, the grim concerns about the unsolved serial murders in the foothills.

"So you don't think there's any chance your island murder fits into that?" Trask asked.

"Doesn't look that way. No weapon, for one thing, except a rock. No knife or gun. And all of yours were campers or joggers—people enjoying the outdoors."

"That Hayden guy—he was a developer?" Trask asked. "What was he going to develop?"

"A huge luxury resort up on the hill above Avalon."

"What'll happen now?"

"Depends on who inherits. And the county planning process."

"Hmmh."

They lapsed into silence again.

When Trask pulled the patrol car into the sally port at the Los Angeles County Jail and Rhys MacFarlane opened the back door of the vehicle, Margaret started awake but instantly composed herself. She smiled wanly at the two men.

"Thank you," she said. "I needed that sleep."

"I'm glad you got some rest," Rhys told her. "It'll get a little crazy while they check you into the jail. But there's an infirmary wing. You'll go there as soon as you're booked, and I asked your daughter to get in touch with your doctor so he can talk to staff. You'll have to appear in court for identification, but aside from that you should be able to rest, and it's possible under the circumstances that you could be released on bail. You'll be comparatively comfortable, I hope."

"You're being very kind to an admitted murderess," she said.

Rhys couldn't find an answer to that, so he said nothing. Uniformed guards were waiting, and he and Trask watched as they escorted her down a corridor until they turned the corner.

"Armed and dangerous she wasn't," Trask said. "Just sad. My god, think what those kids of hers are going through."

"Yeah. At least they don't have to think their dad's a murderer too."

Chapter 44

As Rhys and his driver were en route to the ferry landing, Price phoned again. "Well," he began, "the hospital has kicked Canham out. One of the patrol guys drew the short straw and is sharing a suite with him here in the hotel for the night. The doctors didn't want to put him on the boat just yet, and they didn't want him alone in case of heart complications. The suite was cheaper than a helicopter ride. So we'll see him in the morning."

"I can hardly wait."

"Two more things," Price said. "Remember that woman at the Inn who says she saw Edgar Ruiz and a tall blonde woman both there the night Hayden was murdered? First off, I interviewed Edgar Ruiz after you left. It doesn't look too good for him."

Rhys shifted his phone to speaker and began to take notes as Price continued. "We talked to Ruiz. He told us exactly how Hayden's been operating. In his case, he got an offer from a mortgage company to finance his homes in The Arroyo at a remarkably low interest rate. The package was presented to him as being a special rate for green homes underwritten by an individual who wanted to support environmentally friendly construction practices. But what it really was—" Price stopped and cleared his throat—"was a nasty little trap Hayden laid for Ruiz. It put a city councilman in his pocket."

"Explain," Rhys said. He hadn't realized how tired he was. Images of Margaret Cameron at the door, then disappearing into the bowels of the L.A. County Jail, kept appearing in front of him. Roger Cameron was on Hayden's list too. It felt like a network of wrong and ruin was expanding like wildfire on the island. He worked at focusing as Price explained.

"The underwriter for that mortgage was a friend of Hayden's. Hayden made no bones about the arrangement once his project was coming up for a vote." Price snorted. "Some choice he gave poor Ruiz: approve a project that would involve a huge environmental impact, and keep that great interest rate—or oppose him, and end up owing more every month than he has coming in."

"So why was Ruiz looking for Hayden at the Inn? Was he going to cave?"

"He said he was going to try to talk to Hayden, try to buy some time, maybe even threaten to expose his tactics, but he had second thoughts and went home. His wife says he was home by eight, which is about the time Ellen Storey saw Hayden alive up on the ridge. Of course Alice Ruiz would say he was home—she's his wife, after all. We have to take that with a grain of salt."

"Yeah. Okay. Jeez, Price, is there anybody who didn't have a motive to off this guy?"

"Well, there's us."

"Speak for yourself. I'd happily have murdered him for hitting on Lexi."

"Oh, right. I'll add you to the list. And there's more."

"More?"

"Well, there's the blonde woman in your report, the one who was around about the same time Ruiz was."

"Umh."

"It's looking worse for Andrea, Rhys. The state lab sent word that what little they could get to show up on that note could easily be Andrea Benet's writing."

"A sample that small?"

"That's what they say. Not a definite identification, but definitely not a rule-out. And they're sending it out to a specialist who has a retrieval process that's been pretty successful."

"Woah." Rhys was dismayed. "So I suppose Canham's all set to haul her in?"

"He would be. But maybe he won't be up to getting into all the reports for a while. I suggested he should make a slow start tomorrow, maybe go home and take it easy. I told him it's supposed to take a week or two to really get over food poisoning."

"Good."

"Oh, yeah, there's another thing," Price added. "Viktor Sentik's alibi—it's toast. The bouncer came in all shame-faced and told us it was Thursday night last week, not Friday, that he'd carried Viktor back to The Bell. Seems he doesn't usually work Wednesdays and Thursdays. It was the first night of his work week so he'd thought of it as Friday, but he had to come in on Thursday because the other bouncer-barman sprained his ankle."

"Hmmh. Well, I don't really see Viktor as a suspect, but maybe there's something to all that dark brooding after all."

"Well, maybe by tomorrow we'll come up with something substantial. You think you'll make it to Long Beach in time to get back here this evening?"

"Oh, man, I hope so."

The Express was idling at the dock, with crew standing by to cast off for the day's last run, when Rhys MacFarlane leaped out of Deputy Trask's patrol car, waved his thanks, and sprinted through the terminal.

On board, he bolted a sandwich from the galley, watching the wake as the catamaran cut its way across the open water, fidgeted in the baggage area as the boat entered Avalon Harbor, and was back at the operations center within three minutes of disembarking.

"What a day you've had," Price said.

"Yeah," MacFarlane said. "How about you?"

"Bunch of routine. Nothing much turned up. One thing, though. We haven't found out where Viktor Sentik was on Friday evening."

An hour later, he and Price had reviewed and re-reviewed the list of suspects and were dismayed to find that aside from Viktor Sentik, whom neither of them really suspected, Andrea Benet and Edgar Ruiz topped their list. "Motive and opportunity," Price muttered. "They've got both. But I just can't see it."

"They're both good people," Rhys said miserably. "I refuse to think that either one of them could commit a murder."

"This time yesterday," Price countered, "wouldn't you have said that about Margaret Cameron?" Rhys nodded. What was there to say?

Chapter 45

Thursday, June 12

By the next morning, the mood in the operations center was disintegrating. The serial killer had struck again; a hiker was found dead on the trail in Azusa Canyon, her throat slit. But the novelty of the multiple cases in the mountains was wearing off, and the *L.A. Times* had sicced an ambitious young reporter onto the island's case.

SECOND MURDER ON CATALINA, trumpeted the *Times*.

NO ANSWERS IN DEATH OF DEVELOPER, reported the first sub-head.

FELL OR WAS PUSHED? inquired the article's second sub.

"Sheesh," Price grumbled. "Don't they have anything better to do with all that space?"

He read from the article, "A leading scientist with Catalina Island's prestigious Island Conservancy was found dead in his home Wednesday morning. The Los Angeles County Sheriff's office has confirmed that Roger Cameron, 50, died of a gunshot wound to the chest."

"Well," MacFarlane said, "they got that one right."

"An arrest was made later Wednesday, but no details were forthcoming," Price continued. "It was the second murder in less than a week in the sleepy town of Avalon."

"So far so good, but now the reporter gets going," Price intoned. "No leads have emerged in the mysterious death of a

Colorado land developer found dead Saturday at the foot of a steep incline above the east side of town.

"LACSO Detective Inspector James Canham, heading the Santa Catalina investigation while the department continues to seek a serial killer at large on the mainland, had no major developments to report four days into the investigation.

"A medical examiner for L.A. County, Dr. Amy Porcuincula, indicated that in addition to a broken neck and multiple injuries from his fall, Warner Kendall Hayden, 55, suffered a blunt-force trauma to the temple 'not consistent with a fall.'

"Inspector Canham was unavailable for comment."

The publicity hadn't sweetened Detective Inspector Canham's temper. "Unavailable for comment," he groused. "Stinking media. Half dead in the hospital and they call it 'unavailable for comment.' They sure as hell didn't try to get in touch with us Tuesday."

"Except for those two calls in the morning," Pierce reminded him.

"We were busy." Canham wiped sweat from his forehead. Pierce and MacFarlane exchanged glances. No good would come of pursuing that issue.

"Right, sir," both deputies agreed.

"But hey," Price added, "you don't want them reporting that you were in the hospital, do you?"

Canham muttered, and both detectives looked relieved when the phone rang.

"Got it," Price said.

The import of the call was fairly clear, even before Price hung up the phone with a glum look. "That was the crime lab. No fingerprints on the rock."

"Rocks are never good, especially in dusty places like this. We knew it was a long shot," Rhys said.

"Oh," Canham said, searching among some papers on the desk. "I can't find it but we got the tox results. Positive for cocaine, enough to affect his balance. In addition to the alcohol." He glared at the deputies. "Cocaine in his system. Alcohol. Drunk and high. Has it occurred to you two that this Hayden person just might have fallen onto that rock, that this might be the accident I said it was right at the start?" He was breathing heavily.

How tempting it was, Rhys thought, to agree with him. Just get rid of the notebook with its pages full of motives, with information ripe for destroying half a dozen lives, and let the death of a totally unscrupulous individual go unsolved. After all, blackmailing was a felony. Let his death be considered judgment; let it be called an accident. Put the damned Moleskine back where he got it.

No, he realized, he couldn't.

"But sir," Price was protesting. "There was the M.E.'s report. What're the chances that he could fall at just exactly the right angle, in just the right place, to get a wound like that to the temple? And the report says he was already dead when it was inflicted?" Canham was still pale, and didn't answer. "You feeling okay, sir?" Price asked.

"Hell, no!" Canham burst out. "You don't have your guts turned inside out and spend 24 hours tethered to an IV full of antibiotics and come out feeling hunky-dory. I feel like shit," he said, and to underline his declaration, wobbled out of the room. They heard the now-familiar banging of the restroom door. Did Canham always slam doors?

"Okay, you two," Canham said on his return, "Fill me in with anything you've got. I'm going to make an early day of it. The docs said I need rest and I plan to be on the noon boat off this wretched little island. Lida's going to meet the boat, so I'd better not miss it."

Rhys took the Moleskine journal from his pocket. He stared at it for a moment. "Sir, I found this hidden in Hayden's luggage. There are half a dozen motives in here for murder."

"Well, it's about time we got something to move us forward on this case. What else?"

Canham didn't actually seem interested. The two detectives went over their reports with him, and Canham latched on, as Rhys had feared he would, to Edgar Ruiz's and Andrea Benet's presence at the Inn.

"Too bad about your bug doctor," he said, glaring at MacFarlane, "but it looks like we've got a couple of hot ones here. Probably in cahoots. Now look," he said, fixing each detective in turn with his characteristic stare, "I don't want you working like mad to find excuses for these people. If they're guilty, they're guilty. And that goes for your little photographer, too," he added, glaring at Rhys.

He wiped his brow and shuffled through the stack of reports for half an hour longer. By 11:15 he had taken his leave of the operations center.

"Okay," Price said. "Let's see this sweet little find of yours." MacFarlane handed over the slender notebook.

"There are some pages torn out," he told Price. "I don't think this is the first project Hayden used it for."

Price took the Moleskine in hand with something like awe. He turned pages and looked at Rhys with a grin. "This has to be the key to the whole thing," he gloated. "I'd think you'd be crowing about it."

Rhys wasn't. "I'm just glad Canham is out of the way for a while," he said. "I hate this. All this personal stuff out in the

265

daylight. We'll have to interview all these people, and even if one of them is guilty, there'll be all the others whose lives we've invaded."

"Yeah," agreed Price. "Stirring up the muck at the bottom of the pond."

"Oh, well. Better get on with it."

Some of the initials in Hayden's journal were obvious, and matched the notations in his calendar. Others, they could guess at. Then there were references that didn't match anything in their investigation. Rhys found himself hoping that one of those would suddenly become clear, provide a major clue to a heretofore unknown perpetrator. They pulled out the list of phone numbers found on Hayden's Blackberry for additional reference, then put their two chairs at the desk with the department computer and began a new file for each entry. "Maybe some of these are acronyms we can find online," Rhys said hopefully.

"Not likely," Price said. "But hey, here's 'A.B.' We can be pretty sure that's Andrea. And we know some of the issues there, so let's see how he lists it."

There were two digits that would fit with the era of Andrea's membership in the Green Cell, and "aslt1/misd." would mean first-degree assault, the charge first filed against her, and misdemeanor, the resolution of her case. There were several recent dates with "t" and one with "l." The "l" was obviously a reference to the letter he'd already heard about, and "t" could have been "talk" or "telephone." One of the dates coincided with calls on the ruined cell phone.

"I think it's going to be reasonably easy," Rhys said. "This little tome sure as heck wasn't something he left lying around." Together they began to puzzle out more of the cryptic notes in the little gray Moleskine journal. They had just begun assembling a master list when their Commander phoned. "Anything new out there?"

"Well, sir," Rhys responded, "We're working on some cryptic material from a little Moleskine that Hayden kept hidden in a secret compartment in a rolling carry-on. It's got notes on people he was pressuring—well, blackmailing actually—to get them to support his resort project. Or to work with him on it," he added, cringing inwardly at the addition.

"And how did this come to light?"

"Well, sir, I just kept thinking there had to be something. His appointment calendar was all initials. And then we talked to a P.I. he'd hired to shadow some people, and a volunteer at the Conservancy field office said he'd been looking at some things there and making notes in a little gray notebook, and nothing like that had turned up in his belongings, and so I, ah, had another go at this luggage, and there it was."

"The luggage that was in evidence?"

"Yes, sir. I re-checked it and found the notebook hidden in one of the dividers in an overnight bag."

"Nice work, MacFarlane."

"Thank you, sir."

"I understand Canham's on his way home. He'll probably be back at work tomorrow, but he won't be any too perky, obviously. Let me know what you find and we'll work out a schedule of interviews. I'll see if I can get anybody out to help you two, but we're stretched thinner all the time, so don't count on it."

"No, sir."

The Commander signed off and MacFarlane and Price took out the little notebook and got to work.

Chapter 46

"MLP. Do we know of anybody with those initials?" Macfarlane and Price had paged through the little black journal, and now MacFarlane was puzzling over the initial entry.

"MLP. Cktls 3/5. Dn Pltr 3/27. SLUE. Mk intrn SZ. ???"

"I had a crush on a Mary Lou Partlow in third grade," Price said helpfully. "I remember carving those initials into the bark of a tree in the park. Got in trouble for it, too."

"Mary Lou. Bingo," Rhys said.

"Huh?"

"We could have gone ages with this if you hadn't had that crush," Rhys said with a grin. "California Assemblywoman from Long Beach. Mary Louise Pace."

"Interesting," Price mumbled. Hayden had written his journal entries in a kind of shorthand he appeared to have invented, something shorter than texting abbreviations and often utterly cryptic. However, from the notation "dn 4/3," Price and MacFarlane deduced that Hayden had wined and dined Ms. Pace. After puzzling over SLUE. Mk intrn SZ, they Googled SLUE and came up with Simmons Land Use Engineering. A bit more digging confirmed that the company was one that Hayden used regularly for his projects, and that he had arranged an internship for a Mark Pace as assistant to a biochemist named Zennor. It took only one more phone call to sew up the package with the information that Mark Pace was Mary Louise Pace's nephew.

At the end of Hayden's journal entry were two question marks.

"What do you think those are for?"

"He doesn't know whether she'll support him or not. I'm guessing, of course. A little underhanded but not any reason to think she'd have anything against Hayden," Rhys said. "I don't think she goes on our list of possibles. If it'd been her own kid, or her husband…"

"Husband. From what we hear about Hayden's methods, might there be a jealous husband in the wings?"

"When found, make a note of."

"Meaning?"

"Dickens. Sorry. If there is a husband, I suppose he might as well go on our list."

"Right. We'll check that out later." Price shrugged. "Who's next?"

MacFarlane turned the page and whistled. Wordlessly, he shoved the journal in front of Price.

"The mayor? Wow. 'Sq.Cl.?' 'N.D.'? What do you suppose that is?"

"How about 'squeaky clean' and 'no dice?' Or 'no deal?' There's nothing more after that." MacFarlane turned the page.

"Brilliant." Price was grinning. "Next."

"'A. M. Nrsry.' That's easy. That'd be Andrew Martin, and nursery, huh? 'Cruz, A, J, S. Illgl confmd. Ddln 6/9.' Then 'ICE Celovik' and a phone number. A couple of question marks crossed out. Then a big 'YES!' What do you think?"

"'ICE Celovik.' We could do a lookup but I bet that's some crony of his in Immigration."

"Let's see. Ddln and a date—that's got to be deadline, don't you think?"

"Yeah, probably." Price was scribbling furiously.

"Oh, and Cruz: that's the name of the brothers that work for him. 'Illegal confirmed,' huh?" Rhys was on a roll now.

"The Cruzes? Juan and his brothers? So they're not legal—so what? Jeez, those guys have never been in a bit of trouble. They've all got wives and families and beautiful vegetable gardens. They go to church every Sunday. They're the volunteer groundskeepers at St. Catherine's. They're volunteer firemen and soccer coaches, for crying out loud." Price was indignant.

"Does that make any difference to ICE?"

"Nope. ICE'd haul in their grandmothers if they didn't have their papers in order," Price groused. "And hold them for months so they have to make huge payments to get out. Don't get me started."

"And this big 'YES!' With an exclamation point. You think Andy caved?"

"Looks like it. Not sure I wouldn't do the same. Anyhow, we'll have to get him in here or go out and talk to him. Maybe he was just buying time until he could shove Hayden off a cliff."

"I hate this." Rhys turned another page in the Moleskine. "How about R.C.? That'd be Roger Cameron, right?"

"For sure. I suppose Hayden leaned on him to skew the field studies or something. What's Hayden got for him?"

"Hoo, boy." Rhys held out the notebook for Price to see. "P/U. We know that. But 'S.M.' Whips and dominatrixes for Cameron, you think?"

"Maybe." Rhys gave a short laugh. "But hey, no. We already know that's Sarah Martin. Says here 'Monterey. pic. $1175.' There's a phone number. Area code looks like Monterey or Carmel. Then another number. L.A. Well, there's one we don't need to follow up on." The number was that of the private investigator, Ella Ketchem. "So back to our little book."

"It's like looking in at bedroom windows. Jeez, Price, we're in an invasive line of work. I don't want to know this stuff."

"Me either. But hey. If it gets us to where we need to go." Price shrugged. "But man, I hope that photo isn't circulating somewhere."

"It was in a manila envelope in the notebook. I entered it into evidence."

"Whew. We don't want anybody hanging that on the island grapevine." Price was turning pages in his own note-taking. "I'm curious. Does it look like Hayden was indicating whether Cameron was going to support him?"'

"Still a question mark at the end," Rhys said. "But maybe that refers what comes before it. 'Mg.' Margaret, obviously."

"Ah." Price looked up. "Do you suppose he contacted Margaret? Would that explain—"

"Who knows." Rhys got up and paced.

While Price made notes of what they'd deciphered thus far, MacFarlane continued pacing. He waved the notebook at Price. "This is blackmail. Pure and simple. My god, Price, Hayden deserved whatever it was he got. However he got it."

"Yep. Who else is in Hayden's little Who's Who?"

"'E.R. C. Ccl.'"

"That's easy. Ruiz, city council."

"Not much here. Initials 'A.R./N.Mrtg' That can't be Ruiz; he's Edgar. Then 'No(!)' and 'So 3.5 to 7 per.' What do you suppose – oh, of course. You were telling me about that mortgage. Talk about motive." Hands to his temples, Rhys was the picture of despair.

"Never mind," Price said, impatient. "We've got a bunch of people to talk to, and we're only halfway through this poisonous little tome."

"Keep going."

By the time they had finished with Hayden's notebook, they'd figured out at least part of the meaning of his notations in the gray Moleskine. There was the scandal attached to Andrea's college years that Ella Ketchem had described ferreting out as Hayden's private investigator. It appeared that Hayden had some kind of financial deal he was dangling over the head of the California Secretary for Resources but had apparently hit no pay dirt with two of the secretary's underlings. There were a couple of initials that might belong to people involved in the Island Company. MacFarlane and Price couldn't make out why Bianca Alvarez was in Hayden's notebook, if the "B.A." and the phone number of The Bell referred to the steamy Mexican painter; there were no comments following the listing.

"Maybe it was just a convenient place to write her number," Price suggested.

Infuriating to Rhys was the presence of Lexi's initials on one of the pages. An escalating set of numbers must, he decided, represent the figures for the retainer Hayden had apparently been offering her at intervals. Two were crossed out; the third and largest was followed by a question mark. Well, if that was the case, at least she hadn't signed on with him. Good for her. But he wished it had had the "No!" he'd seen on the listing for Ruiz.

"Should we keep trying on these other initials?" Price was rubbing his temples.

"Not now. We'd just make the list longer."

"Okay, let's start interviewing," Price said.

But the phone rang. The dispatcher from the sheriff's station announced the arrival on the island of Hayden's personal attorney. He'd flown to LAX from Denver, then taken a helicopter to the island. He would talk to the detectives immediately if it was convenient.

It would have to be.

Could they come to his hotel room? They could.

Chapter 47

Rhys MacFarlane experienced an uncanny sense of déjà vu as he and Price entered the attorney's room at the Inn.

Immaculately groomed and tailored, the man stepped around a table set up in front of the wing chair from which he'd obviously risen when they knocked. "Warren Shellgrove. Porter, Shellgrove and Porter. I've handled Warner Hayden's family and personal business for many years now," he introduced himself, proferring a hand first to Price, then to MacFarlane as they, in turn, introduced themselves.

He motioned the detectives to a capacious sofa opposite the chair where he sat. "I hope you'll forgive me," he said with a charming smile. "On such short notice, I couldn't get a business-class seat, and breakfast was about five a.m., Mountain Time. Of course I went immediately to talk with Mr. Hayden's daughter. So I've taken the liberty of ordering room-service lunch. Can I get anything for you gentlemen?"

When they declined, he seated himself, smoothing the back of his gray suit jacket with a deft gesture. It was then that MacFarlane realized he was looking at a person remarkably like Warner Kendall Hayden: well-cut wavy hair silvering at the temples, expensive suit, well-kept physique. He looked like someone who belonged in a glossy magazine article. Forbes 500, perhaps. No, he decided as Bill Gates and Warren Buffett came to mind. Perhaps a slick advertisement for—what?— top-drawer attorneys, he supposed. He realized Shellgrove was speaking and made himself focus his attention on the attorney.

"It took until yesterday for Mr. Hayden's office to reach me," he told the detectives. "I've been out of the country," he added apologetically. "When I learned that his daughter was here on the island, I got in touch with her and came out on the first flight I could get. She'll be coming by in—" he consulted what appeared to be a Rolex Oyster on his wrist—"in about 20 minutes."

"I assume," Price said with a smile, "that you've already talked with her?"

"We discussed Mr. Hayden's will, of course," Shellgrove said. "Except for bequests of the standard sort—a small pension to an aging housekeeper, gifts outright to the young man who served as his driver and to his private secretary—he left everything to his daughter. He told me he hadn't seen her since he and her mother divorced, when she was—ah, still an infant. But that's not unusual in the circles—ah, the circles in which he moved." Shellgrove looked embarrassed, as if he'd said more than he intended.

Before Price could ask more questions, there was a knock at the door and the announcement, "Room Service."

MacFarlane registered the avid look the attorney cast at the tray that was brought in. Something au gratin bubbled in a ramekin, accompanied by a green salad studded with tiny tomatoes, a miniature loaf of crusty bread, and a split of white wine.

"I hope you'll forgive me," Shellgrove said, diving into the meal. "I'm famished."

"You must be."

"Go right head," MacFarlane and Price said at the same time, then laughed. MacFarlane hoped his stomach wouldn't growl too audibly. There was no way they could have accepted the attorney's offer, but he couldn't help envying the lunch. Meanwhile, Shellgrove ate with remarkable efficiency, buttering the bread without shedding crumbs, forking up the casserole without spilling, and chewing romaine and endive without attaching any shreds of salad greens to his gleaming, even teeth.

Between bites, he observed, "I expect you're wondering about the extent of the estate Emilie Oleson will inherit. It's upwards of $500 million in terms of net worth, although a great deal of that is tied up in property."

He smiled at the expressions on the detectives' faces as he delicately mopped up the last of the sauce with a crust of bread. "Not exactly Forbes 500," he said, and MacFarlane wondered if Shellgrove had read his mind. "But enough to make her a very, very rich young woman.

"And I am well aware," he said, maneuvering a final bit of salad onto his fork, "that in your line of work, the first question when a person dies under—shall we say suspicious circumstances?—is 'Who benefits?' And so, as her attorney, I will be present when you talk with Emilie Oleson," he concluded amiably. He chewed the last bite of salad slowly, folded his napkin, and rose to carry his lunch tray to a table that stood by the door.

"I have ordered coffee and cheesecake for all of us," he said. "Please do me the honor of enjoying that with me as we talk with Emilie."

Warner Hayden's daughter and the waiter with coffee and dessert arrived at the same time. Emilie Oleson was a sweet-looking young woman, slender, with long golden hair. Her eyes, however, were shadowed, and she looked tired.

The attorney seated her in the wing chair he'd just vacated as the waiter poured coffee and handed it round, followed by plates of baked cheesecake topped with a scattering of raspberries. This time Price and MacFarlane didn't refuse the offering of refreshment.

Shellgrove took a seat next to Emilie and said to her gently, "Emilie, as I told you earlier when we talked about your father's will, the sheriff's department here is investigating his death. While we assume his fall was an accident," he said smoothly, "it's also possible that he was pushed. He had plans for a project that, I'm sorry to say, was—ah—somewhat controversial here on the island. And what a remarkable coincidence," he added, "that you were planning to be married here." Emilie Oleson looked up sharply at his use of the past tense, but she let it pass.

Price and MacFarlane looked at one another, then at the attorney.

"Go ahead." Shellgrove nodded.

"There's not much to all of this," Price said, as MacFarlane sat poised with his notebook open. "It's merely routine. We need to confirm your whereabouts last Friday afternoon and evening."

Emilie drew in her breath sharply. "You don't think I—"

"As I said, Miss Oleson, this is just routine. We've asked the same question of everyone we can find who had any connection at all with Mr. Hayden."

"But I had none," the young woman objected. "He's just a name. I was only a baby when he and my mother divorced. I didn't even know him. I mean I knew he was my father, and I know he paid support to my mother for me, and I know now he left his estate to me, but I don't want it." She jumped from her chair and paced, wringing her hands. "I don't want it, and I've already made arrangements with Mr.—Mr. Shellgrove here to—"

"Emilie," the attorney said softly, taking her hand, "it's all right. Do sit down. It's just a matter of going through the motions, my dear. They have to ask, and since you have nothing at all to hide, you should just answer. You told me where you were, remember? And you have nothing at all to worry about."

So she'd been coached. Price and MacFarlane exchanged glances again.

"I'm sorry," Price apologized. "I know this is stressful for you. Just think back to Friday, if you would, and tell us about your evening. Suppose you start about 5 o'clock."

"All right," she said, shifting in her chair and stretching a bit, like a cat whose repose has been interrupted. "I was in Long Beach with some friends from college. I came up from San Diego on the train and met them about four-thirty or so. We went for some drinks at a place down by the water—I don't know Long Beach well, so I can't tell you where it was, but Stevie could. Stevie was my roommate at school; she lives in San Pedro. After a while we met up with my mother and then we had dinner with her at her hotel. Which was pretty hotel-ish, but she'd been traveling and said she didn't want to go out."

"And that was?"

"The dinner?"

"The hotel."

"Oh, of course. The Westin."

"Do you remember what time it was?"

"Our dinner reservation was for seven-thirty."

"And was your husband-to-be in this party?"

Emilie raised her eyebrows. "Heavens, no. Jared's not even out here yet. He's finishing up his master's at Washington University in St. Louis, and he had sessions with his degree committee all afternoon Friday. I didn't even get to talk to him until about five—five our time, that is—and he was meeting one of his advisors after that." She seemed to have overcome her attack of nerves. Rhys wrote rapidly as she recited her fiance's phone number.

"And the rest of the evening, after dinner?"

"We left Mother behind—she said she had to get her beauty rest. We went to a little club where there's live music for dancing, but it was kind of loud and crowded, and we didn't know anybody there, so after a while we called it a night. I stayed over with Stevie at her place—her parents' place actually—and they took me to the boat in the morning. That's why Mother and I weren't on the same boat; she was in Long Beach and I was in San Pedro."

"And what time did you leave your—leave the Westin to go to the club Friday evening?"

"About—oh, I think about nine, maybe a little later." Price and MacFarlane exchanged glances again.

"So you came over to the island the next day?"

"Yes. Mother and I were meeting my photographer, Lexi Yoshimoto. Lexi was at school with us, too."

Price didn't look at MacFarlane. Rhys gripped his pen and focused on his notebook.

"But she wasn't with you the previous night?" Price asked. "No. Actually, she was going to be," Emilie said, "but she called Friday afternoon and said she couldn't make it."

Chapter 48

"I thought you said Lexi was with this Emilie and her friends on Friday night," Price said to MacFarlane when they had left the interview with Emilie Oleson and her attorney.

"I thought she was," Rhys said in a small voice. He shook his head miserably. "There was that concert in the park Friday, and I asked her if she'd like to go, and she told me she had to go over town for this dinner with a college friend who was also a client."

"Things come up," Price said. "Don't worry about it, buddy."

They returned to talk of the interview. They'd been surprised when the attorney had confirmed that Emilie was adamant that she did not want the inheritance. After Emilie's vehement outburst about the estate, Shellgrove had quietly explained that he would be helping her to hire a financial advisor who would handle the sale of stocks and properties and advise her on charities. He had already talked her into setting up an annuity that would see her comfortably through life, and she planned, the attorney added, to create another for her mother.

And Emilie, he told the detectives, wanted to deed the site of Hayden's would-be luxury resort to the Island Conservancy. Other properties would likely be donated to other conservancy organizations, he said, looking mildly disapproving. "We'll hold off on those for a while, and see how she feels about that six months, a year from now," he said.

Emilie, her mother and her fiancé, Mr. Shellgrove agreed, all had sufficient motive for the murder of Warner Hayden, but none, apparently, had the opportunity. A phone call to Jared Lee's degree-committee chair confirmed that he had been, and remained, in St. Louis.

So the two detectives were back to the names that had turned up on Hayden's phone and in his deadly little Moleskine. And Lexi Yoshimoto's name could not be eliminated from the list.

"That's not one for you to tackle," Price said. "I'll check it out. Meanwhile, we'd better go through the rest of the list. Who's first?"

"Let's go with the first one we phone who can see us right away," MacFarlane suggested. Twice, Price dialed numbers, made notes, left messages. On the third try, he got through to Andrew Martin.

"Mr. Martin? Detective Price with the sheriff's department here. Are you at the nursery or at home? I wonder if we might have a word with you. You can see us now? We'll be there in a few minutes. Thank you." He looked up. "He'll see us in the nursery office. These notes: 'ICE' and then the 'Yes.' This should be interesting."

Price drove. MacFarlane was quiet, and as they pulled into the landscaped drive of the nursery, Price said, "Hey, buddy. Don't worry about Lexi. She's okay. I'm sure of it."

"You have to admit it's bad either way," MacFarlane said miserably. "Either she's hiding something about where she was that night, or she just didn't want to go out with me."

Price aimed a light punch at MacFarlane's shoulder. "Or," he said, "something came up. Have a little faith, man."

Andrew Martin was in the doorway when the detectives slid out of their vehicle. The scent of lavender, sages, and currant wafted in with them as he showed the men into his tidy office. They heard the spatter sound of water against the back wall as Andy's crew made afternoon irrigation rounds, and occasionally heard a few words of Spanish as workers called to one another.

"What can I do for you?" Martin asked. He seemed calm but wary, MacFarlane thought.

"We're still talking to anyone who had dealings of any sort with Warner Hayden, who might have seen him on Friday, who might have some idea about what was going on with him in the days before his death."

Andrew Martin shook his head. "As you know, I'm on the planning commission. We're named—we were named—as an interested party to the resort project Mr. Hayden proposed. He was of course very anxious that he have our approval. But I suppose that's on hold now that he's deceased. I don't know for sure when I last saw him. Probably at one of the commission briefings."

"Had you had any specific contact with Mr. Hayden in regard to the commission, or your vote?"

Martin ran a hand across his mouth. He looked from Price to MacFarlane. "What kind of specific contact do you mean?" Price pulled out the dove-gray Moleskine. He opened it. "There are the initials A.M. here, with an April date. The name Cruz, with three initials, the initials of the Cruz brothers who work for you. And there's a notation that we read as 'illegal confirmed.' Then the name of a man we know is an agent with Immigration and Customs Enforcement. Mention of a June 9 deadline. And then a big 'YES' with an exclamation point."

Andrew Martin was sweating. He leaned back, looked at the ceiling, and drew breath. Then he sat ramrod straight and said, "I'm sure you've worked out what a lot of that refers to. I'm ashamed to say this, but Mr. Hayden would have had my vote when the project came before us. I prayed I'd be outvoted, and I don't know if he'd have kept his word, but the yes is what you think it is. I agreed to his terms: support his project with my vote in exchange for the well-being of the three best employees I've ever had."

Price and MacFarlane looked on in silence as Martin turned and took three framed photos of kids' soccer teams off the wall. "Here they are. Coaches the kids adore. Family men. All of them ushers at St. Catherine's and the first to volunteer when there's any kind of need. Those guys fought the island fire last year for 48 hours straight. They're working like crazy to get everything lined up for real green cards. They've been paying an immigration attorney in Long Beach off the top of their paychecks for three years, and he says there's only one step left to go. You think I'm going to let someone turn them in to INS? Pardon me, ICE? Let them fester behind bars while their wives and kids suffer?"

"So that was what Hayden threatened you with?"

"Yeah. I was on the wire to their immigration lawyer right away, but he said there was no way to speed up getting their green cards. And if they got hauled in, they wouldn't just be back to square one in the process, they'd be out of it altogether. They'd have to pay huge fines, and at the end of it, be deported."

"Did you try to reason with Hayden?"

Martin exhaled a short, mirthless laugh. "He made it clear there was no room for negotiation. He wanted only that vote."

"Can you be a little more specific about the last time you saw Mr. Hayden?"

"I saw him at last month's council meeting, and probably at the briefing two weeks ago. Not to speak to, though. He did most of his—his wretched business—by letter or phone call."

"Have you kept the letters?"

"The latest one." Martin rummaged in his desk, extracted a folder, and pulled from it an envelope neatly slit and slightly dog-eared. "Here it is." He extracted the letter, unfolded it, and read, "You may also be surprised by the possibility that ICE could arrest any non-citizens in your employ whose documentation cannot be authenticated." He handed it to MacFarlane, who handed it to Price.

"Nice, huh? And I suppose now the Cruz brothers are in for it anyhow."

Price stood. He handed the letter back to Martin. "You've been the victim of extortion, Mr. Martin. That is a crime within our jurisdiction, but the perpetrator isn't around to be charged." Price shrugged. "Whatever his claims in this letter, that is outside our jurisdiction. If he didn't pass along his information to Agent Celovik, we certainly don't intend to. I'd encourage you to do all you can to get the Cruzes' legal status regularized for their safety. They're good men." He smiled.

"I don't think we have reason to bother you any more at this point, Mr. Martin." The two detectives rose. "We'll see ourselves out."

A russet-haired woman in cropped jeans and a linen shirt buried her face in a pot of golden Spanish broom as the detectives passed. She turned and looked after them, then walked quickly into her husband's office.

"What on earth is going on, Andy?"

"Just some routine questions," he assured her. "They know Hayden was pressuring me to vote for approval of his resort scheme. Just when did you see him last, that sort of thing."

Sarah sat down opposite him. "And what did you tell them?"

"What did I tell them?" He furrowed his brow. "At the council meeting at the end of last month, and at the planning board briefing." He shrugged. "We didn't speak. 'Saw' is the operative word."

"But—"

"But where was I the night he died?"

Sarah picked up a polished agate paperweight from Andy's desk and passed it from one hand to the other. "You weren't home until awfully late."

"I know. I actually was here, trying to figure out what I'd say to the planning board. I filled the wastebasket with draft after draft." He rubbed his head with both hands.

"You were actually writing down what you'd say? My god, Andy, what part of 'no' couldn't you—couldn't you say in one word?"

"That's just it." Andy faced her. "I hate telling you this, Sarah. I wasn't going to vote no, and I felt like I'd have to explain myself. But I couldn't find anything to say that I could stand to say."

Sarah leaped to her feet. "You weren't going to vote no? You were going to let that total slimeball go ahead and ruin this island with his big pretentious pleasure palace?"

"Slimeball is right." Andy pulled out a handkerchief and wiped his forehead. "Sarah, you have no idea what whoever murdered Warner Hayden saved me from. If I wouldn't support his project, he was going to—to turn the Cruz brothers in to ICE."

"Oh, Andy."

"I know it was the wrong thing to do, and I can't tell you how ashamed I am, but I was going to—He phoned me and I told him I'd vote yes when it came before the board. First reading would have been at this Friday's meeting. I'd decided the only thing to do was to vote and then resign from the council as soon as I could."

Sarah stared at him for a long, long time without speaking. "Don't look at me like that, darling," he burst out. "I can't bear for you to be disappointed with me."

"I'm just thinking how loyal you are, what a good man you are, and how horrible it must have been for you." She got up and put her arms around him.

"And you know what?" she added, her voice muffled as she pressed her face into his embrace. "If you did murder him, I'll stand behind you all the way."

He looked at her, not knowing whether she was serious.

She looked back at him and smiled, knowing she was deadly serious.

Chapter 49

Friday, June 13

Detective Rhys MacFarlane woke early. Spending most of Wednesday off-island was a diversion he hadn't needed, but it had taken his mind off the circular whos and what ifs of the Hayden case. Yesterday's decoding of Hayden's vicious little Moleskine had got his brain cells invigorated, and he was cheered by the idealism in Emilie Oleson's rejection of her father's fortune and by Andrew Martin's defense of his employees. The world was full of good people; sometimes a cop had to be reminded of that. He couldn't wait to get on with the day and whatever revelations it might bring.

Walking to the operations center, he found Jill Reinhardt herding a small swarm of artists into an Island Conservancy bus. "End of the week," Jill muttered to Rhys. "Next to the last day and now just about everybody wants to go to Two Harbors."

"Not us!" The two French painters marched past, smiling. "Beach and bell tower for us today!"

Viktor Sentik arrived carrying an easel and battered paintbox, offered Jill a grumbled "morning," ignored Rhys, and climbed aboard the bus.

"I assume we'll have a ten-minute wait for Bianca," Jill said to Rhys. "If we're lucky."

"They have a beautiful day for painting, anyway," Rhys said. "You going?"

"I wasn't going to. This is the point where Maribeth and I are up to our ears in cataloguing and hanging paintings. But Maribeth insisted she can finish the cataloguing, and that there's no point in hanging anything until we see what comes in at the end of today's work. So I get to go along." She grinned. "Maybe she couldn't face the prospect of being cooped up with me knowing I'd rather be painting."

"Hope it goes well," Rhys said and continued on toward the operations center.

When he arrived, the room was empty, but he had no sooner set to work than his cell phone began to vibrate. Price was calling from the sheriff's station. He was conferring with the Commander, who would be heading out soon for the boat and a briefing on the mainland. "I'll join you in about half an hour," Price said.

"No problem," Rhys said. "I've got a ton of forms to fill out after yesterday. The fax machine was practically choking with them this morning." He set to work. Before long the office phone rang.

It was D. I. Canham. "How are you feeling, sir?" MacFarlane asked dutifully.

"Like shit."

"Oh. I'm sorry, sir."

"Yeah, well, I'm told that's how it'll be for a while. Listen, Rice. I'm not coming over till the noon boat. I've been reading your reports, and I'm busy with paperwork here in case we need warrants. I think we've got this sewed up. Everything points to that blonde, the Benet woman, and she's probably done it in cahoots with Ruiz. They've got the most to lose, they don't have alibis, there's a lot to explain in how they were hanging around that poncy little hotel where Hayden was staying Friday night. We'll keep it low key, call it assisting with the investigation if you're concerned about your island grapevine, but I want them where I can keep an eye on them before anybody else gets bumped off."

"Yes, sir. But surely—"

"Oh, yeah, yeah. I know you got the Cameron woman for offing her old man. Hell hath no fury, et cetera."

"But sir—"

"You listen to me, Rice. You've got to be the most obstructive little punk a D.I. ever had to put up with. Now here's the thing. You or somebody pointed out the other day that Viktor Sentik, that artist guy, the one with the little fireball girlfriend, doesn't have an alibi for Friday evening. We gotta get all our Is dotted and our Ts crossed before we pull anybody in. We can't afford egg on our faces at this point. The press is already on our tails. So I want you to talk to this Sentik and find out just exactly what he was up to that night. Who knows, maybe he's seen something that's useful."

"He's just left for Two Harbors, sir," MacFarlane said.

"For where?"

"Two Harbors. About half an hour beyond the airport. They'll be painting out there all day."

"Well, no rush. Get your paperwork done first. Then I want you to get a car and get out there and tackle Sentik. Maybe he's our murderer," Canham continued. "But I very much doubt it. I don't think an artist like that would have the guts."

"Then why are you—"

"To get you out of my hair, MacFarlane. I do not need you obstructing this case."

"Yes, sir," said MacFarlane furiously and slammed the phone back onto its base as Price ambled in.

An hour later, paperwork finished for the time being, Rhys was heading for the sheriff's station when he all but bumped into Lexi.

"Hi," she said, reaching for his hand. "Rhys, we've got to help Andrea. She's not eating. She startles at the least little thing. She's hiding from all her friends. Francesca rearranged the whole cheese cooler yesterday and Andrea didn't even notice, much less comment. If she didn't have the big Plein Air brunch to cater tomorrow morning, I don't think she'd even get out of bed."

Rhys drew a deep breath.

"Look," he said. "You don't think she's guilty. I don't think she's guilty. But that's because she's our friend, someone we've known for a long time." He thought about Price's comment and added, "We wouldn't have thought Margaret Cameron would go shooting her husband, either. But she told me she did. Said it as matter-of-factly as if she was telling me she had bought tomatoes at the grocery store."

"Flat affect," Lexi said. "Shock."

"You and your psych terms," Rhys teased. He realized he was still holding the hand she'd reached out to him. "Well," he said seriously, "maybe you shouldn't go telling me about how Andrea's acting because it's just looking blacker and blacker for her."

Lexi backed away. A furrow appeared between her brows as she looked up at him. "I'm sorry," she said. "I know you're investigating and you have to be impartial. But, oh, Rhys, I'm so worried and scared."

"Are you scared that she's looking and acting like she killed Hayden when she didn't," Rhys said soberly, "or are you scared that she did?"

She stared.

"Scared she did?—No, Rhys. I'm not. I'm really not."

"I thought so. Then see if you can't find out what's really eating away at her. Ask John what he thinks. Maybe she'll talk to him."

"Will you come too?"

"I can't. I need to go pick up a car. I have to go to Two Harbors to interview Viktor Sentik. Canham's orders. The man hates me. And he thinks I'm interfering with his case because I just can't think Andrea's—involved," he concluded lamely, realizing he'd said too much when he saw the stricken look on Lexi's face.

"Canham suspects her?"

"Don't worry," he told her. "Just see if you can't get her to talk about what's bothering her. If it doesn't have anything to do with the murder, we can stop worrying about that. If it does, get her to talk to us before anything gets more complicated than it already is."

"Okay. Thanks, Rhys," Lexi said. Rhys turned and watched her as she walked away, small and resolute.

One long, bumpy drive later, Rhys arrived at Two Harbors. It was undeniably picturesque, the way the broad sweep of Isthmus Cove almost intersected with the northeast-pointing arrowhead-shaped Catalina Harbor, the isthmus itself almost an afterthought. Its green oasis of palms and shade trees contrasted with the dusty chapparal and red hills that surrounded it. The day was becoming uncomfortably hot, and Rhys was glad he wasn't in uniform. There was at least that advantage to being a detective, he admitted. He saw the bus first, parked near the sprawling yacht club building, and walked toward Isthmus Cove. Nearby, he spotted a trio of painters on the hillside, laughing and chatting as they worked. He thought of asking them if they'd seen Viktor, but he didn't want to draw attention to his visit.

He ambled past the dive shop and restaurant, having caught sight of a white umbrella near the water. He found Jill Reinhardt at work on a small canvas, a view across the cove at the rust-colored cliffs at its northwest edge.

"Jill, I'm sorry to interrupt, but I need to find Viktor Sentik. Do you know where he might be working?"

She didn't look pleased at the interruption, but rose to walk with him back toward his vehicle and the bus. "The last I saw him, he was heading up beyond Banning House. He said something about the light reflecting off Catalina Harbor." She shaded her eyes and looked up the slope, shrugged, and turned toward the cove and her work. "I can't see him, but that's the direction he went. Come back if you can't find him and I'll help you look."

"Thanks. I don't need to bother you any more than I already have."

"Okay. Good luck." She saluted him with paint-stained fingers and quickly returned to her campstool and her easel.

Rhys thought about walking the rest of the way, but driving to the hotel's parking area would save time and he was anxious to return to Avalon. He drove up the hill, got out of the vehicle and looked around. The slope toward the narrow harbor seemed deserted, and he was about to turn back when he spotted Viktor, wearing a broad-brimmed hat, on the hillside above the hotel. He had neither stool nor umbrella, but stood at his easel, painting industriously. The artist didn't stop work as the detective approached.

"Mr. Sentik. I'm sorry to interrupt you. May I have a word?" At that, Sentik looked up, frowning irritably. Then, to Rhys's surprise, the irritation in the artist's face changed to horror. He seemed to be looking beyond Rhys. Before the detective could turn, something hit him, hard.

Yes, there were stars when you got hit on the head, he thought, amazed. And then even that light was swallowed up in absolute blackness.

Chapter 50

Her conversation with Rhys MacFarlane replayed itself in Lexi's mind as she tried to sort through proofs from her latest job. The inspector was sending him off to the other end of the island, Rhys had told her, because he still believed in Andrea's innocence.

Rhys had said, "He thinks I'm interfering with his case because I just can't think Andrea's—" and then he'd stumbled over the next word. "Involved," he'd said. "Guilty" was what he was going to say. Which meant, she realized, that Inspector Canham thought Andrea was guilty of shoving Warner Hayden off the cliff. Of murdering him.

Could Andrea have committed murder? Lexi knew about the tree-spiking incident, knew how passionate Andrea was about keeping the island pristine, but could not believe the kind, considerate woman who shared her home so freely, who cared so much about her employees and friends and the environment, could have killed Hayden. But if not, how could she explain Andrea's bizarre behavior?

She forced herself to recall as much as she could. At first she had thought only that Andrea's concern was because she, Lexi, had found the body. And unpleasant as that was—she still shuddered at the thought of it—she thought the vehemence of Andrea's response was something more than sympathy.

Pacing the floor, muttering to herself, jumping at the slightest sound, withdrawing from her friends, being irritable and weepy by turns—all of that, Lexi realized, was out of character. It must mean something. If not guilt, what?

"It's just looking blacker and blacker for her," Rhys had said. He had also suggested that Lexi talk to her grandfather. She knew Rhys honored her *pappoús*, thought him almost mystically knowing, but Lexi knew Zorba was troubled by the murders, and troubled even more by Andrea's reaction to Hayden's death. Nevertheless, he was her beloved grandfather and her refuge, and the wisest man she knew. She was glad to put photos of nervously smiling bridesmaids and giggling flower girls aside and go find him.

Finding John Karatsos at home meant finding Yiayia Stina as well. That meant taking time for Stina's strong coffee and, on this particular morning, slices of a sweet, dense, egg-yolk-hued bread with swirls of a poppy-seed filling.

"I haven't had this before, Yiayia," Lexi said. "What's it called?"

"Old-world Poppy-seed Bread," Celestina told her with a wry smile. "Got the recipe on the food channel."

"It's very good," John beamed, gesturing with a half-eaten slice. "You can keep making that one, Stina. But think up a Greek name for it. We have our reputation to live up to."

Lexi looked up, worried that John might reach for another slice, which would require another cup of coffee. But he smiled gently at her and rose. "Excuse us, my dear," he said to Celestina. "Lexi and I are going to go talk with Andrea. Do you want to come?"

"No," Stina said. "I have things I need to do." Then she shook her head. "With you, Andrea might share what she knows. Not with a bigger audience."

295

As they walked, Lexi realized that her grandfather looked older. As if sensing her thoughts, he remarked, "This is a hard time. You were right to fear that man, Lexi. He brought evil to this island, and evil is something that feeds on itself and grows. Now we have lost two of our own to that evil."

"You think there was a connection?"

"Yes," John said. "I do not know what it was, but it was there. And I am afraid. What if there is more?"

"We have to help," Lexi said. "Rhys asked me to help." Her grandfather stopped, gave her a long look, and smiled.

Their first stop was La Cucina but Andrea wasn't there. It was a lull time in the ordinarily bustling shop, and Francesca was cutting a Coppa ham on the mandoline, the paper-thin slices curling off the blade onto a tray. Beside her sat an as-yet unsliced sopressata, the fragrant sausage's signature flattened shape catching Lexi's attention. Francesca saw her eyeing it. "We just brought that in from the kitchen," she said. "It's been drying for three months."

"You made it yourselves?"

Francesca smiled. "First time. Come back at lunch time and we'll sample it, see if it's fit for tomorrow's brunch."

"Love to," Lexi said. "Right now we're looking for Andrea. Is she over in her office?"

Francesca's smile faded. "I hope so."

Lexi and John exchanged glances. "You're worried about her," John said lightly.

Francesca stopped slicing and wiped her hands on a bar cloth. "I am."

There was a silence. Then, "She can't possibly be involved in this thing, but…" Francesca's voice trailed off.

296

"I know." Lexi spoke up. "I see it too. She acts like—I mean, we all just wanted him to go away. I hated being around him, and I know she did too." Francesca nodded. "But she wouldn't kill him," Lexi said. "I know she wouldn't."

"I know," Francesca agreed. "That's not Andrea. But why is she acting the way she is? She's always been so up front, so open, and now she's withdrawing into herself. She won't talk any more, not to me."

"She doesn't seem to be talking to anybody," Lexi agreed. "Something's on her mind."

"On her mind, and tearing her apart," Francesca said. "Detective Price was here yesterday. Here, and over at Edgar's office too. I don't like the feel of it. People are beginning to talk as if it's someone local. One of us. And then Roger, and Margaret—" She paused. "For a while, I hoped that it would all just die down. That we could decide it was just a freak thing, a fall. But now everyone's looking at everyone else, and wondering.

"And I'm realizing," she said, "that there's somebody out there who isn't wondering."

"And you are worried," John said, "that Andrea knows something."

"I think," said Francesca, "that it's something like that. I hope it's something like that. If she'll talk to anyone, she'll talk to you," she added hopefully.

"We have to try, anyway," John said, giving Francesca a farewell hug as they left the shop.

Turning into the little side street where a discreet sign that read Insula: A Catering Company hung from a wrought-iron bracket, grandfather and granddaughter let themselves in at the mango-colored door. "Andrea?" John called out.

"Zorba? I'm in here," she called. "Stockroom. Putting together the service sets for tomorrow morning."

John headed there. Lexi followed.

Andrea turned as they entered the storage area. "Hello, John. Oh, and Lexi. Both of you. What's up?"

"We need to talk," John said.

"We do?" She turned her back and reached for a stack of apricot-colored linen napkins. It was obvious she was stalling.

"We do. Come into your office, will you please?"

"I'm running behind. I really—"

"Andrea, please."

She shrugged and led the way into her office. Lexi, walking behind her, noticed that her twill slacks bagged in back. She'd clearly lost weight. Andrea seated herself atop her desk and indicated the two upholstered chairs in front of it. "Sit, then," she said. There were shadows beneath her eyes and her cheekbones jutted.

Lexi looked at John. He nodded imperceptibly.

"You're not sleeping," Lexi began. "You're pacing the floor at night. You're not eating."

"You're pulling away from people who love you," John added. "You're keeping something locked inside that is eating away at you—"

"Has it occurred to you two," Andrea interrupted angrily, "that I am the perfect murder suspect? Blackmailed by a person I obviously loathed, hiding a guilty secret from my dark and speckled past, undoubtedly seen hanging about the hotel where the victim was staying? Isn't that reason enough to be—to be less than my happy, carefree self?" She stood up

298

and started to pace in the tiny space, like someone in a cage. Or a cell.

"It has," John said calmly. "But since we know perfectly well that you are not the kind of person to do murder, we wonder what it is that you are keeping to yourself."

Andrea surprised both of them by bursting into tears. She grabbed a striped dishtowel and hid her face in it while she shook with sobs. But when she recovered, she was adamant, despite their pleas. "I simply cannot talk about it," she said. "Please go."

They looked at one another. John nodded, and wordlessly, they left. Once they were back at the Karatsos home, John said, "You know what's going on, don't you." It wasn't a question.

Lexi nodded. "She knows who did it. She's protecting someone. Shall I talk to Rhys?"

John nodded.

Lexi smiled. "As soon as he's back from Two Harbors."

Chapter 51

It seemed to Detective Rhys MacFarlane that he had awakened with a terrible hangover, knowing he was supposed to be somewhere doing something about some kind of investigation. He must be late, for the sun was well up, and shining in his eyes. He shut them again. His bed was far from comfortable. And there were women's voices. What was going on?

"I think he's coming around," one of the voices said. "Oh, good."

He knew that voice. Of course. Jill. But what was she doing in—He tried to sit up, but stars appeared again, whirling. He tensed and lay still until the stars subsided, but the pain and nausea remained.

"Easy." That was a different voice. "Lie still. Don't try to get up yet."

Then the unfamiliar voice again. "Go ahead and open your eyes." He did, and the sun's glare was subdued by a pale blue umbrella. He recalled that Jill had been sitting under a white one to paint. A face, not hers, was close to his. "Hmm. Pupils don't quite match. You probably have a concussion, Detective MacFarlane." He closed his eyes.

Background sound, which he'd gradually become aware of, increased at this point: a woman sobbing.

"Oh, hush, Bianca," the woman who'd spoken to him said, turning away from Rhys. "He'll be all right."

"I will be arrested, thrown in prison. Deported." The sobs intensified.

"Arrested, maybe. Jail, perhaps. No prison. And you were made citizen last year, so you will not be deported." That was a man's voice, also familiar. Viktor Sentik. He remembered what it was he was supposed to be doing. D.I. Canham had said he had to interview Viktor.

"Viktor, Jill, now that he's come to, can you help me get Detective MacFarlane over to Banning House?" He opened his eyes again. The woman was looking at him. "You're only a little way from the hotel. They've got a sofa for you, and probably some Tylenol and an ice bag for your head."

Sitting up this time, with strong hands helping him, wasn't as bad. The world spun around him and he had a world-class headache, but Sentik, Jill, and the woman called Ellen, who he realized was the celebrated artist Ellen Storey, helped him to his feet and supported him. He found he was able to move his legs in an efficient enough simulation of walking. Soon he was lowered onto a comfortably padded craftsman divan in a cool, slightly dark room. Someone put a second pillow under his head and shifted him into a more comfortable position.

"That's probably enough for now," Ellen Storey told him. "Relax. Sleep if you can. We'll wake you, though, every fifteen minutes or so to make sure you're okay."

"Fine," he said drowsily. "I'm supposed to interview Viktor Sentik, so don't let me oversleep." And he was out again.

He was dimly aware of Ellen speaking to him, and pressing his eyelids back to check on his pupils; then he slept again. The next time he was checked, Rhys woke.

"Looking better," Ellen told him.

"Let me see if I can sit up," he said, and he could. The horrible whirling sensation was gone, or nearly so. "Whew," he said. "What happened?"

"You arrived and found Viktor. You approached him and said you needed to speak with him. But Bianca came up behind you and hit you over the head with her steel water bottle. It was full, and you were out cold."

"Good grief. But Viktor's still here."

"Of course he's here," said Jill Reinhardt, joining Ellen beside him. "He'll talk with you whenever you feel up to it."

Gingerly, Rhys fingered the back of his head. It felt damp. He looked quickly at his hand.

"No blood," Ellen told him. "Just condensation from your ice pack. They didn't have one of those cloth ice bags, but they had a hot-water bottle and filled it with crushed ice. Great service here." She smiled at him, then at Jill. "I think the patient's pretty much recovered. I'm going back to my picture. Shout if you need me."

"Thanks, Ellen," Jill said. To Rhys, she added, "Ellen took care of a sister who wasn't well for a number of years. She says she doesn't have nursing credentials, but she's had a lot of experience. And a paramedic is coming in on a boat Bay Watch sent out; he should be here in ten or fifteen minutes now. A little late for EMT service, but we did all right by you, I think. Can I get you anything? Water or a 7-Up?"

"I'm good for now," Rhys said. "But thanks." He leaned back, winced, and turned his head to the side.

"You'll have quite a goose-egg, I think. Incidentally, I let the dispatcher know what happened to you, so Bianca will probably find herself in a bit of hot water." Jill sounded slightly self-satisfied.

Rhys laughed. "After trying like mad to get us to arrest Viktor for killing Hayden, I think she was trying to keep me from doing just that."

"You were going to arrest Viktor? Oh, my gosh!"

"Oh—No, Jill. I just had orders from the inspector to find out his whereabouts last Friday. Just a rule-out. Just routine." And, he thought wryly, just a piece of make-work to get me out of the way. Maybe Canham hired Bianca to knock him out to prolong his absence, he thought, and laughed at himself for thinking it. An hour later, Rhys had finished off the toast and tea Seth Forman had advised as a safe alternative to the burger the Banning House manager offered to bring him from the cafe. Seth brought Viktor in to the hotel's sitting room, and Rhys, propped upright on the divan, began the interview he'd been sent to conduct.

"You want an alibi for the night of the murder, and I haven't got one," Viktor said. He grimaced. "I was angry with Bianca and, oh, out of sorts in general. She'd been flirting with that Hayden person for two days; she was always flirting with someone to make me jealous. But she said he was talking about buying one of her paintings, so I thought I'd better leave her to it." He looked sidelong at Rhys. "I was jealous, of course; I always am."

"And Friday evening?"

"Yes. Anyway. I walked to Descanso Beach and up Saint Catherine Way." He stretched. "I hadn't been out that direction before, and I thought it connected with the Chimes Tower Road. But instead," he continued with a bitter laugh, "I wound up at Hamilton Cove and had to retrace my footsteps."

"Did you encounter anyone along the way? Anyone who might remember seeing you?"

"I saw a few people, but I didn't speak to anyone. I wasn't in the mood for cheery good evenings, and I sure as hell wasn't in the mood for conversation."

"Tell me about anyone you saw, anyway." Rhys was taking notes as they talked, though he still felt shaky and wondered if they'd be coherent when it was time to transcribe them.

"I remember two teenagers running—like they were practicing cross-country or something. There was a guy wheeling a garbage can out behind one of the condos, and a woman walking with a little white dog. It was one of those little dogs like a husky. The kind that always barks."

"Can you recall where that was? The woman might remember seeing you, since her dog barked."

Viktor thought for a moment. "That was when I was leaving Hamilton Cove. She could live there or she could have come from anywhere. Like me." He sounded discouraged. "I don't think any of that will help."

"And you left the hotel at what time?"

"About seven, I think. Maybe seven-thirty."

"And walked pretty steadily?"

"Yeah."

"Well," said Rhys, "we'll send one of the foot patrol guys out this evening to walk your route. Dog-walkers usually have a routine, so we might find her."

"Is it so crucial?" Sentik was trying to sound casual, amused, but MacFarlane sensed the tension in his voice. Maybe there was a point to the interview after all. Maybe Bianca's reaction had its roots in a real suspicion, maybe even knowledge, that Viktor had killed Hayden. It would be a relief to find it wasn't someone local. He'd have to remember to have someone talk to Bianca. As her assault victim, he wouldn't be allowed to question her. At least he hoped that would be the case. His head hurt.

"We just try to verify everything," he said. "It'll be a relief to you, I'm sure, if we can find her and she remembers seeing someone that night."

"A long shot," Sentik said gloomily.

"I think," Seth Forman said gently, "that that will do for the time being. I'd like to get Detective MacFarlane back to town." He turned to Rhys. "Your keys, please."

"But what will—oh, yeah. You came by boat." Rhys handed his keys to the medic.

"Detective MacFarlane," Viktor Sentik said, and this time the tension in his voice was painfully obvious, "What's going to happen to Bianca? You know that wasn't premeditated; she just acted on impulse. Will you press charges?"

"I—" Rhys began, but Forman cut him off.

"That's not a decision that Detective MacFarlane will make," he said firmly. "That will be up to the prosecutor. Don't try to leave the island, either of you, for the time being." Seth Forman made sure Bianca and Viktor were back at their easels, he on the slope and she in the hotel garden. He drove Rhys's patrol car up to the hotel door, where he gently maneuvered MacFarlane into the passenger seat.

"If I put the headrest all the way down, you should be able to put your head back," he said. "Let me know if it gets too uncomfortable. And get ready for a long ride. I'm going to go slow to keep from bumping you around."

"Don't lose a lot of time on my account," Rhys said. "I need to get back."

"What you need to get is some rest," Seth countered. "Wait. Turn your head this way. Great. Pupils just about match."

Good, Rhys thought. He needed to think. What was it about the end of his conversation with Viktor that rang a little bell for him? Impulse. Acting on impulse. He tried to keep hold of the thread of the thought, but it eluded him.

As his patrol car eased its way up the slope, Rhys caught sight of the New Englander in her white hat, head thrown back in a laugh, as Ellen and several of the other painters stood looking at her work. He smiled, closed his eyes, and slept.

Chapter 52

Lexi Yoshimoto just happened to be walking along the street when the patrol car pulled up alongside the operations center. She had just happened to be out for a walk, circling the block, for the past 40 minutes. She had stopped in at the operations center twice earlier in the afternoon, finding no one there the first time and leaving hastily the second time when Detective Inspector Canham, who had just arrived, asked what she wanted.

Now, seeing the patrol vehicle, Lexi waited for Rhys to emerge from the driver's seat and stood back, perplexed, when it was Seth Forman who got out. Seth didn't seem to notice her as he came around to the passenger side of the vehicle to help Rhys out.

"Rhys! What's happened?" She hovered anxiously as Forman eased Rhys to a standing position.

"I'm fine," Rhys assured both of them.

"He'll be okay," Seth echoed, steering Rhys toward the hotel's side door.

Lexi followed the two inside, ignoring Seth's startled look. "What on earth—?" She tried again, but Seth held up a warning hand. "Miss Yoshimoto, would you do us a great favor? Would you go over to the pharmacy and pick up an ice bag? Detective MacFarlane has suffered a mild concussion."

"I have one at home," she said. "That'll be quicker." And she was off.

"That young woman," the paramedic observed as he helped Rhys into a chair, "appeared to be lying in wait."

"Mmmh."

"You have a not-so-secret admirer? A stalker?"

"Oh, no," Rhys said hastily. "Not at all—nothing like that. No. She—I—"

"Okay. Got it. Nice." Seth smiled broadly.

"Maybe," Rhys said hopefully, "she's managed to find out something."

"It'll wait."

"I'm not so sure. Oh, gosh," he said, looking around. "Canham's not here. No Price, either. You don't suppose—"

"Price radioed while we were driving back. Guess you were out of it. He's gone to pick up some reports from the crime lab. He'll be back on the last boat. And Canham's still feeling rocky. He's over at the sheriff's station now, and I think he was going to go straight to the boat from there, but he told Price he'd be over first thing in the morning with a warrant to arrest Andrea Benet. No surprise about that," Seth said.

"What?"

"Francesca says she's been a cat on the proverbial hot tin roof all week."

"Right, but—"

"Well, of course she's not guilty. You and I know that. But Canham doesn't."

"But Seth, arresting her would—people won't forget it. Her business—"

"People will remember that some dipstick inspector from off the island arrested her. If it doesn't blow over entirely, they'll sympathize with her. Don't worry."

"I do worry. We've just got to find out who killed Hayden. We think Andrea's protecting someone, but we don't know who."

"Have you asked Andrea straight out?"

"Not yet."

"Well, look. I don't want it getting back, but Francesca's brother works for the credit union Edgar Ruiz belongs to in Long Beach. He said Edgar was in there about two weeks ago inquiring about a second mortgage or a refinance package. I don't know how it came out; he wasn't the loan officer involved."

"Uhmmm. That fits with information we—" Rhys started to rub his head and drew his hand away hastily.

"Yeah. It's gonna hurt like hell for a while, friend. Try not to use the old noggin for a bit if you can avoid it."

"I'll try."

"Sure you will," Forman laughed. "Not likely. Here comes that young lady of yours, and she's looking mighty determined."

"Think this'll do it?" Lexi walked in and held up a blue and green plaid ice bag. "Sorry, it's Campbell plaid. No MacFarlane plaid available."

"Well done," Forman told her, noting with approval that she'd filled it with crushed ice. "I want the patient to apply this for 20 minutes every hour for the rest of the day. Rhys, you can have a couple of Tylenol in another hour, and again in about six hours. And for God's sake take it easy."

He turned to Lexi. "I expect you to enforce that." And to MacFarlane, "Call me and let me know how you're doing, okay?"

"Okay. Thanks, Seth."

Lexi waited until Seth had left. "You had me scared, there," she said. "What on earth happened to you?"

Rhys hesitated. "To be honest, I'm not exactly sure. Canham sent me out to check on Viktor's alibi. I found him on the isthmus, and started to ask him about where he was—I'm not sure I even got to that—and whap! I didn't know what hit me. In fact I didn't know anything at all for a while. But I gather that Bianca Alvorado came up behind me and coshed me with her water bottle. That'll teach me to protect my back, maybe." He laughed ruefully.

"Wait a minute. I thought Bianca was going around telling everyone that Viktor murdered Mr. Hayden because he was jealous."

"Ah, that was just blowing smoke."

"He had an alibi? Oh, wait. You didn't get a chance to ask him, did you."

"Well, actually, I did question him, later. And no, he doesn't have one," Rhys said. "Not that I think he—"

"But wait a minute. Look, Rhys." Lexi's voice rose. "If he did it, then it's obvious Andrea didn't."

"In which case, how come Andrea's acting the way she is? She doesn't have any connection at all to Viktor, does she?"

Lexi's face fell. "I'm grasping at straws, aren't I?"

"I'm afraid so."

"Well, John and I have a theory," she said. "Do you feel up to hearing it?"

An hour later, Lexi and Rhys sat in Lexi's grandparents' comfortable living room, with Andrea Benet and Edgar Ruiz seated across from them looking anything but comfortable.

"Rhys, it's time for another round with the ice bag," Lexi announced. "He was injured in the line of duty," she informed the others.

"I'm not wearing an ice bag during an interview," Rhys said.

"It's not an interview," Lexi countered. "It's a conversation. Right, Pappoús?"

"Rhys has to call the shots here," John Karatsos said. "But we'd like just to explore some territory, and we'd like him to sit in on it. Is that okay with everyone?"

Both Andrea and Edgar nodded.

"I don't know what we should be calling it," Rhys said. "I probably shouldn't be doing this, and I may have to stop you in the middle if we get into what could be evidence. But whatever. Okay, Lexi. Bring on the ice. It really does help. Sorry," he added.

"Okay," Lexi said. "Rhys can correct us if we're wrong, but my grandfather and I think the investigation is focusing in on Andrea and Edgar as having the best motives for killing Warner Hayden. We know they didn't, but we don't know how to prove it. And we have heard—sorry, Rhys, but it's a small island here—that both of you, Andrea and Edgar, were seen around the Inn on the night Mr. Hayden died."

Andrea and Edgar both looked startled, then both appeared to relax somewhat as they looked at one another.

"Did either of you see the other?" Rhys asked.

"Do you want to go first, or shall I?" Andrea asked.

"Your pleasure," Edgar said. "Ladies first, perhaps?"

"All right." Andrea looked first at John, then at Lexi, and finally at Rhys.

"First off, no, I didn't see Edgar. But I was there. I suppose you know that Warner Hayden wanted me to agree to be his food service manager, and that when I declined, he was using outright blackmail to pressure me into changing my mind. He wanted me in his camp, I suppose especially because I was running for council. I hated the man. I hated the idea of a resort like his up there overshadowing the Inn, overshadowing all of Avalon. I hated it that he would even think I'd ever go to work for him.

"And here's the ironic thing," she said, smiling grimly. "I wanted, really wanted, to shove him off his own cliff. I even wrote a note asking him to show me the site." She looked at Rhys, and he nodded. "I had it all worked out that I was going to meet him, up where the trail to his site left the road and... and then I came to my senses. I realized that wouldn't solve anything, really. I went to the Inn but it was pretty clear he'd already left. So I went home and did some work on the statement I would make at the next city council candidates' debate." She handed an envelope to Rhys.

"I don't suppose there's any way to prove when that was written," she said, "but I wanted to show him for what he was." Andrea added, looking at Lexi. "While I was over town last weekend, I decided I was going to tell everyone what I'd done when I was in college, and why; I was also going to explain why I was telling everyone now."

She looked at John, who slowly rose and enveloped her in a long hug. Then he turned to Edgar. "Your turn."

"Nothing in what I can tell you is really much help to me or to you," Edgar Ruiz said. "I, too, was there at the Inn. I wanted to find Hayden, but he wasn't in his room and he wasn't in the bar. It was a nice evening and I thought he might have gone up to the site so I walked up that way, but I didn't see him."

"Did you see anyone?" Rhys asked.

"No," Ruiz said, and held the detective's gaze. "Not up there. I thought I saw Andrea when I left the Inn but I also thought I might be mistaken."

"Why did you want to find Hayden?"

"I was going to tell him that I could not vote for his project," Ruiz said. "I had been hoping I could tell him I had other financing for the next houses in my series, but the truth is it's very unlikely I'll be able to get it. You people have already discovered, Detective MacFarlane, that Mr. Hayden was behind the financing for The Arroyo, and that he was in effect buying my vote. Or thought he was.

"But I couldn't live with myself if I voted for that project," he said. "We'd likely have had to sell our house here, maybe sell the company. I'd told Alice Ann in the afternoon. She was so upset at first that I thought she might lose the baby. But she's a trooper. She said if I'd asked her she'd have told me to do the same." He drew a deep breath. "I know it looks like I'm guilty as hell. And I think I could have been. If I'd found Hayden up on that slope, I'm not sure I wouldn't have given him a good push. Easy answer."

"You wouldn't have," Andrea said.

"I'd have been more likely to do it than you," Ruiz told her.

John Karatsos burst out laughing. "Look at the two of you," he said. "We thought you were covering for each other. And now you're playing 'oh yes I would have.' Well, I'm relieved."

Andrea and Edgar looked at one another and shook their heads. Rhys and Lexi did the same.

"But there's still tomorrow," Rhys said. "Canham's coming over with a warrant."

"Let him," John advised. "Edgar, go home and give Alice Ann a hug from me."

Edgar Ruiz stood, awkward in the moment. "I—thank you, Zorba. Detective MacFarlane."

Rhys stuck out his hand and Ruiz gripped it with both of his. "Good night." They watched Ruiz go out.

John turned to Andrea. "You are still keeping a secret," he told her, "but I think you will not be able to keep it much longer. And I know if someone you know to be innocent is arrested, you will not keep it to their detriment." She gazed at him, unblinking, and he held her gaze for a long moment. "You have a busy morning ahead of you tomorrow."

"Do you need an extra hand?" Lexi asked.

"As a matter of fact, I probably do. I doubt that the kindly D.I. Canham would hold off an arrest until after brunch." She forced a smile. "Don't you agree, Detective Rhys?"

He nodded, as unhappy as he could remember being. "I'm afraid so."

Chapter 53

Saturday, June 14

In the courtyard of the Islander, Andrea Benet was here, there, and everywhere, making sure the Plein-Air artists had enough of everything. The artists munched their way through a buffet arrangement of tiny frittatas, a baked omelet, poached eggs in nests of shredded potatoes and ham, plates of thin-sliced Coppa and the house-made sopressata. They browsed bowls of fresh strawberries, cut mangos, and figs, crescents of melon, and Greek yoghurt with blueberries, and helped themselves from baskets of croissants and cream-cheese Danish, whole-grain pull-aparts, bran muffins, and fruit scones. The air was fragrant, with the scents of fruit and spices underlying the smell of coffee.

Francesca and Lexi helped Andrea, refilling and refreshing buffet bowls and platters, bringing fresh pots of Americano from the portable espresso machine, putting out more plates for grazers who returned to the buffet, and removing the painters' deserted, empty plates. They exchanged worried glances now and then.

Not Andrea, who was shining in her natural element, moving among the artists as they devoured her handiwork. Jill Reinhardt approached her. "Andrea, this is incredible. Way more varied than we bargained for. Those gluten-free scones are delicious. You must have been up all night."

"Yep," Andrea said with a smile. "Baking's a great cure for insomnia." Then she was off to fill Eve's coffee cup and deliver a tiny demitasse of espresso to Ellen, who had lost her taste for American-style coffee. She passed a plate of flaky pastries to René and Jean-Marc, apologizing that they likely weren't up to French standard. She was assured that *oui*, they were. She persuaded the man from Willapa to try some fresh mango. "Tree-ripened," she said. "You won't get that up in Rain Country."

"I haven't seen her that animated for weeks," Lexi murmured to Francesca.

"Whistling in the dark," Francesca whispered back.

On the other side of the building, detectives Ted Price and Rhys MacFarlane sat at their desks, writing reports of the previous day's interviews and eyeing the clock. They heard the incoming Express announce its arrival.

"If he made it to the 8:30, he'll be here in just a few minutes," Rhys said. "Him and his damned warrant."

"Maybe he'll catch the later boat. If he's still feeling puny."

"He's so damned sure of himself. I'll bet he couldn't wait."

"Did you get the crime lab reports filed?"

"Yeah," Rhys said. "Canham loves reports. I put copies in a file on his desk. Oh, shit, Ted. Isn't there any way we can stop him?"

"Probably not. But he'll end up with egg on his face. We just have to figure out how to prove she's innocent. Or find the real perp."

"We've been trying, God knows."

"We've got to have some kind of breakthrough," Price said. "And it's gotta be soon."

"I hate this." Rhys ran his hands through his hair. "Poor Andrea."

The door opened. Detective Inspector Canham had arrived. He stood in the doorway of the operations center, his sheriff's-department badge shining on a dressy, navy blue suit. Rhys wondered if he had brought photographers from the *Times* along. The D.I. brandished a wide manila envelope.

"Price. It's action time. MacFarlane, you—uh—you'd better stick around here. Oh, here's the last report from the lab on the note your nice Ms. Benet wrote to the deceased. Looks like she'd arranged to meet him up on the bluff. We couldn't ask any clearer statement of intent than that. You can file it with the evidence. C'mon, Price. There's a department boat coming in at the mole in about 15 minutes. Let's go get her."

"Sir, she's still serving breakfast to the painters here for the Plein-Air Festival. Couldn't we—"

"Couldn't we wait until it's convenient? For a murderer? I'd expect that from bleeding-heart MacFarlane here, but you know better than that. Let's move it."

The two left the room.

Rhys waited a moment, then slipped through the hallway to the other side of the building to stand in the doorway to the courtyard. Andrea Benet, head high, stood between the resplendent Canham and Detective Price. Then Canham took her by the arm and they walked out toward the street. It was a quiet scene. A confused, milling group of artists sat or stood, stunned, watching their departure. All but one, who had quietly slipped away.

Realizing Canham and Price would probably take Andrea back to the op center before they left for the dock, and that a car might be required, Rhys darted back through the hotel and came in the side door as they entered from the street.

"Get the car," Canham ordered him, triumph evident in his voice.

"Yes, sir."

Bringing the vehicle up to the door, he got out and stood aside. Canham motioned to Price to take the wheel. Canham held the door as Andrea climbed into the back, then got into the passenger seat in the front. Rhys returned to the operations center. A moment later, Lexi burst into the office. The the phone rang as she entered.

"Sheriff's office. MacFarlane," he answered, gesturing to Lexi to have a seat.

The voice at the other end of the line was muffled but audible. A woman's voice, he was certain. "Your inspector has arrested the wrong woman."

"Yes?"

"There's a letter waiting for you at the desk at the Inn," the voice said. The line went dead; the caller had hung up.

Quickly, Rhys dialed the sheriff's station. Yes, there was another car available. "Come on," he told Lexi. There was a strict speed limit on the steep, narrow street that led up the side of Mount Ada, but Rhys drove as fast as he dared, telling Lexi what the caller had said. Lexi nodded and asked no questions, just averted her eyes as the walls on the high side of the cantilevered street rushed past.

No one was in the lobby when they reached the Inn. Rhys rang the bell, waited impatiently, rang again. A young woman sauntered up, smoothing her hair.

"I'm looking for a letter," he said. "It's probably addressed to the sheriff's office."

"Oh, yes, a guy who works down at the Mariner brought this in a little while ago," the clerk said blandly, pulling a creamy envelope from a slot in the desk. "Detective Rhys MacFarlane? Would that be you?"

"Yes," he said, reaching for the letter. The girl handed it over with a disinterested nod.

The letter was hand-written, and covered most of a standard-sized page. He scanned it, his eyes traveling to the signature.

"My God!"

Lexi, at his side now, didn't even look at the letter.

"The airport!" she shouted. They ran to the car. While Rhys drove the tight curves of the descent into town, Lexi frantically keyed the numbers he gave her into his cell phone to tell Canham and Price where they were headed. They wove their way through town with lights flashing and siren screaming. Once they had begun zigzagging up the Stagecoach Road ascent, they realized Price was driving behind them in the other patrol car.

Chapter 54

"I didn't read it. Barely scanned it," Rhys told Lexi. They were at the top of the island now, and Rhys deftly steered the car over rough patches, around hairpin curves ghostly with the stunted skeletons of fire-killed trees, and past steep dropoffs with deadly histories. "Just to see who it was from. Can you manage to read it to me now?"

"Let's wait," Lexi said. "I get carsick trying to read when the car's moving. Especially when it's moving like this."

"I'm learning new things about you every day," Rhys said absently. Whenever the road offered a straight stretch, he and Lexi both peered at the sky ahead of them. And so they both saw it at the same time: a buttercup-yellow dot against the blue sky. It rose and rose. "Get the binoculars," Rhys said. "Try to keep it in sight; if we figure out what direction it's headed, we can call for spotters on the mainland."

Gradually, the plane came closer, following the island's coastline south and east. Rhys pulled the car over at the next wide spot, and Price pulled his car in behind. Everyone got out: Rhys and Lexi, Price, Canham and Andrea. The plane gained altitude; for a few moments they could hear the whine of its accelerating engine, and then it veered out over the ocean. There was a sudden silence as it arced over and down. "What's she doing? Goddamn it, she's taking it down," Canham shouted.

320

Nobody answered. They watched the golden plane plummet, and it slipped into the Pacific with barely a splash. An hour later, after a slow return to the operations center and a flurry of phoning, the inspector, the two detectives and Lexi and Andrea sat crowded into the room that had served as the sheriff's operations center.

They all read once more through Ellen Storey's brief letter.

To whom it may concern:

It would have been nice if everyone could have thought Warner Kendall Hayden had fallen to his death accidentally. I owe you all an apology for wasted time, and for the misallocation of guilt. Most especially I apologize to Andrea Benet, my friend; I am sorry that suspicion fell upon her, of all people. I will not apologize for killing Warner Hayden. I want it to be clear that I, and no one else, was involved. Mr. Hayden had the luxury of dying quickly. My sister, whose life he stole, suffered a sort of death every day she lived.

Even so, my killing him was entirely unpremeditated. An unexpected meeting on an evening when the deceased had drunk enough to be more than usually obnoxious; a conveniently steep slope: you might call it a precipitous situation. I had never known the name of the individual who got my sister pregnant and then talked her into an abortion. I found a photograph of him among her things after she died, but I only recognized him Friday evening after he made a reference to an English teacher he'd once dated that made me realize why he looked familiar. I should stay and face the legal consequences, but I fear an attorney might want to bring out the story behind this story, and I will not have Elise subjected to that, even this long after her death. So my call to judgment will be elsewhere.

Ellen Story

321

"You knew, didn't you?" Canham glared at Andrea.

"I only guessed," Andrea said. "And I felt incredibly guilty, because I'd told her what I really wanted to do with this creep who was blackmailing me—to shove him off his own cliff. And she had made me see reason. She said if I regretted the tree-spiking, I would more than regret doing something that was—deliberate. And then that night when I went up there to the Inn, I realized she was right.—" Andrea swallowed hard. She looked at John as she continued, "You had said Hayden really had nothing he could hurt me with, that I could talk about what happened in Oregon and still hold up my head. Between the two of you, you set me straight. And then—and then when I came back from Long Beach, he was dead and I knew I'd been a part of it."

"Why didn't you tell us you suspected her?"

"And what if it hadn't been her?"

Canham looked away. His face reddened but he said nothing for a while. Then he glared at the two detectives.

"If you people would all get out from underfoot, I might get the paperwork on this case done in time to catch the two o'clock boat."

"We can't just leave it at that," Lexi said as she and Andrea, Ted Price, and Rhys ambled out to the street. It probably wasn't coincidence that the street they chose to wander down passed the Karatsos home.

"Let's tell them," Andrea said.

In John and Celestina's living room, over coffee and honey yoghurt cake, Andrea continued the story.

"They were so close, growing up," Andrea said. "Both so talented. Ellen drew pictures, Elise wrote stories. Once Ellen

322

showed me a neighborhood newspaper they'd created and sold. And then Ellen started painting, and Elise started writing poetry."

"More *yiauortopita*?" Stina asked as she brought in coffee and a bowl of cherries.

Smiling her thanks, Andrea shook her head, sat back and closed her eyes, remembering conversations with Ellen. "Lise went off to the University of Iowa for its writing program, and Ellen went to Hanover, because of its spring program in Paris. After she graduated, she got an artist visa so she could stay.

"By then, Lise had won some young-artist award, I don't remember which, but it was a big one. She had short stories in magazines like the *New Yorker*, and won a teaching fellowship at Bard. So there they were," Andrea continued, "both of them with these really creative careers going. And letters almost every day, both directions."

"What a book those would make," John commented.

"Oh, yeah," Rhys agreed. "I wonder what will happen to the letters now."

"So what happened?" Price was impatient.

"Ellen was living in Le Havre. She told me she woke up one morning—it was fall—with this weird feeling of dread. She'd been getting ecstatic letters from Elise about having met this wonderful man, and then they stopped; she hadn't had a letter in a week. She'd tried and tried to phone Elise and couldn't reach her, which just never happened. So she caught the first plane she could get on. There was a note from a friend of Lise's waiting for her at Lise's apartment. Lise was in the hospital, in intensive care. This friend had gone looking for her when Elise missed classes for a couple of days and found her curled up in a corner of her room, bleeding, running a high fever. Lise fought her, said she deserved it, refused to seek help, but the friend called medics and they got her into a hospital. By then she was in toxic shock, but she survived.

"Well, Ellen got Elise's friends together and some of them knew she'd been seeing a man they didn't know, very handsome, not an academic—nobody knew where she'd met him. She would never say who he was, but eventually she told Ellen that he was married. She hadn't known that, of course, not until she told him she was pregnant. He'd pressured her until she agreed to the abortion. Took her there, to be sure she went through with it. Paid for it, even."

John got up and refilled coffee cups. Andrea sipped for a moment before continuing. "Elise never recovered. Ellen and their brother found a nursing home in the country that treated patients with serious depression. Ellen stayed on and visited Elise every day. And eventually Lise got better, and started teaching again, and Ellen came back to Le Havre. That was the year I met her," Andrea added. "I remember one day I asked her how she could reconcile being a women's libber with being anti-abortion, and she told me what was behind Lise's depression.

"Ellen was going to go home that summer and they'd planned to travel. I remember Ellen being worried when Lise's letters slowed down again, so she didn't wait till June. She hated leaving France in May, when everything was so beautiful, but she did."

"And you kept in touch?"

"Yes. Ellen wrote that Elise barely got through spring quarter. They decided to explore the West Coast, and see if a change of scene would help. It seemed to. They settled in Carmel, and Ellen thought Elise was doing much better. And then one day when Ellen was away, she walked into the ocean." Andrea put her coffee cup down. "You've probably seen some of the paintings Ellen did in California, the Woman in White series? The woman, of course, was her sister." Tears streaked Andrea's face as she spoke.

"You brought her here to paint after that, didn't you?" John asked, covering her hand with his. Andrea nodded.

"And that," Lexi asked, "was when she painted the picture that Hayden wanted her to repeat?"

Andrea nodded again. "And I persuaded her to come for the Plein-Air. I met her at the airport to bring her into town. We were talking, and she'd said how he was pressuring her to paint a version of that picture of the bay from up above the Inn, and how angry it made her. I told her—I told her how Hayden was pressuring us to work for him," she added, looking at Lexi. "I told her about the blackmail." Andrea choked back tears. "I told her he drank a lot, and that I heard him bragging about his coke, and how I came up with the idea of getting him to take me up to his property, and then shoving him off the cliff. But she talked me out of it. I had no idea—"

"Of course you didn't," Celestina exclaimed.

"And you can stop feeling guilty." It was the first thing Price had said, and Andrea looked at him in amazement. "You tested yourself. And you realized you couldn't do it without even going up there."

"But if I had—" she said, and the terror came back into her face, "maybe I could have stopped her."

"No. Delayed, maybe. Not stopped. Especially after she realized—" Price consulted Ellen's letter—"that the 'English teacher he'd once dated' was her sister."

They were all quiet as they imagined Ellen recognizing Hayden, realizing what he'd done.

"Okay," Andrea said with the closest thing to a smile that her friends had seen in weeks. "Then can I say something else?"

"Yeah."

"I'm glad she got away," Andrea said, tears flowing again. "I just wish—"

Everyone nodded.

Chapter 55

Sunday, June 15

High clouds rolled across the sky as the little town of Avalon basked in the evening sun. Art lovers, many of them carrying large boxed or paper-wrapped parcels and triumphant grins, milled around the doorway of the Casino. Inside, the Plein Air Festival committee was tallying up the take in the best auction ever.

An oil painting of a woman in a white gown, leaning against a tree on Mount Ada and looking down at Avalon Harbor— the last work from the brush of noted painter Ellen Storey— brought a record price, and there had been hot competition for the rest of her pieces as well.

A view of Catalina Harbor, painted in Viktor Sentik's slightly abstract style, also brought a fine price, perhaps because for the first time in years, he had returned to a full-spectrum palette: his water glittered with brilliant blues and greens. It sold for twice the highest price paid for one of Bianca Alvarez's paintings, but Bianca didn't care. She and Viktor, she announced to everyone she encountered, were leaving for Mexico City, where they would be married. Even Viktor was smiling.

So was Eve Jones, who was making plans for a trip to France to participate in a plein-air painting event in the troglodyte village of Trôo in the Loire Valley. René would be meeting her plane.

Jill Reinhardt and Maribeth Phillips, all smiles, were bidding the last of the festival's benefactors farewell at the door of the Casino when *Islander* editor Carl Merriman appeared, notebook in hand. "Well done, ladies," he beamed. "And can we say there will definitely be another festival next year?"

Jill and Maribeth looked at one another. Then, in unison, they shook their heads.

"Definitely not," Jill said.

Back in Insula's workroom, an exhausted Francesca and Andrea stowed equipment while their helpers washed goblets and canapé platters.

They were interrupted by a loud knock at the door and looked up to see Detective Inspector James Canham and Detective Ted Price walk in, both in full uniform.

"Ms. Benet," Canham began. "I assume you are aware you have put yourself in a position of accessory to murder—"

"Shut up," interrupted Price.

"What the—" Canham was as purple as he'd ever been.

"The case is finished," Price told Andrea, ignoring his superior. "That was just the D.I.'s inappropriate prelude. What Inspector Canham has come to tell you is that we are closing the book on this homicide. The last detail that remains is to turn over to you a piece of evidence that was confiscated at the airport yesterday. It's addressed to you. We apologize," he added, with a sideways glance at Canham, "for the fact that it has been opened."

The D.I. had the grace to blush. "We had to copy it for the file. Sorry," he muttered. He handed Andrea a small square envelope.

She opened it. A simple engraved "Thank you" card, it bore just a few lines in Ellen Storey's distinctive handwriting.

"Please do not blame yourself," Ellen had written. "I thank you for making it possible for me to do the two things I have wanted to do ever since Elise's death."

On the hillside above the Casino, Lexi Yoshimoto and Rhys MacFarlane picked up the scraps and wrappings of a picnic supper they'd shared at The Chimes Tower.

They gazed across the harbor at Mount Ada.

"Can you imagine it with a huge resort up there?" Rhys said.

"No. Avalon's quite perfect as it is," Lexi said, slipping her hand into Rhys's, which was conveniently close.

"Perfect? With murders and extortion and suspicion all over the place?"

"That," Lexi said, "was a passing aberration."

"Speaking of aberrations," Rhys said, "I haven't asked you how you knew we should go to the airport when you hadn't seen Ellen's letter."

"You don't miss much," Lexi said.

"And?"

"I was helping with the breakfast, remember?"

"Well, yes, but—"

"When the police came for Andrea, everybody kind of froze. I looked around, thinking what a photo it would make. And Ellen wasn't there. Simple as that."

"But you didn't say anything when you came in the office."

"No," she said. "You were on the phone. I knew when you got that call that it would all come out. And she needed the time to get to her plane. Look," she added, pointing down the steps at Crescent Avenue, where they could see her grandparents walking hand-in-hand along the seafront. "Yiayia's joined him for his evening stroll. All's right with the world."

Rhys said nothing, just looked at her. She snuggled closer to him, and they sat looking down at Avalon, rosy in the early evening light. Finally he broke the silence. "Say, are you still photographing Emilie Oleson's wedding?"

"Sure. Why?"

"Her attorney suggested she might not want to have it here. After everything."

"Her attorney?"

"Well, yeah. He was Hayden's personal attorney. When you look at who benefits, she's first in line. A very wealthy young woman now. So of course she had an attorney with her when we questioned her about Friday night."

"Of course," Lexi said. Then her eyes widened. "Friday night."

"Yeah."

"And she said I wasn't at dinner and I'd told you—"

"Things come up," Rhys said. He looked down at her hand, still in his.

"It was still a classmate I had dinner with" Lexi said gently. "Grade school. Middle school. A family friend. My best buddy in the neighborhood when we were little. He came down from San Francisco to tell me that the girl he's been in love with since college is coming back from Spain, and they're going to be married. I'm going to take their pictures, of course."

330

"Oh."

"Rhys. Were you—were you thinking—"

"Never mind," he said. He put his arm around her. Lexi pulled his face down to hers, and the kiss she gave assured him that all was, indeed, right with the world.

The sun dropped behind the ridge on Avalon's west edge. Beyond it the sea took on the deep blue of evening.

And out in the Pacific, the slanting rays of sun picked out the buttercup yellow of the tail of a Cessna as it bobbed in the waves.

Acknowledgements

A book does not happen in a vacuum. I owe great debts of gratitude to many people:

First and foremost, to Michael Maddux, whose idea it was in the first place, who nudged and nagged his mom until it happened, and who put his mind to getting it between covers and into the world.

To the late Marie Whittington for a wise and careful first proofreading of the earliest draft; to writers-group companions Linda Haverstock, Jean Busch, David Snider, Maitri Sojourner, Liz Dykstra, and the late Ed Aceto and Bill Young, for their critiques and encouragement as bits and pieces of this manuscript were written, rewritten, and re-re-written; to fellow writer Linda Warren, for a careful proofing; and to my fellow mystery-lovers, alas no longer with us, Judy Williams and Janice Jackson, for their perceptive readings.

To Mason County Detective Inspector Nick Patterson, for advice on cell phones; to Coroner Wes Stockwell, for reading and advising me on post-mortem issues, and to Captain Douglas Fetteroll, Retired, of the Los Angeles County Sheriff's Office, Avalon Station, for his patient corrections and invaluable information on local procedures. Any implausible procedural details are my own invention and not products of their advice.

To long-time friend and mentor Robert Michael Pyle, for graciously agreeing to appear in these pages even after he read the manuscript, and for his continued encouragement. Only a narrow-minded idiot like Inspector Canham could ever suspect Bob of murder.

To Sue Rikalo, the most hospitable and dearest friend and collaborator anyone could have, for morning trips around Santa Catalina to ensure reasonable locations for the action and for afternoons making sure writing was happening, for reading and re-reading, and for quantities of good advice.

To Lauren Kent, whose lovely plein air painting—from just the right vantage point—graces the cover; to Julia Kent, for her thoughtful cover design; and to Bojan "Arty" Kratofil, for page design and patient fixing of typos.

To the late Sam Rikalo, the inspiration for it all.

And to my beloved husband Donald Maddux, who read, critiqued, and patiently supported me through the process.

About the Author

Carolyn Maddux is a mostly retired journalist who lives with her husband and their Shetland sheepdog in Shelton near Washington's Salish Sea. She teaches creative writing at Olympic College Shelton, and enjoys cooking, gardening, and volunteering with Hypatia-in-the-Woods, a small nonprofit providing residencies for women in the arts and academia. She has written two books of nonfiction and two of poetry. This is her first venture into fiction.

Printed in Great Britain
by Amazon

11655641R00193